EX LIBRIS

Andrea Whittle

FAVORITE POEMS OLD AND NEW

FAVORITE

Selected for boys

POEMS
OLD AND NEW

and girls by HELEN FERRIS

Illustrated by Leonard Weisgard

A Doubleday Book for Young Readers

A Doubleday Book for Young Readers
Published by Delacorte Press
Bantam Doubleday Dell Publishing Group, Inc.,
1540 Broadway, New York, New York 10036

Doubleday and the portrayal of an anchor with a dolphin are
trademarks of Bantam Doubleday Dell Publishing Group, Inc.

ISBN: 0-385-07696-7 Trade
      0-385-06249-4 Prebound

Library of Congress Catalog Card Number 57-11418

Designed by Alma Reese Cardi.

Printed in the United States of America

40   39   38   37

BVG

FOR TIB

who with me inscribes this,
our book, to our family's
youngest generation

ANNE

BOBBY

CRAIG

HOLLY

JANICE

JIMMY

KIMMY

MARY

MICHAL

NANCY

RICKY

TIBBY

TIM

Poetry at our house

This book had its beginning years ago when two parents, loving poetry, made it as much a part of their children's every day as getting up in the morning, eating breakfast, going to school, playing outdoors until suppertime.

It is evening. My brother Fred and I are in bed, propped up against the pillows. Mama is sitting by the table, with the lamp's red shade throwing a rosy glow over her face and the book from which she is reading.

> *"Little Jack Horner*
> *Sat in a corner . . ."*

Fred and I know it by heart, just as we know by heart all the others in the Mother Goose Book. But to have Mama read them aloud gives us a warm feeling of the day ending as it should end. And to our profound satisfaction in hearing the familiar words over and over again is added our pleasure in the cadence of her voice.

When Papa can be with us, it is an event, all too seldom realized. For Papa is a minister with many evening meetings in the small Nebraska town where we live.

Not even Mama can make the shivers run down our backbones as he does with:

> *" 'Twas a misty, moisty morning,*
> *And cloudy was the weather."*

There is ominous portent in his deep tones. Fred and I push closer together.

> "I chanced to meet an old man,
> Clad all in leather.
> Clad all in leather
> With a STRAP beneath his chin."

A strap—goodness! But the mood quickly brightens, for now Fred and I have our turn:

> "How d'ye do"—bow to Mama and Papa.
> "How d'ye do"—bow to each other.
> "How d'ye do again"—bow every which way as fast as we can.

One night Papa came in to hear Mama read:

> "Tom, Tom, the piper's son,
> Stole a pig and away he ran."

"My dear Min," he protested. Mama's name was Minnie. "What are you doing? The word is 'run.'"

Mama's hazel eyes flashed. "Elmer Ferris," she told him firmly, "if you think I am going to expose our children to bad grammar in this house, you are mistaken."

"Better that than expose them to bad rhyme," declared Papa no less firmly.

It was a difference of opinion that was never resolved. But, as with many such at our house, it became a source of merriment. Every now and then when supper was ready Mama would beckon to Fred and me, and the three of us would tiptoe to Papa's study, where he sat reading the paper. Soundlessly Mama's lips would form the words, "Tom, Tom."

Then she would declaim: "Tom, Tom, the piper's son, stole a pig and away he——"

"Ran, ran, ran, ran," Fred and I would shout, swarming over Papa to the definite detriment of the newspaper. Papa would throw back his head and laugh and laugh. And Fred and I were never to forget the importance either of good grammar or good rhyme.

Memory of the poems that accompanied and followed Mother Goose in our bedtime hours is a tapestry, lovely but with no set design. Later I was to learn that Mama had an articulate theory about reading poetry aloud to children, a theory not surprising for she was a pianist. It did not matter, she was convinced, if we could not understand all the words. We could enjoy the beautiful sound of them. So it was that for Fred and me Mother Goose flowed easefully into Alfred Tennyson, Henry Wadsworth Longfellow into Shakespeare.

Shakespeare was especially Papa's. When he was working his way through the old University of Chicago he took on an extra job in order to buy the *Complete Works*. It was a large, worn, and precious part of our library. During many a family celebration Papa would take down the Shakespeare book, unerringly turn the pages to a certain passage, and new meaning was added to the occasion.

Like the sunshine and the softness of twilight, like the wind and the rain and the snow, the poetry of the Bible belongs to the warp and woof of Fred's and my growing up. Mama, reading, "I will lift up mine eyes unto the hills . . ." She loved the Wisconsin hills of her girlhood, and Fred and I were sure the Psalmist meant Wisconsin. Papa, slim and serious in the pulpit of the little prairie church: "The Heavens declare the glory of God . . ."

I often wonder how Mama and Papa knew which of the new books to buy for us. There was no library in that small Nebraska town, no librarian to consult, no bookstore. Nor did the periodicals of those days carry many reviews of children's books. Yet new books regularly appeared for us, often those of poetry, which only rarely failed to enchant us. Perhaps Papa asked questions on his trips.

From one of those trips Papa came home with exciting news. We were going to move to Wisconsin to live. "In the city of La Crosse, which is on the mighty Mississippi River," he told us. From then on it was one word to me, "Mightymississippi."

Having the Mightymississippi so close was as exciting as Papa had predicted. "Papa," I asked him one morning at breakfast, "does the Mightymississippi come from haunts of coot and hern?"

"Certainly," he replied, "and it bickers down a valley, too—up North."

After that, whenever I went alone to the island out in the river, which was the city's Pettibone Park—as I was by then old enough to do—my routine was always the same. Hopping off my bike in the middle of the long bridge, leaning out over the railing, facing north, I told the Mightymississippi, so wide and ceaselessly flowing far below: "You come from haunts of coot and hern. You bicker down a valley."

There were no Camp Fire Girls or Girl Scouts in those days, but there was a Junior Audubon Society, of which my best friend, Addie Dean, and I were ardent members. One rainy day—to get us out from under foot, I am sure—Mama suggested, "Why don't you two bird watchers go to the library and see how many poems about birds you can find for your Audubon notebooks?"

We must have been a pest to Miss Hanson, the librarian, for day after day until we ran out of notebook pages we put in an appearance. But I can remember only her kindness and interest as she guided our search.

Friday afternoon at school was recitation time. Nor was there ever a lapse in any program when measles, mumps, or whooping cough laid low the scheduled performer. There was at hand an ever-eager, ever-ready volunteer named Helen to fill the gap. I loved reciting the dramatic poems—"One if by land, two if by sea"; " 'But spare your country's flag,' she said." The sad ones—"The little toy dog is covered with dust." Those with enviable elocutionary opportunity, "Have you ever heard the wind go 'Yooooooo'?" And the nonsense, " 'Twas brillig, and the slithy toves."

To achieve effective rendition, rehearsing was called for. This took place in my room on the second floor of the parsonage. Standing by my bed, I faced the door, opened into the hall. But it was not the hall that was outside. It was a vast auditorium, crowded with an enrapt throng. And it was my pleasure—nay, my duty—to make certain that those in the most remote corners could hear me with ease.

Then one afternoon: "Daughter!" It was Papa at the foot of the stairs. "If you must bellow, kindly close the door. You are driving every idea out of my head."

Bellow! That was crushing. But without protest I closed the door. All the family knew the importance of ideas to Papa's sermons.

The years passed. Somewhere along the way "Mama" became "Mother" to Fred and me; "Papa," "Dad." But there was no change in our delight in bringing home new poetry that we had discovered. I from Vassar, with all the books by Sara Teasdale that I could squeeze out of my allowance. Fred from Brown, with William Henry Drummond and his *Wreck of the "Julie Plante."*

We moved to New York, on Morningside Drive, with the sweep of the great city beneath our windows and the sunrise on the distant horizon. One afternoon I opened the door of the apartment to see Dad pacing the floor, an open book in his hand. "When I lived in Chicago," he was telling Mother, "the air was electric. I and my friends were young and going places. Chicago was young and going places. And this man Sandburg has caught it. What a poet! Listen to this . . ."

Mother liked Sandburg, too, but she preferred what she called his quiet poems. " 'The fog comes in on little cat feet'—isn't that exactly the way it does down there in the street?"

In time Fred's children stood beside her at the window. "Look, Helen. Look, Frederick. The stars! 'Shall we ride to the blue star or the white star?' " And then to her and Dad's great-grandchildren at the same window: "Look, Ricky. Look, Kimmy. The stars! 'Shall we ride to the blue star or the white star?' "

Other memories, too, entered into the making of this book. Memories of hours when leaders of the Camp Fire Girls and I read poetry together and talked of the poems most meaningful for their girls. Memories of evening campfires, when by the light of high, leaping flames I read poetry to Girl Scouts from near and far and asked them to choose poems later to appear in their magazine, *The American Girl*.

When, in time, I became editor of the Junior Literary Guild, there was for me but one way in which to start each issue of *Young Wings*, our Junior Guild magazine. Many a letter from our young members enthusiastically mentioned this poem and that, which had appeared on the inside front cover. "Please have more like the one last month." When we sent books of poetry to them, as Junior Literary Guild selections, their warm response was immediate. Of Ruth Barnes's collection of traditional poems from our country, *I Hear America Singing*, one boy wrote, "These poems are swell." Of Carl Sandburg's *Early Moon* a girl said, "I didn't know poetry could be like this. I have read *Early Moon* six times and am going to read it lots more." The old and the new.

I cannot remember just when the plan took shape to gather together the poems of these cherished memories. But so it was, and so it is that of much of this book it can truly be said, "Remembered by Helen Ferris." To the remembering, as I made my final choices, were added still further happy discoveries, poems by the newest poets of all, poems from days gone by not come upon before.

To all who helped me in my searching and discovering, my heartfelt thanks. To my husband, Albert B. Tibbets, my enduring gratitude for his belief, for his stalwart encouragement in those inevitable moments when it seemed to me that no one, least of all myself, could possibly choose from among the overwhelming number of lovely poems today awaiting young readers.

My deep appreciation goes to Margaret Lesser, my editor, whose own remembering was a delight. To Barbara A. Huff, whose love of poetry and whose unflagging zeal made her a valued fellow searcher. To Alida Malkus, who led me to the poets of Latin America, and on around the world. To the librarians of New York City's Public Library, who never failed to find the books of my need, and in especial to Maria Cimino of the Children's Room at Forty-second Street. To those others who so generously shared with me their memories of the poems they loved in their younger days—Nora Beust, Ann Durell, Muriel Fuller, Sidonie M. Gruenberg, Sallie Marks, Ken McCormick, Dora and Angelo Patri, Eleanor Roosevelt. And to Leonard Weisgard, for his sensitive understanding.

To my staff in the Junior Literary Guild, I am more indebted than I can express. They found every paper I lost, took meticulous care of every detail—Thérèse Doumenjou, Rose Engle, Ruth Clement Hoyer, Barbara A. Huff. My gratitude is with Alma Cardi, as well, designer of my book; with Elfry Zaeyen, for her able work in obtaining the many permissions to include here the poems of my choice; and with Blanche Van Buren, guardian of proof and schedules.

Helen Ferris

Hollow House Farm

Contents

IT'S FUN TO PLAY

LITTLE THINGS THAT CREEP AND CRAWL AND SWIM AND SOMETIMES FLY

FROM THE GOOD EARTH GROWING

MY BROTHER THE SUN, MY SISTER THE MOON, THE STARS, AND MOTHER EARTH

PEOPLE TO KNOW, FRIENDS TO MAKE

Myself and I

ME
Walter de la Mare

As long as I live
I shall always be
My Self—and no other,
Just me.

Like a tree.

Like a willow or elder,
An aspen, a thorn,
Or a cypress forlorn.

Like a flower,
For its hour
A primrose, a pink,
Or a violet—
Sunned by the sun,
And with dewdrops wet.

Always just me.

EVERYBODY SAYS
Dorothy Aldis

Everybody says
I look just like my mother.
Everybody says
I'm the image of Aunt Bee.
Everybody says
My nose is like my father's,
But *I* want to look like *me*.

MY INSIDE-SELF
Rachel Field

My Inside-Self and my Outside-Self
   Are different as can be.
My Outside-Self wears gingham smocks,
   And very round is she,
With freckles sprinkled on her nose,
   And smoothly parted hair,
And clumsy feet that cannot dance
   In heavy shoes and square.

But, oh, my little Inside-Self—
   In gown of misty rose
She dances lighter than a leaf
   On blithe and twinkling toes;
Her hair is blowing gold, and if
   You chanced her face to see,
You would not think she could belong
   To staid and sober me!

WASHING
John Drinkwater

What is all this washing about,
Every day, week in, week out?
From getting up till going to bed,
I'm tired of hearing the same thing said.
Whether I'm dirty or whether I'm not.
Whether the water is cold or hot,
Whether I like or whether I don't,
Whether I will or whether I won't,
"Have you washed your hands, and washed your face?"
I seem to *live* in the washing-place.

Whenever I go for a walk or ride,
As soon as I put my nose inside
The door again, there's some one there
With a sponge and soap, and a lot they care
If I have something better to do,
"Now wash your face and your fingers too."

Before a meal is ever begun,
And after ever a meal is done,
It's time to turn on the waterspout,

Please, what *is* all this washing about?

I WANT TO KNOW
John Drinkwater

I want to know why when I'm late
For school, they get into a state,
But if invited out to tea
I must'n ever early be.

Why, if I'm eating nice and slow,
It's "Slow-coach, hurry up, you know!"
But if I'm eating nice and quick
It's "Gobble-gobble, you'll be sick!"

Why, when I'm walking in the street
My clothes must always be complete,
While at the seaside I can call
It right with nothing on at all.

Why I must always go to bed
When other people don't instead,
And why I have to say good-night
Always before I'm ready, quite.

Why seeds grow up instead of down,
Why sixpence isn't half a crown,
Why kittens are so quickly cats
And why the angels have no hats.

It seems, however hard they try,
That nobody can tell me why,
So I know really, I suppose,
As much as anybody knows.

SOMEWHERE
Walter de la Mare

Could you tell me the way to Somewhere—
   Somewhere, Somewhere,
   I have heard of a place called Somewhere—
   But know not where it can be.
      It makes no difference,
      Whether or not
      I go in dreams
      Or trudge on foot:
Would you tell me the way to Somewhere,
   The Somewhere meant for me.

There's a little old house in Somewhere—
   Somewhere, Somewhere,
A queer little house, with a Cat and a Mouse—
   Just room enough for three.
      A kitchen, a larder,
      A bin for bread,
      A string of candles,
      Or stars instead,
      A table, a chair,
      And a four-post bed—
There's room for us all in Somewhere,
   For the Cat and the Mouse and Me.

Puss is called *Skimme* in Somewhere,
  In *Somewhere, Somewhere;*
  Miaou, miaou, in Somewhere,
  S—K—I—M—M—E.
    Miss Mouse is scarcely
    One inch tall,
    So *she* never needed
    A name at all;
    And though you call,
    And call, and call,
    There squeaks no answer,
    Great or small—
Though her tail is a sight times longer
  Than this is likely to be:

                    FOR

I want to be *off* to Somewhere,
To far, lone, lovely Somewhere,
  No matter where Somewhere be.
    It makes no difference
    Whether or not
    I go in dreams
    Or trudge on foot,
    Or this time to-morrow
    How far I've got,
    Summer or Winter,
    Cold, or hot,
    Where, or When,
    Or Why, or What—
Please, tell me the way to Somewhere—
  *Some*where, *Some*where;
Somewhere, *Some*where, *Somewhere*, SOMEWHERE—
  The Somewhere meant for me!

HALFWAY DOWN
A. A. Milne

Halfway down the stairs
Is a stair
Where I sit.
There isn't any
Other stair
Quite like
It.
I'm not at the bottom,
I'm not at the top;
So this is the stair
Where
I always
Stop.

Halfway up the stairs
Isn't up,
And isn't down.
It isn't in the nursery,
It isn't in the town.
And all sorts of funny thoughts
Run round my head:
"It isn't really
Anywhere!
It's somewhere else
Instead!"

THIS IS MY ROCK
David McCord

This is my rock
And here I run
To steal the secret of the sun;

This is my rock
And here come I
Before the night has swept the sky;

This is my rock,
This is the place
I meet the evening face to face.

THE SECRET CAVERN
Margaret Widdemer

Underneath the boardwalk, way, way back,
There's a splendid cavern, big and black—
If you want to get there, you must crawl
Underneath the posts and steps and all
When I've finished paddling, there I go—
None of all the other children know!

There I keep my treasures in a box—
Shells and colored glass and queer-shaped rocks,
In a secret hiding place I've made,
Hollowed out with clamshells and a spade,
Marked with yellow pebbles in a row—
None of all the other children know!

It's a place that makes a splendid lair,
Room for chests and weapons and one chair.
In the farthest corner, by the stones,
I shall have a flag with skulls and bones
And a lamp that casts a lurid glow—
None of all the other children know!

Sometime, by and by, when I am grown,
I shall go and live there all alone;
I shall dig and paddle till it's dark,
Then go out and man my private bark:
I shall fill my cave with captive foe—
None of all the other children know!

THE LAND OF STORY BOOKS
Robert Louis Stevenson

At evening when the lamp is lit,
Around the fire my parents sit;
They sit at home and talk and sing,
And do not play at anything.

Now, with my little gun, I crawl
All in the dark along the wall,
And follow round the forest track
Away behind the sofa back.

There, in the night, where none can spy,
All in my hunter's camp I lie,
And play at books that I have read
Till it is time to go to bed.

These are the hills, these are the woods,
These are my starry solitudes;
And there the river by whose brink
The roaring lions come to drink.

I see the others far away
As if in firelit camp they lay,
And I, like to an Indian scout,
Around their party prowled about.

So, when my nurse comes in for me,
Home I return across the sea,
And go to bed with backward looks
At my dear Land of Story Books.

I'D LEAVE
Andrew Lang

I'd leave all the hurry,
   the noise and the fray
For a house full of books
   and a garden of flowers.

A BOOK
Emily Dickinson

There is no frigate like a book
    To take us lands away,
Nor any coursers like a page
    Of prancing poetry.
This traverse may the poorest take
    Without oppress of toll;
How frugal is the chariot
    That bears a human soul!

MY SHADOW
Robert Louis Stevenson

I have a little shadow that goes in and out with me,
And what can be the use of him is more than I can see.
He is very, very like me from the heels up to the head;
And I see him jump before me, when I jump into my bed.

The funniest thing about him is the way he likes to grow—
Not at all like proper children, which is always very slow;
For he sometimes shoots up taller like an India-rubber ball,
And he sometimes gets so little that there's none of him at all.

He hasn't got a notion of how children ought to play,
And can only make a fool of me in every sort of way.
He stays so close beside me, he's a coward you can see;
I'd think shame to stick to nursie as that shadow sticks to me!

One morning, very early, before the sun was up,
I rose and found the shining dew on every buttercup;
But my lazy little shadow, like an arrant sleepyhead,
Had stayed at home behind me and was fast asleep in bed.

THE INVISIBLE PLAYMATE
Margaret Widdemer

When the other children go,
   Though there's no one seems to see
And there's no one seems to know,
   Fanny comes and plays with me.

She has yellow curly hair
   And her dress is always blue.
And she always plays quite fair
   Everything I tell her to.

People say she isn't there—
   They step over her at play
And they sit down in her chair
   In the very rudest way.

It is queer they cannot know
   When she's there for me to see!
When the other children go
   Fanny comes and plays with me.

WISHING
William Allingham

Ring—ting! I wish I were a primrose,
A bright yellow primrose blooming in the spring!
   The stooping boughs above me,
   The wandering bee to love me,
The fern and moss to creep across,
And the elm tree for our king!

Nay—stay! I wish I were an elm tree,
A great, lofty elm tree with green leaves gay!
   The winds would set them dancing,
   The sun and moonshine glance in,
The birds would house among the boughs,
And ever sweetly sing!

Oh—no! I wish I were a robin,
A robin or a little wren, everywhere to go;
  Through forest, field, or garden,
  And ask no leave or pardon,
Till winter comes with icy thumbs
To ruffle up our wings!

Well—tell! Where should I fly to,
Where go to sleep in the dark wood or dell?
  Before a day was over,
  Home comes the rover,
For Mother's kiss—sweeter this
Than any other thing.

RATHERS
Mary Austin

I know very well what I'd rather be
If I didn't always have to be me!
I'd rather be an owl,
A downy feathered owl,
A wink-ity, blink-ity, yellow-eyed owl
In a hole in a hollow tree.
I'd take my dinner in chipmunk town,
And wouldn't I gobble the field mice down,
If I were a wink-ity, blink-ity owl,
And didn't always have to be me!

I know very well what I'd like to do
If I didn't have to do what I do!
I'd go and be a woodpecker,
A rap-ity, tap-ity, red-headed woodpecker
In the top of a tall old tree.
And I'd never take a look
At a lesson or a book,
And I'd scold like a pirate on the sea,
If I only had to do what I like to do,
And didn't always have to be me!

15

Or else I'd be an antelope,
A pronghorned antelope,
With lots of other antelope
Skimming like a cloud on a wire-grass plain.
But if I were an antelope,
A bounding, bouncing antelope,
You'd never get me back to my desk again!

Or I might be a puma,
A singe-colored puma,
A slinking, sly-foot puma
As fierce as fierce could be!
And I'd wait by the waterholes where antelope drink
In the cool of the morning
And I *do*
      not
        think
That ever any antelope could get away from me.

But if I were a hunter,
A red Indian hunter—
I'd *like* to be a hunter,—
I'd have a bow made of juniper wood
From a lightning-blasted tree,
And I'd creep and I'd creep on that puma asleep
And I'd shoot him with an arrow,
A flint tipped arrow,
An eagle feathered arrow,
For a puma kills calves and a puma kills sheep,
And he'd never eat any more antelope
If he once met up with me!

A WORD FITLY SPOKEN
The Bible

A word fitly spoken
Is like apples of gold in pictures of silver.

THE CAVE-BOY
Laura E. Richards

I dreamed I was a cave-boy
  And lived in a cave,
A mammoth for my saddle horse,
  A monkey for my slave.
And through the tree-fern forests
  A-riding I would go,
When I was once a cave-boy,
  A million years ago.

I dreamed I was a cave-boy;
  I hunted with a spear
The sabre-toothed tiger,
  The prehistoric deer.
A wolf-skin for my dress suit,
  I thought me quite a beau,
When I was once a cave-boy,
  A million years ago.

I dreamed I was a cave-boy;
  My dinner was a bone,
And how I had to fight for it,
  To get it for my own!
We banged each other o'er the head,
  And oft our blood did flow,
When I was once a cave-boy,
  A million years ago.

I dreamed I was a cave-boy.
  The torches' smoky light
Shone on the dinner table,
  A pile of bones so white.
I lapped some water from the spring,
  The easiest way, you know,
When I was once a cave-boy,
  A million years ago.

I dreamed—but now I am awake;
    A voice is in my ear.
"Come out and have a game of ball!
    The sun is shining clear.
We'll have some doughnuts afterwards,
    And then a-swimming go!"
I'm glad I'm *not* a cave-boy,
    A million years ago!

I AM
Hilda Conkling

I am willowy boughs
For coolness;
I am gold-finch wings
For darkness;
I am a little grape
Thinking of September,
I am a very small violet
Thinking of May.

A LITTLE SONG OF LIFE
Lizette Woodworth Reese

Glad that I live am I;
    That the sky is blue;
Glad for the country lanes,
    And the fall of dew.

After the sun the rain,
    After the rain the sun;
This is the way of life,
    Till the work be done.

All that we need to do,
Be we low or high,
Is to see that we grow
Nearer the sky.

FOR A CHILD
Fannie Stearns Davis

Your friends shall be the Tall Wind,
The River and the Tree;
The Sun that laughs and marches,
The Swallows and the Sea.

Your prayers shall be the murmur
Of grasses in the rain;
The song of wildwood thrushes
That makes God glad again.

And you shall run and wander,
And you shall dream and sing
Of brave things and bright things
Beyond the swallow's wings.

And you shall envy no man,
Nor hurt your heart with sighs,
For I will keep you simple
That God may make you wise.

PRIMER LESSON
Carl Sandburg

Look out how you use proud words.
When you let proud words go, it is not easy to call them back.
They wear long boots, hard boots; they walk off proud; they can't
hear you calling—
Look out how you use proud words.

THE DAY BEFORE APRIL
Mary Carolyn Davies

> The day before April
> Alone, alone,
> I walked in the woods
> And I sat on a stone.
>
> I sat on a broad stone
> And sang to the birds.
> The tune was God's making
> But I made the words.

BEAUTY
E-Yeh-Shure

> Beauty is seen
> In the sunlight,
> The trees, the birds,
> Corn growing and people working
> Or dancing for their harvest.
>
> Beauty is heard
> In the night,
> Wind sighing, rain falling,
> Or a singer chanting
> Anything in earnest.
>
> Beauty is in yourself.
> Good deeds, happy thoughts
> That repeat themselves
> In your dreams,
> In your work,
> And even in your rest.

BARTER
Sara Teasdale

Life has loveliness to sell,
    All beautiful and splendid things,
Blue waves whitened on a cliff,
    Soaring fire that sways and sings,
And children's faces looking up
Holding wonder like a cup.

Life has loveliness to sell,
    Music like a curve of gold,
Scent of pine trees in the rain,
    Eyes that love you, arms that hold,
And for your spirit's still delight,
Holy thoughts that star the night.

Spend all you have for loveliness,
    Buy it and never count the cost;
For one white singing hour of peace
    Count many a year of strife well lost,
And for a breath of ecstasy
Give all you have been, or could be.

GOOD COMPANY
Karle Wilson Baker

Today I have grown taller from walking with the trees,
The seven sister-poplars who go so softly in a line;
And I think my heart is whiter for its parley with a star
That trembled out at nightfall and hung above the pine.

The call-note of a redbird from the cedars in the dusk
Woke his happy note within me to answer free and fine;
And a sudden angel beckoned from a column of blue smoke—
Lord, who am I that they should stoop—these holy folk of thine?

MEASURE ME, SKY
Leonora Speyer

Measure me, sky!
   Tell me I reach by a song
Nearer the stars;
   I have been little so long.

Weigh me, high wind!
   What will your wild scales record?
Profit of pain,
   Joy by the weight of a word.

Horizon, reach out!
   Catch at my hands, stretch me taut,
Rim of the world:
   Widen my eyes by a thought.

Sky, be my depth,
   Wind, be my width and my height,
World, my heart's span;
   Loveliness, wings for my flight.

HOLD FAST YOUR DREAMS
Louise Driscoll

Hold fast your dreams!
Within your heart
Keep one still, secret spot
Where dreams may go,
And sheltered so,
May thrive and grow—
Where doubt and fear are not.
Oh, keep a place apart
Within your heart,
For little dreams to go.

A CHILD'S THOUGHT OF GOD
Elizabeth Barrett Browning

They say that God lives very high!
   But if you look above the pines
You cannot see our God. And why?

And if you dig down in the mines
   You never see Him in the gold,
Though from Him all that's glory shines.

God is so good, He wears a fold
   Of heaven and earth across His face—
Like secrets kept, for love untold.

But still I feel that His embrace
   Slides down by thrills, through all things made,
Through sight and sound of every place:

As if my tender mother laid
   On my shut lids her kisses' pressure,
Half-waking me at night and said,
   "Who kissed you through the dark, dear guesser?"

MY GIFT
Christina Rossetti

What can I give Him
Poor as I am;
If I were a shepherd,
I would give Him a lamb.
If I were a wise man,
I would do my part.
But what can I give Him?
I will give my heart.

A SONG OF GREATNESS
A Chippewa Indian song
Transcribed by Mary Austin

When I hear the old men
Telling of heroes,
Telling of great deeds
Of ancient days,
When I hear them telling,
Then I think within me
I too am one of these.

When I hear the people
Praising great ones,
Then I know that I too
Shall be esteemed,
I too when my time comes
Shall do mightily.

HE THAT IS SLOW TO ANGER
The Bible

He that is slow to anger is better than the mighty;
And he that ruleth his spirit than he that taketh a city.

A CHILD'S PRAYER
John Banister Tabb

Make me, dear Lord, polite and kind
To every one, I pray.
And may I ask you how you find
Yourself, dear Lord, to-day?

A GRACE FOR A CHILD
Robert Herrick

Here a little child I stand,
Heaving up my either hand,
Cold as paddocks though they be,
Here I lift them up to Thee,
For a benison to fall
On our meat and on us all.

THE LORD IS MY SHEPHERD
The Bible: Psalm 23

The Lord is my shepherd;
I shall not want.
He maketh me to lie down in green pastures;
He leadeth me beside the still waters.
He restoreth my soul.

He leadeth me in the paths of righteousness
For his name's sake.
Yea, though I walk through the valley of the shadow of death,
I will fear no evil:
For thou art with me;
Thy rod and thy staff
They comfort me.

Thou preparest a table before me
In the presence of mine enemies;
Thou anointest my head with oil;
My cup runneth over.

Surely goodness and mercy shall follow me
All the days of my life:
And I will dwell in the house of the Lord
For ever.

*My family
and I*

SONG FOR A LITTLE HOUSE
Christopher Morley

I'm glad our house is a little house,
  Not too tall nor too wide;
I'm glad the hovering butterflies
  Feel free to come inside.

Our little house is a friendly house,
  It is not shy or vain;
It gossips with the talking trees,
  And makes friends with the rain.

And quick leaves cast a shimmer of green
  Against our whited walls,
And in the phlox the courteous bees
  Are paying duty calls.

WE THANK THEE

For mother-love and father-care,
For brothers strong and sisters fair,
For love at home and here each day,
For guidance lest we go astray,
  Father in Heaven, we thank Thee.

For this new morning with its light,
For rest and shelter of the night,
For health and food, for love and friends,
For ev'rything His goodness sends,
  Father in Heaven, we thank Thee.

For flowers that bloom about our feet,
For tender grass, so fresh, so sweet,
For song of bird and hum of bee,
For all things fair we hear or see,
    Father in Heaven, we thank Thee.

For blue of stream and blue of sky,
For pleasant shade of branches high,
For fragrant air and cooling breeze,
For beauty of the blooming trees,
    Father in Heaven, we thank Thee.

LET'S BE MERRY
Christina Rossetti

Mother shake the cherry-tree,
    Susan catch a cherry;
Oh how funny that will be,
    Let's be merry!

One for brother, one for sister,
    Two for mother more,
Six for father, hot and tired,
    Knocking at the door.

WHAT DO THEY DO?
Christina Rossetti

What does the bee do?
    Bring home honey.
And what does Father do?
    Bring home money.
And what does Mother do?
    Lay out the money.
And what does baby do?
    Eat up the honey.

ONLY ONE MOTHER
George Cooper

Hundreds of stars in the pretty sky,
　　Hundreds of shells on the shore together,
Hundreds of birds that go singing by,
　　Hundreds of lambs in the sunny weather.

Hundreds of dewdrops to greet the dawn,
　　Hundreds of bees in the purple clover,
Hundreds of butterflies on the lawn,
　　But only one mother the wide world over.

MOTHER
Theresa Helburn

I have praised many loved ones in my song,
　　And yet I stand
Before her shrine, to whom all things belong,
　　With empty hand.

Perhaps the ripening future holds a time
　　For things unsaid;
Not now; men do not celebrate in rhyme
　　Their daily bread.

WHEN MOTHER READS ALOUD

When Mother reads aloud, the past
　　Seems real as every day;
I hear the tramp of armies vast,
I see the spears and lances cast,
　　I join the trilling fray;
Brave knights and ladies fair and proud
I meet when Mother reads aloud.

When Mother reads aloud, far lands
  Seem very near and true;
I cross the desert's gleaming sands,
Or hunt the jungle's prowling bands,
  Or sail the ocean blue.
Far heights, whose peaks the cold mists shroud,
I scale, when Mother reads aloud.

When Mother reads aloud, I long
  For noble deeds to do—
To help the right, redress the wrong;
It seems so easy to be strong,
  So simple to be true.
Oh, thick and fast the visions crowd
My eyes, when Mother reads aloud.

HER WORDS
Anna Hempstead Branch

My mother has the prettiest tricks
  Of words and words and words.
Her talk comes out as smooth and sleek
  As breasts of singing birds.

She shapes her speech all silver fine
  Because she loves it so,
And her own eyes begin to shine
  To hear her stories grow.

And if she goes to make a call
  Or out to take a walk,
We leave our work when she returns
  And run to hear her talk.

We had not dreamed these things were so
  Of sorrow and of mirth.
Her speech is as a thousand eyes
  Through which we see the earth.

God wove a web of loveliness,
    Of clouds and stars and birds,
But made not anything at all
    So beautiful as words.

They shine around our simple earth
    With golden shadowings,
And every common thing they touch
    Is exquisite with wings.

There's nothing poor and nothing small
    But is made fair with them.
They are the hands of living faith
    That touch the garment's hem.

They are as fair as bloom or air,
    They shine like any star,
And I am rich who learned from her
    How beautiful they are.

FATHER'S STORY
Elizabeth Madox Roberts

We put more coal on the big red fire,
    And while we are waiting for dinner to cook,
Our father comes and tells us about
    A story that he has read in a book.

And Charles and Will and Dick and I
    And all of us but Clarence are there.
And some of us sit on Father's legs,
    But one has to sit on the little red chair.

And when we are sitting very still,
    He sings us a song or tells a piece;
He sings "Dan Tucker Went to Town,"
    Or he tells us about the golden fleece.

He tells us about the golden wool,
  And some of it is about a boy
Named Jason, and about a ship,
  And some is about a town called Troy.

And while he is telling or singing it through,
  I stand by his arm, for that is my place.
And I push my fingers into his skin
  To make little dents in his big round face.

FATHER
Frances Frost

My father's face is brown with sun,
His body is tall and limber.
His hands are gentle with beast or child
And strong as hardwood timber.

My father's eyes are the colors of sky,
Clear blue or gray as rain:
They change with the swinging change of days
While he watches the weather vane.

That galleon, golden upon our barn,
Veers with the world's four winds.
My father, his eyes on the vane, knows when
To fill our barley bins,

To stack our wood and pile our mows
With redtop and sweet tossed clover.
He captains our farm that rides the winds,
A keen-eyed brown earth-lover.

AUTOMOBILE MECHANICS
Dorothy W. Baruch

Sometimes
 I help my dad
Work on our automobile.
  We unscrew
  The radiator cap
   And we let some water run—
   Swish—from a hose
   Into the tank.

   And then we open up the hood
   And feed in oil
   From a can with a long spout.
   And then we take a lot of rags
   And clean all about.
    We clean the top
    And the doors
    And the fenders and the wheels
    And the windows and floors. . . .
     We work *hard*
     My dad
     And I.

DADDY FELL INTO THE POND
Alfred Noyes

Everyone grumbled. The sky was grey.
We had nothing to do and nothing to say.
We were nearing the end of a dismal day,
And there seemed to be nothing beyond,
            THEN
    Daddy fell into the pond!

And everyone's face grew merry and bright,
And Timothy danced for sheer delight.
"Give me the camera, quick, oh quick!
He's crawling out of the duckweed." *Click!*

Then the gardener suddenly slapped his knee,
And doubled up, shaking silently,
And the ducks all quacked as if they were daft
And it sounded as if the old drake laughed.

O, there wasn't a thing that didn't respond
WHEN
Daddy fell into the pond!

TO MY SON, AGED THREE YEARS
AND FIVE MONTHS
Thomas Hood

Thou happy, happy elf!
(But stop,—first let me kiss away that tear)—
Thou tiny image of myself!
(My love, he's poking peas into his ear!)
Thou merry laughing sprite!
With spirits feather light,
Untouched by sorrow, and unsoiled by sin—
(Good Heavens! the child is swallowing a pin!)

Thou little tricksy Puck!
With antic toys so funnily bestuck,
Light as the singing bird that wings the air—
(The door! the door! he'll tumble down the stair!)
Thou darling of thy sire!
(Why, Jane, he'll set his pinafore afire!)
Thou imp of mirth and joy!
In love's dear chain, so strong and bright a link,
Thou idol of thy parents—(Drat the boy!
There goes my ink!)

Thy father's pride and hope!
(He'll break the mirror with that skipping-rope!)
With pure heart newly stamped from Nature's mint—
(Where *did* he learn that squint?)
 Thou young domestic dove!
(He'll have that jug off with another shove!)
  Dear nursling of the Ilymeneal nest!
  (Are those torn clothes his best?)
  Little epitome of man!
(He'll climb upon the table, that's his plan!)
Touched with the beauteous tints of dawning life
  (He's got a knife!)

 Thou pretty opening rose!
(Go to your mother, child, and wipe your nose!)
Balmy and breathing music like the South,
(He really brings my heart into my mouth!)
Fresh as the morn, and brilliant as its star,—
(I wish that window had an iron bar!)
Bold as the hawk, yet gentle as the dove,—
  (I'll tell you what, my love,
I cannot write unless he's sent above!)

INFANT JOY
William Blake

        "I have no name;
        I am but two days old."
        What shall I call thee?
        "I happy am,
        Joy is my name."
        Sweet joy befall thee!

        Pretty joy!
        Sweet joy, but two days old.
        Sweet joy I call thee;
        Thou dost smile,
        I sing the while;
        Sweet joy befall thee!

37

A BABY'S FEET
Algernon Charles Swinburne

A baby's feet, like sea-shells pink,
  Might tempt, should heaven see meet
An angel's lips to kiss, we think,
  A baby's feet.

Like rose-hued sea-flowers toward the heat
  They stretch and spread and wink
Their ten soft buds that part and meet.

No flower-bells that expand and shrink
  Gleam half so heavenly sweet,
As shine on life's untrodden brink
  A baby's feet.

LITTLE
Dorothy Aldis

I am the sister of him
  And he is my brother.
He is too little for us
  To talk to each other.

So every morning I show him
  My doll and my book;
But every morning he still is
  Too little to look.

IN GO-CART SO TINY
Kate Greenaway

In go-cart so tiny
  My sister I drew;
And I've promised to draw her
  The wide world through.

38

We have not yet started—
I own it with sorrow—
Because our trip's always
Put off till to-morrow.

SLIPPERY
Carl Sandburg

The six month child
Fresh from the tub
Wriggles in our hands.
This is our fish child.
Give her a nickname: Slippery.

SISTERS
Eleanor Farjeon

"Come!" cried Helen, eager Helen.
"*Time enough,*" said careful Ann.
But oh, the lilac-buds were swelling
And all the birds had started telling—
"Listen! look!" cried eager Helen,
Pointing where the spring began.
"*Well, and what of that,*" said Ann.
"Something's happening—oh, let's go!"
"*When it happens we shall know.*"
"Ah, but that's so slow!" cried Helen,
"Come on, come!" cried eager Helen.
   "*Time enough,*" said Ann.
"I must go!" "*And I will wait.*
You'll be too soon." "You'll be too late!"
"*Who knows?*" said Ann. "Come on!" cried Helen,
   And ran and ran and ran.

TWO IN BED
A. B. Ross

When my brother Tommy
Sleeps in bed with me,
He doubles up
And makes
himself
exactly
like
a
V

And 'cause the bed is not so wide,
A part of him is on my side.

OUR SILLY LITTLE SISTER
Dorothy Aldis

To begin with she wouldn't have fallen in
If she hadn't been acting so silly.
First thing we saw was her hair ribbon there
On top like a water lily.

In less than a minute we'd gotten her out
And set her down quickly to drain,
And do you know what she said through her dripping hair?
"I want to go swimming again."

"Swimming?" we cried. "Do you think *you* can swim?"
She sat there so scowly and black.
"*Much better than you can, besides I don't care!*"
We couldn't think what to say back.

BIG BROTHER
Elizabeth Madox Roberts

Our brother Clarence goes to school;
    He has a slate and a blue schoolbag.
He has a book and a copybook
    And a scholar's companion and a little slate rag.

He knows a boy named Joe B. Kirk,
    And he learns about *c-a-t* cat,
And how to play one-two-sky-blue,
    And how to make a football out of a hat.

We climb up on the fence and gate
    And watch until he's small and dim,
Far up the street, and he looks back
    To see if we keep on watching him.

THE QUARREL
Eleanor Farjeon

I quarreled with my brother,
I don't know what about,
One thing led to another
And somehow we fell out.
The start of it was slight,
The end of it was strong,
He said he was right,
I knew he was wrong!

We hated one another.
The afternoon turned black.
Then suddenly my brother
Thumped me on the back,
And said, "Oh, *come* along!
We can't go on all night—
I was in the wrong."
So he was in the right.

41

THE CUPBOARD
Walter de la Mare

I know a little cupboard,
With a teeny tiny key,
And there's a jar of Lollipops
  For me, me, me.

It has a little shelf, my dear,
As dark as dark can be,
And there's a dish of Banbury Cakes
  For me, me, me.

I have a small fat grandmamma,
With a very slippery knee,
And she's Keeper of the Cupboard,
  With the key, key, key.

And when I'm very good, my dear,
As good as good can be,
There's Banbury Cakes, and Lollipops
  For me, me, me.

AFTERNOON WITH GRANDMOTHER
Barbara A. Huff

I always shout when Grandma comes,
But Mother says, "Now please be still
And good and do what *Grandma* wants."
And I say, "Yes, I will."

So off we go in Grandma's car.
"There's a brand new movie quite near by,"
She says, "that I'd rather like to see."
And I say, "So would I."

The show has horses and chases and battles;
We gasp and hold hands the whole way through.
She smiles and says, "I liked that lots."
And I say, "I did, too."

"It's made me hungry, though," she says,
"I'd like a malt and tarts with jam.
By any chance are you hungry, too?"
And I say, "Yes, I am."

Later at home my Mother says,
"I hope you were careful to do as bid.
Did you and Grandma have a good time?"
And I say, "YES, WE DID!!!"

ANIMAL CRACKERS
Christopher Morley

Animal crackers, and cocoa to drink,
That is the finest of suppers, I think;
When I'm grown up and can have what I please
I think I shall always insist upon these.

What do *you* choose when you're offered a treat?
When Mother says, "What would you like best to eat?"
Is it waffles and syrup, or cinnamon toast?
It's cocoa and animal crackers that *I* love most!

The kitchen's the cosiest place that I know:
The kettle is singing, the stove is aglow,
And there in the twilight, how jolly to see
The cocoa and animals waiting for me.

Daddy and Mother dine later in state,
With Mary to cook for them, Susan to wait;
But they don't have nearly as much fun as I
Who eat in the kitchen with Nurse standing by;
And Daddy once said, he would like to be me
Having cocoa and animals once more for tea!

SETTING THE TABLE
Dorothy Aldis

Evenings
When the house is quiet
I delight
To spread the white
Smooth cloth and put the flowers on the table.

I place the knives and forks around
Without a sound.
I light the candles.

I love to see
Their small reflected torches shine
Against the greenness of the vine
And garden.

Is that the mignonette, I wonder,
Smells so sweet?

And then I call them in to eat.

MANNERS
Mariana Griswold Van Rensselaer

I have an uncle I don't like,
   An aunt I cannot bear:
She chucks me underneath the chin,
   He ruffles up my hair.

Another uncle I adore,
   Another aunty, too:
She shakes me kindly by the hand,
   He says, "How do you do?"

I'VE GOT A NEW BOOK FROM
MY GRANDFATHER HYDE
Leroy F. Jackson

I've got a new book from my Grandfather Hyde.
It's skin on the cover and paper inside,
And reads about Arabs and horses and slaves,
And tells how the Caliph of Bagdad behaves.
I'd not take a goat and a dollar beside
For the book that I got from my Grandfather Hyde.

A CHILD'S GRACE
Robert Burns

Some hae meat and canna eat,
    And some wad eat that want it;
But we hae meat and we can eat,
    And sae the Lord be thankit.

A POP CORN SONG
Nancy Byrd Turner

Sing a song of pop corn
    When the snowstorms rage;
Fifty little brown men
    Put into a cage.
Shake them till they laugh and leap
    Crowding to the top;
Watch them burst their little coats
    Pop!! Pop!! Pop!!

Sing a song of pop corn
    In the firelight;
Fifty little fairies
    Robed in fleecy white.

45

Through the shining wires see
How they skip and prance
To the music of the flames;
Dance! Dance! Dance!

Sing a song of pop corn
Done the frolicking;
Fifty little fairies
Strung upon a string.
Cool and happy, hand in hand,
Sugar-spangled, fair;
Isn't that a necklace fit
For any child to wear?

WHEN YOUNG MELISSA SWEEPS
Nancy Byrd Turner

When young Melissa sweeps a room
I vow she dances with the broom!

She curtsies in a corner brightly
And leads her partner forth politely.

Then up and down in jigs and reels,
With gold dust flying at their heels,

They caper. With a whirl or two
They make the wainscot shine like new;

They waltz beside the hearth, and quick
It brightens, shabby brick by brick.

A gay gavotte across the floor,
A Highland fling from door to door,

And every crack and corner's clean
Enough to suit a dainty queen.

If ever you are full of gloom,
Just watch Melissa sweep a room!

I LIKE HOUSECLEANING
Dorothy Brown Thompson

It's fun to clean house.
   The food isn't much,
And paint's all about
   That we mustn't touch;
But strange stored-away things,
Not like everyday things,
Make marvelous playthings
   From attics and such.

The boxes come out
   From closets and chests,
With odd sorts of clothes
   Like old hats and vests,
And photographed faces,
And ribbons and laces,
And postcards of places,
   And cards left by guests.

Then Mother says, "Throw
   The whole lot away!"
And Father says, "Wait—
   I'll need this someday."
But either way's meaning
A chance to go gleaning
Among the housecleaning
   For new things to play.

MUMPS
Elizabeth Madox Roberts

I had a feeling in my neck,
   And on the sides were two big bumps;
I couldn't swallow anything
   At all because I had the mumps.

And Mother tied it with a piece.
   And then she tied up Will and John,
And no one else but Dick was left
   That didn't have a mump rag on.

He teased at us and laughed at us,
   And said, whenever he went by,
"It's vinegar and lemon drops
   And pickles!" just to make us cry.

But Tuesday Dick was very sad
   And cried because his neck was sore,
And not a one said sour things
   To anybody any more.

THE LAND OF COUNTERPANE
Robert Louis Stevenson

When I was sick and lay abed,
I had two pillows at my head,
And all my toys beside me lay
To keep me happy all the day.

And sometimes for an hour or so
I watched my leaden soldiers go,
With different uniforms and drills,
Among the bedclothes, through the hills;

And sometimes sent my ships in fleets
All up and down among the sheets;
Or brought my trees and houses out,
And planted cities all about.

I was the giant great and still
That sits upon the pillow-hill,
And sees before him, dale and plain,
The pleasant Land of Counterpane.

MR. NOBODY

I know a funny little man,
　　As quiet as a mouse,
Who does the mischief that is done
　　In everybody's house!
There's no one ever sees his face,
　　And yet we all agree
That every plate we break was cracked
　　By Mr. Nobody.

'Tis he who always tears our books,
　　Who leaves the door ajar,
He pulls the buttons from our shirts,
　　And scatters pins afar;
That squeaking door will always squeak,
　　For, prithee, don't you see,
We leave the oiling to be done
　　By Mr. Nobody.

The finger marks upon the door
　　By none of us are made;
We never leave the blinds unclosed,
　　To let the curtains fade.
The ink we never spill; the boots
　　That lying round you see
Are not our boots—they all belong
　　To Mr. Nobody.

LITTLE BROTHER'S SECRET
Katherine Mansfield

When my birthday was coming
Little Brother had a secret:
He kept it for days and days
And just hummed a little tune when I asked him.

But one night it rained
And I woke up and heard him crying:
Then he told me.
"I planted two lumps of sugar in your garden
Because you love it so frightfully.
I thought there would be a whole sugar tree for your birthday.
And now it will all be melted."
O the darling!

THE BIRTHDAY CHILD
Rose Fyleman

Everything's been different
All the day long,
Lovely things have happened,
Nothing has gone wrong.

Nobody has scolded me,
Everyone has smiled.
Isn't it delicious
To be a birthday child?

SEVEN TIMES ONE
Jean Ingelow

There's no dew left on the daisies and clover,
There's no rain left in heaven;
I've said my "seven times" over and over,
Seven times one are seven.

I am old, so old, I can write a letter;
My birthday lessons are done;
The lambs play always, they know no better;
They are only one times one.

O Moon! in the night I have seen you sailing
  And shining so round and low;
You were bright! ah, bright! but your light is failing—
  You are nothing now but a bow.

You Moon, have you done something wrong in heaven
  That God has hidden your face?
I hope if you have you will soon be forgiven,
  And shine again in your place.

O velvet Bee, you're a dusty fellow,
  You've powdered your legs with gold!
O brave Marsh Marybuds, rich and yellow,
  Give me your money to hold!

O Columbine, open your folded wrapper,
  Where two twin turtledoves dwell!
O Cuckoo pint, toll me the purple clapper
  That hangs in your clear green bell!

And show me your nest with the young ones in it;
  I will not steal them away;
I am old! you may trust me, Linnet, Linnet—
  I am seven times one today.

THE CHILDREN'S HOUR
Henry Wadsworth Longfellow

> Between the dark and the daylight,
>   When the night is beginning to lower,
> Comes a pause in the day's occupations
>   That is known as the Children's Hour.
>
> I hear in the chamber above me
>   The patter of little feet,
> The sound of a door that is opened,
>   And voices soft and sweet.

From my study I see in the lamplight,
　　Descending the broad hall stair,
Grave Alice, and laughing Allegra,
　　And Edith with golden hair.

A whisper, and then a silence:
　　Yet I know by their merry eyes
They are plotting and planning together
　　To take me by surprise.

A sudden rush from the stairway,
　　A sudden raid from the hall!
By three doors left unguarded
　　They enter my castle wall!

They climb up into my turret
　　O'er the arms and back of my chair;
If I try to escape, they surround me;
　　They seem to be everywhere.

They almost devour me with kisses,
　　Their arms about me entwine,
Till I think of the Bishop of Bingen
　　In his Mouse-Tower on the Rhine!

Do you think, O blue-eyed banditti,
　　Because you have scaled the wall,
Such an old mustache as I am
　　Is not a match for you all?

I have you fast in my fortress,
　　And will not let you depart,
But put you down into the dungeon
　　In the round-tower of my heart.

And there I will keep you forever,
　　Yes, forever and a day,
Till the wall shall crumble to ruin,
　　And molder in dust away!

NIGHT
William Blake

The sun descending in the west,
   The evening star does shine;
The birds are silent in their nest,
   And I must seek for mine.
The moon, like a flower,
In heaven's high bower,
With silent delight
Sits and smiles on the night.

Farewell, green fields and happy groves,
   Where flocks have took delight.
Where lambs have nibbled, silent moves
   The feet of angels bright;
Unseen they pour blessing,
And joy without ceasing,
On each bud and blossom,
And each sleeping bosom.

GOOD NIGHT
Victor Hugo

Good night! Good night!
Far flies the light;
But still God's love
Shall flame above,
Making all bright.
Good night! Good night!

SWEET AND LOW
Alfred Tennyson

Sweet and low, sweet and low,
   Wind of the western sea!
Low, low, breathe and blow,
   Wind of the western sea!
Over the rolling waters go,
Come from the dying moon, and blow,
   Blow him again to me;
While my little one, while my pretty one sleeps.

Sleep and rest, sleep and rest,
   Father will come to thee soon;
Rest, rest, on mother's breast,
   Father will come to thee soon;
Father will come to his babe in the nest,
Silver sails all out of the west
   Under the silver moon:
Sleep, my little one, sleep, my pretty one, sleep.

CRADLE SONG
Sarojini Naidu

From groves of spice,
O'er fields of rice,
Athwart the lotus stream,
I bring for you,
Aglint with dew,
A little lovely dream.

Sweet, shut your eyes,
The wild fireflies
Dance through the fairy neem;
From the poppybole
For you I stole
A little lovely dream.

Dear eyes, good night,
In golden light
The stars around you gleam;
On you I press
With soft caress
A little lovely dream.

WYNKEN, BLYNKEN, AND NOD
Eugene Field

Wynken, Blynken, and Nod one night
Sailed off in a wooden shoe,—
Sailed on a river of crystal light
Into a sea of dew.
"Where are you going, and what do you wish?"
The old moon asked the three.
"We have come to fish for the herring fish
That live in this beautiful sea;
Nets of silver and gold have we!"
Said Wynken,
Blynken,
And Nod.

The old moon laughed and sang a song,
As they rocked in the wooden shoe;
And the wind that sped them all night long
Ruffled the waves of dew.
The little stars were the herring fish
That lived in that beautiful sea—
"Now cast your nets wherever you wish,—
Never afeard are we!"
So cried the stars to the fishermen three,
Wynken,
Blynken,
And Nod.

All night long their nets they threw
  To the stars in the twinkling foam,—
Then down from the skies came the wooden shoe,
  Bringing the fishermen home:
'Twas all so pretty a sail, it seemed
  As if it could not be;
And some folk thought 'twas a dream they'd dreamed
  Of sailing that beautiful sea;
  But I shall name you the fishermen three:
          Wynken,
          Blynken,
          And Nod.

Wynken and Blynken are two little eyes,
  And Nod is a little head,
And the wooden shoe that sailed the skies
  Is a wee one's trundle-bed;
So shut your eyes while Mother sings
  Of wonderful sights that be,
And you shall see the beautiful things
  As you rock in the misty sea
  Where the old shoe rocked the fishermen three:—
          Wynken,
          Blynken,
          And Nod.

SLUMBER SONG
Louis V. Ledoux

    Drowsily come the sheep
  From the place where the pastures be,
    By a dusty lane
    To the fold again,
  First one, and then two, and three:
    First one, then two, by the paths of sleep
    Drowsily come the sheep.

Drowsily come the sheep,
And the shepherd is singing low:
    After eight comes nine
    In the endless line,
They come, and then in they go.
    First eight, then nine, by the paths of sleep
    Drowsily come the sheep.

Drowsily come the sheep
And they pass through the sheepfold door;
    After one comes two,
    After one comes two,
Comes two and then three and four.
    First one, then two, by the paths of sleep,
    Drowsily come the sheep.

PRAYER FOR THIS HOUSE
Louis Untermeyer

May nothing evil cross this door,
    And may ill-fortune never pry
About these windows; may the roar
    And rains go by.

Strengthened by faith, the rafters will
    Withstand the battering of the storm.
This hearth, though all the world grow chill
    Will keep you warm.

Peace shall walk softly through these rooms,
    Touching your lips with holy wine,
Till every casual corner blooms
    Into a shrine.

Laughter shall drown the raucous shout
    And, though the sheltering walls are thin,
May they be strong to keep hate out
    And hold love in.

My almanac

TIME, YOU OLD GYPSY MAN
Ralph Hodgson

Time, you old gypsy man,
  Will you not stay,
Put up your caravan
  Just for one day?

All things I'll give you
Will you be my guest:
Bells for your jennet
Of silver the best;
Goldsmiths shall beat you
A great golden ring;
Peacocks shall bow to you;
Little boys sing.
Oh, and sweet girls will
Festoon you with may.
Time, you old gypsy,
Why hasten away?

Last week in Babylon,
Last night in Rome,
Morning, and in the crush
Under Paul's dome;
Under Paul's dial
You tighten your rein—
Only a moment,
And off once again;
Off to some city
Now blind in the womb,
Off to another
Ere that's in the tomb.

Time, you old gypsy man,
  Will you not stay,
Put up your caravan
  Just for one day?

61

THE MONTHS
Christina Rossetti

January cold and desolate;
February dripping wet;
March wind ranges;
April changes;
Birds sing in tune
To flowers of May,
And sunny June
Brings longest day;
In scorched July
The storm-clouds fly,
Lightning-torn;
August bears corn,
September fruit;
In rough October
Earth must disrobe her;
Stars fall and shoot
In keen November;
And night is long
And cold is strong
In bleak December.

MARJORIE'S ALMANAC
Thomas Bailey Aldrich

Robins in the treetop,
    Blossoms in the grass,
Green things a-growing
    Everywhere you pass;
Sudden little breezes,
    Showers of silver dew,
Black bough and bent twig
    Budding out anew;

Pine tree and willow tree,
    Fringed elm and larch,—
Don't you think that Maytime's
    Pleasanter than March?

Apples in the orchard
    Mellowing one by one;
Strawberries upturning
    Soft cheeks to the sun;
Roses faint with sweetness,
    Lilies fair of face,
Drowsy scents and murmurs
    Haunting every place;
Lengths of golden sunshine,
    Moonlight bright as day,—
Don't you think that summer's
    Pleasanter than May?

Roger in the cornpatch
    Whistling Negro songs;
Pussy by the hearthside
    Romping with the tongs;
Chestnuts in the ashes
    Bursting through the rind;
Red leaf and gold leaf
    Rustling down the wind;
Mother "doin' peaches"
    All the afternoon,—
Don't you think that autumn's
    Pleasanter than June?

Little fairy snowflakes
    Dancing in the flue;
Old Mr. Santa Claus,
    What's keeping you?
Twilight and firelight
    Shadows come and go;
Merry chime of sleigh bells
    Tinkling through the snow;

Mother knitting stockings
(Pussy's got the ball),—
Don't you think that winter's
Pleasanter than all?

THE BELLS
FROM THE BELLS
Edgar Allan Poe

Hear the sledges with the bells—
Silver bells!
What a world of merriment their melody foretells!
How they tinkle, tinkle, tinkle,
In the icy air of night!
While the stars that oversprinkle
All the heavens seem to twinkle
With a crystalline delight;
Keeping time, time, time,
In a sort of Runic rhyme,
To the tintinnabulation that so musically wells
From the bells, bells, bells, bells,
Bells, bells, bells—
From the jingling and the tinkling of the bells.

RING OUT, WILD BELLS
FROM RING OUT, WILD BELLS
Alfred Tennyson

Ring out, wild bells, to the wild sky,
The flying cloud, the frosty light;
The year is dying in the night;
Ring out, wild bells, and let him die.

64

Ring out the old, ring in the new,
   Ring, happy bells, across the snow;
   The year is going, let him go;
Ring out the false, ring in the true.

WHEN ICICLES HANG BY THE WALL
William Shakespeare

When icicles hang by the wall,
   And Dick the shepherd blows his nail,
And Tom bears logs into the hall,
   And milk comes frozen home in pail,
When blood is nipped and ways be foul,
Then nightly sings the staring owl,
   "Tu-whit, tu-whoo!" A merry note,
While greasy Joan doth keel the pot.

When all aloud the wind doth blow,
   And coughing drowns the parson's saw,
And birds sit brooding in the snow,
   And Marian's nose looks red and raw;
When roasted crabs hiss in the bowl,
Then nightly sings the staring owl,
   "Tu-whit, tu-whoo!" A merry note,
While greasy Joan doth keel the pot.

THE FIRST SNOW-FALL
FROM THE FIRST SNOW-FALL
James Russell Lowell

The snow had begun in the gloaming,
   And busily all the night
Had been heaping field and highway
   With a silence deep and white.

Every pine and fir and hemlock
  Wore ermine too dear for an earl,
And the poorest twig on the elm-tree
  Was ridged inch deep with pearl.

WHITE FIELDS
James Stephens

1.

In the winter time we go
Walking in the fields of snow;

Where there is no grass at all;
Where the top of every wall,

Every fence and every tree,
Is as white as white can be.

2.

Pointing out the way we came,
Everyone of them the same—

All across the fields there be
Prints in silver filigree;

And our mothers always know,
By our footprints in the snow,

Where the children go.

VELVET SHOES
Elinor Wylie

Let us walk in the white snow
  In a soundless space;
With footsteps quiet and slow,
  At a tranquil pace,
  Under veils of white lace.

I shall go shod in silk,
  And you in wool,
White as a white cow's milk,
  More beautiful
  Than the breast of a gull.

We shall walk through the still town
  In a windless peace;
We shall step upon white down,
  Upon silver fleece,
  Upon softer than these.

We shall walk in velvet shoes:
  Wherever we go
Silence will fall like dews
  On white silence below.
  We shall walk in the snow.

STOPPING BY WOODS ON A SNOWY EVENING
Robert Frost

Whose woods these are I think I know.
His house is in the village though;
He will not see me stopping here
To watch his woods fill up with snow.

The little horse must think it queer
To stop without a farmhouse near
Between the woods and frozen lake
The darkest evening of the year.

He gives his harness bells a shake
To ask if there is some mistake.
The only other sound's the sweep
Of easy wind and downy flake.

The woods are lovely and dark and deep.
But I have promises to keep,
And miles to go before I sleep.
And miles to go before I sleep.

FEBRUARY TWILIGHT
Sara Teasdale

I stood beside a hill
  Smooth with new-laid snow,
A single star looked out
  From the cold evening glow.

There was no other creature
  That saw what I could see—
I stood and watched the evening star
  As long as it watched me.

MY VALENTINE
Robert Louis Stevenson

I will make you brooches and toys for your delight
Of bird song at morning and starshine at night.
I will make a palace fit for you and me,
  Of green days in forests
  And blue days at sea.

SONG
William Shakespeare

Tomorrow is Saint Valentine's day,
  All in the morning betime,
And I a maid at your window,
  To be your Valentine.

WRITTEN IN MARCH
William Wordsworth

The cock is crowing,
The stream is flowing,
The small birds twitter,
The lake doth glitter,
The green field sleeps in the sun;
The oldest and youngest
Are at work with the strongest;
The cattle are grazing,
Their heads never raising;
There are forty feeding like one!

Like an army defeated
The snow hath retreated,
And now doth fare ill
On the top of the bare hill;
The ploughboy is whooping—anon—anon—
There's joy in the mountains;
There's life in the fountains;
Small clouds are sailing,
Blue sky prevailing;
The rain is over and gone!

WHO HAS SEEN THE WIND?
Christina Rossetti

Who has seen the wind?
Neither I nor you:
But when the leaves hang trembling,
The wind is passing through.

Who has seen the wind?
Neither you nor I:
But when the trees bow down their heads,
The wind is passing by.

THE NIGHT WIND
Eugene Field

Have you ever heard the wind go "Yooooo"?
   'Tis a pitiful sound to hear!
It seems to chill you through and through
   With a strange and speechless fear.
'Tis the voice of the night that broods outside
   When folk should be asleep,
And many and many's the time I've cried
To the darkness brooding far and wide
   Over the land and the deep:
   "Whom do you want, O lonely night,
   That you wail the long hours through?"
And the night would say in its ghostly way:
      "Yoooooooo!
      Yoooooooo!
      Yoooooooo!"

My mother told me long ago
   (When I was a little tad)
That when the night went wailing so,
   Somebody had been bad;
And then, when I was snug in bed,
   Whither I had been sent,
With the blankets pulled up round my head,
I'd think of what my mother'd said,
   And wonder what boy she meant!
And "Who's been bad to-day?" I'd ask
   Of the wind that hoarsely blew,
And the voice would say in its meaningful way:
      "Yoooooooo!
      Yoooooooo!
      Yoooooooo!"

That this was true I must allow—
   You'll not believe it, though!
Yes, though I'm quite a model now,
   I was not always so.

And if you doubt what things I say,
   Suppose you make the test;
Suppose, when you've been bad some day
And up to bed are sent away
   From mother and the rest—
Suppose you ask, "Who has been bad?"
   And then you'll hear what's true;
For the wind will moan in its ruefulest tone:
      "Yoooooooo!
      Yoooooooo!
      Yoooooooo!"

LO, THE WINTER IS PAST
The Bible

For, lo, the winter is past,
The rain is over and gone;
The flowers appear on the earth;
The time of the singing of birds is come,
And the voice of the turtle is heard in our land.

SPRING
William Blake

Sound the flute!
Now it's mute.
Birds delight
Day and night;
Nightingale
In the dale,
Lark in sky,—
Merrily,
Merrily, merrily to welcome in the year.

Little boy,
Full of joy;
Little girl,
Sweet and small;
Cock does crow,
So do you.
Merry voice,
Infant noise,
Merrily, merrily, to welcome in the year.

Little lamb,
Here I am;
Come and lick
My white neck;
Let me pull
Your soft wool;
Let me kiss
Your soft face:
Merrily, merrily, we welcome in the year.

AWAKE!
The Bible

Awake, O, north wind;
And come, thou south;
Blow upon my garden.

PIPPA'S SONG
Robert Browning

The year's at the spring,
And day's at the morn;
Morning's at seven;
The hillside's dew-pearled;

The lark's on the wing;
The snail's on the thorn:
God's in His Heaven—
All's right with the world!

CHANSON INNOCENTE
e. e. Cummings

in Just-
spring   when the world is mud-
luscious the little
lame balloonman

whistles   far   and wee

and eddieandbill come
running from marbles and
piracies and it's
spring

when the world is puddle-wonderful

the queer
old balloonman whistles
far   and   wee
and bettyandisbel come dancing

from hop-scotch and jump-rope and

it's
spring
and
    the

        goat-footed

balloonMan   whistles
far
and
wee

ON EASTER DAY
Celia Thaxter

Easter lilies! Can you hear
What they whisper, low and clear?
In dewy fragrance they unfold
Their splendor sweet, their snow and gold.
Every beauty-breathing bell
News of heaven has to tell.
Listen to their mystic voice,
Hear, oh mortal, and rejoice!
Hark, their soft and heavenly chime!
Christ is risen for all time!

APRIL
Sara Teasdale

The roofs are shining from the rain,
    The sparrows twitter as they fly,
And with a windy April grace
    The little clouds go by.

Yet the back yards are bare and brown
    With only one unchanging tree—
I could not be so sure of Spring
    Save that it sings in me.

APRIL RAIN SONG
Langston Hughes

Let the rain kiss you.
Let the rain beat upon your head with silver liquid drops.
Let the rain sing you a lullaby.

The rain makes still pools on the sidewalk.
The rain makes running pools in the gutter.
The rain plays a little sleep-song on our roof at night—

And I love the rain.

THE RAINBOW
David McCord

The rainbow arches in the sky,
But in the earth it ends;
But if you ask the reason why,
They'll tell you: "That depends."

It never comes without the rain,
Nor goes without the sun;
But though you try with might and main,
You'll never catch me one.

Perhaps you'll see it once a year,
Perhaps you'll say: "No, twice";
But every time it does appear,
It's very clean and nice.

If I were God, I'd like to win
At sun-and-moon croquet:
I'd drive the rainbow-wickets in
And ask someone to play.

I WILL SING PRAISE
The Bible: from Psalm 9

I will praise thee, O Lord, with my whole heart;
I will shew forth all thy marvellous works.
I will be glad and rejoice in thee:
I will sing praise to thy name, O thou most High.

'TIS MERRY IN GREENWOOD
Walter Scott

'Tis merry in greenwood—thus runs the old lay,—
In the gladsome month of lively May,
When the wild birds' song on stem and spray
    Invites to forest bower;
Then rears the ash his airy crest,
Then shines the birch in silver vest,
And the beech in glistening leaves is drest,
And dark between shows the oak's proud breast,
    Like a chieftain's frowning tower;
Though a thousand branches join their screen,
Yet the broken sunbeams glance between,
And tip the leaves with lighter green,
    With brighter tints the flowers;
Dull is the heart that loves not then
The deep recess of the wildwood glen,
Where roe and red-deer find sheltering den,
    When the sun is in his power.

THE CLOUD
Percy Bysshe Shelley

I bring fresh showers for the thirsting flowers,
    From the seas and the streams;
I bear light shade for the leaves when laid
    In their noonday dreams.
From my wings are shaken the dews that waken
    The sweet buds every one,
When rocked to rest on their mother's breast,
    As she dances about the sun.
I wield the flail of the lashing hail,
    And whiten the green plains under;
And then again I dissolve it in rain,
    And laugh as I pass in thunder.

A DAY IN JUNE
FROM THE VISION OF SIR LAUNFAL
James Russell Lowell

> And what is so rare as a day in June?
> Then, if ever, come perfect days;
> Then Heaven tries earth if it be in tune,
> And over it softly her warm ear lays;
> Whether we look, or whether we listen,
> We hear life murmur, or see it glisten;
> Every clod feels a stir of might,
> An instinct within it that reaches and towers,
> And, groping blindly above it for light,
> Climbs to a soul in grass and flowers.

JULY: THE SUCCESSION
OF THE FOUR SWEET MONTHS
Robert Herrick

> First, April, she with mellow showers
> Opens the way for early flowers;
> Then after her comes smiling May,
> In a more rich and sweet array;
> Next enters June, and brings us more
> Gems than those two, that went before:
> Then, lastly, July comes, and she
> More wealth brings in than all those three.

AUGUST
Celia Thaxter

> Buttercup nodded and said good-by,
> Clover and daisy went off together,
> But the fragrant water lilies lie
> Yet moored in the golden August weather.

The swallows chatter about their flight,
  The cricket chirps like a rare good fellow,
The asters twinkle in clusters bright,
  While the corn grows ripe and the apples mellow.

LEISURE
William H. Davies

What is this life if, full of care,
We have no time to stand and stare?

No time to stand beneath the boughs
And stare as long as sheep or cows.

No time to see, when woods we pass,
Where squirrels hide their nuts in grass.

No time to see, in broad daylight,
Streams full of stars, like skies at night.

No time to turn at Beauty's glance,
And watch her feet, how they can dance.

No time to wait till her mouth can
Enrich that smile her eyes began.

A poor life this if, full of care,
We have no time to stand and stare.

SEPTEMBER
Helen Hunt Jackson

The goldenrod is yellow;
  The corn is turning brown;
The trees in apple orchards
  With fruit are bending down.

The gentian's bluest fringes
　　Are curling in the sun;
In dusty pods the milkweed
　　Its hidden silk has spun.

The sedges flaunt their harvest
　　In every meadow nook;
And asters by the brook-side
　　Make asters in the brook.

From dewy lanes at morning
　　The grapes' sweet odors rise;
At noon the roads all flutter
　　With yellow butterflies.

By all these lovely tokens
　　September days are here,
With summer's best of weather,
　　And autumn's best of cheer.

SCHOOL-BELL
Eleanor Farjeon

Nine-o'clock Bell!
Nine-o'clock Bell!
All the small children and big ones as well,
Pulling their stockings up, snatching their hats,
Cheeking and grumbling and giving back-chats,
Laughing and quarreling, dropping their things,
These at a snail's pace and those upon wings,
Lagging behind a bit, running ahead,
Waiting at corners for lights to turn red,
　　Some of them scurrying,
　　Others not worrying,
Carelessly trudging or anxiously hurrying,
All through the streets they are coming pell-mell
　　At the Nine-o'clock
　　　Nine-o'clock
　　　Nine-o'clock
　　　　Bell!

ARITHMETIC
FROM ARITHMETIC
Carl Sandburg

Arithmetic is where numbers fly like pigeons in and out of your head.
Arithmetic tells you how many you lose or win if you know how
    many you had before you lost or won.
Arithmetic is seven eleven all good children go to heaven—or five
    six bundle of sticks.
Arithmetic is numbers you squeeze from your head to your hand to
    your pencil to your paper till you get the answer.
Arithmetic is where the answer is right and everything is nice and
    you can look out the window and see the blue sky—or the an-
    swer is wrong and you have to start all over and try again and
    see how it comes out this time.

OUR HISTORY
Catherine Cate Coblentz

Our history sings of centuries
Such varying songs it sings!
It starts with winds, slow moving sails,
It ends with skies and wings.

GEOGRAPHY
Eleanor Farjeon

Islands and peninsulas, continents and capes,
Dromedaries, cassowaries, elephants and apes,
Rivers, lakes and waterfalls, whirlpools and the sea,
Valley-beds and mountain-tops—are all Geography!

The capitals of Europe with so many curious names,
The North Pole and the South Pole and Vesuvius in flames,
Rice-fields, ice-fields, cotton-fields, fields of maize and tea,
The Equator and the Hemispheres—are all Geography!

80

The very streets I live in, and the meadows where I play,
Are just as much Geography as countries far away,
Where yellow girls and coffee boys are learning about *me*,
The little white-skinned stranger who is in Geography!

AUTUMN
Emily Dickinson

The morns are meeker than they were,
    The nuts are getting brown;
The berry's cheek is plumper,
    The rose is out of town.

The maple wears a gayer scarf,
    The field a scarlet gown.
Lest I should be old-fashioned,
    I'll put a trinket on.

A VAGABOND SONG
Bliss Carman

There is something in the autumn that is native to my blood—
Touch of manner, hint of mood;
And my heart is like a rhyme,
With the yellow and the purple and the crimson keeping time.

The scarlet of the maples can shake me like a cry
Of bugles going by.
And my lonely spirit thrills
To see the frosty asters like smoke upon the hills.

There is something in October sets the gypsy blood astir;
We must rise and follow her,
When from every hill of flame
She calls and calls each vagabond by name.

THE MIST AND ALL
Dixie Willson

I like the fall,
The mist and all.
I like the night owl's
Lonely call—
And wailing sound
Of wind around.

I like the gray
November day,
And bare, dead boughs
That coldly sway
Against my pane.
I like the rain.

I like to sit
And laugh at it—
And tend
My cozy fire a bit.
I like the fall—
The mist and all.—

FOG
Carl Sandburg

The fog comes
on little cat feet.

It sits looking
over harbor and city
on silent haunches
and then, moves on.

HALLOWE'EN
Harry Behn

Tonight is the night
When dead leaves fly
Like witches on switches
Across the sky,
When elf and sprite
Flit through the night
On a moony sheen.

Tonight is the night
When leaves make a sound
Like a gnome in his home
Under the ground,
When spooks and trolls
Creep out of holes
Mossy and green.

Tonight is the night
When pumpkins stare
Through sheaves and leaves
Everywhere,
When ghoul and ghost
And goblin host
Dance round their queen.
It's Hallowe'en.

NOVEMBER NIGHT
Adelaide Crapsey

Listen . . .
With faint dry sound,
Like steps of passing ghosts,
The leaves, frost-crisp'd, break from the trees
And fall.

THANKSGIVING DAY
Lydia Maria Child

Over the river and through the wood,
  To grandfather's house we go;
    The horse knows the way
    To carry the sleigh
  Through the white and drifted snow.

Over the river and through the wood—
  Oh, how the wind does blow!
    It stings the toes
    And bites the nose,
  As over the ground we go.

Over the river and through the wood,
  To have a first-rate play.
    Hear the bells ring,
    "Ting-a-ling-ding!"
  Hurrah for Thanksgiving Day!

Over the river and through the wood
  Trot fast, my dapple-gray!
    Spring over the ground,
    Like a hunting-hound!
  For this is Thanksgiving Day.

Over the river and through the wood,
  And straight through the barnyard gate.
    We seem to go
    Extremely slow,—
  It is so hard to wait!

Over the river and through the wood—
  Now grandmother's cap I spy!
    Hurrah for the fun!
    Is the pudding done?
  Hurrah for the pumpkin-pie!

BE THANKFUL UNTO HIM
The Bible: Psalm 100

Make a joyful noise unto the Lord, all ye lands.
Serve the Lord with gladness!
Come before his presence with singing!

Know ye that the Lord he is God:
It is he that hath made us, and not we ourselves;
We are his people, and the sheep of his pasture.

Enter into his gates with thanksgiving, and into his courts with
    praise!
Be thankful unto him, and bless his name.

For the Lord is good;
His mercy is everlasting;
And his truth endureth to all generations.

CHRISTMAS BELLS
Henry Wadsworth Longfellow

I heard the bells on Christmas Day
Their old, familiar carols play,
        And wild and sweet
        The words repeat
Of peace on earth, good-will to men!

And thought how, as the day had come,
The belfries of all Christendom
        Had rolled along
        The unbroken song
Of peace on earth, good-will to men!

Till, ringing, singing on its way,
The world revolved from night to day,
        A voice, a chime,
        A chant sublime
Of peace on earth, good-will to men!

Then from each black, accursèd mouth
The cannon thundered in the South,
    And with the sound
    The carols drowned
Of peace on earth, good-will to men!

It was as if an earthquake rent
The hearth stones of a continent,
    And made forlorn
    The households born
Of peace on earth, good-will to men!

And in despair I bowed my head;
"There is no peace on earth," I said;
    "For hate is strong,
    And mocks the song
Of peace on earth, good-will to men!"

Then pealed the bells more loud and deep:
"God is not dead, nor doth He sleep!
    The Wrong shall fail,
    The Right prevail,
With peace on earth, good-will to men!"

A VISIT FROM ST. NICHOLAS
Clement Clarke Moore

'Twas the night before Christmas, when all through the house
Not a creature was stirring, not even a mouse;
The stockings were hung by the chimney with care,
In hopes that St. Nicholas soon would be there.
The children were nestled all snug in their beds,
While visions of sugar-plums danced in their heads;
And mamma in her 'kerchief, and I in my cap,
Had just settled our brains for a long winter's nap,
When out on the lawn there arose such a clatter,
I sprang from my bed to see what was the matter.

Away to the window I flew like a flash,
Tore open the shutters and threw up the sash.
The moon on the breast of the new-fallen snow
Gave the luster of midday to objects below,
When, what to my wondering eyes should appear,
But a miniature sleigh, and eight tiny reindeer,
With a little old driver, so lively and quick,
I knew in a moment it must be St. Nick.
More rapid than eagles his coursers they came,
And he whistled, and shouted, and called them by name:
"Now, Dasher! now, Dancer! now, Prancer and Vixen!
On, Comet! on, Cupid! on, Donder and Blitzen!
To the top of the porch! to the top of the wall!
Now dash away! dash away! dash away all!"
As dry leaves that before the wild hurricane fly,
When they meet with an obstacle, mount to the sky,
So up to the housetop the coursers they flew,
With the sleigh full of toys, and St. Nicholas, too.
And then, in a twinkling, I heard on the roof
The prancing and pawing of each little hoof.
As I drew in my head, and was turning around,
Down the chimney St. Nicholas came with a bound.
He was dressed all in fur, from his head to his foot,
And his clothes were all covered with ashes and soot;
A bundle of toys he had flung on his back,
And he looked like a peddler just opening his pack.
His eyes—how they twinkled! his dimples how merry!
His cheeks were like roses, his nose like a cherry!
His droll little mouth was drawn up like a bow,
And the beard on his chin was as white as the snow;
The stump of a pipe he held tight in his teeth,
And the smoke it encircled his head like a wreath;
He had a broad face and a little round belly
That shook, when he laughed, like a bowlful of jelly.
He was chubby and plump, a right jolly old elf,
And I laughed when I saw him, in spite of myself;
A wink of his eye and a twist of his head,
Soon gave me to know I had nothing to dread;

He spoke not a word, but went straight to his work,
And filled all the stockings; then turned with a jerk,
And laying his finger aside of his nose
And giving a nod, up the chimney he rose;
He sprang to his sleigh, to his team gave a whistle,
And away they all flew like the down of a thistle.
But I heard him exclaim, ere he drove out of sight,
"Happy Christmas to all, and to all a good night."

AN OLD CHRISTMAS GREETING

Sing hey! Sing hey!
For Christmas Day
Twine mistletoe and holly
For friendship glows
In winter snows,
And so let's all be jolly.

CHRISTMAS CAROL
Kenneth Grahame

Villagers all, this frosty tide,
Let your doors swing open wide,
Though wind may follow and snow betide,
Yet draw us in by your fire to bide:
    Joy shall be yours in the morning.

Here we stand in the cold and the sleet,
Blowing fingers and stamping feet,
Come from far away, you to greet—
You by the fire and we in the street—
    Bidding you joy in the morning.

For ere one half of the night was gone,
Sudden a star has led us on,
Raining bliss and benison—
Bliss tomorrow and more anon,
    Joy for every morning.

Good man Joseph toiled through the snow—
Saw the star o'er the stable low;
Mary she might not farther go—
Welcome thatch and litter below!
    Joy was hers in the morning.

And then they heard the angels tell,
"Who were the first to cry noel?
Animals all as it befell,
In the stable where they did dwell!
    Joy shall be theirs in the morning."

ON CHRISTMAS MORN
Adapted from an old Spanish carol
Ruth Sawyer

Shall I tell you who will come
    to Bethlehem on Christmas Morn,
Who will kneel them gently down
    before the Lord, new-born?

One small fish from the river
    with scales of red, red gold.
One wild bee from the heather,
    one grey lamb from the fold,
One ox from the high pasture,
    one black bull from the herd,
One goatling from the far hills,
    one white, white bird.

And many children, God give them grace—
bringing tall candles to light Mary's face.

Shall I tell you who will come
   to Bethlehem on Christmas Morn,
Who will kneel them gently down
   before the Lord, new-born?

HERE WE COME A-CAROLING

Here we come a-caroling
   Among the leaves so green;
Here we come a-wand'ring
   So fair to be seen.

Love and joy come to you
And a joyful Christmas, too;
And God bless you and send
You a Happy New Year—
And God send you a Happy New Year.

We are not daily beggars
   That beg from door to door;
But we are neighbors' children
   That you have seen before.

Love and joy come to you
And a joyful Christmas, too;
And God bless you and send
You a Happy New Year—
And God send you a Happy New Year.

God bless the master of the house
   Likewise the mistress, too;
And all the little children
   That round the table go.

Love and joy come to you
And a joyful Christmas, too;
And God bless you and send
You a Happy New Year—
And God send you a Happy New Year.

TIDINGS OF GREAT JOY
The Bible

And there were in the same country
Shepherds abiding in the field,
Keeping watch over their flock by night.

And, lo, the angel of the Lord came upon them;
And the glory of the Lord shone round about them;
And they were sore afraid.

And the angel said unto them, "Fear not!
For, behold, I bring you tidings of great joy,
Which shall be to all people.

"For unto you is born this day in the city of David
A Saviour, which is Christ the Lord.

"And this shall be a sign unto you:
Ye shall find the babe wrapped in swaddling clothes,
Lying in a manger."

And suddenly there was with the angel
A multitude of the heavenly host
Praising God, and saying,

"Glory to God in the highest,
And on earth peace,
Good will toward men!"

LONG, LONG AGO

Winds through the olive trees
   Softly did blow,
Round little Bethlehem
   Long, long ago.

Sheep on the hillside lay
   Whiter than snow;
Shepherds were watching them,
   Long, long ago.

Then from the happy sky,
    Angels bent low,
Singing their songs of joy,
    Long, long ago.

For in a manger bed,
    Cradled we know,
Christ came to Bethlehem,
    Long, long ago.

THE FRIENDLY BEASTS
An old carol from France

Jesus our brother, kind and good,
Was humbly born in a stable rude;
The friendly beasts around Him stood,
Jesus our brother, kind and good.

"I," said the donkey, shaggy and brown,
"I carried His Mother up hill and down;
I carried her safely to Bethlehem town,
I," said the donkey, shaggy and brown.

"I," said the cow, all white and red,
"I gave Him my manger for His bed;
I gave Him my hay to pillow His head.
I," said the cow, all white and red.

"I," said the sheep with the curly horn,
"I gave Him my wool for a blanket warm.
He wore my coat on Christmas morn.
I," said the sheep with the curly horn.

"I," said the dove from the rafters high,
"I cooed Him to sleep so He would not cry,
I cooed Him to sleep, my mate and I.
I," said the dove from the rafters high.

And every beast, by some good spell,
In the stable dark was glad to tell,
Of the gift he gave Immanuel,
The gift he gave Immanuel.

A CHRISTMAS FOLK SONG
Lizette Woodworth Reese

The little Jesus came to town;
The wind blew up, the wind blew down;
Out in the street the wind was bold;
Now who would house Him from the cold?

Then opened wide a stable door,
Fair were the rushes on the floor;
The Ox put forth a horned head:
"Come, little Lord, here make Thy bed."

Up rose the Sheep were folded near:
"Thou Lamb of God, come, enter here."
He entered there to rush and reed,
Who was the Lamb of God indeed.

The little Jesus came to town;
With ox and sheep He laid Him down;
Peace to the byre, peace to the fold,
For that they housed Him from the cold!

CRADLE HYMN
Martin Luther

Away in a manger, no crib for a bed,
The little Lord Jesus laid down His sweet head.
The stars in the bright sky looked down where He lay—
The little Lord Jesus asleep on the hay.

The cattle are lowing, the Baby awakes,
But little Lord Jesus, no crying He makes.
I love Thee, Lord Jesus! look down from the sky,
And stay by my cradle till morning is nigh.

IT CAME UPON THE MIDNIGHT CLEAR
E. H. Sears

It came upon the midnight clear,
    That glorious song of old,
From angels bending near the earth
    To touch their harps of gold;

Peace on earth, good-will to men,
    From heaven's all-gracious King;
The world in solemn stillness lay
    To hear the angels sing.

O LITTLE TOWN OF BETHLEHEM
Phillips Brooks

O little town of Bethlehem,
    How still we see thee lie!
Above thy deep and dreamless sleep
    The silent stars go by;
Yet in thy dark streets shineth
    The everlasting Light;
The hopes and fears of all the years
    Are met in thee tonight.

For Christ is born of Mary,
　　And, gathered all above,
While mortals sleep, the angels keep
　　Their watch of wondering love.
O morning stars, together
　　Proclaim the holy birth!
And praises sing to God the King,
　　And peace to men on earth.

How silently, how silently,
　　The wondrous gift is given!
So God imparts to human hearts
　　The blessings of His heaven.
No ear may hear His coming,
　　But in this world of sin,
Where meek souls will receive Him still,
　　The dear Christ enters in.

O holy Child of Bethlehem!
　　Descend to us, we pray;
Cast out our sin, and enter in,
　　Be born in us today.
We hear the Christmas angels
　　The great tidings tell;
Oh, come to us, abide with us,
　　Our Lord Emmanuel!

It's fun to play

FROLIC
A. E. (G. W. Russell)

> The children were shouting together
>> And racing along the sands,
> A glimmer of dancing shadows,
>> A dovelike flutter of hands.
>
> The stars were shouting in heaven,
>> The sun was chasing the moon:
> The game was the same as the children's,
>> They danced to the self-same tune.
>
> The whole of the world was merry,
>> One joy from the vale to the height,
> Where the blue woods of twilight encircled
>> The lovely lawns of the light.

PLAY TIME
William Blake

> When the voices of children are heard on the green
>> And laughing is heard on the hill,
> My heart is at rest within my breast,
>> And everything else is still.
>
> "Then come home, my children, the sun is gone down,
>> And the dews of night arise;
> Come, come, leave off play, and let us away
>> Till the morning appears in the skies."
>
> "No, no, let us play, for it is yet day,
>> And we cannot go to sleep;
> Besides in the sky the little birds fly,
>> And the hills are all covered with sheep."

"Well, well, go and play till the light fades away,
  And then go home to bed."
The little ones leaped and shouted and laughed;
  And all the hills echoed.

ALLIE
Robert Graves

Allie, call the birds in,
  The birds from the sky!
Allie calls, Allie sings,
  Down they all fly:
First there came
Two white doves,
  Then a sparrow from his nest,
Then a clucking bantam hen,
  Then a robin red-breast.

Allie, call the beasts in,
  The beasts, every one!
Allie calls, Allie sings,
  In they all run:
First there came
Two black lambs,
  Then a grunting Berkshire sow,
Then a dog without a tail,
  Then a red and white cow.

Allie, call the fish up,
  The fish from the stream!
Allie calls, Allie sings,
  Up they all swim:
First there came
Two gold fish,
  A minnow and a miller's thumb,
Then a school of little trout,
  Then the twisting eels come.

Allie, call the children,
    Call them from the green!
Allie calls, Allie sings,
    Soon they run in:
First there came
Tom and Madge,
    Kate and I who'll not forget
How we played by the water's edge
    Till the April sun set.

RING-A-RING
Kate Greenaway

Ring-a-ring of little boys,
    Ring-a-ring of girls;
All around—all around,
    Twists and twirls.

You are merry children.
    "Yes, we are."
Where do you come from?
    "Not very far.

"We live in the mountain,
    We live in the tree;
And I live in the river bed
    And you won't catch me!"

A GOOD PLAY
Robert Louis Stevenson

We built a ship upon the stairs,
All made of back-bedroom chairs,
And filled it full of sofa pillows
To go a-sailing on the billows.

We took a saw and several nails,
And water in the nursery pails;
And Tom said, "Let us also take
An apple and a slice of cake";—
Which was enough for Tom and me
To go a-sailing on, till tea.

We sailed along for days and days,
And had the very best of plays;
But Tom fell out and hurt his knee,
So there was no one left but me.

HIDING
Dorothy Aldis

I'm hiding, I'm hiding,
   And no one knows where;
For all they can see is my
   Toes and my hair.

And I just heard my father
   Say to my mother—
"But, darling, he must be
   Somewhere or other;

"Have you looked in the inkwell?"
   And Mother said, "Where?"
"In the *inkwell*," said Father. But
   I was not there.

Then "Wait!" cried my mother—
   "I think that I see
Him under the carpet." But
   It was not me.

"Inside the mirror's
   A pretty good place,"
Said Father and looked, but saw
   Only his face.

"We've hunted," sighed Mother,
   "As hard as we could
And I *am* so afraid that we've
   Lost him for good."

Then I laughed out aloud
   And I wiggled my toes
And Father said—"Look, dear,
   I wonder if those

"Toes could be Benny's?
   There are ten of them, see?"
And they *were* so surprised to find
   Out it was me!

BLOCK CITY
Robert Louis Stevenson

What are you able to build with your blocks?
Castles and palaces, temples and docks.
Rain may keep raining, and others go roam,
But I can be happy and building at home.

Let the sofa be mountains, the carpet be sea,
There I'll establish a city for me:
A kirk and a mill and a palace beside,
And a harbor as well where my vessels may ride.

Great is the palace with pillar and wall,
A sort of a tower on the top of it all,
And steps coming down in an orderly way
To where my toy vessels lie safe in the bay.

This one is sailing and that one is moored:
Hark to the song of the sailors on board!
And see on the steps of my palace, the kings
Coming and going with presents and things!

Now I have done with it, down let it go!
All in a moment the town is laid low.
Block upon block lying scattered and free,
What is there left of my town by the sea?

Yet as I saw it, I see it again,
The kirk and the palace, the ships and the men,
And as long as I live, and where'er I may be,
I'll always remember my town by the sea.

EXTREMES
James Whitcomb Riley

A little boy once played so loud
That the thunder, up in a thundercloud,
Said, "Since I can't be heard, why, then
I'll never, never thunder again!"

And a little girl once kept so still
That she heard a fly on the window sill
Whisper and say to a ladybird,—
"She's the stillest child I ever heard!"

THE BEAR HUNT
Margaret Widdemer

I played I was two polar bears
Who lived inside a cave of chairs,

And Brother was the hunter-man
Who tried to shoot us when we ran.

The tenpins made good bones to gnaw,
I held them down beneath my paw.

Of course, I had to kill him quick
Before he shot me with his stick.

So all the cave fell down, you see,
On Brother and the bones and me—

So then he said he wouldn't play—
But it was teatime, anyway!

THE LITTLE JUMPING GIRLS
Kate Greenaway

Jump—jump—jump—
  Jump away
From this town into
  The next, today.

Jump—jump—jump—
  Jump over the moon;
Jump all the morning
  And all the noon.

Jump—jump—jump—
  Jump all night;
Won't our mothers
  Be in a fright?

Jump—jump—jump—
  Over the sea;
What wonderful wonders
  We shall see.

Jump—jump—jump—
  Jump far away;
And all come home
  Some other day.

MARCHING SONG
Robert Louis Stevenson

Bring the comb and play upon it!
  Marching, here we come!
Willie cocks his highland bonnet,
  Johnnie beats the drum.

Mary Jane commands the party,
  Peter leads the rear;
Feet in time, alert and hearty,
  Each a Grenadier!

All in the most martial manner
  Marching double-quick;
While the napkin, like a banner,
  Waves upon the stick!

Here's enough of fame and pillage,
  Great commander Jane!
Now that we've been round the village,
  Let's go home again.

ROLLER SKATES
John Farrar

Rumble, rumble, rumble, goes the gloomy "L"
And the street car rattles as well,
Motor-trucks wheeze and limousines purr,
Everything is noisy—all the world's astir!
Bang-whirr, bang-whirr, we'll all join too,
The pavement may be dirty, but the sky's clean blue!
Whiz by the lady with the funny little girl,
Swing around the corner in a gleeful whirl!
Don't bump the fat man, jump the other way,
Yell a little, shout a little, "Hip-Hooray!"
Everybody's busy—we'll be busy, too,
The pavement may be dirty, but the sky's clean blue.

DIFFERENT BICYCLES
Dorothy W. Baruch

When I ride my bicycle
I pedal and pedal
Knees up, knees down.
Knees up, knees down.

But when the boy next door
Rides his,
It's whizz—
A chuck a chuck—

And away
He's gone
With his
Knees steady-straight
In one place . . .
Because—
   His bicycle has
   A motor fastened on.

THE PLAYHOUSE KEY
Rachel Field

This is the key to the playhouse
  In the woods by the pebbly shore,
It's winter now, I wonder if
  There's snow about the door?

I wonder if the fir trees tap
  Green fingers on the pane,
If sea gulls cry and the roof is wet
  And tinkle-y with rain?

I wonder if the flower-sprigged cups
  And plates sit on their shelf,
And if my little painted chair
  Is rocking by itself?

THE LOST DOLL
Charles Kingsley

I once had a sweet little doll, dears,
  The prettiest doll in the world;
Her cheeks were so red and so white, dears,
  And her hair was so charmingly curled.
But I lost my poor little doll, dears,
  As I played on the heath one day;
And I cried for her more than a week, dears,
  But I never could find where she lay.

I found my poor little doll, dears,
  As I played on the heath one day;
Folks say she is terribly changed, dears,
  For her paint is all washed away,
And her arm trodden off by the cows, dears,
  And her hair not the least bit curled;
Yet for old time's sake, she is still, dears,
  The prettiest doll in the world.

PIRATE STORY
Robert Louis Stevenson

Three of us afloat in the meadow by the swing,
  Three of us aboard in the basket on the lea.
Winds are in the air, they are blowing in the spring,
  And waves are on the meadow like the waves there are at sea.

Where shall we adventure, to-day that we're afloat,
  Wary of the weather and steering by a star?
Shall it be to Africa, a-steering of the boat,
  To Providence, or Babylon, or off to Malabar?

Hi! but here's a squadron a-rowing on the sea—
  Cattle on the meadow a-charging with a roar!
Quick, and we'll escape them, they're as mad as they can be,
  The wicket is the harbour and the garden is the shore.

THE ARCHER
Clinton Scollard

When May has come, and all around
The dandelions dot the ground,
Then out into the woods I go,
And take my arrows and my bow.

Of hickory my bow is made,
Deep in a darksome forest glade
Cut from a sapling slim and tall,
And feathered are my arrows all.

And sometimes I am Robin Hood,
That olden archer brave and good;
And sometimes I'm an Indian sly,
Who waits to shoot the passers-by.

So up and down the woods I roam
Till sunset bids me hurry home
Before the pathway through the glen
Is peopled by the shadow-men.

And when at night my bow unstrung,
Is close beside my quiver hung,
To bed I slip and slumber well,
And dream that I am William Tell.

THE KITE
Harry Behn

How bright on the blue
Is a kite when it's new!

With a dive and a dip
It snaps its tail

Then soars like a ship
With only a sail

As over tides
Of wind it rides,

Climbs to the crest
Of a gust and pulls,

Then seems to rest
As wind falls.

When string goes slack
You wind it back

And run until
A new breeze blows

And its wings fill
And up it goes!

How bright on the blue
Is a kite when it's new!

But a raggeder thing
You never will see

When it flaps on a string
In the top of a tree.

A SWING SONG
William Allingham

Swing, swing,
Sing, sing,
Here! my throne and I am a king!
Swing, sing,
Swing, sing,
Farewell, earth, for I'm on the wing!

Low, high,
Here I fly,
Like a bird through sunny sky;
Free, free,
Over the lea,
Over the mountain, over the sea!

Up, down,
Up and down,
Which is the way to London Town?
Where? Where?
Up in the air,
Close your eyes and now you are there!

Soon, soon,
Afternoon,
Over the sunset, over the moon;
Far, far,
Over all bar,
Sweeping on from star to star!

No, no,
Low, low,
Sweeping daisies with my toe.
Slow, slow,
To and fro,
Slow—slow—slow—slow.

THE FISHING POLE
Mary Carolyn Davies

A fishing pole's a curious thing;
It's made of just a stick and string;
A boy at one end and a wish,
And on the other end a fish.

SWIMMING
Clinton Scollard

When all the days are hot and long
And robin bird has ceased his song,
I go swimming every day
And have the finest kind of play.

I've learned to dive and I can float
As easily as does a boat;
I splash and plunge and laugh and shout
Till Daddy tells me to come out.

It's much too soon; I'd like to cry
For I can see the ducks go by,
And Daddy Duck—how I love him—
He lets his children swim and swim!

I feel that I would be in luck
If I could only be a duck!

MY PLAN
Marchette Chute

When I'm a little older
  I plan to buy a boat,
And up and down the river
  The two of us will float.

I'll have a little cabin
  All painted white and red
With shutters for the window
  And curtains for the bed.

I'll have a little cookstove
  On which to fry my fishes,
And all the Hudson River
  In which to wash my dishes.

AT THE SEA-SIDE
Robert Louis Stevenson

When I was down beside the sea
A wooden spade they gave to me
  To dig the sandy shore.

My holes were empty like a cup.
In every hole the sea came up,
  Till it could come no more.

LULLABY
Robert Hillyer

The long canoe
Toward the shadowy shore,
One . . . two . . .
Three . . . four . . .
The paddle dips,
Turns in the wake,
Pauses, then
Forward again,
Water drips
From the blade to the lake.
Nothing but that,
No sound of wings;
The owl and bat
Are velvet things.
No wind awakes,
No fishes leap,
No rabbits creep
Among the brakes.

The long canoe
At the shadowy shore,
One . . . two . . .
Three . . . four . . .

A murmur now
Under the prow
Where rushes bow
To let us through.
One . . . two . . .
Upon the shore,
Three . . . four . . .
Upon the lake,
No one's awake,
No one's awake,
One . . .
Two . . .
No one,
Not even
You.

PAPER BOATS
Rabindranath Tagore
Who was awarded the Nobel Prize for Literature

Day by day I float my paper boats one by one down the running
stream.
In big black letters I write my name on them and the name of the
village where I live.
I hope that someone in some strange land will find them and know
who I am.
I load my little boats with *shiuli* flowers from our garden, and hope
that these blooms of dawn will be carried safely to land in the
night.
I launch my paper boats and look up into the sky and see the little
clouds setting their white bulging sails.
I know not what playmate of mine in the sky sends them down the
air to race with my boats!
When night comes I bury my face in my arms and dream that my
paper boats float on and on under the midnight stars.
The fairies of sleep are sailing in them, and the lading is their baskets
full of dreams.

THE KAYAK

Over the briny wave I go,
In spite of the weather, in spite of the snow:
What cares the hardy Eskimo?
In my little skiff, with paddle and lance,
I glide where the foaming billows dance.

Round me the sea-birds slip and soar;
Like me, they love the ocean's roar.
Sometimes a floating iceberg gleams
Above me with its melting streams;
Sometimes a rushing wave will fall
Down on my skiff and cover it all.

But what care I for a wave's attack?
With my paddle I right my little kayak,
And then its weight I speedily trim,
And over the water away I skim.

A SLEDDING SONG
Norman C. Schlichter

Sing a song of winter,
    Of frosty clouds in air!
Sing a song of snowflakes
    Falling everywhere.

Sing a song of winter!
    Sing a song of sleds!
Sing a song of tumbling
    Over heels and heads.

Up and down a hillside
    When the moon is bright,
Sledding is a tiptop
    Wintertime delight.

SKATING
Herbert Asquith

When I try to skate,
My feet are so wary
They grit and they grate:
And then I watch Mary
Easily gliding,
Like an ice-fairy;
Skimming and curving,
Out and in,
With a turn of her head,
And a lift of her chin,
And a gleam of her eye,
And a twirl and a spin;
Sailing under
The breathless hush
Of the willows, and back
To the frozen rush;
Out to the island
And round the edge,
Skirting the rim
Of the crackling sedge,
Swerving close
To the poplar root,
And round the lake
On a single foot,
With a three, and an eight,
And a loop and a ring;
Where Mary glides,
The lake will sing!
Out in the mist
I hear her now
Under the frost
Of the willow-bough
Easily sailing,
Light and fleet,
With the song of the lake
Beneath her feet.

COUNTING-OUT RHYMES

Eenie, meenie, minie, mo,
Catch a tiger by the toe,
If he hollers let him go,
Eenie, meenie, minie, mo.

Out goes the rat,
Out goes the cat,
Out goes the lady
With the big green hat.
Y, O, U, spells you;
O, U, T, spells out!

One potato, two potato,
Three potato, four;
Five potato, six potato,
Seven potato, MORE.

One-ery, Ore-ery, Ickery, Ann,
Phillip-son, Phollop-son, Nicholas, John,
    Queevy, Quavy,
    English Navy,
Zinglum, Zanglum, Bolun, Bun.

Hinty, minty, cuty, corn,
Apple seed, and apple thorn,
Wire, briar, limber lock,
Three geese in a flock.
One flew east, and one flew west,
One flew over the cuckoo's nest.

Little things that creep

and crawl and swim

and sometimes fly

FEATHER OR FUR
John Becker

When you watch for
Feather or fur
Feather or fur
Do not stir
Do not stir.

Feather or fur
Come crawling
Creeping
Some come peeping
Some by night
And some by day.
Most come gently
All come softly
Do not scare
A friend away.

When you watch for
Feather or fur
Feather or fur
Do not stir
Do not stir.

AT THE GARDEN GATE
David McCord

Who so late
at the garden gate?
Emily, Kate,
and John.
"John,
where have you been?
It's after six;
Supper is on,
And you've been gone
An hour,
John!"
"We've been, we've been,
We've just been over
The field," said
John.
(Emily, Kate,
and John.)

Who so late
at the garden gate?
Emily, Kate,
and John.
"John,
what have you got?"
"A whopping toad.
Isn't he big?
He's a terrible
Load.
(We found him
A little ways
Up the road,"
said Emily,
Kate,
and John.)

Who so late
at the garden gate?
Emily, Kate,
and John.
"John,
put that thing down!
Do you want to get warts?"
(They all three have 'em
By last
Reports.)
Still, finding toads
Is the best of
Sports,
Say Emily,
Kate,
and John.

OUR LITTLE KINSMEN
Emily Dickinson

Our little kinsmen after rain
In plenty may be seen,
A pink and pulpy multitude
The tepid ground upon;

A needless life it seemed to me
Until a little bird
As to a hospitality
Advanced and breakfasted.

As I of he, so God of me,
I pondered, may have judged,
And left the little angleworm
With modesties enlarged.

FOUR THINGS
The Bible

There be four things which are little upon the earth,
But they are exceeding wise:

The ants are a people not strong,
Yet they prepare their meat in the summer;

The conies are but a feeble folk,
Yet make they their houses in the rocks;

The locusts have no king,
Yet go they forth all of them by bands;

The spider taketh hold with her hands,
And is in kings' palaces.

THE ANT VILLAGE
Marion Edey and Dorothy Grider

Somebody up in the rocky pasture
  Heaved the stone over.
Here are the cells and a network of furrows
  In the roots of the clover.

Hundreds of eggs lie fitted in patterns,
  Waxy and yellow.
Hundreds of ants are racing and struggling.
  One little fellow

Shoulders an egg as big as his body,
  Ready for hatching.
Darkness is best, so everyone's rushing,
  Hastily snatching

Egg after egg to the lowest tunnels.
  And suddenly, where
Confusion had been, there now is nothing.
  Ants gone. Cells bare.

124

GO TO THE ANT
The Bible

Go to the ant, thou sluggard;
Consider her ways, and be wise:
Which having no guide,
Overseer, or ruler,
Provideth her meat in the summer,
And gathereth her food in the harvest.

THE HUMBLE-BEE
FROM THE HUMBLE-BEE
Ralph Waldo Emerson

Burly dozing humble-bee
Where thou art is clime for me.
Let them sail for Porto Rique,
Far-off heats through seas to seek;
I will follow thee alone,
Thou animated torrid zone!
Zigzag steerer, desert cheerer,
Let me chase thy waving lines;
Keep me nearer, me thy hearer,
Singing over shrubs and vines.

HOW DOTH THE LITTLE BUSY BEE
FROM AGAINST IDLENESS AND MISCHIEF
Isaac Watts

How doth the little busy bee
  Improve each shining hour
And gather honey all the day
  From every passing flower!

How skilfully she builds her cell;
How neat she spreads the wax!
And labours hard to store it well
With the sweet food she makes.

THE BEES
Lola Ridge

Bees over the gooseberry bushes,
Bees with golden thighs
Climbing out of pale flowers
(Bees singing to you for a long while,
You sitting quite still,
Holding the sun in your lap),
Bees, take care!
You may catch fire in the sun,
If you venture so high in the blue air.

THE BEETLE
FROM THE BEETLE
James Whitcomb Riley

The shrilling locust slowly sheathes
His dagger-voice, and creeps away
Beneath the brooding leaves where breathes
The zephyr of the dying day:
One naked star has waded through
The purple shallows of the night,
And faltering as falls the dew
It drips its misty light.
   O'er garden blooms,
   On tides of musk,
The beetle booms adown the glooms
And bumps along the dusk.

LITTLE BLACK BUG
Margaret Wise Brown

Little black bug,
Little black bug,
Where have you been?
I've been under the rug,
Said the little black bug.
Bug-ug-ug-ug.

Little green fly,
Little green fly,
Where have you been?
I've been way up high,
Said little green fly.
Bzzzzzzzz.

Little old mouse,
Little old mouse,
Where have you been?
I've been all through the house,
Said little old mouse.
Squeak-eak-eak-eak-eak.

CATERPILLAR
Christina Rossetti

Brown and furry
Caterpillar in a hurry
Take your walk
To the shady leaf, or stalk,
Or what not,
Which may be the chosen spot.
No toad spy you,
Hovering bird of prey pass by you;
Spin and die,
To live again a butterfly.

ONLY MY OPINION
Monica Shannon

> Is a caterpillar ticklish?
>> Well, it's always my belief
> That he giggles, as he wiggles
>> Across a hairy leaf.

LITTLE CHARLIE CHIPMUNK
Helen Cowles Le Cron

Little Charlie Chipmunk was a *talker*. Mercy me!
He chattered after breakfast and he chattered after tea!
He chattered to his father and he chattered to his mother!
He chattered to his sister and he chattered to his brother!
He chattered till his family was almost driven *wild*.
Oh, little Charlie Chipmunk was a *very* tiresome child!

SPRING CRICKET
Frances Rodman

> He put away his tiny pipe
> Last autumn, when the gale was chill:
> And now in rusty coat and brown
> He tries his strength upon the hill.
>
> With fiddle tucked beneath a wing
> He staggers over a stubbled ground:
> He climbs upon a sunny stone,
> Shakes winter off, and looks around.
>
> He polishes his dingy coat
> And scrapes a valiant tune and high
> To tell his tiny universe
> That April's due to saunter by.

SPLINTER
Carl Sandburg

> The voice of the last cricket
> across the first frost
> is one kind of good-by.
> It is so thin a splinter of singing.

WHITE BUTTERFLIES
Algernon Charles Swinburne

> Fly, white butterflies, out to sea,
> Frail, pale wings for the wind to try,
> Small white wings that we scarce can see,
> > Fly!
>
> Some fly light as a laugh of glee,
> Some fly soft as a long, low sigh;
> All to the haven where each would be,
> > Fly!

THE CHAMELEON
A. P. Herbert

> The chameleon changes his color;
> > He can look like a tree or a wall;
> He is timid and shy and he hates to be seen,
> So he simply sits down on the grass and grows green,
> > And pretends he is nothing at all.
>
> I wish l could change my complexion
> > To purple or orange or red:
> I wish I could look like the arm of a chair
> So nobody ever would know I was there
> > When they wanted to put me to bed.

I wish I could be a chameleon
And look like a lily or rose;
I'd lie on the apples and peaches and pears,
But not on Aunt Margaret's yellowy chairs—
I should have to be careful of those.

The chameleon's life is confusing;
He is used to adventure and pain;
But if he ever sat on Aunt Maggie's cretonne
And found what a curious color he'd gone,
I don't think he'd do it again.

THE PUZZLED CENTIPEDE

A centipede was happy quite,
Until a frog in fun
Said, "Pray, which leg comes after which?"
This raised her mind to such a pitch,
She lay distracted in the ditch
Considering how to run.

A DRAGON-FLY
Eleanor Farjeon

When the heat of the summer
Made drowsy the land,
A dragon-fly came
And sat on my hand,
With its blue jointed body,
And wings like spun glass,
It lit on my fingers
As though they were grass.

FIREFLIES
Carolyn Hall

Little lamps of the dusk,
   You fly low and gold
When the summer evening
   Starts to unfold.
So that all the insects,
   Now, before you pass,
Will have light to see by,
   Undressing in the grass.

But when the night has flowered,
   Little lamps agleam,
You fly over treetops
   Following a dream.
Men wonder from their windows
   That a firefly goes so far—
They do not know your longing
   To be a shooting star.

THE SPRING
Rose Fyleman

A little mountain spring I found
That fell into a pool;
I made my hands into a cup
And caught the sparkling water up—
It tasted fresh and cool.

A solemn little frog I spied
Upon the rocky brim;
He looked so boldly in my face,
I'm certain that he thought the place
Belonged by rights to him.

131

ALAS, ALACK!
Walter de la Mare

Ann, Ann!
  Come! quick as you can!
There's a fish that *talks*
  In the frying pan.
Out of the fat,
  As clear as glass,
He put up his mouth
  And moaned "Alas!"
Oh, most mournful,
  "Alas, alack!"
Then turned to his sizzling
  And sank him back.

GRASSHOPPER GREEN

Grasshopper Green is a comical chap;
  He lives on the best of fare.
Bright little trousers, jacket, and cap,
  These are his summer wear.
Out in the meadow he loves to go,
  Playing away in the sun;
It's hopperty, skipperty, high and low,
  Summer's the time for fun.

Grasshopper Green has a quaint little house;
  It's under the hedge so gay.
Grandmother Spider, as still as a mouse,
  Watches him over the way.
Gladly he's calling the children, I know,
  Out in the beautiful sun;
It's hopperty, skipperty, high and low,
  Summer's the time for fun.

AN EXPLANATION OF THE GRASSHOPPER
Vachel Lindsay

> The Grasshopper, the Grasshopper,
> I will explain to you:—
> He is the Brownies' racehorse,
> The Fairies' Kangaroo.

TO THE LADY-BIRD

> Lady-bird! Lady-bird! fly away home;
>   The field-mouse is gone to her nest,
> The daisies have shut up their sleepy red eyes,
>   And the birds and the bees are at rest.
>
> Lady-bird! Lady-bird! fly away home;
>   The glow-worm is lighting her lamp,
> The dew's falling fast, and your fine speckled wings
>   Will flag with the close-clinging damp.
>
> Lady-bird! Lady-bird! fly away home;
>   The fairy-bells tinkle afar;
> Make haste, or they'll catch you and harness you fast
>   With a cobweb to Oberon's car.

CLOCK-A-CLAY
Who is a lady-bird
John Clare

> In the cowslip pips I lie,
> Hidden from the buzzing fly,
> While green grass beneath me lies,
> Pearled with dew like fishes' eyes,
> Here I lie, a clock-a-clay,
> Waiting for the time of day.

While grassy forest quakes surprise,
And the wild wind sobs and sighs,
My gold home rocks as like to fall,
On its pillar green and tall;
When the pattering rain drives by
Clock-a-clay keeps warm and dry.

Day by day and night by night,
All the week I hide from sight;
In the cowslip pips I lie,
In rain and dew still warm and dry;
Day and night, and night and day,
Red, black-spotted clock-a-clay.

My home shakes in wind and showers,
Pale green pillar topped with flowers,
Bending at the wild wind's breath,
Till I touch the grass beneath;
Here I live, lone clock-a-clay,
Watching for the time of day.

MINNOWS
John Keats

. . . Swarms of minnows show their little heads,
Staying their waxy bodies 'gainst the streams,
To taste the luxury of sunny beams
Tempered with coolness. How they ever wrestle
With their own sweet delight, and ever nestle
Their silver bellies on the pebbly sand.
If you but scantily hold out the hand,
That very instant not one will remain;
But turn your eye, and they are there again.
The ripples seem right glad to reach those cresses,
And cool themselves among the em'rald tresses;
The while they cool themselves, they freshness give,
And moisture, that the bowery green may live.

THE LOCUST
FROM THE ZUNI AMERICAN INDIAN
Translated by Frank Cushing

Locust, locust, playing a flute,
Locust, locust, playing a flute!
Away up on the pine-tree bough,
Closely clinging,
Playing a flute,
Playing a flute!

THE LOBSTER QUADRILLE
Lewis Carroll

"Will you walk a little faster?" said a whiting to a snail,
"There's a porpoise close behind us, and he's treading on my tail.
See how eagerly the lobsters and the turtles all advance!
They are waiting on the shingle—will you come and join the dance?
Will you, won't you, will you, won't you,
will you join the dance?
Will you, won't you, will you, won't you,
won't you join the dance?

"You can really have no notion how delightful it will be
When they take us up and throw us, with the lobsters out to sea!"
But the snail replied, "Too far, too far!" and gave a look askance—
Said he thanked the whiting kindly, but he would not join the dance.
Would not, could not, would not, could not,
would not join the dance.
Would not, could not, would not, could not,
could not join the dance.

"What matters it how far we go?" his scaly friend replied.
"There is another shore, you know, upon the other side.
The further off from England the nearer is to France—
Then turn not pale, beloved snail, but come and join the dance.

Will you, won't you, will you, won't you,
    will you join the dance?
Will you, won't you, will you, won't you,
    won't you join the dance?"

MICE
Rose Fyleman

I think mice
Are rather nice.

    Their tails are long,
    Their faces small,
    They haven't any
    Chins at all.
    Their ears are pink,
    Their teeth are white,
    They run about
    The house at night.
    They nibble things
    They shouldn't touch
    And no one seems
    To like them much.

But I think mice
Are nice.

THE MOUSE
Elizabeth Coatsworth

I heard a mouse
Bitterly complaining
In a crack of moonlight
Aslant on the floor—

"Little I ask
And that little is not granted.
There are few crumbs
In this world any more.

"The bread-box is tin
And I cannot get in.

"The jam's in a jar
My teeth cannot mar.

"The cheese sits by itself
On the pantry shelf—

"All night I run
Searching and seeking,
All night I run
About on the floor.

"Moonlight is there
And a bare place for dancing,
But no little feast
Is spread any more."

THE FIELD MOUSE
William Sharp

When the moon shines o'er the corn
And the beetle drones his horn,
And the flittermice swift fly,
And the nightjars swooping cry,
And the young hares run and leap,
We waken from our sleep.

And we climb with tiny feet
And we munch the green corn sweet
With startled eyes for fear
The white owl should fly near,
Or long slim weasel spring
Upon us where we swing.

We do not hurt at all;
Is there not room for all
Within the happy world?
All day we lie close curled
In drowsy sleep, nor rise
Till through the dusky skies
The moon shines o'er the corn
And the beetle drones his horn.

THE CITY MOUSE AND THE GARDEN MOUSE
Christina Rossetti

The city mouse lives in a house;—
   The garden mouse lives in a bower,
He's friendly with the frogs and toads,
   And sees the pretty plants in flower.

The city mouse eats bread and cheese;—
   The garden mouse eats what he can;
We will not grudge him seeds and stocks,
   Poor little timid furry man.

ALL BUT BLIND
Walter de la Mare

All but blind
   In his chambered hole
Gropes for worms
   The four-clawed Mole.

All but blind
   In the evening sky,
The hooded Bat
   Twirls softly by.

All but blind
   In the burning day
The Barn-Owl blunders
   On her way.

And blind as are
   These three to me,
So, blind to Some-one
   I must be.

GREEN MOTH
Winifred Welles

The night the green moth came for me,
   A creamy moon poured down the hill,
The meadow seemed a silver sea,
Small pearls were hung in every tree,
   And all so still, so still—

He floated in on my white bed,
   A strange and soundless fellow.
I saw the horns wave on his head,
   He stepped across my pillow
In tiny ermine boots, and spread
   His cape of green and yellow.

He came so close that I could see
   His golden eyes, and sweet and chill,
His faint breath wavered over me.
"Come Child, my Beautiful," said he,
   And all so still, so still—

LITTLE SNAIL
Hilda Conkling

I saw a snail
Come down the garden walk,
He wagged his head this way . . . that way . . .
Like a clown in a circus.
He looked from side to side
As though he were from a different country.
I have always said he carries his house on his back . . .
Today in the rain
I saw that it was his umbrella!

SNAIL
Langston Hughes

Little snail,
Dreaming you go.
Weather and rose
Is all you know.

Weather and rose
Is all you see,
Drinking
The dewdrop's
Mystery.

THE SILENT SNAKE

The birds go fluttering in the air,
  The rabbits run and skip,
Brown squirrels race along the bough,
  The May-flies rise and dip;
But while these creatures play and leap,
The silent snake goes *creepy-creep!*

140

The birdies sing and whistle loud,
    The busy insects hum,
The squirrels chat, the frogs say "Crook!"
    But the snake is always dumb.
With not a sound through grasses deep
The silent snake goes *creepy-creep!*

STARFISH
Winifred Welles

Last night I saw you in the sky.
I watched you jumping from so high,
Falling so far it made me cry.
I said that star will be so hurt,
Cut on the stones and buried in dirt,
He'll wish he had not been so pert,
So proud, so sure. I said no star
Should take such chances, it's too far,
Even for stars. Yet here you are,
Quietly curling. You are found
Upon this soft and sandy mound,
Cooled by the spray, all safe and sound.
And not one point in all your five
Is even nicked; you sprawl alive,
Not even dented by your dive.
Brave Star, I hope that you will lie
Lazily here and never try
To jump back up into the sky.

OF A SPIDER
Wilfrid Thorley

The spider weaves his silver wire
Between the cherry and the brier.

He runs along and sees the thread
Well-fastened on each hawser-head.

And then within his wheel he dozes
Hung on a thorny stem of roses,

While fairies ride the silver ferry
Between the rose-bud and the cherry.

THE TREE TOAD
Monica Shannon

The Tree Toad is a creature neat,
With tidy rubbers on his feet.
Embarrassment is all he knows—
His color comes, his color goes.

The Tree Toad is quite small, at least,
Unless his girth has just increased.
The truth is always hard to seek,
For things are changing every week.

THE SONG OF THE TOAD
John Burroughs

Have you heard the blinking toad
    Sing his solo by the river
When April nights are soft and warm,
    And spring is all a-quiver?
If there are jewels in his head,
    His wits they often muddle,
For his mate will lay her eggs
    Into a drying puddle.

The jewel's in his throat, I ween,
    And song in ample measure,
For he can make the welkin ring,
    And do it at his leisure.
At ease he sits upon the pool,
    And, void of fuss or trouble,
Makes vesper music fit for kings
    From out an empty bubble:

A long-drawn-out and tolling cry,
    That drifts above the chorus
Of shriller voices from the marsh
    That April nights send o'er us;
A tender monotone of song
    With vernal longings blending,
That rises from the ponds and pools,
    And seems at times unending;

A linked chain of bubbling notes,
    When birds have ceased their calling,
That lulls the ear with soothing sound
    Like voice of water falling.
It is the knell of winter dead;
    Good-by, his icy fetter.
Blessings on thy warty head:
    No bird could do it better.

A FRIEND IN THE GARDEN
Juliana Horatia Ewing

He is not John the gardener,
    And yet the whole day long
Employs himself most usefully
    The flower-beds among.

143

He is not Tom the pussy-cat;
   And yet the other day,
With stealthy stride and glistening eye,
   He crept upon his prey.

He is not Dash, the dear old dog,
   And yet, perhaps, if you
Took pains with him and petted him,
   You'd come to love him, too.

He's not a blackbird, though he chirps,
   And though he once was black;
But now he wears a loose, grey coat,
   All wrinkled on the back.

He's got a very dirty face,
   And very shining eyes!
He sometimes comes and sits indoors;
   He looks—and p'r'aps is—wise.

But in a sunny flower-bed
   He has his fixed abode;
He eats the things that eat my plants—
   He is a friendly TOAD.

LITTLE HORNED TOAD
FROM THE NAVAJO AMERICAN INDIAN
Transcribed by Hilda Faunce Wetherill

Little horned toad
Living in the sand
Tell me a story
Tell me of the time
When you spoke like a man,
When you knew Mr. Coyote.
Tell me how you teased him
And how you ran away,
And how he cried with anger
All day, all day.

Little bluebird
Take me with you,
Show me where you live,
Give me feathers from your coat
And to you I'll give
Many hairs from my white goat
To line your nest with.

THE LITTLE TURTLE
Vachel Lindsay

There was a little turtle.
He lived in a box.
He swam in a puddle.
He climbed on the rocks.

He snapped at a mosquito.
He snapped at a flea.
He snapped at a minnow.
And he snapped at me.

He caught the mosquito.
He caught the flea.
He caught the minnow.
But he didn't catch me.

THE TORTOISE IN ETERNITY
Elinor Wylie

Within my house of patterned horn
I sleep in such a bed
As men may keep before they're born
And after they are dead.

Sticks and stones may break their bones,
And words may make them bleed;
There is not one of them who owns
An armour to his need.

Tougher than hide or lozenged bark,
Snow-storm and thunder proof,
And quick with sun, and thick with dark,
Is this my darling roof.

Men's troubled dreams of death and birth
Pulse mother-o'-pearl to black;
I hear the rainbow bubble Earth
Square on my scornful back.

THE WASP
William Sharp

When the ripe pears droop heavily,
    The yellow wasp hums loud and long
    His hot and drowsy autumn song:
A yellow flame he seems to be,
    When darting suddenly from high
    He lights where fallen peaches lie.

Yellow and black—this tiny thing's
A tiger-soul on elfin wings.

THE WORM
Ralph Bergengren

When the earth is turned in spring
The worms are fat as anything.

And birds come flying all around
To eat the worms right off the ground.

They like worms just as much as I
Like bread and milk and apple pie.

And once, when I was very young,
I put a worm right on my tongue.

I didn't like the taste a bit,
And so I didn't swallow it.

But oh, it makes my Mother squirm
Because she *thinks* I ate that worm!

LITTLE TALK
Aileen Fisher

Don't you think it's probable
that beetles, bugs, and bees
talk about a lot of things—
you know, such things as these:

The kind of weather where they live
in jungles tall with grass
and earthquakes in their villages
whenever people pass!

Of course, we'll never know if bugs
talk very much at all,
because our ears are far too big
for talk that is so small.

HE PRAYETH BEST
FROM THE RIME OF THE ANCIENT MARINER
Samuel Taylor Coleridge

He prayeth best, who loveth best
All things both great and small;
For the dear God who loveth us,
He made and loveth all.

NEAR DUSK
Joseph Auslander

Gold, red and green flies
Tease each other in the copse,
While a tanager takes the air
In three hops.

Heavy bees go mumbling,
Orange, black and brown;
Little tads go tumbling
Up and down.

White moths whirr and flutter
In the glowworm light,
Bronze beetles plod and pass
Out of sight.

END-OF-SUMMER POEM
Rowena Bastin Bennett

The little songs of summer are all gone today.
The little insect instruments are all packed away:
The bumblebee's snare drum, the grasshopper's guitar,
The katydid's castanets—I wonder where they are.
The bullfrog's banjo, the cricket's violin,
The dragonfly's cello have ceased their merry din.
Oh, where is the orchestra? From harpist down to drummer
They've all disappeared with the passing of the summer.

LITTLE THINGS
James Stephens

Little things, that run, and quail,
And die, in silence and despair!

Little things, that fight, and fail,
And fall, on sea, and earth, and air!

All trapped and frightened little things,
The mouse, the coney, hear our prayer!

As we forgive those done to us,
—The lamb, the linnet, and the hare—

Forgive us all our trespasses,
Little creatures, everywhere!

HURT NO LIVING THING
Christina Rossetti

Hurt no living thing:
    Ladybird, no butterfly,
Nor moth with dusty wing,
    No cricket chirping cheerily,
Nor grasshopper so light of leap,
    Nor dancing gnat, no beetle fat,
Nor harmless worms that creep.

Animal pets
and otherwise

PUPPY AND I
A. A. *Milne*

I met a man as I went walking;
We got talking,
Man and I.
"Where are you going to, Man?" I said
  (I said to the Man as he went by).
"Down to the village, to get some bread.
  Will you come with me?" "No, not I."

I met a Horse as I went walking;
We got talking,
Horse and I.
"Where are you going to, Horse, to-day?"
  (I said to the Horse as he went by).
"Down to the village to get some hay.
  Will you come with me?" "No, not I."

I met a Woman as I went walking;
We got talking,
Woman and I.
"Where are you going to, Woman, so early?"
  (I said to the Woman as she went by).
"Down to the village to get some barley.
  Will you come with me?" "No, not I."

I met some Rabbits as I went walking;
We got talking,
Rabbits and I.
"Where are you going in your brown fur coats?"
  (I said to the Rabbits as they went by).
"Down to the village to get some oats.
  Will you come with us?" "No, not I."

I met a Puppy as I went walking;
We got talking,
Puppy and I.
"Where are you going this nice fine day?"
    (I said to the Puppy as he went by).
"Up in the hills to roll and play."
    "*I'll* come with you, Puppy," said I.

MY DOG
Marchette Chute

His nose is short and scrubby;
    His ears hang rather low;
And he always brings the stick back,
    No matter how far you throw.

He gets spanked rather often
    For things he shouldn't do,
Like lying-on-beds, and barking,
    And eating up shoes when they're new.

He always wants to be going
    Where he isn't supposed to go.
He tracks up the house when it's snowing—
    Oh, puppy, I love you so.

THE HAIRY DOG
Herbert Asquith

My dog's so furry I've not seen
His face for years and years:
His eyes are buried out of sight,
I only guess his ears.

When people ask me for his breed,
I do not know or care:
He has the beauty of them all
Hidden beneath his hair.

DOGS AND WEATHER
Winifred Welles

I'd like a different dog
  For every kind of weather—
A narrow greyhound for a fog,
    A wolfhound strange and white,
  With a tail like a silver feather
    To run with in the night,
    When snow is still, and winter stars are bright.

In the fall I'd like to see
  In answer to my whistle,
A golden spaniel look at me.
    But best of all for rain
  A terrier, hairy as a thistle,
    To trot with fine disdain
    Beside me down the soaked, sweet-smelling lane.

LONE DOG
Irene Rutherford McLeod

I'm a lean dog, a keen dog, a wild dog, and lone;
I'm a rough dog, a tough dog, hunting on my own;
I'm a bad dog, a mad dog, teasing silly sheep;
I love to sit and bay the moon, to keep fat souls from sleep.

I'll never be a lap dog, licking dirty feet,
A sleek dog, a meek dog, cringing for my meat,
Not for me the fireside, the well-filled plate,
But shut door, and sharp stone, and cuff and kick and hate.

Not for me the other dogs, running by my side,
Some have run a short while, but none of them would bide,
Oh, mine is still the lone trail, the hard trail, the best,
Wide wind, and wild stars, and hunger of the quest!

LITTLE PUPPY
FROM THE NAVAJO AMERICAN INDIAN
Transcribed by Hilda Faunce Wetherill

Little puppy with the black spots,
Come and herd the flock with me.
We will climb the red rocks
And from the top we'll see
The tall cliffs, the straight cliffs,
The fluted cliffs,
Where the eagles live.
We'll see the dark rocks,
The smooth rocks,
That hold the rain to give us
Water, when we eat our bread and meat,
When the sun is high.
Little spotted dog of mine,
Come and spend the day with me.
When the sun is going down
Behind the pointed hill,
We will follow home the flock.
They will lead the way
To the hogans where the fires burn
And the square cornbread is in the ashes,
Waiting our return.

THE KITTEN AT PLAY
William Wordsworth

See the kitten on the wall,
Sporting with the leaves that fall,
Withered leaves, one, two and three
Falling from the elder tree,
Through the calm and frosty air
Of the morning bright and fair.

See the kitten, how she starts,
Crouches, stretches, paws and darts;
With a tiger-leap half way
Now she meets her coming prey.
Lets it go as fast and then
Has it in her power again.

Now she works with three and four,
Like an Indian conjurer;
Quick as he in feats of art,
Gracefully she plays her part;
Yet were gazing thousands there;
What would little Tabby care?

THE RUM TUM TUGGER
T. S. Eliot

The Rum Tum Tugger is a Curious Cat:
If you offer him pheasant he would rather have grouse.
If you put him in a house he would much prefer a flat,
If you put him in a flat then he'd rather have a house.
If you set him on a mouse then he only wants a rat,
If you set him on a rat then he'd rather chase a mouse.
Yes the Rum Tum Tugger is a Curious Cat—
　　And there isn't any call for me to shout it:
　　　　For he will do
　　　　As he do do
　　　　　　And there's no doing anything about it!

157

The Rum Tum Tugger is a terrible bore:
When you let him in, then he wants to be out;
He's always on the wrong side of every door,
As soon as he's at home, then he'd like to get about.
He likes to lie in the bureau drawer,
But he makes such a fuss if he can't get out.
Yes the Rum Tum Tugger is a Curious Cat—
   And it isn't any use for you to doubt it:
     For he will do
     As he do do
       And there's no doing anything about it!

The Rum Tum Tugger is a curious beast:
His disobliging ways are a matter of habit.
If you offer him fish then he always wants a feast;
When there isn't any fish then he won't eat rabbit.
If you offer him cream then he sniffs and sneers,
For he only likes what he finds for himself;
So you'll catch him in it right up to the ears,
If you put it away on the larder shelf.
The Rum Tum Tugger is artful and knowing,
The Rum Tum Tugger doesn't care for a cuddle;
But he'll leap on your lap in the middle of your sewing,
For there's nothing he enjoys like a horrible muddle.
Yes the Rum Tum Tugger is a Curious Cat—
   And there isn't any need for me to spout it:
     For he will do
     As he do do
       And there's no doing anything about it!

THE MYSTERIOUS CAT
Vachel Lindsay

   I saw a proud, mysterious cat,
   I saw a proud, mysterious cat,
   Too proud to catch a mouse or rat—
      Mew, mew, mew.

But catnip she would eat, and purr,
But catnip she would eat, and purr.
And goldfish she did much prefer—
     Mew, mew, mew.

I saw a cat—'twas but a dream,
I saw a cat—'twas but a dream,
Who scorned the slave that brought her cream—
     Mew, mew, mew.

Unless the slave were dressed in style,
Unless the slave were dressed in style,
And knelt before her all the while—
     Mew, mew, mew.

Did you ever hear of a thing like that?
Did you ever hear of a thing like that?
Did you ever hear of a thing like that?
Oh, what a proud, mysterious cat.
Oh, what a proud, mysterious cat.
Oh, what a proud, mysterious cat.
     Mew . . . Mew . . . Mew.

POEM
William Carlos Williams

       As the cat
       climbed over
       the top of

       the jamcloset
       first the right
       forefoot

       carefully
       then the hind
       stepped down

       into the pit of
       the empty
       flower pot

THE BAD KITTENS
Elizabeth Coatsworth

You may call, you may call,
But the little black cats won't hear you,
The little black cats are maddened
By the bright green light of the moon,
They are whirling and running and hiding,
They are wild who were once so confiding,
They are crazed when the moon is riding—
You will not catch the kittens soon.
They care not for saucers of milk,
They think not of pillows of silk,
Your softest, crooningest call
Is less than the buzzing of flies.
They are seeing more than you see,
They are hearing more than you hear,
And out of the darkness they peer
With a goblin light in their eyes.

HEARTH
Peggy Bacon

A cat sat quaintly by the fire
    And watched the burning coals
And watched the little flames aspire
    Like small decrepit souls.
Queer little fire with coals so fat
    And crooked flames that rise,
No queerer than the little cat
    With fire in its eyes.

THE RUNAWAY
Robert Frost

Once, when the snow of the year was beginning to fall,
We stopped by a mountain pasture to say "Whose colt?"
A little Morgan had one forefoot on the wall,
The other curled at his breast. He dipped his head
And snorted to us. And then he had to bolt.
We heard the miniature thunder where he fled
And we saw him or thought we saw him dim and gray,
Like a shadow against the curtain of falling flakes.
"I think the little fellow's afraid of the snow.
He isn't winter-broken. It isn't play
With the little fellow at all. He's running away.
I doubt if even his mother could tell him, 'Sakes,
It's only weather.' He'd think she didn't know.
Where is his mother? He can't be out alone."
And now he comes again with a clatter of stone
And mounts the wall again with whited eyes
And all his tail that isn't hair up straight.
He shudders his coat as if to throw off flies.
"Whoever it is that leaves him out so late,
When other creatures have gone to stall and bin,
Ought to be told to come and take him in."

NOONDAY SUN
Kathryn and Byron Jackson

Oh, I've ridden plenty of horses
    And I've broken a score in my time,
But there never was one
    Like the colt Noonday Sun—
Now there was a horse that was prime!
    Oh, yippi ippi ai—Oh, yippi ippi ay,
Now there was a horse that was prime!

161

She'd run up the side of a mountain
  Or she'd tackle a wildcat alone.
Oh, she stood twelve hands high
  And her proud shining eye
Would soften the heart of a stone.
  Oh, yippi ippi ai—Oh, yippi ippi ay,
Would soften the heart of a stone.

She'd splash through a treach'rous river,
  Or she'd tease for an apple or sweet,
She'd buck and she'd prance,
  Or she'd do a square dance
On her four little white little feet.
  Oh, yippi ippi ai—Oh, yippi ippi ay,
On her four little white little feet.

But one night the rustlers stole her,
  They stole her and took her away.
Now the sun never shines,
  And the wind in the pines
Says, "You've lost your colt, lack-a-day!"
  Oh, yippi ippi ai—Oh, yippi ippi ay,
Says, "You've lost your colt, lack-a-day!"

Someday I'll ride through the prairie.
  Someday I'll pull out my gun,
And I'll plug him—bang-bang!—
  And I may even hang—
The outlaw who stole Noonday Sun.
  Oh, yippi ippi ai—Oh, yippi ippi ay,
The outlaw that stole Noonday Sun.

Oh, I still have her bridle and saddle,
  And I still have her bare empty stall.
But there'll never be one
  Like the colt Noonday Sun,
And she'll never more come to my call!
  Oh, yippi ippi ai—Oh, yippi ippi ay,
And she'll never more come to my call!

THE HORSE
The Bible

Hast thou given the horse strength?
Hast thou clothed his neck with thunder?
Canst thou make him afraid as a grasshopper?
The glory of his nostrils is terrible.
He paweth in the valley, and rejoiceth in his strength;
He goeth on to meet the armed men.
He swalloweth the ground with fierceness and rage;
Neither believeth he that it is the sound of the trumpet.
He saith among the trumpets, "Ha, Ha!"
And he smelleth the battle afar off,
The thunder of the captains, and the shouting.

BURRO WITH THE LONG EARS
FROM THE NAVAJO AMERICAN INDIAN
Transcribed by Hilda Faunce Wetherill

Ja-Nez—burro with the long ears—
Come with me to the water hole.
I will fill the kegs with water
And you will carry them home.
Down the crooked trail,
Through the deep hot sand,
Past the fragrant piñon trees,
Winding this way, winding that way,
Do not step into the cactus.
Now I wade into the water
Where it is clearest; I dip and pour.
While you drink I fill the kegs.
They are heavy as I lift them to your back again.
Now we wander through the cactus,
Past the fragrant trees,
Up the sandy trail, winding slowly.
At the hogan my mother sees
Us coming home with water.

THE COW
Robert Louis Stevenson

The friendly cow all red and white,
　I love with all my heart;
She gives me cream with all her might,
　To eat with apple tart.

She wanders lowing here and there,
　And yet she cannot stray,
All in the pleasant open air,
　The pleasant light of day;

And blown by all the winds that pass
　And wet with all the showers,
She walks among the meadow grass
　And eats the meadow flowers.

MILK-WHITE MOON, PUT THE COWS TO SLEEP
Carl Sandburg

Milk-white moon, put the cows to sleep.
Since five o'clock in the morning,
Since they stood up out of the grass,
Where they slept on their knees and hocks,
They have eaten grass and given their milk
And eaten grass again and given milk,
And kept their heads and teeth at the earth's face.
　Now they are looking at you, milk-white moon.
　Carelessly as they look at the level landscapes,
　Carelessly as they look at a pail of new white milk,
　They are looking at you, wondering not at all, at all,
　If the moon is the skim face top of a pail of milk,
　Wondering not at all, carelessly looking.
　Put the cows to sleep, milk-white moon,
　Put the cows to sleep.

HOOSEN JOHNNY

De little black bull kem down de medder,
    Hoosen Johnny, Hoosen Johnny.
De little black bull kem down de medder,
    Long time ago.

Long time ago, long time ago,
De little black bull kem down de medder,
    Long time ago.

Fust he paw and den he beller,
    Hoosen Johnny, Hoosen Johnny,
Fust he paw and den he beller,
    Long time ago.

He whet his horn on a white oak saplin',
    Hoosen Johnny, Hoosen Johnny.
He whet his horn on a white oak saplin',
    Long time ago.

He shake his tail, he jar de ribber,
    Hoosen Johnny, Hoosen Johnny.
He shake his tail, he jar de ribber,
    Long time ago.

He paw de dirt in de heifers' faces,
    Hoosen Johnny, Hoosen Johnny.
He paw de dirt in de heifers' faces,
    Long time ago.

THE LAMB
William Blake

Little Lamb, who made thee?
Dost thou know who made thee?
Gave thee life, and bade thee feed
By the stream and o'er the mead;

Gave thee clothing of delight,
Softest clothing, woolly, bright;
Gave thee such a tender voice,
Making all the vales rejoice?
   Little Lamb, who made thee?
   Dost thou know who made thee?

Little Lamb, I'll tell thee;
Little Lamb, I'll tell thee:
He is called by thy name,
For He calls Himself a Lamb.
He is meek, and He is mild,
He became a little child.
I a child, and thou a lamb,
We are called by His name.
   Little Lamb, God bless thee!
   Little Lamb, God bless thee!

THE UNKNOWN COLOR
Countee Cullen

I've often heard my mother say,
When great winds blew across the day,
And, cuddled close and out of sight,
The young pigs squealed with sudden fright
Like something speared or javelined,
"Poor little pigs, they see the wind."

RABBIT
Tom Robinson

I'd like to run like a rabbit in hops
With occasional intermediate stops.
He is so cute when he lifts his ears
And looks around to see what he hears.

WHITE SEASON
(For Tony)
Frances Frost

In the winter the rabbits match their pelts to the earth,
With ears laid back, they go
Blown through the silver hollow, the silver thicket,
Like puffs of snow.

TO A SQUIRREL AT KYLE-NA-NO
W. B. Yeats

Come play with me;
Why should you run
Through the shaking tree
As though I'd a gun
To strike you dead?
When all I would do
Is to scratch your head
And let you go.

THE SQUIRREL

Whisky Frisky,
Hippity hop,
Up he goes
To the tree top!

Whirly, twirly,
Round and round,
Down he scampers
To the ground.

Furly, curly,
What a tail!
Tall as a feather,
Broad as a sail!

Where's his supper?
In the shell,
Snap, cracky,
Out it fell.

THE SKUNK
Robert P. Tristram Coffin

When the sun has slipped away
And the dew is on the day,
Then the creature comes to call
Men malign the most of all.

The little skunk is very neat,
With his sensitive, plush feet
And a dainty, slim head set
With diamonds on bands of jet.

He walks upon his evening's duty
Of declaring how that beauty
With her patterns is not done
At the setting of the sun.

He undulates across the lawn,
He asks nobody to fawn
On his graces. All that he
Asks is that men let him be.

He knows that he is very fine
In every clean and rippling line,
He is a conscious black and white
Little symphony of night.

THE JOLLY WOODCHUCK
Marion Edey and Dorothy Grider

The woodchuck's very very fat
But doesn't care a pin for that.

When nights are long and the snow is deep.
Down in his hole he lies asleep.

Under the earth is a warm little room
The drowsy woodchuck calls his home.

Rolls of fat and fur surround him,
With all his children curled around him,

Snout to snout and tail to tail.
He never awakes in the wildest gale;

When icicles snap and the north wind blows
He snores in his sleep and rubs his nose.

THE BROWN BEAR
Mary Austin

Now the wild bees that hive in the rocks
    Are winding their horns, elfin shrill,
And hark, at the pine tree the woodpecker knocks,
    And the speckled grouse pipes on the hill.
Now the adder's dull brood wakes to run,
    Now the sap mounts abundant and good,
And the brown bear has turned his side to the sun
    In his lair in the depth of the wood—
    Old Honey-Paw wakes in the wood.

"Oh, a little more slumber," says he,
    "And a little more turning to sleep,"
But he feels the spring fervor that hurries the bee
    And the hunger that makes the trout leap;

So he ambles by thicket and trail,
  So he noses the tender young shoots,
In the spring of the year at the sign of the quail
  The brown bear goes digging for roots—
  For sappy and succulent roots.

Oh, as still goes the wolf on his quest,
  As the spotted snake glides through the rocks,
And the deer and the sheep count the lightest foot best,
  And slinking and sly trots the fox.
But fleet-foot and light-foot will stay,
  And fawns by their mothers will quail
At the saplings that snap and the thickets that sway
  When Honey-Paw takes to the trail—
  When he shuffles and grunts on the trail.

He has gathered the ground squirrel's hoard,
  He has rifled the store of the bees,
He has caught the young trout at the shoals of the ford
  And stripped the wild plums from the trees;
So robbing and ranging he goes,
  And the right to his pillage makes good
Till he rounds out the year at the first of the snows
  In his lair in the depth of the wood—
  Old Honey-Paw sleeps in the wood.

GRIZZLY BEAR
Mary Austin

            If you ever, ever, ever meet a grizzly bear,
            You must never, never, never ask him *where*
            He is going,
            Or *what* he is doing;
            For if you ever, ever dare
            To stop a grizzly bear,
            You will never meet *another* grizzly bear.

TWELFTH NIGHT: SONG OF THE CAMELS
Elizabeth Coatsworth

Not born to the forest are we,
Not born to the plain,
To the grass and the shadowing tree
And the splashing of rain.
Only the sand we know
And the cloudless sky.
The mirage and the deep-sunk well
And the stars on high.

To the sound of our bells we came
With huge soft stride,
Kings riding upon our backs,
Slaves at our side.
Out of the east drawn on
By a dream and a star,
Seeking the hills and the groves
Where the fixed towns are.

Our goal was no palace gate,
No temple of old,
But a child on his mother's lap
In the cloudy cold.
The olives were windy and white,
Dust swirled through the town,
As all in their royal robes
Our masters knelt down.

THE DEER
Mary Austin

Under the pines and hemlocks
So thick the needles lie
You scarcely hear
The shy, dun deer
With its young go softly by.

"Twelfth Night: Song of the Camels" from *Country Poems*, by Elizabeth Coatsworth. Copyright 1942 by Elizabeth Coatsworth. Courtesy of The Macmillan Company.

Follow, follow,
By hill and hollow,
The dun buck bells to the doe,
The moon is bright,
And we feed tonight
Where the buckthorn thickets grow.

Under the pines and the hemlocks
The thick, white cloud mists creep,
And drip all down
The needles brown
Where the dun deer lies asleep.
Follow, follow,
By hill and hollow,
The doe to her spotted fawn;
'Tis dark o' the moon,
But day comes soon
For I sniff the breath of the dawn.

Under the pines and hemlocks
Flickers through light and shade
The deer to his lair
In the deep fern there,
Or to pasture in open glade.
Follow, follow,
By hill and hollow,
Dun buck, and fawn and doe.
The sun is high
And by day we lie
Where only the deer must know.

HOLDING HANDS
Lenore M. Link

Elephants walking
Along the trails

Are holding hands
By holding tails.

Trunks and tails
Are handy things

When elephants walk
In Circus rings.

Elephants work
And elephants play

And elephants walk
And feel so gay.

And when they walk—
It never fails

They're holding hands
By holding tails.

NIGHT OF WIND
Frances Frost

How lost is the little fox at the borders of night,
Poised in the forest of fern, in the trample of the wind!
Caught by the blowing cold of the mountain darkness,
He shivers and runs under tall trees, whimpering,
Brushing the tangles of dew. Pausing and running,
He searches the warm and shadowy hollow, the deep
Home on the mountain's side where the nuzzling, soft
Bodies of little foxes may hide and sleep.

FOUR LITTLE FOXES
Lew Sarett

Speak gently, Spring, and make no sudden sound;
For in my windy valley, yesterday I found
New-born foxes squirming on the ground—
    Speak gently.

Walk gently, March; forbear the bitter blow;
Her feet within a trap, her blood upon the snow,
The four little foxes saw their mother go—
    Walk softly.

Go lightly, Spring; oh, give them no alarm;
When I covered them with boughs to shelter them from harm,
The thin blue foxes suckled at my arm—
    Go lightly.

Step softly, March, with your rampant hurricane;
Nuzzling one another, and whimpering with pain,
The new little foxes are shivering in the rain—
    Step softly.

THE SING-SONG OF OLD MAN KANGAROO
Rudyard Kipling

This is the mouth-filling song of the race that was run by a Boomer,
Run in a single burst—only event of its kind—
Started by Big God Nqong from Warrigaborrigarooma,
Old Man Kangaroo first, Yellow-Dog Dingo behind.

Kangaroo bounded away, his back legs working like pistons—
Bounded from morning till dark, twenty-five feet to a bound.
Yellow-Dog Dingo lay like a yellow cloud in the distance—
Much too busy to bark. My! but they covered the ground!

Nobody knows where they went, or followed the track that they
    flew in,
For that Continent hadn't been given a name.
They ran thirty degrees, from Torres Straits to the Leeuwin
(Look at the Atlas, please), and they ran back as they came.

S'posing you could trot
From Adelaide to the Pacific,
For an afternoon's run—
Half what these gentlemen did—

You would feel rather hot,
But your legs would develop terrific—
Yes, my importunate son,
You'd be a Marvellous Kid!

THE LION
Mary Howitt

When Lion sends his roaring forth,
Silence falls upon the earth;
For the creatures, great and small,
Know his terror-breathing call;
And, as if by death pursued,
Leave him to a solitude.

Lion, thou art made to dwell
In hot lands, intractable,
And thyself, the sun, the sand,
Are a tyrannous triple band;
Lion-king and desert throne,
All the region is your own!

THE MONKEYS AND THE CROCODILE
Laura E. Richards

Five little monkeys
    Swinging from a tree;
Teasing Uncle Crocodile,
    Merry as can be.
Swinging high, swinging low,
    Swinging left and right:
"Dear Uncle Crocodile,
    Come and take a bite!"

Five little monkeys
 Swinging in the air;
Heads up, tails up,
 Little do they care.
Swinging up, swinging down,
 Swinging far and near:
"Poor Uncle Crocodile,
 Aren't you hungry, dear?"

Four little monkeys
 Sitting in a tree;
Heads down, tails down,
 Dreary as can be.
Weeping loud, weeping low,
 Crying to each other:
"Wicked Uncle Crocodile
 To gobble up our brother!"

PRAIRIE-DOG TOWN
Mary Austin

Old Peter Prairie-Dog
Builds him a house
In Prairie-Dog Town,
With a door that goes down
And down and down,
And a hall that goes under
And under and under,
Where you can't see the lightning,
You can't hear the thunder,
For they don't *like* thunder
In Prairie-Dog Town.

Old Peter Prairie-Dog
Digs him a cellar
In Prairie-Dog Town,
With a ceiling that is arched

And a wall that is round,
And the earth he takes out he makes into a mound.
And the hall and the cellar
Are dark as dark,
And you can't see a spark,
Not a single spark;
And the way to them cannot be found.

Old Peter Prairie-Dog
Knows a very clever trick
Of behaving like a stick
When he hears a sudden sound,
Like an old dead stick;
And when you turn your head
He'll jump quick, quick,
And be another stick
When you look around.
It *is* a clever trick,
And it keeps him safe and sound
In the cellar and the halls
That are under the mound
In Prairie-Dog Town.

SEAL LULLABY
Rudyard Kipling

Oh! hush thee, my baby, the night is behind us,
    And black are the waters that sparkled so green.
The moon, o'er the combers, looks downward to find us
    At rest in the hollows that rustle between.
Where billow meets billow, there soft be thy pillow;
    Ah, weary wee flipperling, curl at thy ease!
The storm shall not wake thee, nor shark overtake thee,
    Asleep in the arms of the slow-swinging seas.

THE TIGER
William Blake

Tiger! Tiger! burning bright,
In the forests of the night,
What immortal hand or eye
Could frame thy fearful symmetry?

In what distant deeps or skies
Burnt the fire of thine eyes?
On what wings dare he aspire?
What the hand dare seize the fire?

And what shoulder, and what art,
Could twist the sinews of thy heart?
And when thy heart began to beat,
What dread hand and what dread feet?

What the hammer? what the chain?
In what furnace was thy brain?
What the anvil? What dread grasp
Dare its deadly terrors clasp?

When the stars threw down their spears,
And watered heaven with their tears,
Did He smile His work to see?
Did He who made the Lamb, make thee?

Tiger! Tiger! burning bright,
In the forests of the night,
What immortal hand or eye
Dare frame thy fearful symmetry?

THE WOLF CRY
Lew Sarett

The Arctic moon hangs overhead;
The wide white silence lies below.
A starveling pine stands lone and gaunt,
Black-penciled on the snow.

Weird as the moan of sobbing winds,
A lone long call floats up from the trail;
And the naked soul of the frozen North
Trembles in that wail.

THE PEACEABLE KINGDOM
The Bible

The wolf also shall dwell with the lamb,
and the leopard shall lie down with the kid;
and the calf and the young lion
and the fatling together;
and a little child shall lead them.

On the way to anywhere

ROADS GO EVER ON AND ON
J. R. R. Tolkien

Roads go ever on and on,
   Over rock and under tree,
By caves where sun has never shone,
   By streams that never find the sea;
Over snow by winter sown,
   And through the merry flowers of June,
Over grass and over stone,
   And under mountains in the moon.

ROADS
Rachel Field

A road might lead to anywhere—
   To harbor towns and quays,
Or to a witch's pointed house
   Hidden by bristly trees.
It might lead past the tailor's door,
   Where he sews with needle and thread,
Or by Miss Pim the milliner's,
   With her hats for every head.
It might be a road to a great, dark cave
   With treasure and gold piled high,
Or a road with a mountain tied to its end,
   Blue-humped against the sky.
Oh, a road might lead you anywhere—
   To Mexico or Maine.
But then, it might just fool you, and—
   Lead you back home again!

THERE ARE SO MANY WAYS OF GOING PLACES
Leslie Thompson

Big yellow trolley limbers along,
Long black subway sings an under song,
Airplanes swoop and flash in the sky,
Noisy old elevated goes rocketing by,
Boats across the river—back and forth they go,
Big boats and little boats, fast boats and slow.
Trains puff and thunder; their engines have a headlight;
They have a special kind of car where you can sleep all night.
Tall fat buses on the Avenue,
They will stop for anyone—even—just—you.
All kinds of autos rush down the street.
And then there are always—your own two feet.

SONG FOR A BLUE ROADSTER
Rachel Field

Fly, Roadster, fly!
  The sun is high,
Gold are the fields
  We hurry by,
Green are the woods
  As we slide through
Past harbor and headland,
  Blue on blue.

Fly, Roadster, fly!
  The hay smells sweet,
And the flowers are fringing
  Each village street,
Where carts are blue
  And barns are red,
And the road unwinds
  Like a twist of thread.

Fly, Roadster, fly!
  Leave Time behind;
Out of sight
  Shall be out of mind.
Shine and shadow
  Blue sea, green bough,
Nothing is real
  But Here and Now.

STOP-GO
Dorothy W. Baruch

Automobiles
In
   a
     row
Wait to go
While the signal says:
                    STOP

Bells ring
Tingaling!
Red light's gone!
Green light's on!
Horns blow!
And the row
Starts
       to
                    GO

FUNNY THE WAY DIFFERENT CARS START
Dorothy W. Baruch

Funny the way
Different cars start.
Some with a chunk and a jerk,
Some with a cough and a puff of smoke
Out of the back,
Some with only a little click—with hardly any noise.

Funny the way
Different cars run.
Some rattle and bang,
Some whirrr,
Some knock and knock.
Some purr
And hummmmm
Smoothly on with hardly any noise.

TRUCKS
James S. Tippett

Big trucks for steel beams,
Big trucks for coal,
Rumbling down the broad streets,
Heavily they roll.

Little trucks for groceries,
Little trucks for bread,
Turning into every street,
Rushing on ahead.

Big trucks, little trucks,
In never ending lines,
Rumble on and rush ahead
While I read their signs.

B'S THE BUS
Phyllis McGinley

B's the Bus,
The bouncing Bus,
   That bears a shopper store-ward.
It's fun to sit
In back of it
   But seats are better forward.
Although it's big as buildings are
   And looks both bold and grand,
It has to stop obligingly
   If you but raise your hand.

THE LOCOMOTIVE
Emily Dickinson

I like to see it lap the miles,
And lick the valleys up,
And stop to feed itself at tanks;
And then, prodigious, step

Around a pile of mountains,
And, supercilious, peer
In shanties by the sides of roads;
And then a quarry pare

To fit its sides, and crawl between,
Complaining all the while
In horrid, hooting stanza;
Then chase itself downhill

And neigh like Boanerges;
Then, punctual as a star,
Stop—docile and omnipotent—
At its own stable door.

TRAINS
James S. Tippett

Over the mountains,
Over the plains,
Over the rivers,
Here come the trains.

Carrying passengers,
Carrying mail,
Bringing their precious loads
In without fail.

Thousands of freight cars
All rushing on
Through day and darkness,
Through dusk and dawn.

Over the mountains,
Over the plains,
Over the rivers,
Here come the trains.

SONG OF THE TRAIN
David McCord

Clickety-clack,
Wheels on the track,
This is the way
They begin the attack:
Click-ety-clack,
Click-ety-clack,
Click-ety, *clack*-ety,
Click-ety
Clack.

Clickety-clack,
Over the crack,
Faster and faster
The song of the track:

Clickety-clack,
Clickety-clack,
Clickety, clackety,
Clackety.
Clack.

Riding in front,
Riding in back,
Everyone hears
The song of the track:
Clickety-clack,
Clickety-clack,
Clickety, *clickety,*
Clackety
Clack.

FROM A RAILWAY CARRIAGE
Robert Louis Stevenson

Faster than fairies, faster than witches,
Bridges and houses, hedges and ditches;
And charging along like troops in a battle
All through the meadows the horses and cattle:
All of the sights of the hill and the plain
Fly as thick as driving rain;
And ever again, in the wink of an eye,
Painted stations whistle by.

Here is a child who clambers and scrambles,—
All by himself and gathering brambles;
Here is a tramp who stands and gazes;
And there is the green for stringing the daisies!
Here is a cart run away in the road
Lumping along with man and load;
And here is a mill, and there is a river:
Each a glimpse and gone for ever!

TRAVEL
Edna St. Vincent Millay

The railroad track is miles away,
    And the day is loud with voices speaking,
Yet there isn't a train goes by all day
    But I hear its whistle shrieking.

All night there isn't a train goes by,
    Though the night is still for sleep and dreaming,
But I see its cinders red on the sky,
    And hear its engine steaming.

My heart is warm with the friends I make,
    And better friends I'll not be knowing,
Yet there isn't a train I wouldn't take,
    No matter where it's going.

SEA FEVER
John Masefield

I must go down to the seas again, to the lonely sea and the sky,
And all I ask is a tall ship and a star to steer her by,
And the wheel's kick and the wind's song and the white sail's
    shaking,
And a gray mist on the sea's face, and a gray dawn breaking.

I must go down to the seas again, for the call of the running tide
Is a wild call and a clear call that may not be denied;
And all I ask is a windy day with the white clouds flying,
And the flung spray and the blown spume, and the sea gulls crying.

I must go down to the seas again, to the vagrant gypsy life,
To the gull's way and the whale's way where the wind's like a
    whetted knife;
And all I ask is a merry yarn from a laughing fellow-rover,
And quiet sleep and a sweet dream when the long trick's over.

THE SEA GYPSY
Richard Hovey

I am fevered with the sunset,
I am fretful with the bay,
For the wander-thirst is on me
And my soul is in Cathay.

There's a schooner in the offing,
With her top-sails shot with fire,
And my heart has gone aboard her
For the Islands of Desire.

I must forth again tomorrow!
With the sunset I must be,
Hull down on the trail of rapture
In the wonder of the Sea.

A WINDY DAY
Winifred Howard

Have you been at sea on a windy day
    When the water's blue
    And the sky is too,
And showers of spray
    Come sweeping the decks
And the sea is dotted
    With little flecks
Of foam, like daisies gay;

When there's salt on your lips,
    In your eyes and hair,
And you watch other ships
    Go riding there?
Sailors are happy,
    And birds fly low
To see how close they can safely go
To the waves as they heave and roll.

Then, wheeling, they soar
  Mounting up to the sky,
Where billowy clouds
  Go floating by!
Oh, there's fun for you
And there's fun for me
  At sea
On a windy day!

ON A STEAMER
Dorothy W. Baruch

Once
I went for an ocean trip
On a big steamer.

Its whistle blew
With a loud
A woo. . . .

  When dinner time came
  I didn't get off.
  No—
    I ate my dinner
    Right on the boat.

When bed time came
I didn't get off
No—
  I went to sleep
  Right on the boat.

    I had a little room
    With a closet in it
    Where I could hang up my suit
    And my hat
    And my coat.

And when I climbed into bed that night
And put my ear
Down—tight—
Then—
  All at once—
    I could hear
    The engines go
    Way far below
    Throbadoba throbadoba
      Never stopping
      Always throbbing
      Throbadoba throbadoba
      Throba doba dob.

BACK AND FORTH
Lucy Sprague Mitchell

        Back and forth
        go the ferries,
        back and forth
        from shore to shore,
        hauling people, trucks and autos,
        back and forth
        from shore to shore.

                Back and forth
                go the ferries,
                either end
                is bow or stern;
                good old poky, clumsy ferries
                they don't even
                have to turn.

        Back and forth
        go the ferries,
        Here's a freighter!

There's a barge!
Nosing through the harbor traffic,
tugs and steamers
small and large.

Back and forth
go the ferries;
anxiously
the captains steer
poking slowly through the fog bank,
coasting, bump!
into the pier.

Back and forth
go the ferries;
clang the bell
and close the door.
Streaks of foam across the harbor.
Open gate,
They've reached the shore.

RIDING IN A MOTOR BOAT
Dorothy W. Baruch

A putta putta putt—
The motor boat
Splashes
A spray behind it.

A putta putta putt—
I go for a ride
And watch
The beach slide by.

I see a man upside down on his head,
And a boy turning somersaults,
And umbrellas
That stand
Like high mushrooms
In the sand.

A putta putt putt—
I reach my hand
Over the side of the boat
Into the slipping water.

It feels
Tingly
And cold.

TUGS
James S. Tippett

Chug! Puff! Chug!
Push, little tug.
Push the great ship here
Close to its pier.

Chug! Puff! Chug!
Pull, strong tug.
Drawing all alone
Three boat-loads of stone.

Busy harbor tugs,
Like round water bugs,
Hurry here and there,
Working everywhere.

FREIGHT BOATS
James S. Tippett

Boats that carry sugar
And tobacco from Havana;
Boats that carry coconuts
And coffee from Brazil;
Boats that carry cotton
From the city of Savannah;
Boats that carry anything
From any place you will.

Boats like boxes loaded down
With tons of sand and gravel;
Boats with blocks of granite
For a building on the hill;
Boats that measure many thousand
Lonesome miles of travel
As they carry anything
From any place you will.

CARGOES
John Masefield

Quinquireme of Nineveh from distant Ophir
Rowing home to haven in sunny Palestine,
With a cargo of ivory,
And apes and peacocks,
Sandalwood, cedarwood, and sweet white wine.

Stately Spanish galleon coming from the Isthmus,
Dipping through the Tropics by the palm-green shores,
With a cargo of diamonds,
Emeralds, amethysts,
Topazes, and cinnamon, and gold moidores.

Dirty British coaster with a salt-caked smokestack
Butting through the Channel in the mad March days,
With a cargo of Tyne coal,
Road-rails, pig-lead,
Firewood, iron-ware, and cheap tin trays.

THEY THAT GO DOWN TO THE SEA
The Bible: from Psalm 107

They that go down to the sea in ships,
That do business in great waters;
These see the works of the Lord,
And his wonders in the deep.

THE AIRPLANE
Rowena Bastin Bennett

An airplane has gigantic wings
But not a feather on her breast;
She only mutters when she sings
And builds a hangar for a nest.
I love to see her stop and start;
She has a little motor heart
That beats and throbs and then is still.
She wears a fan upon her bill.

No eagle flies through sun and rain
So swiftly as an airplane.
I wish she would come swooping down
Between the steeples of the town
And lift me right up off my feet
And take me high above the street,
That all the other boys might see
The little speck that would be me.

THE DIRIGIBLE
Ralph Bergengren

The only real airship
    That I've ever seen
Looked more like a fish
    Than a flying machine.

It made me feel funny,
    And just as if we
Were all of us down
    On the floor of the sea.

A big whale above us
    Was taking a swim,
And we little fishes
    Were staring at him.

GO FLY A SAUCER
FROM GO FLY A SAUCER
David McCord

I've seen one flying saucer. Only when
It flew across our sight in 1910
We little thought about the little men.

But let's suppose the little men were there
To cozy such a disk through foreign air:
Connecticut was dark, but didn't scare.

I wonder what they thought of us, and why
They chose the lesser part of Halley's sky,
And went away and let the years go by

Without return? Or did they not get back
To Mars or Venus through the cosmic flak?
At least they vanished, every spaceman Jack.

SILVER SHIPS
Mildred Plew Meigs

There are trails that a lad may follow
    When the years of his boyhood slip,
But I shall soar like a swallow
    On the wings of a silver ship,

Guiding my bird of metal,
    One with her throbbing frame,
Floating down like a petal,
    Roaring up like a flame;

Winding the wind that scatters
    Smoke from the chimney's lip,
Tearing the clouds to tatters
    With the wings of a silver ship;

Grazing the broad blue sky light
    Up where the falcons fare,
Riding the realms of twilight,
    Brushed by a comet's hair;

Snug in my coat of leather,
    Watching the skyline swing,
Shedding the world like a feather
    From the tip of a tilted wing.

There are trails that a lad may travel
    When the years of his boyhood wane,
But I'll let a rainbow ravel
    Through the wings of my silver plane.

RIDING IN AN AIRPLANE
Dorothy W. Baruch

Azzoomm, azzoomm loud and strong—
Azzoomm, azzoomm a steady song—
  And UP I went
  UP and UP
    For a ride
    In an airplane.

The machinery roarrrred
And whirrred
And jiggled my ears
Yet I
Just sat right
On a chair
Inside that airplane
And made myself
Stare
Out of a window.

There
Way down below
I saw autos
Scuttling along.
  They looked to me
  Like fast little lady bugs—
  So small!
And I saw houses
That seemed to be
  Only as big as match boxes—
    That's all!

But the strangest sight
Was when
We came to some clouds!
We stared *down*
Instead of *up*
To see them,

And they looked
Like puffs of smoke
From giant cigarettes.

COCKPIT IN THE CLOUDS
Dick Dorrance

Two thousand feet beneath our wheels
The city sprawls across the land
Like heaps of children's blocks outflung,
In tantrums, by a giant hand.
To east a silver spire soars
And seeks to pierce our lower wing.
Above its grasp we drift along,
A tiny, droning, shiny thing.

The noon crowds pack the narrow streets.
The el trains move so slow, so slow.
Amidst their traffic, chaos, life,
The city's busy millions go.
Up here, aloof, we watch them crawl.
In crystal air we seem to poise
Behind our motor's throaty roar—
Down there, we're just another noise.

NIGHT PLANE
Frances Frost

The midnight plane with its riding lights
looks like a footloose star
wandering west through the blue-black night
to where the mountains are,

a star that's journeyed nearer earth
to tell each quiet farm
and little town, "Put out your lights,
children of earth. Sleep warm."

PRAYER FOR A PILOT
Cecil Roberts

Lord of Sea and Earth and Air,
Listen to the Pilot's prayer—
Send him wind that's steady and strong,
Grant that his engine sings the song
Of flawless tone, by which he knows
It shall not fail him where he goes;
Landing, gliding, in curve, half-roll—
Grant him, O Lord, a full control,
That he may learn in heights of Heaven
The rapture altitude has given,
That he shall know the joy they feel
Who ride Thy realms on Birds of Steel.

WHEN I CONSIDER THY HEAVENS
The Bible: from Psalm 8

When I consider thy heavens, the work of thy fingers,
The moon and the stars, which thou hast ordained,
What is man, that thou art mindful of him?
And the son of man, that thou visitest him?

For thou hast made him a little lower than the angels,
And hast crowned him with glory and honour.

FLIGHT
Harold Vinal

They are immortal, voyagers like these,
Bound for supreme and royal latitudes;
They soar beyond the eagle, where it broods,
With Venus and the evening Pleiades;
For in the pale blue Indies of the sky,
They plough, gold-prowed, the Arteries of Air,
Finding an unexplored dimension there—
They leave us Star Maps we may voyage by.

Not Galileo, with his dreaming power,
Not great Columbus, master of the gale,
Chartered for Time such harbors for man's flight.
Lured by another Odyssey, a Grail,
They climbed the heavens. Byrd in his white hour,
Lindbergh, an eagle sweeping through the night.

HIGH FLIGHT
John Gillespie Magee, Jr.

Oh, I have slipped the surly bonds of earth,
And danced the skies on laughter-silvered wings;
Sunward I've climbed and joined the tumbling mirth
Of sun-split clouds—and done a hundred things
You have not dreamed of—wheeled and soared and swung
High in the sunlit silence. Hov'ring there
I've chased the shouting wind along and flung
My eager craft through footless halls of air.
Up, up the long delirious burning blue
I've topped the wind-swept heights with easy grace,
Where never lark, or even eagle, flew;
And, while with silent, lifting mind I've trod
The high untrespassed sanctity of space,
Put out my hand, and touched the face of God.

From the good earth

growing

TREES
Joyce Kilmer

I think that I shall never see
A poem lovely as a tree.

A tree whose hungry mouth is pressed
Against the earth's sweet flowing breast;

A tree that looks at God all day
And lifts her leafy arms to pray;

A tree that may in summer wear
A nest of robins in her hair;

Upon whose bosom snow has lain;
Who intimately lives with rain.

Poems are made by fools like me,
But only God can make a tree.

SONG TO A TREE
Edwin Markham

Give me the dance of your boughs, O Tree,
    Whenever the wild wind blows;
And when the wind is gone, give me
    Your beautiful repose.

How easily your greatness swings
    To meet the changing hours;
I, too, would mount upon your wings,
    And rest upon your powers.

I seek your grace, O mighty Tree,
   And shall seek, many a day,
Till I more worthily shall be
   Your comrade on the way.

BE DIFFERENT TO TREES
Mary Carolyn Davies

The talking oak
To the ancients spoke.

But any tree
Will talk to me.

What truths I know
I garnered so.

But those who want to talk and tell,
   And those who will not listeners be,
Will never hear a syllable
   From out the lips of any tree.

STRANGE TREE
Elizabeth Madox Roberts

Away beyond the Jarboe house
   I saw a different kind of tree.
Its trunk was old and large and bent,
   And I could feel it look at me.

The road was going on and on
   Beyond to reach some other place.
I saw a tree that looked at me,
   And yet it did not have a face.

It looked at me with all its limbs;
    It looked at me with all its bark.
The yellow wrinkles on its sides
    Were bent and dark.

And then I ran to get away,
    But when I stopped and turned to see,
The tree was bending to the side
    And leaning out to look at me.

TAPESTRY TREES
William Morris

OAK

I am the rooftree and the keel:
I bridge the seas for woe and weal.

FIR

High o'er the lordly oak I stand,
And drive him on from land to land.

ASH

I heft my brother's iron bane;
I shaft the spear and build the wain.

YEW

Dark down the windy dale I grow,
The father of the fateful bow.

POPLAR

The war shaft and milking bowl
I make, and keep the hay-wain whole.

OLIVE

The King I bless; the lamps I trim;
In my warm wave do fishes swim.

APPLE TREE

I bowed my head to Adam's will;
The cups of toiling men I fill.

VINE

I draw the blood from out the earth;
I store the sun for winter mirth.

ORANGE TREE

Amidst the greenness of my night
My odorous lamps hang round and bright.

FIG TREE

I who am little among trees
In honey-making mate the bees.

MULBERRY TREE

Love's lack hath dyed my berries red:
For love's attire my leaves are shed.

PEAR TREE

High o'er the mead flower's hidden feet
I bear aloft my burden sweet.

BAY

Look on my leafy boughs, the crown
Of living song and dead renown!

UNDER THE GREENWOOD TREE
William Shakespeare

Under the greenwood tree,
Who loves to lie with me,
And turn his merry note
Unto the sweet bird's throat,
Come hither, come hither, come hither!
Here shall he see
No enemy
But winter and rough weather.

Who doth ambition shun,
And loves to live i' the sun,
Seeking the food he eats,
And pleased with what he gets,
Come hither, come hither, come hither;
Here shall he see
No enemy
But winter and rough weather.

WHAT DO WE PLANT?
Henry Abbey

What do we plant when we plant the tree?
We plant the ship which will cross the sea.
We plant the mast to carry the sails;
We plant the planks to withstand the gales—
The keel, the keelson, the beam, the knee;
We plant the ship when we plant the tree.

What do we plant when we plant the tree?
We plant the houses for you and me.
We plant the rafters, the shingles, the floors,
We plant the studding, the lath, the doors,
The beams and siding, all parts that be;
We plant the house when we plant the tree.

What do we plant when we plant the tree?
A thousand things that we daily see;
We plant the spire that out-towers the crag,
We plant the staff for our country's flag,
We plant the shade, from the hot sun free;
We plant all these when we plant the tree.

THE OAK
Alfred Tennyson

Live thy Life,
    Young and old,
Like yon oak,
Bright in spring,
    Living gold;

Summer-rich
    Then; and then
Autumn-changed,
Soberer-hued
    Gold again.

All his leaves
    Fallen at length,
Look, he stands,
Trunk and bough,
    Naked strength.

AUTUMN FANCIES

The maple is a dainty maid,
    The pet of all the wood,
Who lights the dusky forest glade
    With scarlet cloak and hood.

The elm a lovely lady is,
  In shimmering robes of gold,
That catch the sunlight when she moves,
  And glisten, fold on fold.

The sumac is a gypsy queen,
  Who flaunts in crimson dressed,
And wild along the roadside runs,
  Red blossoms in her breast.

And towering high above the wood,
  All in his purple cloak,
A monarch in his splendor is
  The proud and princely oak.

THE WILLOWS
Walter Prichard Eaton

By the little river,
  Still and deep and brown,
Grow the graceful willows,
  Gently dipping down.

Dipping down and brushing
  Everything that floats—
Leaves and logs and fishes,
  And the passing boats.

Were they water maidens
  In the long ago,
That they lean out sadly
  Looking down below?

In the misty twilight
  You can see their hair,
Weeping water maidens
  That were once so fair.

FORESTER'S SONG
A. E. Coppard

> Will you take a sprig of hornbeam?
>   Will you try a twig of pine?
> Or a beam of dusky cedar
>   That the ivy dare not twine?
> My larch is slim and winsome,
>   There is blossom on the sloe;
> Timber tell you, tell you timber,
>   How the trees do grow!
>
> There are thorns on yonder mountain,
>   An olive on the crag,
> And I leave a knotted thicket
>   As a chamber for the stag;
> Lovely oak and spangled sycamore,
>   The quince and mistletoe;
> Willow will you, will you willow,
>   How the trees do grow!

A COMPARISON
John Farrar

> Apple blossoms look like snow,
> They're different, though.
> Snow falls softly, but it brings
> Noisy things:
> Sleighs and bells, forts and fights,
> Cosy nights.
> But apple blossoms when they go,
> White and slow,
> Quiet all the orchard space
> Till the place
> Hushed with falling sweetness seems
> Filled with dreams.

OH, FAIR TO SEE
Christina Rossetti

Oh, fair to see
Bloom-laden cherry tree,
   Arrayed in sunny white:
   An April day's delight,
Oh, fair to see!

Oh, fair to see
Fruit-laden cherry tree,
   With balls of shining red
   Decking a leafy head,
Oh, fair to see!

BABY SEED SONG
Edith Nesbit

Little brown brother, oh! little brown brother,
   Are you awake in the dark?
Here we lie cosily, close to each other:
   Hark to the song of the lark—
"Waken!" the lark says, "waken and dress you;
   Put on your green coats and gay,
Blue sky will shine on you, sunshine caress you—
   Waken! 'tis morning—'tis May!"

Little brown brother, oh! little brown brother,
   What kind of flower will you be?
I'll be a poppy—all white, like my mother;
   Do be a poppy like me.
What! you're a sunflower? How I shall miss you
   When you're grown golden and high!
But I shall send all the bees up to kiss you;
   Little brown brother, good-by.

GREEN RAIN
Mary Webb

Into the scented woods we'll go,
And see the blackthorn swim in snow.
High above, in the budding leaves,
A brooding dove awakes and grieves;
The glades with mingled music stir,
And wildly laughs the woodpecker.
When blackthorn petals pearl the breeze,
There are the twisted hawthorne trees
Thick-set with buds, as clear and pale
As golden water or green hail—
As if a storm of rain had stood
Enchanted in the thorny wood,
And, hearing fairy voices call,
Hang poised, forgetting how to fall.

FLOWER IN THE CRANNIED WALL
Alfred Tennyson

Flower in the crannied wall,
I pluck you out of the crannies,
I hold you here, root and all, in my hand,
Little flower—but *if* I could understand
What you are, root and all, and all in all,
I should know what God and man is.

CYCLE
Langston Hughes

So many little flowers
Drop their tiny heads
But newer buds come to bloom
In their place instead.

I miss the little flowers
That have gone away.
But the newly budding blossoms
Are equally gay.

THE FLOWERS
Robert Louis Stevenson

All the names I know from nurse:
Gardener's garters, shepherd's purse:
Bachelor's buttons, lady's smock,
And the lady hollyhock.

Fairy places, fairy things,
Fairy woods where the wild bee wings,
Tiny trees for tiny dames—
These must all be fairy names!

Tiny woods below whose boughs
Shady fairies weave a house;
Tiny treetops, rose or thyme,
Where the braver fairies climb!

Fair are grown-up people's trees,
But the fairest woods are these;
Where, if I were not so tall,
I should live for good and all.

THE LITTLE ROSE TREE
Rachel Field

Every rose on the little tree
Is making a different face at me!
Some look surprised when I pass by,
And others droop—but they are shy.

These two whose heads together press
Tell secrets I could never guess.
Some have their heads thrown back to sing,
And all the buds are listening.
I wonder if the gardener knows,
Or if he calls each just a rose?

DAFFODILS
William Wordsworth

I wandered lonely as a cloud
    That floats on high o'er vales and hills,
When all at once I saw a crowd,—
    A host of golden daffodils
Beside the lake, beneath the trees,
Fluttering and dancing in the breeze.

Continuous as the stars that shine
    And twinkle on the Milky Way,
They stretched in never-ending line
    Along the margin of a bay:
Ten thousand saw I, at a glance,
Tossing their heads in sprightly dance.

The waves beside them danced, but they
    Outdid the sparkling waves in glee;
A poet could not be but gay
    In such a jocund company;
I gazed—and gazed—but little thought
What wealth the show to me had brought.

For oft, when on my couch I lie,
    In vacant or in pensive mood,
They flash upon that inward eye
    Which is the bliss of solitude;
And then my heart with pleasure fills,
And dances with the daffodils.

QUEEN ANNE'S LACE
Mary Leslie Newton

Queen Anne, Queen Anne, has washed her lace
  (She chose a summer day)
And hung it in a grassy place
  To whiten, if it may.

Queen Anne, Queen Anne, has left it there,
  And slept the dewy night;
Then waked, to find the sunshine fair,
  And all the meadows white.

Queen Anne, Queen Anne, is dead and gone
  (She died a summer's day),
But left her lace to whiten on
  Each weed-entangled way!

A VIOLET BANK
William Shakespeare

I know a bank whereon the wild thyme blows,
Where oxlips and the nodding violet grows:
Quite over-canopied with lush woodbine,
With sweet musk roses and with eglantine.

DANDELION
Hilda Conkling

O little soldier with the golden helmet,
What are you guarding on my lawn?
You with your green gun
And your yellow beard,
Why do you stand so stiff?
There is only the grass to fight!

TO THE DANDELION
FROM TO THE DANDELION
James Russell Lowell

Dear common flower, that grow'st beside the way,
Fringing the dusty road with harmless gold,
    First pledge of blithesome May,
Which children pluck, and, full of pride, uphold,
  High-hearted buccaneers, o'erjoyed that they
An Eldorado in the grass have found,
Which not the rich earth's ample round
    May match in wealth, thou art more dear to me
    Than all the prouder summer blooms may be.

My childhood's earliest thoughts are linked with thee;
The sight of thee calls back the robin's song,
    Who, from the dark old tree
Beside the door, sang clearly all day long,
  And I, secure in childish piety,
Listened as if I heard an angel sing
With news from heaven, which he could bring
    Fresh every day to my untainted ears
    When birds and flowers and I were happy peers.

FRINGED GENTIANS
Amy Lowell

Near where I live there is a lake
As blue as blue can be; winds make
It dance as they go blowing by.
I think it curtsies to the sky.

It's just a lake of lovely flowers,
And my Mamma says they are ours;
But they are not like those we grow
To be our very own, you know.

We have a splendid garden, there
Are lots of flowers everywhere;
Roses, and pinks, and four-o'clocks,
And hollyhocks, and evening stocks.

Mamma lets us pick them, but never
Must we pick any gentians—ever!
For if we carried them away
They'd die of homesickness that day.

THE LILAC
Humbert Wolfe

Who thought of the lilac?
"I," dew said,
"I made up the lilac,
out of my head."

"She made up the lilac!
Pooh!" thrilled a linnet,
and each dew-note had a
lilac in it.

THE GOLDEN ROD
Frank Dempster Sherman

Spring is the morning of the year,
    And summer is the noontide bright;
The autumn is the evening clear,
    That comes before the winter's night.

And in the evening, everywhere
    Along the roadside, up and down,
I see the golden torches flare
    Like lighted street-lamps in the town.

I think the butterfly and bee,
From distant meadows coming back,
Are quite contented when they see
These lamps along the homeward track.

But those who stay too late get lost;
For when the darkness falls about,
Down every lighted street the Frost
Will go and put the torches out!

WINDOW BOXES
Eleanor Farjeon

A window box of pansies
Is such a happy thing.
A window box of wallflowers
Is a garden for a king.
A window box of roses
Makes everyone stand still
Who sees a garden growing
On a window sill.

FLOWERS
Harry Behn

We planted a garden
Of all kinds of flowers
And it grew very well
Because there were showers,
And the bees came and buzzed:
This garden is ours!

But every day
To the honeyed bowers
The butterflies come
And hover for hours
Over the daisies
And hollyhock towers.

So we let the honey
Be theirs, but the flowers
We cut to take
In the house are ours,
Not yours, if you please,
You busy bees!

THE GRASS
Emily Dickinson

The grass so little has to do,—
    A sphere of simple green,
With only butterflies to brood,
    And bees to entertain,

And stir all day to pretty tunes
    The breezes fetch along,
And hold the sunshine in its lap
    And bow to everything;

And thread the dews all night, like pearls,
    And make itself so fine,—
A duchess were too common
    For such a noticing.

And even when it dies, to pass
    In odours so divine,
As lowly spices gone to sleep,
    Or amulets of pine.

And then to dwell in sovereign barns,
And dream the days away,—
The grass so little has to do,
I wish I were the hay!

THE GRASS ON THE MOUNTAIN
FROM THE PAIUTE AMERICAN INDIAN
Transcribed by Mary Austin

Oh, long long
The snow has possessed the mountains.

The deer have come down and the big-horn,
They have followed the Sun to the south
To feed on the mesquite pods and the bunch grass.
Loud are the thunderdrums
In the tents of the mountains.
Oh, long long
Have we eaten chia seeds
And dried deer's flesh of the summer killing.
We are wearied of our huts
And the smoky smell of our garments.

We are sick with desire of the sun
And the grass on the mountain.

SPRING GRASS
Carl Sandburg

Spring grass, there is a dance to be danced for you.
Come up, spring grass, if only for young feet.
Come up, spring grass, young feet ask you.

Smell of the young spring grass,
You're a mascot riding on the wind horses.
You came to my nose and spiffed me. This is your lucky year.

Young spring grass just after the winter,
Shoots of the big green whisper of the year,
Come up, if only for young feet.
Come up, young feet ask you.

WHO MAKETH THE GRASS TO GROW
The Bible: from Psalm 147

Praise ye the Lord!
For it is good to sing praises unto our God;
For it is pleasant; and praise is comely.
Great is our Lord, and of great power;
Who covereth the heaven with clouds,
Who prepareth rain for the earth,
Who maketh grass to grow upon the mountains.
He giveth to the beast his food,
And to the young ravens which cry.
He giveth snow like wool;
He scattereth the hoarfrost like ashes.
He casteth forth his ice like morsels;
Who can stand before his cold?
He sendeth out his word, and melteth them;
He causeth his wind to blow, and the waters flow.
Sing unto the Lord with thanksgiving!
Praise ye the Lord.

Roundabout the country,
roundabout town

MY LAND IS FAIR FOR ANY EYES TO SEE
Jesse Stuart

My land is fair for any eyes to see—
Now look, my friends—look to the east and west!
You see the purple hills far in the west—
Hills lined with pine and gum and black-oak tree—
Now to the east you see the fertile valley!
This land is mine, I sing of it to you—
My land beneath the skies of white and blue.

This land is mine, for I am part of it.
I am the land, for it is part of me—
We are akin and thus our kinship be!
It would make me a brother to the tree!
And far as eyes can see this land is mine.
Not for one foot of it I have a deed—
To own this land I do not need a deed—
They all belong to me—gum, oak, and pine.

BAREFOOT DAYS
Rachel Field

In the morning, very early,
    That's the time I love to go
Barefoot where the fern grows curly
    And grass is cool between each toe,
        On a summer morning-O!
        On a summer morning!

That is when the birds go by
Up the sunny slopes of air,
And each rose has a butterfly
Or a golden bee to wear;
And I am glad in every toe—
Such a summer morning-O!
Such a summer morning!

NEW FARM TRACTOR
Carl Sandburg

Snub nose, the guts of twenty mules are in your cylinders and
transmission.
The rear axles hold the kick of twenty Missouri jackasses.
It is in the records of the patent office and the ads there is twenty
horse power pull here.
The farm boy says hello to you instead of twenty mules—he sings to
you instead of ten span of mules.
A bucket of oil and a can of grease is your hay and oats.
Rain proof and fool proof they stable you anywhere in the fields with
the stars for a roof.
I carve a team of long ear mules on the steering wheel—it's good-by
now to leather reins and the songs of the old mule skinners.

THE PASTURE
Robert Frost

I'm going out to clean the pasture spring;
I'll only stop to rake the leaves away
(And wait to watch the water clear, I may):
I sha'n't be gone long.—You come too.

I'm going out to fetch the little calf
That's standing by the mother. It's so young
It totters when she licks it with her tongue.
I sha'n't be gone long.—You come too.

I WILL GO WITH MY FATHER A-PLOUGHING
Joseph Campbell

I will go with my Father a-ploughing
To the Green Field by the sea,
And the rooks and corbies and seagulls
Will come flocking after me.
I will sing to the patient horses
With the lark in the shine of the air,
And my Father will sing the Plough-Song
That blesses the cleaving share.

I will go with my Father a-sowing
To the Red Field by the sea,
And the merls and robins and thrushes
Will come flocking after me.
I will sing to the striding sowers
With the finch on the flowering sloe,
And my Father will sing the Seed-Song
That only the wise men know.

I will go with my Father a-reaping
To the Brown Field by the sea,
And the geese and pigeons and sparrows
Will come flocking after me.
I will sing to the weary reapers
With the wren in the heat of the sun,
And my Father will sing the Scythe-Song
That joys for the harvest done.

PLOUGHING ON SUNDAY
Wallace Stevens

The white cock's tail
Tosses in the wind.
The turkey-cock's tail
Glitters in the sun.

Water in the fields.
The wind pours down.
The feathers flare
And bluster in the wind.

Remus, blow your horn!
I'm ploughing on Sunday,
Ploughing North America.
Blow your horn!

Tum-ti-tum,
Ti-tum-tum-tum!
The turkey-cock's tail
Spreads to the sun.

The white cock's tail
Streams to the moon.
Water in the fields.
The wind pours down.

THE EARTH IS THE LORD'S
The Bible: from Psalm 24

The earth is the Lord's, and the fulness thereof;
The world, and they that dwell therein.
For he hath founded it upon the seas,
And established it upon the floods.

Who shall ascend into the hill of the Lord?
Or who shall stand in his holy place?
He that has clean hands, and a pure heart.

232

THE HAY APPEARETH
The Bible

The hay appeareth, and the tender grass sheweth itself,
And herbs of the mountains are gathered.

VEGETABLES
Eleanor Farjeon

The country vegetables scorn
   To lie about in shops,
They stand upright as they were born
   In neatly-patterned crops;

And when you want your dinner you
   Don't buy it from a shelf,
You find a lettuce fresh with dew
   And pull it for yourself;

You pick an apronful of peas
   And shell them on the spot.
You cut a cabbage, if you please,
   To pop into the pot.

The folk who their potatoes buy
   From sacks before they sup,
Miss half of the potato's joy,
   And that's to dig it up.

MILLIONS OF STRAWBERRIES
Genevieve Taggard

Marcia and I went over the curve,
Eating our way down
Jewels of strawberries we didn't deserve,
Eating our way down.

Till our hands were sticky, and our lips painted,
And over us the hot day fainted,
And we saw snakes,
And got scratched,
And a lust overcame us for the red unmatched
Small buds of berries,
Till we lay down—
Eating our way down—
And rolled in the berries like two little dogs,
Rolled
In the late gold.
And gnats hummed,
And it was cold,
And home we went, home without a berry,
Painted red and brown,
Eating our way down.

THE POTATOES' DANCE
Vachel Lindsay

I

"Down cellar," said the cricket,
"Down cellar," said the cricket,
"Down cellar," said the cricket,
"I saw a ball last night,
In honor of a lady,
In honor of a lady,
In honor of a lady,
Whose wings were pearly white.
The breath of bitter weather,
The breath of bitter weather,
The breath of bitter weather,
Had smashed the cellar pane.

We entertained a drift of leaves,
We entertained a drift of leaves,
We entertained a drift of leaves,
And then of snow and rain.
But we were dressed for winter,
But we were dressed for winter,
But we were dressed for winter,
And loved to hear it blow
In honor of the lady,
In honor of the lady,
In honor of the lady,
Who makes potatoes grow,
Our guest the Irish lady,
The tiny Irish lady,
The airy Irish lady,
Who makes potatoes grow.

II

"Potatoes were the waiters,
Potatoes were the waiters,
Potatoes were the waiters,
Potatoes were the band,
Potatoes were the dancers
Kicking up the sand,
Kicking up the sand,
Kicking up the sand,
Potatoes were the dancers
Kicking up the sand.
Their legs were old burnt matches,
Their legs were old burnt matches,
Their legs were old burnt matches,
Their arms were just the same.
They jigged and whirled and scrambled,
Jigged and whirled and scrambled,
Jigged and whirled and scrambled,
In honor of the dame,
The noble Irish lady
Who makes potatoes dance,

The witty Irish lady,
The saucy Irish lady,
The laughing Irish lady
Who makes potatoes prance.

III

"There was just one sweet potato
He was golden brown and slim.
The lady loved his dancing,
The lady loved his dancing,
The lady loved his dancing,
She danced all night with him,
She danced all night with him.
Alas, he wasn't Irish.
So when she flew away,
They threw him in the coalbin,
And there he is today,
Where they cannot hear his sighs
And his weeping for the lady,
The glorious Irish lady,
The beauteous Irish lady,
Who
Gives
Potatoes
Eyes."

THE LAST CORN SHOCK
Glenn Ward Dresbach

I remember how we stood
   In the field, while far away
Blue hazes drifted on from hill to hill
And curled like smoke from many a sunset wood,
And the loaded wagon creaked while standing still . . .
   I heard my father say,
   "The last corn shock can stay."

236

We had seen a pheasant there
    In the sun; he went inside
As if he claimed the shock, as if he meant
To show us, with the field so nearly bare,
We had no right to take his rustic tent.
    And so we circled wide
    For home, and let him hide.

The first wild ducks flashed by
    Where the pasture brook could hold
The sunset at the curve, and drifting floss
Escaped the wind and clung. The shocks were dry
And rustled on the wagon. Far across
    The field, against the cold,
    The last shock turned to gold.

EVENING AT THE FARM
John Townsend Trowbridge

Over the hill the farm boy goes,
His shadow lengthens along the land,
A giant staff in a giant hand;
In the poplar tree, above the spring,
The katydid begins to sing;
    The early dews are falling;—
Into the stone heap darts the mink;
The swallows skim the river's brink;
And home to the woodland fly the crows,
When over the hill the farm boy goes,
    Cheerily calling,—
    "Co', boss! co', boss! co'! co'! co'!"
Farther, farther, over the hill,
Faintly calling, calling still,—
    "Co', boss! co', boss! co'! co'!"

Into the yard the farmer goes,
With grateful heart, at the close of day;
Harness and chain are hung away;
In the wagon shed stand yoke and plow;
The straw's in the stack, the hay in the mow,
    The cooling dews are falling;—
The friendly sheep his welcome bleat,
The pigs come grunting to his feet,
The whinnying mare her master knows,
When into the yard the farmer goes,
    His cattle calling,—
    "Co', boss! co', boss! co'! co'! co'!"
While still the cowboy, far away,
Goes seeking those that have gone astray,—
    "Co', boss! co', boss! co'! co'!"

Now to her task the milkmaid goes,
The cattle come crowding through the gate,
Lowing, pushing, little and great;
About the trough, by the farmyard pump,
The frolicsome yearlings frisk and jump,
    While the pleasant dews are falling;—
The new milch heifer is quick and shy,
But the old cow waits with tranquil eye;
And the white stream into the bright pail flows,
When to her task the milkmaid goes,
    Soothingly calling,—
    "So, boss! so, boss! so! so! so!"
The cheerful milkmaid takes her stool,
And sits and milks in the twilight cool,
    Saying, "So! so, boss! so! so!"

To supper at last the farmer goes.
The apples are pared, the paper read,
The stories are told, then all to bed.
Without, the crickets' ceaseless song
Makes shrill the silence all night long;
    The heavy dews are falling;—

The housewife's hand has turned the lock;
Drowsily ticks the kitchen clock;
The household sinks to deep repose;
But still in sleep the farm boy goes
    Singing, calling,—
    "Co', boss! co', boss! co'! co'! co'!"
And oft the milkmaid, in her dreams,
Drums in the pail with the flashing streams,
    Murmuring, "So, boss! so!"

APPLE SONG
Frances Frost

The apples are seasoned
And ripe and sound.
Gently they fall
On the yellow ground.

The apples are stored
In the dusky bin
Where hardly a glimmer
Of light creeps in.

In the firelit, winter
Nights, they'll be
The clear sweet taste
Of a summer tree!

MILKING TIME
Elizabeth Madox Roberts

When supper time is almost come,
But not quite here, I cannot wait,
And so I take my china mug
And go down by the milking gate.

The cow is always eating shucks
And spilling off the little silk.
Her purple eyes are big and soft—
She always smells like milk.

And father takes my mug from me,
And then he makes the stream come out.
I see it going in my mug
And foaming all about.

And when it's piling very high,
And when some little streams commence
To run and drip along the sides,
He hands it to me through the fence.

OLD LOG HOUSE
James S. Tippett

On a little green knoll
At the edge of the wood
My great great grandmother's
First house stood.

The house was of logs
My grandmother said
With one big room
And a lean-to shed.

The logs were cut
And the house was raised
By pioneer men
In the olden days.

I like to hear
My grandmother tell
How they built the fireplace
And dug the well.

They split the shingles;
They filled each chink;
It's a house of which
I like to think.

Forever and ever
I wish I could
Live in a house
At the edge of a wood.

THE HOUSE ON THE HILL
Edwin Arlington Robinson

They are all gone away,
    The house is shut and still,
There is nothing more to say.

Through broken walls and gray
    The winds blow bleak and shrill:
They are all gone away.

Nor is there one today
    To speak them good or ill:
There is nothing more to say.

Why is it then we stray
    Around the sunken sill?
They are all gone away.

And our poor fancy-play
    For them is wasted skill:
There is nothing more to say.

There is ruin and decay
    In the house on the hill:
They are all gone away,
    There is nothing more to say.

THE WAY THROUGH THE WOODS
Rudyard Kipling

They shut the road through the woods
Seventy years ago.
Weather and rain have undone it again,
And now you would never know
There was once a road through the woods
Before they planted the trees.
It is underneath the coppice and heath,
And the thin anemones.
Only the keeper sees
That, where the ring-dove broods,
And the badgers roll at ease,
There was once a road through the woods.

Yet, if you enter the woods
Of a summer evening late,
When the night-air cools on the trout-ringed pools
Where the otter whistles his mate
(They fear not men in the woods,
Because they see so few),
You will hear the beat of the horse's feet,
And the swish of a skirt in the dew,
Steadily cantering through
The misty solitudes,
As though they perfectly knew
The old lost road through the woods . . . . . .
But there is no road through the woods.

FAREWELL TO THE FARM
Robert Louis Stevenson

The coach is at the door at last;
The eager children, mounting fast
And kissing hands, in chorus sing:
Good-by, good-by, to everything!

To house and garden, field and lawn,
The meadow gates we swang upon,
To pump and stable, tree and swing,
Good-by, good-by, to everything!

And fare you well for evermore,
O ladder at the hayloft door,
O hayloft where the cobwebs cling,
Good-by, good-by, to everything!

Crack goes the whip, and off we go;
The trees and houses smaller grow;
Last, round the woody turn we swing;
Good-by, good-by, to everything!

COUNTRY TRUCKS
Monica Shannon

Big trucks with apples
  And big trucks with grapes
Thundering through the mountains
  While every wild thing gapes.

Thundering through the valley,
  Like something just let loose,
Big trucks with oranges
  For city children's juice.

Big trucks with peaches,
  And big trucks with pears,
Frightening all the rabbits
  And giving squirrels gray hairs.

Yet, when city children
  Sit down to plum or prune,
They know more trucks are coming
  As surely as the moon.

SATURDAY MARKET
FROM SATURDAY MARKET
Charlotte Mew

In Saturday Market, there's eggs a-plenty
   And dead-alive ducks with their legs tied down,
Gray old gaffers and boys of twenty—
   Girls and the women of the town—
Pitchers and sugar-sticks, ribbons and laces,
   Posies and whips and dicky-birds' seed,
Silver pieces and smiling faces,
   In Saturday Market they've all they need.

CITY
Langston Hughes

In the morning the city
Spreads its wings
Making a song
In stone that sings.

In the evening the city
Goes to bed
Hanging lights
About its head.

SKYSCRAPERS
Rachel Field

Do skyscrapers ever grow tired
Of holding themselves up high?
Do they ever shiver on frosty nights
With their tops against the sky?
Do they feel lonely sometimes
Because they have grown so tall?
Do they ever wish they could lie right down
And never get up at all?

244

MOTOR CARS
Rowena Bastin Bennett

From a city window, 'way up high,
I like to watch the cars go by.
They look like burnished beetles black,
That leave a little muddy track
Behind them as they slowly crawl.
Sometimes they do not move at all
But huddle close with hum and drone
As though they feared to be alone.
They grope their way through fog and night
With the golden feelers of their light.

F IS THE FIGHTING FIRETRUCK
Phyllis McGinley

F is the fighting Firetruck
    That's painted a flaming red.
When the signals blast
It follows fast
    When the chief flies on ahead.
And buses pull to the curbing
    At the siren's furious cry,
For early or late
They have to wait
    When the Firetruck flashes by.

TAXIS
Rachel Field

Ho, for taxis green or blue,
    Hi, for taxis red,
They roll along the avenue
    Like spools of colored thread!

Jack-o'-lantern yellow,
Orange as the moon,
Greener than the greenest grass
Ever grew in June.
Gaily striped or checked in squares,
Wheels that twinkle bright,
Don't you think that taxis make
A very pleasant sight?
Taxis shiny in the rain,
Scudding through the snow,
Taxis flashing back the sun,
Waiting in a row.

Ho, for taxis red and green,
   Hi, for taxis blue,
I wouldn't be a private car
   In sober black, would you?

BUS RIDE
FROM FERRY RIDE
Selma Robinson

I hailed the bus and I went for a ride
And I rode on top and not inside
As I'd done on every other day:
The air was so sweet and the city so gay
The sun was so hot and the air so mellow
And the shops were bursting with green and yellow.

The shops were the brightest I'd ever seen—
Full of yellow and pink and green,
Yellow in this and green in that,
A dress or a 'kerchief, a tie or a hat,
And I wanted to dance and I wanted to sing
And I bought a flower because it was spring.

PEOPLE
Lois Lenski

Tall people, short people,
Thin people, fat,
Lady so dainty
Wearing a hat,
Straight people, dumpy people,
Man dressed in brown;
Baby in a buggy—
These make a town.

J'S THE JUMPING JAY-WALKER
Phyllis McGinley

J's the jumping Jay-walker,
   A sort of human jeep.
He crosses where the lights are red.
   Before he looks, he'll leap!
Then many a wheel
Begins to squeal,
   And many a brake to slam.
He turns your knees to jelly
   And the traffic into jam.

BOBBY BLUE
John Drinkwater

Sometimes I have to cross the road
   When some one isn't there
Except a man in uniform
   Who takes a lot of care;
I do not call him Officer
   As other people do,
I thank him most politely,
   And call him Bobby Blue.

He's very big, and every one
    Does everything he tells,
The motor-cars with hooters
    And the bicycles with bells;
And even when I cross the road
    With other people too,
I always say as I go by,
    "Good-morning, Bobby Blue."

THE POSTMAN

The whistling postman swings along.
    His bag is deep and wide,
And messages from all the world
    Are bundled up inside.

The postman's walking up our street.
    Soon now he'll ring my bell.
Perhaps there'll be a letter stamped
    In Asia. Who can tell?

ON THEIR APPOINTED ROUNDS
Inscription on the Main Post Office, New York City

Neither snow, nor rain,
nor heat, nor gloom of night
stays these couriers
from the swift completion
of their appointed rounds.

A MAN WITH A LITTLE PLEATED PIANO
Winifred Welles

Lean out the window: down the street
    There's lovely music flowing—
It floods the gutters, wets the feet,
A brook of silver, bright and sweet,
    A jet of jewels blowing,
A gush of golden drops that fly,
It bubbles far, it splashes high
Until it glistens in the eye
Of every twinkling passer-by.

Hold out your hand, let each round note
    Be lightly caught and felt there—
Oh, hear the sprays of soft sound float
Around your hair, against your throat,
    Across your mouth to melt there.
Leap down the stair, the doorstep, run
Along the sidewalk in the sun
To smile upon that strolling one,
Tugging at his accordion.

THE ICE-CREAM MAN
Rachel Field

When summer's in the city,
    And brick's a blaze of heat,
The Ice-Cream Man with his little cart
    Goes trundling down the street.

Beneath his round umbrella,
    Oh, what a joyful sight,
To see him fill the cones with mounds
    Of cooling brown or white;

Vanilla, chocolate, strawberry,
    Or chilly things to drink
From bottles full of frosty-fizz,
    Green, orange, white, or pink.

His cart might be a flower bed
    Of roses and sweet peas,
The way the children cluster round
    As thick as honeybees.

CITY TREES
Edna St. Vincent Millay

The trees along this city street,
    Save for the traffic and the trains,
Would make a sound as thin and sweet
    As trees in country lanes.

And people standing in their shade
    Out of a shower, undoubtedly
Would hear such music as is made
    Upon a country tree.

O little leaves that are so dumb
    Against the shrieking city air,
I watch you when the wind has come—
    I know what sound is there.

THE LIBRARY
Barbara A. Huff

It looks like any building
When you pass it on the street,
Made of stone and glass and marble,
Made of iron and concrete.

But once inside you can ride
A camel or a train,
Visit Rome, Siam, or Nome,
Feel a hurricane,
Meet a king, learn to sing,
How to bake a pie,
Go to sea, plant a tree,
Find how airplanes fly,
Train a horse, and of course
Have all the dogs you'd like,
See the moon, a sandy dune,
Or catch a whopping pike.
Everything that books can bring
You'll find inside those walls.
A world is there for you to share
When adventure calls.

You cannot tell its magic
By the way the building looks,
But there's wonderment within it,
The wonderment of books.

AT THE ZOO
A. A. *Milne*

There are lions and roaring tigers, and enormous camels and things,
There are biffalo-buffalo-bisons, and a great big bear with wings,
There's a sort of tiny potamus, and a tiny nosserus too—
But *I* gave buns to the elephant when *I* went down to the Zoo!

There are badgers and bidgers and bodgers, and a Super-in-tendent's
    House,
There are masses of goats, and a Polar, and different kinds of mouse,
And I think there's a sort of a something which is called a
    wallaboo—
But *I* gave buns to the elephant when *I* went down to the Zoo!

If you try to talk to the bison, he never quite understands;
You can't shake hands with a mingo—he doesn't like shaking hands.
And lions and roaring tigers *hate* saying, "How do you do?"—
But *I* give buns to the elephant when *I* go down to the Zoo!

AT THE AQUARIUM
Max Eastman

Serene the silver fishes glide,
Stern-lipped, and pale, and wonder-eyed.
As, through the aged deeps of ocean,
They glide with wan and wavy motion.
They have no pathway where they go,
They flow like water to and fro,
They watch, with never-winking eyes,
They watch, with staring, cold surprise,
The level people in the air,
The people peering, peering there:
Who wander also to and fro,
And know not why or where they go,
Yet have a wonder in their eyes,
Sometimes a pale and cold surprise.

AT THE THEATER
Rachel Field

The sun was bright when we went in,
    But night and lights were there,
The walls had golden trimming on
    And plush on every chair.

The people talked; the music played,
    Then it grew black as pitch,
Yes, black as closets full of clothes,
    Or caves, I don't know which.

The curtain rolled itself away,
  It went I don't know where,
But, oh, that country just beyond,
  I do wish we lived there!

The mountain peaks more jagged rise,
  Grass grows more green than here;
The people there have redder cheeks,
  And clothes more gay and queer.

They laugh and smile, but not the same,
  Exactly as we do,
And if they ever have to cry
  Their tears are different, too—

More shiny, somehow, and more sad,
  You hold your breath to see
If everything will come out right
  And they'll live happily;

If Pierrot will kiss Pierrette
  Beneath an orange moon,
And Harlequin and Columbine
  Outwit old Pantaloon.

You know they will, they always do,
  But still your heart must beat,
And you must pray they will be saved,
  And tremble in your seat.

And then it's over and they bow
  All edged about with light,
The curtain rattles down and shuts
  Them every one from sight.

It's strange to find the afternoon
  Still bright outside the door,
And all the people hurrying by
  The way they were before!

THE CIRCUS
Elizabeth Madox Roberts

Friday came and the circus was there,
And Mother said that the twins and I
And Charles and Clarence and all of us
Could go out and see the parade go by.

And there were wagons with pictures on,
And you never could guess what they had inside,
Nobody could guess, for the doors were shut,
And there was a dog that a monkey could ride.

A man on the top of a sort of a cart
Was clapping his hands and making a talk.
And the elephant came—he can step pretty far—
It made us laugh to see him walk.

Three beautiful ladies came riding by,
And each one had on a golden dress,
And each one had a golden whip.
They were queens of Sheba, I guess.

A big wild man was in a cage,
And he had some snakes going over his feet.
And somebody said, "He eats them alive!"
But I didn't see him eat.

CITY LIGHTS
Rachel Field

Into the endless dark
The lights of the buildings shine,
Row upon twinkling row,
Line upon glistening line.
Up and up they mount
Till the tallest seems to be
The topmost taper set
On a towering Christmas tree.

PRAYERS OF STEEL
Carl Sandburg

Lay me on an anvil, O God.
Beat me and hammer me into a crowbar.
Let me pry loose old walls;
Let me lift and loosen old foundations.

Lay me on an anvil, O God.
Beat me and hammer me into a steel spike.
Drive me into the girders that hold a skyscraper together.
Take red-hot rivets and fasten me into the central girders.
Let me be the great nail holding a skyscraper through blue nights
     into white stars.

My brother the sun,

my sister the moon,

    the stars,

        and Mother Earth

PRAISE OF CREATED THINGS
Saint Francis of Assisi

Be thou praised, my Lord, with all Thy creatures,
Above all, Brother Sun, who gives the day and lightens us therewith.
And he is beautiful and radiant with great splendor,
Of Thee, Most High, he bears similitude.

Be Thou praised, my Lord, of Sister Moon and the stars,
In the heaven hast Thou formed them,
Clear and precious and comely.

Be Thou praised, my Lord, of our Sister Mother Earth,
Which sustains and hath us in rule,
And produces divers fruits with colored flowers, and herbs.

THE EARTH ABIDETH FOREVER
The Bible

The earth abideth forever.
The sun also ariseth, and the sun goeth down,
And hasteth to his place where he arose.

The wind goeth toward the south,
And turneth about unto the north;
It whirleth about continually,
And the wind returneth again according to his circuits.

All the rivers run into the sea;
Yet the sea is not full;
Unto the place whence the rivers come,
Thither they return again.

THE WONDERFUL WORLD
William Brighty Rands

Great, wide, beautiful, wonderful World,
With the wonderful water round you curled,
And the wonderful grass upon your breast,
World, you are beautifully dressed.

The wonderful air is over me,
And the wonderful wind is shaking the tree—
It walks on the water, and whirls the mills,
And talks to itself on the top of the hills.

You friendly Earth, how far do you go,
With the wheat fields that nod and the rivers that flow,
With cities and gardens and cliffs and isles,
And the people upon you for thousands of miles?

Ah! you are so great, and I am so small,
I hardly can think of you, World, at all;
And yet, when I said my prayers today,
My mother kissed me, and said, quite gay,

"If the wonderful World is great to you,
And great to Father and Mother, too,
You are more than the Earth, though you are such a dot!
You can love and think, and the Earth cannot!"

THE CREATION
Cecil Frances Alexander

All things bright and beautiful,
   All creatures, great and small,
All things wise and wonderful,
   The Lord God made them all.

Each little flower that opens,
  Each little bird that sings,
He made their glowing colors,
  He made their tiny wings;

The rich man in his castle,
  The poor man at his gate,
God made them, high or lowly,
  And ordered their estate.

The purple-headed mountain,
  The river running by,
The sunset and the morning,
  That brightens up the sky;

The cold wind in the winter,
  The pleasant summer sun,
The ripe fruits in the garden—
  He made them every one.

The tall trees in the greenwood,
  The meadows where we play,
The rushes by the water
  We gather every day,—

He gave us eyes to see them,
  And lips that we might tell
How great is God Almighty,
  Who has made all things well!

MORNING
Emily Dickinson

Will there really be a morning?
  Is there such a thing as day?
Could I see it from the mountains
  If I were as tall as they?

Has it feet like water-lilies?
  Has it feathers like a bird?
Is it brought from famous countries
  Of which I have never heard?

Oh, some scholar! Oh, some sailor!
  Oh, some wise man from the skies!
Please to tell a little pilgrim
  Where the place called morning lies.

THE SUN
John Drinkwater

I told the Sun that I was glad,
  I'm sure I don't know why;
Somehow the pleasant way he had
  Of shining in the sky,
Just put a notion in my head
  That wouldn't it be fun
If, walking on the hill, I said
  "I'm happy" to the Sun.

THE SUN'S TRAVELS
Robert Louis Stevenson

The sun is not abed, when I
At night upon my pillow lie;
Still round the earth his way he takes,
And morning after morning makes.

While here at home, in shining day,
We round the sunny garden play,
Each little Indian sleepyhead
Is being kissed and put to bed.

And when at eve I rise from tea,
Day dawns beyond the Atlantic Sea;
And all the children in the West
Are getting up and being dressed.

THE LIGHT IS SWEET
The Bible

Truly the light is sweet,
And a pleasant thing it is
For the eyes to behold the sun.

GIVE ME THE SPLENDID SILENT SUN
Walt Whitman

Give me the splendid silent sun with all its beams full-dazzling,
Give me juicy autumnal fruit ripe and red from the orchard,
Give me a field where the unmowed grass grows,
Give me an arbor, give me the trellised grape,
Give me fresh corn and wheat, give me serene-moving animals
teaching content.
Give me nights perfectly quiet as on high plateaus west of the
Mississippi, and I am looking up at the stars,
Give me odorous at sunrise a garden of beautiful flowers where I
can walk undisturbed.

THE NIGHT WILL NEVER STAY
Eleanor Farjeon

The night will never stay,
The night will still go by,
Though with a million stars
You pin it to the sky;

Though you bind it with the blowing wind
And buckle it with the moon,
The night will slip away
Like sorrow or a tune.

NIGHT
Sara Teasdale

Stars over snow,
    And in the west a planet
Swinging below a star—
    Look for a lovely thing and you will find it,
It is not far—
    It never will be far.

QUESTIONS AT NIGHT
Louis Untermeyer

Why
Is the sky?

What starts the thunder overhead?
Who makes the crashing noise?
Are the angels falling out of bed?
Are they breaking all their toys?

Why does the sun go down so soon?
Why do the night-clouds crawl
Hungrily up to the new-laid moon
And swallow it, shell and all?

If there's a Bear among the stars
As all the people say,
Won't he jump over those Pasture-bars
And drink up the Milky Way?

Does every star that happens to fall
Turn into a fire-fly?
Can't it ever get back to Heaven at all?
And why
Is the sky?

SILVER
Walter de la Mare

Slowly, silently, now the moon
Walks the night in her silver shoon;
This way, and that, she peers, and sees
Silver fruit upon silver trees;
One by one the casements catch
Her beams beneath the silvery thatch;
Couched in his kennel, like a log,
With paws of silver sleeps the dog;
From their shadowy cote the white breasts peep
Of doves in a silver-feathered sleep;
A harvest mouse goes scampering by,
With silver claws, and silver eye;
And moveless fish in the water gleam,
By silver reeds in a silver stream.

THE MOON'S THE NORTH WIND'S COOKY
(What the Little Girl Said)
Vachel Lindsay

The Moon's the North Wind's cooky,
He bites it day by day,
Until there's but a rim of scraps
That crumble all away.

The South Wind is a baker.
He kneads clouds in his den,
And bakes a crisp new moon *that . . . greedy*
North . . . Wind . . . eats . . . again!

MY STAR
Robert Browning

All that I know
   Of a certain star
Is, it can throw
   (Like an angled spar)
Now a dart of red,
   Now a dart of blue;
Till my friends have said
   They would fain see, too,
My star that dartles the red and the blue!

Then it stops like a bird; like a flower, hangs furled:
   They must solace themselves with the Saturn above it.
What matter to me if their star is a world?
   Mine has opened its soul to me; therefore I love it.

STARS
Sara Teasdale

Alone in the night
   On a dark hill
With pines around me
   Spicy and still,

And a heaven full of stars
   Over my head,
White and topaz
   And misty red;

266

Myriads with beating
  Hearts of fire
That aeons
  Cannot vex or tire;

Up the dome of heaven
  Like a great hill,
I watch them marching
  Stately and still,

And I know that I
  Am honored to be
Witness
  Of so much majesty.

BABY TOES
Carl Sandburg

There is a blue star, Janet,
Fifteen years' ride from us,
If we ride a hundred miles an hour.

There is a white star, Janet,
Forty years' ride from us,
If we ride a hundred miles an hour.

Shall we ride
To the blue star
Or the white star?

THE HEAVENS DECLARE THE GLORY OF GOD
The Bible: from Psalm 19

The heavens declare the glory of God
And the firmament sheweth his handywork.

Day unto day uttereth speech,
And night unto night sheweth knowledge.

There is no speech nor language
Where their voice is not heard.

Their line is gone out through all the earth,
And their words to the end of the world.

I NEVER SAW A MOOR
Emily Dickinson

I never saw a moor,
I never saw the sea;
Yet know I how the heather looks,
And what a wave must be.

I never spoke with God,
Nor visited in heaven;
Yet certain am I of the spot
As if the chart were given.

MY PRAIRIES
Hamlin Garland

I love my prairies, they are mine
    From zenith to horizon line,
Clipping a world of sky and sod
    Like the bended arm and wrist of God.

I love their grasses. The skies
    Are larger, and my restless eyes
Fasten on more of earth and air
    Than seashore furnishes anywhere.

I love the hazel thickets; and the breeze,
    The never resting prairie winds. The trees
That stand like spear points high
    Against the dark blue sky

Are wonderful to me. I love the gold
    Of newly shaven stubble, rolled
A royal carpet toward the sun, fit to be
    The pathway of a deity.

I love the life of pasture lands; the songs of birds
    Are not more thrilling to me than the herd's
Mad bellowing or the shadow stride
    Of mounted herdsmen at my side.

I love my prairies, they are mine
    From high sun to horizon line.
The mountains and the cold gray sea
    Are not for me, are not for me.

AFTERNOON ON A HILL
Edna St. Vincent Millay

I will be the gladdest thing
    Under the sun!
I will touch a hundred flowers
    And not pick one.

I will look at cliffs and clouds
    With quiet eyes,
Watch the wind bow down the grass,
    And the grass rise.

And when lights begin to show
    Up from the town,
I will mark which must be mine,
    And then start down.

I STOOD TIPTOE UPON A LITTLE HILL
John Keats

I stood tiptoe upon a little hill;
The air was cooling and so very still,
That the sweet buds which with a modest pride
Pull droopingly, in slanting curve aside,
Their scanty-leaved, and finely-tapering stems,
Had not yet lost their starry diadems
Caught from the early sobbing of the morn.
The clouds were pure and white as flocks new-shorn,
And fresh from the clear brook; sweetly they slept
On the blue fields of heaven, and then there crept
A little noiseless noise among the leaves,
Born of the very sigh that silence heaves;
For not the faintest motion could be seen
Of all the shades that slanted o'er the green.

I WILL LIFT UP MINE EYES
The Bible: Psalm 121

I will lift up mine eyes unto the hills;
From whence cometh my help?
My help cometh from the Lord,
Which made heaven and earth.

He will not suffer thy foot to be moved;
He that keepeth thee will not slumber.
Behold, he that keepeth Israel
Shall neither slumber nor sleep.

The Lord is thy keeper:
The Lord is thy shade upon thy right hand.
The sun shall not smite thee by day,
Nor the moon by night.

The Lord shall preserve thee from all evil;
He shall preserve thy soul.
The Lord shall preserve thy going out and thy coming in,
From this time forth, and even for evermore.

OPEN RANGE
Kathryn and Byron Jackson

Prairie goes to the mountain,
   Mountain goes to the sky.
The sky sweeps across to the distant hills
And here, in the middle,
   Am I.

Hills crowd down to the river,
   River runs by the tree.
Tree throws its shadow on sunburnt grass
And here, in the shadow,
   Is me.

Shadows creep up the mountain,
   Mountain goes black on the sky,
The sky bursts out with a million stars
And here, by the campfire,
   Am I.

THE NOISE OF WATERS
James Joyce

All day I hear the noise of waters
   Making moan,
Sad as the sea-bird is, when going
   Forth alone,
He hears the winds cry to the waters'
   Monotone.

The grey winds, the cold winds are blowing
   Where I go.
I hear the noise of many waters
   Far below.
All day, all night I hear them flowing
   To and fro.

THE BROOK
Alfred Tennyson

I come from haunts of coot and hern,
   I make a sudden sally,
And sparkle out among the fern,
   To bicker down a valley.

By thirty hills I hurry down,
   Or slip between the ridges,
By twenty thorps, a little town,
   And half a hundred bridges.

Till last by Philip's farm I flow
   To join the brimming river,
For men may come and men may go,
   But I go on forever.

I chatter over stony ways,
   In little sharps and trebles,
I bubble into eddying bays,
   I babble on the pebbles.

With many a curve my banks I fret
   By many a field and fallow,
And many a fairy foreland set
   With willow-weed and mallow.

I chatter, chatter, as I flow
   To join the brimming river,
For men may come and men may go,
   But I go on forever.

I wind about and in and out,
   With here a blossom sailing,
And here and there a lusty trout,
   And here and there a grayling,

And here and there a foamy flake
   Upon me, as I travel
With many a silvery water-break
   Above the golden gravel,

And draw them all along, and flow
   To join the brimming river,
For men may come and men may go,
   But I go on forever.

I steal by lawns and grassy plots,
   I slide by hazel covers;
I move the sweet forget-me-nots
   That grow for happy lovers.

I slip, I slide, I gloom, I glance,
   Among my skimming swallows;
I make the netted sunbeam dance
   Against my sandy shallows.

I murmur under moon and stars
   In brambly wildernesses;
I linger by my shingly bars,
   I loiter round my cresses;

And out again I curve and flow
   To join the brimming river,
For men may come and men may go,
   But I go on forever.

THE RIVER-GOD'S SONG
Beaumont and Fletcher

Do not fear to put thy feet
Naked in the river sweet;
Think not leech, or newt, or toad
Will bite thy foot when thou hast trod;
Nor let the water, rising high,
As thou wadest, make thee cry,
And sob; but ever live with me,
And not a wave shall trouble thee.

THE HORSES OF THE SEA
Christina Rossetti

The horses of the sea
   Rear a foaming crest,
But the horses of the land
   Serve us the best.

The horses of the land
   Munch corn and clover,
While the foaming sea-horses
   Toss and turn over.

SEA SHELL
Amy Lowell

Sea Shell, Sea Shell,
   Sing me a song, O please!
A song of ships, and sailormen,
   And parrots, and tropical trees,

Of islands lost in the Spanish Main
Which no man ever may find again,
Of fishes and corals under the waves,
And sea horses stabled in great green caves.

Sea Shell, Sea Shell,
Sing of the things you know so well.

ROLL ON, THOU DARK BLUE OCEAN
FROM CHILDE HAROLD
Lord Byron

Roll on, thou deep and dark blue Ocean—roll!
Ten thousand fleets sweep over thee in vain;
Man marks the earth with ruin—his control
Stops with the shore;—upon the watery plain
The wrecks are all thy deed, nor doth remain
A shadow of man's ravage, save his own,
When, for a moment, like a drop of rain,
He sinks into thy depths with bubbling groan,
Without a grave, unknell'd, uncoffin'd, and unknown.

And I have loved thee, Ocean! and my joy
Of youthful sports was on thy breast to be
Borne, like thy bubbles, onward; from a boy
I wanton'd with thy breakers—they to me
Were a delight; and if the freshening sea
Made them a terror—'twas a pleasing fear,
For I was as it were a child of thee,
And trusted to thy billows far and near,
And laid my hand upon thy mane—as I do here.

Bird-watcher

JOY OF THE MORNING
Edwin Markham

I hear you, little bird,
Shouting a-swing above the broken wall.
Shout louder yet: no song can tell it all.
Sing to my soul in the deep, still wood:
'Tis wonderful beyond the wildest word:
I'd tell it, too, if I could.

Oft when the white, still dawn
Lifted the skies and pushed the hills apart,
I've felt it like a glory in my heart—
(The world's mysterious stir)
But had no throat like yours, my bird,
Nor such a listener.

A BIRD
FROM A BIRD
Emily Dickinson

A bird came down the walk:
He did not know I saw;
He bit an angleworm in halves
And ate the fellow, raw.

And then he drank a dew
From a convenient grass,
And then hopped sidewise to the wall
To let a beetle pass.

BE LIKE THE BIRD
Victor Hugo

Be like the bird, who
Halting in his flight
On limb too slight
Feels it give way beneath him,
Yet sings
Knowing he hath wings.

THREE THINGS TO REMEMBER
William Blake

A Robin Redbreast in a cage
Puts all Heaven in a rage.

A skylark wounded on the wing
Doth make a cherub cease to sing.

He who shall hurt the little wren
Shall never be beloved by men.

THE RIVALS
James Stephens

I heard a bird at dawn
Singing sweetly on a tree,
That the dew was on the lawn,
And the wind was on the lea;
But I didn't listen to him,
For he didn't sing to me.

I didn't listen to him,
For he didn't sing to me
That the dew was on the lawn
And the wind was on the lea!
I was singing at the time,
Just as prettily as he!

I was singing all the time,
Just as prettily as he,
About the dew upon the lawn,
And the wind upon the lea!
So I didn't listen to him
As he sang upon a tree!

THE HENS
Elizabeth Madox Roberts

The night was coming very fast;
It reached the gate as I ran past.

The pigeons had gone to the tower of the church
And all the hens were on their perch,

Up in the barn, and I thought I heard
A piece of a little purring word.

I stopped inside, waiting and staying,
To try to hear what the hens were saying.

They were asking something, that was plain,
Asking it over and over again.

One of them moved and turned around,
Her feathers made a ruffled sound,

A ruffled sound, like a bushful of birds,
And she said her little asking words.

She pushed her head close into her wing,
But nothing answered anything.

THE CHICKENS

Said the first little chicken,
  With a queer little squirm,
"I wish I could find
  A fat little worm."

Said the next little chicken,
  With an odd little shrug,
"I wish I could find
  A fat little slug."

Said the third little chicken,
  With a sharp little squeal,
"I wish I could find
  Some nice yellow meal."

Said the fourth little chicken,
  With a small sigh of grief,
"I wish I could find
  A little green leaf."

Said the fifth little chicken,
  With a faint little moan,
"I wish I could find
  A wee gravel stone."

"Now, see here," said the mother,
  From the green garden patch,
"If you want any breakfast,
  Just come here and scratch."

DUCK'S DITTY
Kenneth Grahame

All along the backwater,
  Through the rushes tall,
Ducks are a-dabbling,
  Up tails all!

Ducks' tails, drakes' tails,
  Yellow feet a-quiver,
Yellow bills all out of sight
  Busy in the river!

Slushy green undergrowth
  Where the roaches swim—
Here we keep our larder,
  Cool and full and dim.

Everyone for what he likes!
  We like to be
Heads down, tails up,
  Dabbling free!

High in the blue above
  Swifts whirl and call—
We are down a-dabbling,
  Up tails all!

THE NEW DUCKLING
Alfred Noyes

"I want to be new," said the duckling.
  "Oho!" said the wise old owl,
While the guinea hen cluttered off chuckling
  To tell all the rest of the fowl.

"I should like a more elegant figure,"
  That child of a duck went on.
"I should like to grow bigger and bigger,
  Until I could swallow a swan.

"I won't be the bondslave of habit,
  I won't have these webs on my toes.
I want to run round like a rabbit,
  A rabbit as red as a rose.

"I don't want to waddle like mother,
   Or quack like my silly old dad.
I want to be utterly other,
   And frightfully modern and mad."

"Do you know," said the turkey, "you're quacking!
   There's a fox creeping up thro' the rye;
And, if you're not utterly lacking,
   You'll make for that duck pond. Good-by!"

But the duckling was perky as perky.
   "Take care of your stuffing!" he called.
(This was horribly rude to a turkey!)
   "But you aren't a real turkey," he bawled.

"You're an early-Victorian sparrow!
   A fox is more fun than a sheep!
I shall show that my mind is not narrow
   And give him my feathers—to keep."

Now the curious end of this fable,
   So far as the rest ascertained,
Though they searched from the barn to the stable,
   Was that only his feathers remained.

So he wasn't the bondslave of habit,
   And he didn't have webs on his toes;
And perhaps he runs round like a rabbit,
   A rabbit as red as a rose.

WILD GEESE
Elinor Chipp

I heard the wild geese flying
   In the dead of the night,
With beat of wings and crying
   I heard the wild geese flying.

And dreams in my heart sighing
    Followed their northward flight.
I heard the wild geese flying
    In the dead of the night.

WHAT ROBIN TOLD
George Cooper

How do robins build their nests?
    Robin Redbreast told me—
First a wisp of yellow hay
In a pretty round they lay;
Then some shreds of downy floss,
Feathers, too, and bits of moss,
Woven with a sweet, sweet song,
This way, that way, and across;
    That's what Robin told me.

Where do robins hide their nests?
    Robin Redbreast told me—
Up among the leaves so deep,
Where the sunbeams rarely creep,
Long before the winds are cold,
Long before the leaves are gold,
Bright-eyed stars will peep and see
Baby robins—one, two, three;
    That's what Robin told me.

THE BLACKBIRD
Humbert Wolfe

In the far corner
Close by the swings,
Every morning
A blackbird sings.

His bill's so yellow,
His coat's so black,
That he makes a fellow
Whistle back.

Ann, my daughter,
Thinks that he
Sings for us two
Especially.

THE LAST WORD OF A BLUEBIRD
Robert Frost

As I went out a Crow
In a low voice said 'Oh,
I was looking for you.
How do you do?
I just came to tell you
To tell Lesley (will you?)
That her little Bluebird
Wanted me to bring word
That the north wind last night
That made the stars bright
And made ice on the trough
Almost made him cough
His tail feathers off.
He just had to fly!
But he sent her Good-by,
And said to be good,
And wear her red hood,
And look for skunk tracks
In the snow with an ax—
And do everything!
And perhaps in the spring
He would come back and sing.'

INVITATION
Harry Behn

Blue jay, fly to my windowsill!
Here's suet and raisins, so eat your fill.
Not that I care for your scratchy call,
And I like your manners least of all,
But when you are hungry, the chickadees
Who ask politely, please, please, please,
Are much too bothered by what you say—
So come have your breakfast, and fly away!

ROBERT OF LINCOLN
William Cullen Bryant

Merrily swinging on brier and weed,
  Near to the nest of his little dame,
Over the mountainside or mead,
  Robert of Lincoln is telling his name:
    Bob-o'-link, bob-o'-link,
    Spink, spank, spink;
Snug and safe is that nest of ours,
Hidden among the summer flowers.
      Chee, chee, chee.

Robert of Lincoln is gaily dressed,
  Wearing a bright black wedding coat;
White are his shoulders and white his crest.
  Hear him call in his merry note:
    Bob-o'-link, bob-o'-link,
    Spink, spank, spink;
Look, what a nice new coat is mine,
Sure there was never a bird so fine.
      Chee, chee, chee.

Robert of Lincoln's Quaker wife,
  Pretty and quiet, with plain brown wings,
Passing at home a patient life,
    Broods in the grass while her husband sings:
      Bob-o'-link, bob-o'-link,
      Spink, spank, spink;
Brood, kind creature; you need not fear
Thieves and robbers while I am here.
        Chee, chee, chee.

Modest and shy as a nun is she;
  One weak chirp is her only note.
Braggart and prince of braggarts is he,
    Pouring boasts from his little throat:
      Bob-o'-link, bob-o'-link,
      Spink, spank, spink;
Never was I afraid of man;
Catch me, cowardly knaves, if you can!
        Chee, chee, chee.

Six white eggs on a bed of hay,
  Flecked with purple, a pretty sight!
There as the mother sits all day,
    Robert is singing with all his might:
      Bob-o'-link, bob-o'-link,
      Spink, spank, spink;
Nice good wife, that never goes out,
Keeping house while I frolic about.
        Chee, chee, chee.

Soon as the little ones chip the shell,
  Six wide mouths are open for food;
Robert of Lincoln bestirs him well,
    Gathering seeds for the hungry brood.
      Bob-o'-link, bob-o'-link,
      Spink, spank, spink;
This new life is likely to be
Hard for a gay young fellow like me.
        Chee, chee, chee.

Robert of Lincoln at length is made
  Sober with work, and silent with care;
Off is his holiday garment laid,
  Half forgotten that merry air:
    Bob-o'-link, bob-o'-link,
    Spink, spank, spink;
Nobody knows but my mate and I
Where our nest and our nestlings lie.
      Chee, chee, chee.

Summer wanes; the children are grown;
  Fun and frolic no more he knows;
Robert of Lincoln's a humdrum crone;
  Off he flies, and we sing as he goes:
    Bob-o'-link, bob-o'-link,
    Spink, spank, spink;
When you can pipe that merry old strain,
Robert of Lincoln, come back again.
      Chee, chee, chee.

WINGS
The Bible: from Psalm 55

Oh that I had wings like a dove!
For then I would fly away and be at rest.
Lo, then would I wander far off.
And remain in the wilderness.

SONG
John Keats

I had a dove and the sweet dove died;
  And I have thought it died of grieving:
O, what could it grieve for? it was tied,
  With a silken thread of my own hand's weaving;

Sweet little red feet! why did you die—
Why would you leave me, sweet dove! why?
You liv'd alone on the forest-tree,
Why, pretty thing! could you not live with me?
I kiss'd you oft and gave you white peas;
Why not live sweetly, as in the green trees?

THE CHICKADEE
Ralph Waldo Emerson

Piped a tiny voice hard by,
Gay and polite, a cheerful cry,
"Chic-chicadee-dee!" Saucy note
Out of a sound heart and a merry throat,
As if it said, "Good day, good sir.
Fine afternoon, old passenger!
Happy to meet you in these places
When January brings new faces!"

HARK, HARK THE LARK
William Shakespeare

Hark! hark! the lark at Heaven's gate sings,
    And Phœbus 'gins arise,
His steeds to water at those springs
    On chalic'd flowers that lies.

And winking Mary-buds begin
    To ope their golden eyes;
With everything that pretty bin:
    My lady sweet, arise;
                    Arise, arise.

THE HUMMING BIRD
Harry Hibbard Kemp

The sunlight speaks, and its voice is a bird:
It glimmers half-guessed, half-seen, half-heard,
Above the flowerbed, over the lawn—
A flashing dip, and it is gone,
And all it lends to the eye is this—
A sunbeam giving the air a kiss.

THE EAGLE
Alfred Tennyson

He clasps the crag with crooked hands;
Close to the sun in lonely lands,
Ringed with the azure world, he stands.

The wrinkled sea beneath him crawls;
He watches from his mountain walls,
And like a thunderbolt he falls.

LOOK AT SIX EGGS
FROM CORNHUSKERS
Carl Sandburg

Look at six eggs
In a mockingbird's nest.

Listen to six mockingbirds
Flinging follies of O-be-joyful
Over the marshes and uplands.

Look at songs
Hidden in eggs.

THE SANDPIPER
Celia Thaxter

Across the narrow beach we flit,
   One little sandpiper and I,
And fast I gather, bit by bit,
   The scattered driftwood bleached and dry.
The wild waves reach their hands for it,
   The wild wind raves, the tide runs high,
As up and down the beach we flit,—
   One little sandpiper and I.

Above our heads the sullen clouds
   Scud black and swift across the sky;
Like silent ghosts in misty shrouds
   Stand out the white lighthouses high.
Almost as far as eye can reach
   I see the close-reefed vessels fly,
As fast we flit along the beach,—
   One little sandpiper and I.

I watch him as he skims along,
   Uttering his sweet and mournful cry.
He starts not at my fitful song,
   Nor flash of fluttering drapery.
He has no thought of any wrong;
   He scans me with a fearless eye:
Staunch friends are we, well tried and strong,
   The little sandpiper and I.

Comrade, where wilt thou be tonight,
   When the loosed storm breaks furiously?
My driftwood fire will burn so bright!
   To what warm shelter canst thou fly?
I do not fear for thee, though wroth
   The tempest rushes through the sky:
For are we not God's children both,
   Thou, little sandpiper, and I?

SONG: THE OWL
Alfred Tennyson

When cats run home and light is come,
   And dew is cold upon the ground,
And the far-off stream is dumb,
   And the whirring sail goes round,
   And the whirring sail goes round;
Alone and warming his five wits,
The white owl in the belfry sits.

When merry milkmaids click the latch,
   And rarely smells the new-mown hay,
And the cock hath sung beneath the thatch
   Twice or thrice his roundelay,
   Twice or thrice his roundelay;
Alone and warming his five wits,
The white owl in the belfry sits.

TO A SKYLARK
Percy Bysshe Shelley

Hail to thee, blithe spirit!
   Bird thou never wert,
That from heaven, or near it,
   Pourest thy full heart
In profuse strains of unpremeditated art.

Higher still and higher
   From the earth thou springest
Like a cloud of fire;
   The blue deep thou wingest,
And singing still dost soar, and soaring ever singest.

In the golden lightning
   Of the setting sun,
O'er which clouds are brightening,
   Thou dost float and run
Like an unbodied joy whose race is just begun.

THE SPARROW
The Bible

1

The sparrow hath found an house,
And the swallow a nest for herself,
Where she may lay her young.

2

Are not two sparrows sold for a farthing?
And one of them shall not fall to the ground
Without your Father.

THE THROSTLE
Alfred Tennyson

"Summer is coming, summer is coming,
    I know it, I know it, I know it.
Light again, leaf again, life again, love again,"
    Yes, my wild little Poet.

Sing the new year in under the blue.
    Last year you sang it as gladly.
"New, new, new, new!" Is it then *so* new
    That you should carol so madly?

"Love again, song again, nest again, young again,"
    Never a prophet so crazy!
And hardly a daisy as yet, little friend,
    See, there is hardly a daisy.

"Here again, here, here, here, happy year!"
    O warble unchidden, unbidden!
Summer is coming, is coming, my dear,
    And all the winters are hidden.

SWALLOW TAILS
Tom Robinson

I lie in the hay,
And watch the way
The swallows fly out and in all day.
From the hay on the floor,
The live-long day,
I watch the way
They swoop in and out through the old barn door.

In their nests of clay,
I hear them say
Whatever they say to the little ones there.
They twitter and cheep,
For that is the way,
Whatever they say,
The swallows put their children—and me—to sleep.

THE BROWN THRUSH
Lucy Larcom

There's a merry brown thrush sitting up in the tree,
He's singing to me! He's singing to me!
And what does he say, little girl, little boy?
"Oh, the world's running over with joy!
　　Don't you hear? Don't you see?
　　Hush! Look! In my tree,
　　I'm as happy as happy can be!"

And the brown thrush keeps singing, "A nest do you see,
And five eggs hid by me in the juniper tree?
Don't meddle! Don't touch, little girl, little boy,
Or the world will lose some of its joy!
　　Now I'm glad! Now I'm free!
　　And I always shall be,
　　If you never bring sorrow to me."

So the merry brown thrush sings away in the tree,
To you and to me, to you and to me;
And he sings all the day, little girl, little boy,
"Oh, the world's running over with joy!
   But long it won't be,
   Don't you know? Don't you see?
   Unless we're as good as can be!"

LITTLE TROTTY WAGTAIL
John Clare

Little trotty wagtail, he went in the rain,
And tittering, tottering sideways he ne'er got straight again.
He stooped to get a worm, and looked up to get a fly,
And then he flew away ere his feathers they were dry.

Little trotty wagtail, he waddled in the mud,
And left his little footmarks, trample where he would.
He waddled in the water-pudge, and waggle went his tail,
And chirrupt up his wings to dry upon the garden rail.

Little trotty wagtail, you nimble all about,
And in the dimpling water-pudge you waddle in and out;
Your home is nigh at hand, and in the warm pigsty,
So, little Master Wagtail, I'll bid you a good-bye.

A WIDOW BIRD
Percy Bysshe Shelley

A widow bird sat mourning for her love
   Upon a wintry bough;
The frozen wind crept on above,
   The freezing stream below.

There was no leaf upon the forest bare,
   No flower upon the ground,
And little motion in the air
   Except the mill wheel's sound.

THE WOODPECKER
Elizabeth Madox Roberts

The woodpecker pecked out a little round hole
And made him a house in the telephone pole.
One day when I watched he poked out his head,
And he had on a hood and a collar of red.

When the streams of rain pour out of the sky,
And the sparkles of lightning go flashing by,
And the big, big wheels of thunder roll,
He can snuggle back in the telephone pole.

LITTLE LADY WREN
Tom Robinson

Little Lady Wren,
Hopping from bough to bough,
Bob your tail for me,
Bob it now!

You carry it so straight
Up in the air and when
You hop from bough to bough
You bob it now and then.

Why do you bob your tail,
Hopping from bough to bough,
And will not bob it when I say,
"Bob it now!"?

People to know,

  friends to make

A BOY'S SONG
James Hogg

Where the pools are bright and deep,
Where the gray trout lies asleep,
Up the river and over the lea—
That's the way for Billy and me.

Where the blackbird sings the latest,
Where the hawthorn blooms the sweetest,
Where the nestlings chirp and flee—
That's the way for Billy and me.

Where the mowers mow the cleanest,
Where the hay lies thick and greenest;
There to trace the homeward bee—
That's the way for Billy and me.

Where the hazel bank is steepest,
Where the shadow lies the deepest,
Where the clustering nuts fall free—
That's the way for Billy and me.

Why the boys should drive away
Little sweet maidens from the play,
Or love to banter and fight so well,
That's the thing I never could tell.

But this I know: I love to play
Through the meadow, among the hay
Up the water and over the lea,
That's the way for Billy and me.

LITTLE GARAINE
Sir Gilbert Parker

"Where do the stars grow, little Garaine?
   The garden of moons, is it far away?
The orchard of suns, my little Garaine,
   Will you take us there some day?"

"If you shut your eyes," quoth little Garaine,
   "I will show you the way to go
To the orchard of suns and the garden of moons
   And the field where the stars do grow.

"But you must speak soft," quoth little Garaine,
   "And still must your footsteps be,
For a great bear prowls in the field of stars,
   And the moons they have men to see.

"And the suns have the Children of Signs to guard,
   And they have no pity at all—
You must not stumble, you must not speak,
   When you come to the orchard wall.

"The gates are locked," quoth little Garaine,
   "But the way I am going to tell!
The key of your heart it will open them all
   And there's where the darlings dwell!"

THE CHILD NEXT DOOR
Rose Fyleman

The child next door has a wreath on her hat;
Her afternoon frock sticks out like that,
   All soft and frilly;
She doesn't believe in fairies at all
(She told me over the garden wall)—
   She thinks they're silly.

The child next door has a watch of her own;
She has shiny hair and her name is Joan;
   (Mine's only Mary).
But doesn't it seem very sad to you
To think that she never her whole life through
   Has seen a fairy?

O TAN-FACED PRAIRIE-BOY
Walt Whitman

O tan-faced prairie-boy,
Before you came to camp came many a welcome gift,
Praises and presents came and nourishing food, till at last among the
    recruits
You came, taciturn, with nothing to give—we but look'd on each
    other,
When lo! more than all the gifts of the world you gave me.

JENNY WHITE AND JOHNNY BLACK
Eleanor Farjeon

          Jenny White and Johnny Black
          Went out for a walk.
          Jenny found wild strawberries,
          And John a lump of chalk.

          Jenny White and Johnny Black
          Clambered up a hill.
          Jenny heard a willow-wren
          And John a workman's drill.

          Jenny White and Johnny Black
          Wandered by the dyke.
          Jenny smelt the meadow-sweet,
          And John a motor-bike.

Jenny White and Johnny Black
Turned into a lane.
Jenny saw the moon by day.
And Johnny saw a train.

Jenny White and Johnny Black
Walked into a storm.
Each felt for the other's hand
And found it nice and warm.

DA BOY FROM ROME
Thomas Augustine Daly

Today ees com' from Eetaly
  A boy ees leeve een Rome,
An' he ees stop an' speak weeth me—
  I weesh he stay at home.

He stop an' say "Hallo," to me,
  An' w'en he standin' dere
I smal da smal of Eetaly
  Steell steechin' een hees hair,
Dat com' weeth heem across da sea,
  An' een da clo'es he wear.

Da peopla bomp heem een da street,
  De noise ees scare heem, too;
He ees so clumsy een da feet
  He don't know w'at to do,
Dere ees so many theeng he meet
  Dat ees so strange, so new.

He sheever an' he ask eef here
  Eet ees so always cold.
Deen een hees eye ees com' a tear—
  He ees no vera old—
An', oh, hees voice ees soun' so queer
  I have no heart for scold.

He look up een da sky so gray,
  But oh, hees eye ees be
So far away, so far away,
  An' w'at he see I see.
Da sky eet ees no gray today
  At home een Eetaly.

He see da glada peopla seet
  Where warma shine da sky—
Oh, while he eesa look at eet
  He ees baygeen to cry.
Eef I no growl an' swear a beet
  So, too, my frand, would I.

Oh, why he stop an' speak weeth me,
  Dees boy dat leeve een Rome,
An' come today from Eetaly?
  I weesh he stay at home.

GIPSY JANE
William Brighty Rands

She had corn flowers in her ear
  As she came up the lane;
"What may be your name, my dear?"
  "O, sir, Gipsy Jane."

"You are berry-brown, my dear."
  "That, sir, well may be;
For I live more than half the year,
  Under tent or tree."

Shine, Sun! blow, Wind!
  Fall gently, Rain!
The year's declined; be soft and kind,
  Kind to Gipsy Jane.

LITTLE PAPOOSE
Hilda Conkling

Little papoose
Swung high in the branches
Hears a song of birds, stars, clouds,
Small nests of birds,
Small buds of flowers.
But he is thinking of his mother with dark hair
Like her horse's mane.

Fair clouds nod to him
Where he swings in the tree,
But he is thinking of his father
Dark and glistening and wonderful,
Of his father with a voice like ice and velvet,
And tones of falling water,
Of his father who shouts
Like a storm.

A FELLER I KNOW
Mary Austin

His name it is Pedro-Pablo-Ignacio-Juan-
Francesco García y Gabaldon,
But the fellers call him Pete;
His folks belong to the Conquistadores
And he lives at the end of our street.

His father's father's great-grandfather
Was friends with the King of Spain
And his father peddles hot tamales
From here to Acequia-Madre Lane.

And Pete knows every one of the signs
For things that are lucky to do,
A charm to say for things that are lost,
And roots that are good to chew.

Evenings we go to Pedro's house
When there's firelight and rain
To hear of the Indians his grandfather fought
When they first came over from Spain.

And how De Vargas with swords and spurs
Came riding down our street,
And Pedro's mother gives us cakes
That are strange and spicy and sweet.

And we hear of gold that is buried and lost
On ranches they used to own,
And all us fellers think a lot
Of Pedro-Pablo-Ignacio-Juan-
Francesco García y Gabaldon.

DARK DANNY
Ivy O. Eastwick

Dark Danny has eyes
As black as the sloe,
And his freckles tell
Where the sunbeams go!

Dark Danny has hair
Like a raven's wing,
And his voice is gay
As the thrush in Spring.

Dark Danny will show
You the first wild rose;
Where the earliest violet
Blooms—he knows!

Where the red fox hides,
Why the nightingale sings . . .
Dark Danny knows all
These lovely things.

TIRED TIM
Walter de la Mare

Poor tired Tim! It's sad for him.
He lags the long bright morning through,
Ever so tired of nothing to do;
He moons and mopes the livelong day,
Nothing to think about, nothing to say;
Up to bed with his candle to creep,
Too tired to yawn, too tired to sleep:
Poor tired Tim! It's sad for him.

GODFREY GORDON GUSTAVUS GORE
William Brighty Rands

Godfrey Gordon Gustavus Gore—
No doubt you have heard the name before—
Was a boy who never would shut a door!

The wind might whistle, the wind might roar,
And teeth be aching and throats be sore,
But still he never would shut the door.

His father would beg, his mother implore,
"Godfrey Gordon Gustavus Gore,
We really *do* wish you would shut the door!"

Their hands they wrung, their hair they tore;
But Godfrey Gordon Gustavus Gore
Was deaf as the buoy out at the Nore.

When he walked forth the folks would roar,
"Godfrey Gordon Gustavus Gore,
Why don't you think to shut the door?"

They rigged out a Shutter with sail and oar,
And threatened to pack off Gustavus Gore
On a voyage of penance to Singapore.

But he begged for mercy, and said, "No more!
Pray do not send me to Singapore
On a Shutter, and then I will shut the door!"

"You will?" said his parents; "then keep on shore!
But mind you do! For the plague is sore
Of a fellow that never will shut the door,
Godfrey Gordon Gustavus Gore!"

FELICIA ROPPS
Gelett Burgess

Funny, how Felicia Ropps
Always handles things in shops!
Always pinching, always poking,
Always feeling, always stroking
Things she has no right to touch!
Goops like that annoy me much!

SOME PEOPLE
Rachel Field

Isn't it strange some people make
   You feel so tired inside,
Your thoughts begin to shrivel up
   Like leaves all brown and dried!

But when you're with some other ones,
   It's stranger still to find
Your thoughts as thick as fireflies
   All shiny in your mind!

OLD ELLEN SULLIVAN
Winifred Welles

Down in our cellar on a Monday and a Tuesday,
  You should hear the slapping and the rubbing and the muttering,
You should see the bubbles and the steaming and the splashing.
  The dark clothes dripping and the white clothes fluttering,
        Where old Ellen Sullivan,
        Cross Ellen Sullivan,
        Kind Ellen Sullivan,
Is washing and ironing, and ironing and washing.

Like a gnarled old root, like a bulb, brown and busy,
  With earth and air and water angrily tussling,
Hissing at the flatirons, getting hot and huffy,
  Then up to the sunlight with the baskets bustling,
        Comes old Ellen Sullivan,
        Cross Ellen Sullivan,
        Kind Ellen Sullivan,
The clothes like blossoms, all sweet and fresh and fluffy.

STRAWBERRY JAM
May Justus

          I went visiting Miss Melinda,
            Miss Melinda Brown.
          She has a cottage out in the country;
            I live here in town.

          "Guess what I've got for your dinner, dearie,"
            Miss Melinda said.
          "Strawberry jam," for my nose had guessed it!
            "Strawberry jam and bread."

310

Strawberry jam in the corner cupboard,
  On the middle shelf.
She let me stand on a chair and tiptoe,
  Get it down myself.

Somehow, visiting Miss Melinda,
  Time goes by on wings.
"What do you do all alone," I asked her.
  "I make jam and things."

When it was time to go home I kissed her.
  "Thanks for the lovely day!"
"Thank you for coming," said Miss Melinda,
  "Come again right away!"

THIS AND THAT
Florence Boyce Davis

Mary McGuire's our cook, you know;
  And Bridget McCann, our neighbor,
Does whatever she finds to do,
  And lives by honest labor;
And every morning when she comes
  To help about the dairy,
"A foine day *this!*" says Bridget McCann.
  "It is *that!*" answers Mary.

It may be June, or it may be March
  With sleet and wild winds blowing,
Whether it's warm and bright and fair,
  Or whether it's cold and snowing,
Bridget McCann comes bouncing in,
  Her cheeks as red as a cherry,
And, "A foine day *this!*" she always says.
  "It is *that!*" answers Mary.

GOODY O'GRUMPITY
Carol Ryrie Brink

When Goody O'Grumpity baked a cake
The tall reeds danced by the mournful lake,
The pigs came nuzzling out of their pens,
The dogs ran sniffing and so did the hens,
And the children flocked by dozens and tens.
They came from the north, the east and the south
With wishful eyes and watering mouth,
And stood in a crowd about Goody's door,
Their muddy feet on her sanded floor.
And what do you s'pose they came to do!
Why, to lick the dish when Goody was through!
And throughout the land went such a smell
Of citron and spice—no words can tell
How cinnamon bark and lemon rind,
And round, brown nutmegs grated fine
A wonderful haunting perfume wove,
Together with allspice, ginger and clove,
When Goody but opened the door of her stove.
The children moved close in a narrowing ring,
They were hungry—as hungry as bears in the spring;
They said not a word, just breathed in the spice,
And at last when the cake was all golden and nice,
Goody took a great knife and cut each a slice.

PORTRAIT BY A NEIGHBOR
Edna St. Vincent Millay

Before she has her floor swept
    Or her dishes done,
Any day you'll find her
    A-sunning in the sun!

It's long after midnight
    Her key's in the lock,
And you never see her chimney smoke
    Till past ten o'clock!

She digs in her garden
    With a shovel and a spoon,
She weeds her lazy lettuce
    By the light of the moon,

She walks up the walk
    Like a woman in a dream,
She forgets she borrowed butter
    And pays you back cream!

Her lawn looks like a meadow,
    And if she mows the place
She leaves the clover standing
    And the Queen Anne's lace!

OUR HIRED MAN
(And His Daughter, Too)
Monica Shannon

            He isn't all Indian,
                He isn't all white,
            But José smokes the bacon,
                And milks every night.

            He chases our rabbits
                (When rabbits get out)
            Over the mountains
                And back with a shout.

            From chasing tame rabbits,
                He limbered up so,
            He catches a cotton-tail
                Just on the go!

You never saw rabbits
  So woolly and wild
As the rabbits he stews
  Every night for his child,

So pink and so plumpy
  (She's three and a half)
And holds both her sides
  When she shakes with a laugh.

MR. WELLS
Elizabeth Madox Roberts

On Sunday morning, then he comes
To church, and everybody smells
The blacking and the toilet soap
And camphor balls from Mr. Wells.

He wears his whiskers in a bunch,
And wears his glasses on his head.
I mustn't call him Old Man Wells—
No matter—that's what Father said.

And when the little blacking smells
And camphor balls and soap begin,
I do not have to look to know
That Mr. Wells is coming in.

MR. MACKLIN'S JACK O'LANTERN
David McCord

Mr. Macklin takes his knife
And carves the yellow pumpkin face:
Three holes bring eyes and nose to life,
The mouth has thirteen teeth in place.

314

Then Mr. Macklin just for fun
Transfers the corn-cob pipe from his
Wry mouth to Jack's, and everyone
Dies laughing! O what fun it is

Till Mr. Macklin draws the shade
And lights the candle in Jack's skull.
Then all the inside dark is made
As spooky and as horrorful

As Halloween, and creepy crawl
The shadows on the tool-house floor,
With Jack's face dancing on the wall.
O Mr. Macklin! where's the door?

MR. COGGS, WATCHMAKER
Edward Verrall Lucas

A watch will tell the time of day,
Or tell it nearly, anyway,
Excepting when it's overwound,
Or when you drop it on the ground.

If any of our watches stop,
We haste to Mr. Coggs's shop;
For though to scold us he pretends
He's quite among our special friends.

He fits a dice box in his eye,
And takes a long and thoughtful spy,
And prods the wheels, and says: "Dear, dear!
More carelessness I greatly fear."

And then he lays the dice box down
And frowns a most prodigious frown;
But if we ask him what's the time,
He'll make his gold repeater chime.

THE SHOEMAKER

As I was a-walking the other day,
   I peeped in a window just over the way
And old and bent and feeble too,
   There sat an old cobbler a-making a shoe.
With a rack-a-tac-tac and a rack-a-tack-too,
   This is the way he makes a shoe.
With a bright little awl he makes a hole,
   Right through the upper and then through the sole.
He puts in a peg, he puts in two,
   And a ha-ha-ha-ha and he hammers it through.

MISTER BEERS
Hugh Lofting

This is Mister Beers;
   And for forty-seven years
He's been digging in his garden like a miner.
   He isn't planting seeds
   Nor scratching up weeds,
He's trying to bore a tunnel down to China.

THE FISHERMAN
Abbie Farwell Brown

The fisherman goes out at dawn
   When every one's abed,
And from the bottom of the sea
   Draws up his daily bread.

His life is strange; half on the shore
   And half upon the sea—
Not quite a fish, and yet not quite
   The same as you and me.

The fisherman has curious eyes;
  They make you feel so queer,
As if they had seen many things
  Of wonder and of fear.

They're like the sea on foggy days,—
  Not gray, nor yet quite blue;
They're like the wondrous tales he tells—
  Not quite—yet maybe—true.

He knows so much of boats and tides,
  Of winds and clouds and sky!
But when I tell of city things,
  He sniffs and shuts one eye!

THE SHEEPHERDER
Lew Sarett

Loping along on the day's patrol,
I came on a herder in Jackson's Hole;
Furtive of manner, blazing of eye,
He never looked up when I rode by;
But counting his fingers, fiercely intent,
Around and around his herd he went:

  One sheep, two sheep, three sheep, four . . .
  Twenty and thirty . . . forty more;
  Strayed—nine ewes; killed—ten rams;
  Seven and seventy lost little lambs.

He was the only soul I could see
On the lonely range for company—
Save one lean wolf and a prairie-dog,
And a myriad of ants at the foot of a log;
So I sat the herder down on a clod—
But his eyes went counting the ants in the sod:

317

One sheep, two sheep, three sheep, four . . .
Fifty and sixty . . . seventy more;
There's not in this flock a good bell-wether!
Then how can a herder hold it together!

Seeking to cheer him in his plight,
I flung my blankets down for the night;
But he wouldn't talk as we sat by the fire—
Corralling sheep was his sole desire;
With fingers that pointed near and far,
Mumbling, he herded star by star:

One sheep, two sheep, three—as before!
Eighty and ninety . . . a thousand more!
My lost little lambs—one thousand seven!—
Are wandering over the hills of Heaven.

SEUMAS BEG
James Stephens

A man was sitting underneath a tree
Outside the village; and he asked me what
Name was upon this place; and said that he
Was never here before— He told a lot

Of stories to me too. His nose was flat!
I asked him how it happened, and he said
—The first mate of the Holy Ghost did that
With a marlin-spike one day; but he was dead;

And jolly good job too; and he'd have gone
A long way to have killed him— Oh, he had
A gold ring in one ear; the other one
—"Was bit off by a crocodile, bedad!"—

That's what he said. He taught me how to chew!
He was a real nice man! He liked me too!

THE PEPPERY MAN
Arthur Macy

The Peppery Man was cross and thin;
He scolded out and scolded in;
He shook his fist, his hair he tore;
He stamped his feet and slammed the door.

Heigh ho, the Peppery Man,
The rabid, crabbed Peppery Man!
Oh, never since the world began
Was anyone like the Peppery Man.

His ugly temper was so sour
He often scolded for an hour;
He gnashed his teeth and stormed and scowled,
He snapped and snarled and yelled and howled.

He wore a fierce and savage frown;
He scolded up and scolded down;
He scolded over field and glen,
And then he scolded back again.

His neighbors, when they heard his roars,
Closed their blinds and locked their doors,
Shut their windows, sought their beds,
Stopped their ears and covered their heads.

He fretted, chafed, and boiled and fumed;
With fiery rage he was consumed,
And no one knew, when he was vexed,
What in the world would happen next.

Heigh ho, the Peppery Man,
The rabid, crabbed Peppery Man!
Oh, never since the world began
Was anyone like the Peppery Man.

ANTIQUE SHOP
Carl Carmer

I knew an old lady
A long time ago
Who rocked while she told me
The things I should know.

She lies in her grave now
And I am a man
But here is her rocker
And here is her fan.

Her fan and her rocker
Are all that remain
But I can still see her
Rock-rocking,
Talk-talking,
Rock-rocking
Again.

AN OLD WOMAN OF THE ROADS
Padraic Colum

O, to have a little house!
To own the hearth and stool and all!
The heaped up sods upon the fire,
The pile of turf against the wall!

To have a clock with weights and chains
And pendulum swinging up and down!
A dresser filled with shining delph,
Speckled and white and blue and brown!

I could be busy all the day
Clearing and sweeping hearth and floor,
And fixing on their shelf again
My white and blue and speckled store!

I could be quiet there at night
Beside the fire and by myself,
Sure of a bed and loth to leave
The ticking clock and the shining delph!

Och! but I'm weary of mist and dark,
And roads where there's never a house nor bush,
And tired I am of bog and road,
And the crying wind and the lonesome hush!

And I am praying to God on high,
And I am praying Him night and day,
For a little house—a house of my own—
Out of the wind's and the rain's way.

THE LAST LEAF
Oliver Wendell Holmes

I saw him once before,
As he passed by the door,
    And again
The pavement stones resound,
As he totters o'er the ground
    With his cane.

They say that in his prime,
Ere the pruning-knife of Time
    Cut him down,
Not a better man was found
By the Crier on his round
    Through the town.

But now he walks the streets,
And he looks at all he meets
    Sad and wan,
And he shakes his feeble head,
That it seems as if he said,
    "They are gone."

The mossy marbles rest
On the lips that he has prest
   In their bloom,
And the names he loved to hear
Have been carved for many a year
   On the tomb.

My grandmamma has said
Poor old lady, she is dead
   Long ago—
That he had a Roman nose,
And his cheek was like a rose
   In the snow;

But now his nose is thin,
And it rests upon his chin
   Like a staff,
And a crook is in his back,
And a melancholy crack
   In his laugh.

I know it is a sin
For me to sit and grin
   At him here;
But the old three-cornered hat,
And the breeches, and all that,
   Are so queer!

And if I should live to be
The last leaf upon the tree
   In the spring,
Let them smile, as I do now,
At the old forsaken bough
   Where I cling.

DOORBELLS
Rachel Field

You never know with a doorbell
    Who may be ringing it—
It may be Great-aunt Cynthia
    To spend the day and knit;
It may be a peddler with things to sell
    (I'll buy some when I'm older),
Or the grocer's boy with his apron on
    And a basket on his shoulder;
It may be the old umbrella-man
    Giving his queer, cracked call,
Or a lady dressed in rustly silk,
    With card-case and parasol.
Doorbells are like a magic game,
    Or the grab-bag at a fair—
You never know when you hear one ring
    Who may be waiting there!

THERE ISN'T TIME
Eleanor Farjeon

There isn't time, there isn't time
To do the things I want to do,
With all the mountain-tops to climb,
And all the woods to wander through,
And all the seas to sail upon,
And everywhere there is to go,
And all the people, every one
Who lives upon the earth, to know.
There's only time, there's only time
To know a few, and do a few,
And then sit down and make a rhyme
About the rest I want to do.

Almost any time

is laughing time

LAUGHING TIME
William Jay Smith

It was laughing time, and the tall Giraffe
Lifted his head, and began to laugh:

Ha! Ha!　　Ha! Ha!

And the Chimpanzee on the gingko tree
Swung merrily down with a *Tee Hee Hee*:

Hee! Hee!　　Hee! Hee!

"It's certainly not against the law!"
Croaked Justice Crow with a loud guffaw:

Haw! Haw!　　Haw! Haw!

The dancing bear who could never say "No"
Waltzed up and down on the tip of his toe:

Ho! Ho!　　Ho! Ho!

The donkey daintily took his paw,
And around they went: Hee-Haw! Hee-Haw!

Hee-Haw!　　Hee-Haw!

The Moon had to smile as it started to climb;
All over the world it was laughing time!

Ho! Ho!　　Ho! Ho!　　Hee-Haw!　　Hee-Haw!
Hee! Hee!　　Hee! Hee!　　Ha! Ha!　　Ha! Ha!

THE WALRUS AND THE CARPENTER
Lewis Carroll

The sun was shining on the sea,
   Shining with all his might:
He did his very best to make
   The billows smooth and bright—
And this was odd, because it was
   The middle of the night.

The moon was shining sulkily,
   Because she thought the sun
Had got no business to be there
   After the day was done—
"It's very rude of him," she said,
   "To come and spoil the fun!"

The sea was wet as wet could be,
   The sands were dry as dry.
You could not see a cloud, because
   No cloud was in the sky:
No birds were flying overhead—
   There were no birds to fly.

The Walrus and the Carpenter
   Were walking close at hand:
They wept like anything to see
   Such quantities of sand:
"If this were only cleared away,"
   They said, "it *would* be grand!"

"If seven maids with seven mops
   Swept it for half a year,
Do you suppose," the Walrus said,
   "That they could get it clear?"
"I doubt it," said the Carpenter,
   And shed a bitter tear.

"O, Oysters, come and walk with us!"
    The Walrus did beseech.
"A pleasant talk, a pleasant walk,
    Along the briny beach:
We cannot do with more than four,
    To give a hand to each."

The eldest Oyster looked at him,
    But never a word he said;
The eldest Oyster winked his eye,
    And shook his heavy head—
Meaning to say he did not choose
    To leave the oyster-bed.

But four young Oysters hurried up,
    All eager for the treat:
Their coats were brushed, their faces washed,
    Their shoes were clean and neat—
And this was odd, because, you know,
    They hadn't any feet.

Four other Oysters followed them,
    And yet another four;
And thick and fast they came at last,
    And more, and more, and more—
All hopping through the frothy waves,
    And scrambling to the shore.

The Walrus and the Carpenter
    Walked on a mile or so,
And then they rested on a rock
    Conveniently low:
And all the little Oysters stood
    And waited in a row.

"The time has come," the Walrus said,
    "To talk of many things:
Of shoes—and ships—and sealing-wax—
    Of cabbages—and kings—
And why the sea is boiling hot—
    And whether pigs have wings."

"But wait a bit," the Oysters cried,
  "Before we have our chat;
For some of us are out of breath,
  And all of us are fat!"
"No hurry!" said the Carpenter.
  They thanked him much for that.

"A loaf of bread," the Walrus said,
  "Is what we chiefly need:
Pepper and vinegar besides
  Are very good indeed—
Now, if you're ready, Oysters dear,
  We can begin to feed."

"But not on us!" the Oysters cried,
  Turning a little blue.
"After such kindness, that would be
  A dismal thing to do!"
"The night is fine," the Walrus said.
  "Do you admire the view?"

"It was so kind of you to come!
  And you are very nice!"
The Carpenter said nothing but
  "Cut us another slice.
I wish you were not quite so deaf—
  I've had to ask you twice!"

"It seems a shame," the Walrus said,
  "To play them such a trick,
After we've brought them out so far,
  And made them trot so quick!"
The Carpenter said nothing but
  "The butter's spread too thick!"

"I weep for you," the Walrus said:
  "I deeply sympathize."
With sobs and tears he sorted out
  Those of the largest size,
Holding his pocket handkerchief
  Before his streaming eyes.

"O Oysters," said the Carpenter,
"You've had a pleasant run!
Shall we be trotting home again?"
But answer came there none—
And this was scarcely odd, because
They'd eaten every one.

THE PANTHER
Ogden Nash

The panther is like a leopard,
Except it hasn't been peppered,
Should you behold a panther crouch,
Prepare to say Ouch.
Better yet, if called by a panther,
Don't anther.

THE RHINOCEROS
Hilaire Belloc

Rhinoceros, your hide looks all undone,
You do not take my fancy in the least:
You have a horn where other brutes have none:
Rhinoceros, you are an ugly beast.

THE OSTRICH IS A SILLY BIRD
Mary E. Wilkins Freeman

The ostrich is a silly bird,
With scarcely any mind.
He often runs so very fast,
He leaves himself behind.

And when he gets there has to stand
And hang about till night,
Without a blessed thing to do
Until he comes in sight.

JOHNNIE CRACK AND FLOSSIE SNAIL
FROM UNDER MILK WOOD
Dylan Thomas

Johnnie Crack and Flossie Snail
Kept their baby in a milking pail
Flossie Snail and Johnnie Crack
One would pull it out and one would put it back.

O it's my turn now said Flossie Snail
To take the baby from the milking pail
And it's my turn now said Johnnie Crack
To smack it on the head and put it back.

Johnnie Crack and Flossie Snail
Kept their baby in a milking pail
One would put it back and one would pull it out
And all it had to drink was ale and stout
For Johnnie Crack and Flossie Snail
Always used to say that stout and ale
Was *good* for a baby in a milking pail.

THE TALE OF CUSTARD THE DRAGON
Ogden Nash

Belinda lived in a little white house,
With a little black kitten and a little gray mouse,
And a little yellow dog and a little red wagon,
And a realio, trulio, little pet dragon.

Now the name of the little black kitten was Ink,
And the little gray mouse, she called her Blink,
And the little yellow dog was sharp as Mustard,
But the dragon was a coward, and she called him Custard.

Custard the dragon had big sharp teeth,
And spikes on top of him and scales underneath,
Mouth like a fireplace, chimney for a nose,
And realio, trulio daggers on his toes.

Belinda was as brave as a barrel full of bears,
And Ink and Blink chased lions down the stairs,
Mustard was as brave as a tiger in a rage,
But Custard cried for a nice safe cage.

Belinda tickled him, she tickled him unmerciful,
Ink, Blink and Mustard, they rudely called him Percival,
They all sat laughing in the little red wagon
At the realio, trulio, cowardly dragon.

Belinda giggled till she shook the house,
And Blink said Weeck! which is giggling for a mouse,
Ink and Mustard rudely asked his age,
When Custard cried for a nice safe cage.

Suddenly, suddenly they heard a nasty sound,
And Mustard growled, and they all looked around.
Meowch! cried Ink, and Ooh! cried Belinda,
For there was a pirate, climbing in the winda.

Pistol in his left hand, pistol in his right,
And he held in his teeth a cutlass bright,
His beard was black, one leg was wood;
It was clear that the pirate meant no good.

Belinda paled, and she cried Help! Help!
But Mustard fled with a terrified yelp,
Ink trickled down to the bottom of the household,
And little mouse Blink strategically mouseholed.

But up jumped Custard, snorting like an engine,
Clashed his tail like irons in a dungeon,
With a clatter and a clank and a jangling squirm
He went at the pirate like a robin at a worm.

The pirate gaped at Belinda's dragon,
And gulped some grog from his pocket flagon,
He fired two bullets, but they didn't hit,
And Custard gobbled him, every bit.

Belinda embraced him, Mustard licked him,
No one mourned for his pirate victim.
Ink and Blink in glee did gyrate
Around the dragon that ate the pyrate.

Belinda still lives in her little white house,
With her little black kitten and her little gray mouse,
And her little yellow dog and her little red wagon,
And her realio, trulio, little pet dragon.

Belinda is as brave as a barrel full of bears,
And Ink and Blink chase lions down the stairs.
Mustard is as brave as a tiger in a rage,
But Custard keeps crying for a nice safe cage.

JABBERWOCKY
Lewis Carroll

'Twas brillig, and the slithy toves
    Did gyre and gimble in the wabe:
All mimsy were the borogoves,
        And the mome raths outgrabe.

"Beware the Jabberwock, my son!
    The jaws that bite, the claws that catch!
Beware the Jubjub bird, and shun
        The frumious Bandersnatch!"

He took his vorpal sword in hand:
   Long time the manxome foe he sought—
So rested he by the Tumtum tree,
   And stood awhile in thought.

And, as in uffish thought he stood,
   The Jabberwock, with eyes of flame,
Came whiffling through the tulgey wood,
   And burbled as it came!

One, two! One, two! And through and through
   The vorpal blade went snicker-snack!
He left it dead, and with its head
   He went galumphing back.

"And hast thou slain the Jabberwock?
   Come to my arms, my beamish boy!
O frabjous day! Callooh! Callay!"
   He chortled in his joy.

'Twas brillig, and the slithy toves
   Did gyre and gimble in the wabe:
All mimsy were the borogoves,
   And the mome raths outgrabe.

JONATHAN BING
Beatrice Curtis Brown

Poor old Jonathan Bing
Went out in his carriage to visit the King,
But everyone pointed and said, "Look at that!
Jonathan Bing has forgotten his hat!"
(He'd forgotten his hat!)

Poor old Jonathan Bing
Went home and put on a new hat for the King,
But up by the palace a soldier said, "Hi!
You can't see the King; you've forgotten your tie!"
(He'd forgotten his tie!)

335

Poor old Jonathan Bing,
He put on a *beautiful* tie for the King,
But when he arrived an Archbishop said, "Ho!
You can't come to court in pyjamas, you know!"

Poor old Jonathan Bing
Went home and addressed a short note to the King:

If you please will excuse me
I won't come to tea;
For home's the best place for
All people like me!

THE STRANGE MAN

His face was the oddest that ever was seen,
His mouth stood across 'twixt his nose and his chin;
Whenever he spoke it was then with his voice,
And in talking he always made some sort of noise.

Derry down.

He'd an arm on each side to work when he pleased,
But he never worked hard when he lived at his ease;
Two legs he had got to make him complete,
And what is more odd, at each end were his feet.

His legs, as folks say, he could move at his will,
And when he was walking he never stood still.
If you were to see him, you'd laugh till you burst,
For one leg or the other would always be first.

If this whimsical fellow had a river to cross,
If he could not get over, he stayed where he was,
He seldom or ever got off the dry ground,
So great was his luck that he never was drowned.

But the reason he died and the cause of his death
Was owing, poor soul, to the want of more breath;
And now he is left in the grave for to molder,
Had he lived a day longer, he'd have been a day older.

Derry down.

THE MODERN HIAWATHA
George A. Strong

He killed the noble Mudjokovis,
With the skin he made him mittens,
Made them with the fur side inside,
Made them with the skin side outside,
He, to get the warm side inside,
Put the inside skin side outside:
He, to get the cold side outside,
Put the warm side fur side inside:
That's why he put the fur side inside,
Why he put the skin side outside,
Why he turned them inside outside.

THE INGENIOUS LITTLE OLD MAN
John Bennett

A little old man of the sea
Went out in a boat for a sail:
The water came in
Almost up to his chin
And he had nothing with which to bail.
But this little old man of the sea
Just drew out his jack-knife so stout,
And a hole with its blade
In the bottom he made,
So that all of the water ran out.

ARCHY, THE COCKROACH, SPEAKS
FROM CERTAIN MAXIMS OF ARCHY
Don Marquis

i heard a
couple of fleas
talking the other
days says one come
to lunch with
me i can lead you
to a pedigreed
dog says the
other one
i do not care
what a dog s
pedigree may be
safety first
is my motto what
i want to know
is whether he
has got a
muzzle on
millionaires and
bums taste
about alike to me

HOW TO TELL THE WILD ANIMALS
Carolyn Wells

If ever you should go by chance
    To jungles in the East;
And if there should to you advance
    A large and tawny beast,
If he roars at you as you're dyin'
You'll know it is the Asian Lion.

Or if sometime when roaming round,
    A noble wild beast greets you,
With black stripes on a yellow ground,
    Just notice if he eats you.
This simple rule may help you learn
The Bengal Tiger to discern.

If strolling forth, a beast you view,
    Whose hide with spots is peppered,
As soon as he has lept on you,
    You'll know it is the Leopard.
'Twill do no good to roar with pain,
He'll only lep and lep again.

If when you're walking round your yard,
    You meet a creature there,
Who hugs you very, very hard,
    Be sure it is the Bear.
If you have any doubt, I guess
He'll give you just one more caress.

Though to distinguish beasts of prey
    A novice might nonplus,
The Crocodiles you always may
    Tell from Hyenas thus:
Hyenas come with merry smiles;
But if they weep, they're Crocodiles.

The true Chameleon is small,
    A lizard sort of thing;
He hasn't any ears at all,
    And not a single wing.
If there is nothing on the tree,
'Tis the Chameleon you see.

THE YAK
Hilaire Belloc

As a friend to the children, commend me the Yak;
   You will find it exactly the thing;
It will carry and fetch, you can ride on its back,
   Or lead it about with a string.

The Tartar who dwells on the plains of Thibet
   (A desolate region of snow),
Has for centuries made it a nursery pet,
   And surely the Tartar should know!

Then tell your papa where the Yak can be got,
   And if he is awfully rich,
He will buy you the creature—or else he will not
   (I cannot be positive which).

THE OCTOPUSSYCAT
Kenyon Cox

I love Octopussy, his arms are so long;
There's nothing in nature so sweet as his song.
'Tis true I'd not touch him—no, not for a farm!
If I keep at a distance he'll do me no harm.

THERE WAS A YOUNG LADY WHOSE NOSE
Edward Lear

There was a Young Lady, whose Nose
Continually prospers and grows;
   When it grew out of sight,
   She exclaimed in a fright,
"Oh! Farewell to the end of my Nose!"

THE JELLYFISH
Ogden Nash

> Who wants my jellyfish?
> I'm not sellyfish.

THERE WAS AN OLD PERSON WHOSE HABITS
Edward Lear

> There was an Old Person whose habits
> Induced him to feed upon rabbits;
>   When he'd eaten eighteen,
>   He turned perfectly green,
> Upon which he relinquished those habits.

THE PLAINT OF THE CAMEL
Charles Edward Carryl

> Canary-birds feed on sugar and seed,
>   Parrots have crackers to crunch;
> And, as for the poodles, they tell me the noodles
>   Have chickens and cream for their lunch.
>   But there's never a question
>   About *my* digestion—
>   *Anything* does for me!
>
> Cats, you're aware, can repose in a chair,
>   Chickens can roost upon rails;
> Puppies are able to sleep in a stable,
>   And oysters can slumber in pails.
>   But no one supposes
>   A poor Camel dozes—
>   *Any place* does for me!

Lambs are enclosed where it's never exposed,
    Coops are constructed for hens;
Kittens are treated to houses well heated,
    And pigs are protected by pens.
        But a Camel comes handy
        Wherever it's sandy—
        Anywhere does for me!

People would laugh if you rode a giraffe,
    Or mounted the back of an ox;
It's nobody's habit to ride on a rabbit,
    Or try to bestraddle a fox.
        But as for a Camel, he's
        Ridden by families—
        Any load does for me!

A snake is as round as a hole in the ground,
    And weasels are wavy and sleek;
And no alligator could ever be straighter
    Than lizards that live in a creek.
        But a Camel's all lumpy
        And bumpy and humpy—
        Any shape does for me!

THE SONG OF MR. TOAD
Kenneth Grahame

The world has held great Heroes,
    As history-books have showed;
But never a name to go down to fame
    Compared with that of Toad!

The clever men at Oxford
    Know all that there is to be knowed.
But they none of them knew one half as much
    As intelligent Mr. Toad!

The animals sat in the Ark and cried,
  Their tears in torrents flowed.
Who was it said, "There's land ahead"?
  Encouraging Mr. Toad!

The Army all saluted
  As they marched along the road.
Was it the King? Or Kitchener?
  No. It was Mr. Toad!

The Queen and her Ladies-in-waiting
  Sat at the window and sewed.
She cried, "Look! who's that *handsome* man?"
  They answered, "Mr. Toad."

A NAUTICAL BALLAD
Charles Edward Carryl

A capital ship for an ocean trip,
  Was the Walloping Window blind.
No gale that blew dismayed her crew,
  Nor troubled the captain's mind.

The man at the wheel was taught to feel
  Contempt for the wildest blow;
And it often appeared—when the weather had cleared—
  He had been in his bunk below.

The boatswain's mate was very sedate,
  Yet fond of amusement, too;
And he played hopscotch with the starboard watch,
  While the captain tickled the crew.

And the gunner we had was apparently mad,
  For he sat on the after rail
And fired salutes with the captain's boots
  In the teeth of the booming gale.

The captain sat on the commodore's hat,
    And dined in a royal way,
Off toasted pigs and pickles and figs
    And gunnery bread each day.

The cook was Dutch and behaved as such,
    For the diet he gave the crew
Was a number of tons of hot cross-buns,
    Served up with sugar and glue.

All nautical pride we laid aside,
    And we cast our vessel ashore,
On the Gulliby Isles, where the Poo-Poo smiles
    And the Rumpletum-Bunders roar.

We sat on the edge of a sandy ledge,
    And shot at the whistling bee:
And the cinnamon bats wore waterproof hats,
    As they danced by the sounding sea.

On Rug-gub bark, from dawn till dark,
    We fed, till we all had grown
Uncommonly shrunk; when a Chinese junk
    Came in from the Torrible Zone.

She was stubby and square, but we didn't much care,
    So we cheerily put to sea;
And we left the crew of the junk to chew
    The bark of the Rug-gub tree.

THE FROG
Hilaire Belloc

Be kind and tender to the Frog,
    And do not call him names,
As "Slimy-Skin," or "Polly-wog,"
    Or likewise, "Ugly James,"

Or "Gape-a-grin," or "Toad-gone-wrong,"
 Or "Billy-Bandy-knees";
The Frog is justly sensitive
 To epithets like these.

No animal will more repay
 A treatment kind and fair,
At least, so lonely people say
Who keep a frog (and, by the way,
 They are extremely rare).

THE ELF AND THE DORMOUSE
Oliver Herford

Under a toadstool
 Crept a wee Elf,
Out of the rain
 To shelter himself.

Under the toadstool,
 Sound asleep,
Sat a big Dormouse
 All in a heap.

Trembled the wee Elf,
 Frightened, and yet
Fearing to fly away
 Lest he get wet.

To the next shelter—
 Maybe a mile!
Sudden the wee Elf
 Smiled a wee smile,

Tugged till the toadstool
 Toppled in two.
Holding it over him
 Gaily he flew.

Soon he was safe home
Dry as could be.
Soon woke the Dormouse—
"Good gracious me!

Where is my toadstool?"
Loud he lamented.
—And that's how umbrellas
First were invented.

THE MELANCHOLY PIG
Lewis Carroll

There was a Pig that sat alone,
Beside a ruined Pump.
By day and night he made his moan:
It would have stirred a heart of stone
To see him wring his hoofs and groan,
Because he could not jump.

ELETELEPHONY
Laura E. Richards

Once there was an elephant,
Who tried to use the telephant—
No! no! I mean an elephone
Who tried to use the telephone—
(Dear me! I am not certain quite
That even now I've got it right.)

Howe'er it was, he got his trunk
Entangled in the telephunk;
The more he tried to get it free,
The louder buzzed the telephee—
(I fear I'd better drop the song
Of elephop and telephong!)

THE EMBARRASSING EPISODE OF
LITTLE MISS MUFFET
Guy Wetmore Carryl

Little Miss Muffet discovered a tuffet,
    (Which never occurred to the rest of us)
And, as 'twas a June day, and just about noonday,
    She wanted to eat—like the best of us:
Her diet was whey, and I hasten to say
    It is wholesome and people grow fat on it.
The spot being lonely, the lady not only
    Discovered the tuffet, but sat on it.

A rivulet gabbled beside her and babbled,
    As rivulets always are thought to do,
And dragon flies sported around and cavorted,
    As poets say dragon flies ought to do;
When, glancing aside for a moment, she spied
    A horrible sight that brought fear to her,
A hideous spider was sitting beside her,
    And most unavoidably near to her!

Albeit unsightly, this creature politely
    Said: "Madam, I earnestly vow to you,
I'm penitent that I did not bring my hat. I
    Should otherwise certainly bow to you."
Though anxious to please, he was so ill at ease
    That he lost all his sense of propriety,
And grew so inept that he clumsily stept
    In her plate—which is barred in Society.

This curious error completed her terror;
    She shuddered, and growing much paler, not
Only left tuffet, but dealt him a buffet
    Which doubled him up in a sailor knot.
It should be explained that at this he was pained:
    He cried: "I have vexed you, no doubt of it!
Your fist's like a truncheon." "You're still in my luncheon,"
    Was all that she answered. "Get out of it!"

And the *Moral* is this: Be it madam or miss
 To whom you have something to say,
You are only absurd when you get in the curd
 But you're rude when you get in the whey!

THE DUEL
Eugene Field

The gingham dog and the calico cat
Side by side on the table sat;
'T was half-past twelve, and (what do you think!)
Nor one nor t' other had slept a wink!
 The old Dutch clock and the Chinese plate
 Appeared to know as sure as fate
There was going to be a terrible spat.
 (*I wasn't there; I simply state*
 What was told to me by the Chinese plate!)

The gingham dog went, "bow-wow-wow!"
And the calico cat replied, "mee-ow!"
The air was littered, an hour or so,
With bits of gingham and calico,
 While the old Dutch clock in the chimney-place
 Up with its hands before its face,
For it always dreaded a family row!
 (*Now mind: I'm only telling you*
 What the old Dutch clock declares is true!)

The Chinese plate looked very blue,
And wailed, "Oh, dear! what shall we do!"
But the gingham dog and the calico cat
Wallowed this way and tumbled that,
 Employing every tooth and claw
 In the awfullest way you ever saw—
And, oh! how the gingham and calico flew!
 (*Don't fancy I exaggerate—*
 I got my news from the Chinese plate!)

Next morning, where the two had sat
They found no trace of dog or cat;
And some folks think unto this day
That burglars stole that pair away!
   But the truth about the cat and pup
   Is this: they ate each other up!
Now what do you really think of that!
   (The old Dutch clock it told me so,
   And that is how I came to know.)

THE DUKE OF PLAZA-TORO
W. S. *Gilbert*

In enterprise of martial kind,
   When there was any fighting,
He led his regiment from behind—
   He found it less exciting.

But when away his regiment ran,
   His place was at the fore, O—
      That celebrated,
      Cultivated,
      Underrated
         Nobleman,
   The Duke of Plaza-Toro!

In the first and foremost flight, ha, ha!
You always found that knight, ha, ha!
      That celebrated,
      Cultivated,
      Underrated
         Nobleman,
   The Duke of Plaza-Toro!

When, to evade Destruction's hand,
   To hide they all proceeded,
No soldier in that gallant band
   Hid half as well as he did.

349

He lay concealed throughout the war,
　And so preserved his gore, O!
　　That unaffected,
　　Undetected,
　　Well-connected
　　　Warrior,
　The Duke of Plaza-Toro!

In every doughty deed, ha, ha!
He always took the lead, ha, ha!
　　That unaffected,
　　Undetected,
　　Well-connected
　　　Warrior,
　The Duke of Plaza-Toro!

FATHER WILLIAM
Lewis Carroll

"You are old, Father William," the young man said,
　"And your hair has become very white;
And yet you incessantly stand on your head—
　Do you think, at your age, it is right?"

"In my youth," Father William replied to his son,
　"I feared it might injure the brain;
But now that I'm perfectly sure I have none,
　Why, I do it again and again."

"You are old," said the youth, "as I mentioned before,
　And have grown most uncommonly fat;
Yet you turned a back somersault in at the door—
　Pray, what is the reason for that?"

"In my youth," said the sage, as he shook his gray locks,
　"I kept all my limbs very supple
By the use of this ointment—one shilling the box—
　Allow me to sell you a couple."

"You are old," said the youth, "and your jaws are too weak
  For anything tougher than suet;
Yet you finished the goose, with the bones and the beak;
  Pray, how did you manage to do it?"

"In my youth," said his father, "I took to the law,
  And argued each case with my wife;
And the muscular strength which it gave to my jaw,
  Has lasted the rest of my life."

"You are old," said the youth; "one would hardly suppose
  That your eye was as steady as ever;
Yet you balanced an eel on the end of your nose—
  What made you so awfully clever?"

"I have answered three questions, and that is enough,"
  Said his father; "don't give yourself airs!
Do you think I can listen all day to such stuff?
  Be off, or I'll kick you downstairs!"

THE FABLE OF THE MAGNET AND THE CHURN
W. S. *Gilbert*

A magnet hung in a hardware shop,
And all around was a loving crop
Of scissors and needles, nails and knives,
Offering love for all their lives;
But for iron the magnet felt no whim,
Though he charmed iron, it charmed not him;
From needles and nails and knives he'd turn,
For he'd set his love on a Silver Churn!

His most aesthetic,
Very magnetic
Fancy took this turn—
"If I can wheedle
A knife or a needle,
Why not a Silver Churn?"

And Iron and Steel expressed surprise,
The needles opened their well-drilled eyes,
The penknives felt "shut up," no doubt,
The scissors declared themselves "cut out,"
The kettles boiled with rage, 'tis said,
While every nail went off its head,
And hither and thither began to roam,
Till a hammer came up—and drove them home.

While this magnetic,
Peripatetic
Lover he lived to learn,
By no endeavor
Can a magnet ever
Attract a Silver Churn!

THE CENTIPEDE
Ogden Nash

I objurgate the centipede,
A bug we do not really need.
At sleepy-time he beats a path
Straight to the bedroom or the bath.
You always wallop where he's not,
Or, if he is, he makes a spot.

HOW DOTH THE LITTLE CROCODILE
Lewis Carroll

How doth the little crocodile
Improve his shining tail,
And pour the waters of the Nile
On every golden scale!

How cheerfully he seems to grin,
How neatly spreads his claws,
And welcomes little fishes in
With gently smiling jaws!

A TRAGIC STORY
Albert Von Chamisso
Translated by William Makepeace Thackeray

There lived a sage in days of yore,
And he a handsome pigtail wore;
But wondered much, and sorrowed more,
Because it hung behind him.

He mused upon this curious case,
And swore he'd change the pigtail's place,
And have it hanging at his face,
Not dangling there behind him.

Says he, "The mystery I've found,—
I'll turn me round,"—he turned him round,
But still it hung behind him.

Then round and round, and out and in,
All day the puzzled sage did spin;
In vain—it mattered not a pin—
The pigtail hung behind him.

And right and left, and roundabout,
And up and down and in and out
He turned; but still the pigtail stout
Hung steadily behind him.

And though his efforts never slack,
And though he twist, and twirl, and tack,
Alas! still faithful to his back,
The pigtail hangs behind him.

THE OWL AND THE PUSSYCAT
Edward Lear

The Owl and the Pussycat went to sea
   In a beautiful pea-green boat:
They took some honey, and plenty of money
   Wrapped up in a five-pound note.
The Owl looked up to the stars above,
   And sang to a small guitar,
"O lovely Pussy, O Pussy, my love,
   What a beautiful Pussy you are,
           You are,
           You are!
   What a beautiful Pussy you are!"

Pussy said to the Owl, "You elegant fowl,
   How charmingly sweet you sing!
Oh! let us be married; too long we have tarried:
   But what shall we do for a ring?"
They sailed away, for a year and a day,
   To the land where the bong tree grows;
And there in a wood a Piggy-wig stood,
   With a ring at the end of his nose,
           His nose,
           His nose,
   With a ring at the end of his nose.

"Dear Pig, are you willing to sell for one shilling
   Your ring?" Said the Piggy, "I will."
So they took it away, and were married next day
   By the Turkey who lives on the hill.
They dined on mince and slices of quince,
   Which they ate with a runcible spoon;
And hand in hand, on the edge of the sand,
   They danced by the light of the moon,
           The moon,
           The moon,
   They danced by the light of the moon.

THE TWINS
Henry S. Leigh

In form and feature, face and limb,
    I grew so like my brother,
That folks got taking me for him,
    And each for one another.
It puzzled all our kith and kin,
    It reached a fearful pitch;
For one of us was born a twin,
    Yet not a soul knew which.

One day, to make the matter worse,
    Before our names were fixed,
As we were being washed by nurse,
    We got completely mixed;
And thus, you see, by fate's decree,
    Or rather nurse's whim,
My brother John got christened me,
    And I got christened him.

This fatal likeness even dogged
    My footsteps when at school,
And I was always getting flogged,
    For John turned out a fool.
I put this question, fruitlessly,
    To everyone I knew,
"What *would* you do, if you were me,
    To prove that you were *you?*"

Our close resemblance turned the tide
    Of my domestic life,
For somehow, my intended bride
    Became my brother's wife.
In fact, year after year the same
    Absurd mistakes went on,
And when I died, the neighbors came
    And buried brother John.

THE LAMA
Ogden Nash

The one-l lama,
He's a priest.
The two-l llama,
He's a beast.
And I will bet
A silk pajama
There isn't any
Three-l lllama.

CALICO PIE
Edward Lear

Calico Pie,
The little Birds fly
Down to the calico tree,
Their wings were blue,
And they sang "Tilly-loo!"
Till away they flew,—
And they never came back to me!
They never came back!
They never came back!
They never came back to me!

Calico Jam,
The little Fish swam
Over the syllabub sea,
He took off his hat
To the Sole and the Sprat,
And the Willeby-wat,—
But he never came back to me!
He never came back!
He never came back!
He never came back to me!

Calico Ban,
The little Mice ran,
To be ready in time for tea,
Flippity flup,
They drank it all up,
And danced in the cup,—
But they never came back to me!
They never came back!
They never came back!
They never came back to me!

Calico Drum,
The Grasshoppers come,
The Butterfly, Beetle, and Bee,
Over the ground,
Around and round,
With a hop and a bound,—
But they never came back!
They never came back!
They never came back!
They never came back to me!

THE FLY
Ogden Nash

The Lord in His wisdom made the fly
And then forgot to tell us why.

THE EEL
Ogden Nash

I don't mind eels
Except as meals.
And the way they feels.

SONG OF THE POP-BOTTLERS
Morris Bishop

Pop bottles pop-bottles
  In pop shops;
The pop-bottles Pop bottles
  Poor Pop drops.

When Pop drops pop-bottles,
  Pop-bottles plop!
Pop-bottle-tops topple!
  Pop mops slop!

Stop! Pop'll drop bottle!
  Stop, Pop, stop!
When Pop bottles pop-bottles,
  Pop-bottles pop!

PETER PIPER

Peter Piper picked a peck of pickled peppers;
A peck of pickled peppers Peter Piper picked;
If Peter Piper picked a peck of pickled peppers,
Where's the peck of pickled peppers Peter Piper picked?

IF A WOODCHUCK WOULD CHUCK

How much wood would a woodchuck chuck
If a woodchuck could chuck wood?
He would chuck what wood a woodchuck would chuck,
If a woodchuck would chuck wood.

AFTER THE PARTY
William Wise

Jonathan Blake
Ate too much cake,
He isn't himself today;
He's tucked up in bed
With a feverish head,
And he doesn't much care to play.

Jonathan Blake
Ate too much cake,
And three kinds of ice cream too—
From latest reports
He's quite out of sorts,
And I'm sure the reports are true.

I'm sorry to state
That he also ate
Six pickles, a pie, and a pear;
In fact I confess
It's a reasonable guess
He ate practically everything there.

Yes, Jonathan Blake
Ate too much cake,
So he's not at his best today;
But there's no need for sorrow—
If you come back tomorrow,
I'm sure he'll be out to play.

OLD MAN WITH A BEARD
Edward Lear

There was an Old Man with a beard
Who said, "It is just as I feared!
    Two Owls and a Hen,
    Four Larks and a Wren,
Have all built their nests in my beard!"

A YOUNG LADY OF NORWAY
Edward Lear

There was a Young Lady of Norway
Who casually sat in a doorway;
    When the door squeezed her flat,
    She exclaimed, "What of that?"
This courageous Young Lady of Norway.

THE YOUNG LADY OF NIGER

There was a young lady of Niger
Who smiled as she rode on a tiger;
    They returned from the ride
    With the lady inside,
And the smile on the face of the tiger.

ONCE A BIG MOLICEPAN

Once a big molicepan
Saw a bittle lum,
Sitting on the sturbcone
Chewing gubble bum.

"Hi!" said the molicepan.
"Better simmie gome."
"Tot on your nintype!"
Said the bittle lum.

THERE WAS AN OLD MAN WHO SAID "DO"

There was an old man who said, "Do
Tell me *how* I should add two and two?
   I think more and more
   That it makes about four—
But I fear that is almost too few."

A YOUNG LADY NAMED BRIGHT

There was a young lady named Bright,
Who traveled much faster than light.
   She started one day
   In the relative way,
And returned on the previous night.

ALGY MET A BEAR

Algy met a bear,
The bear was bulgy,
The bulge was Algy.

SHE CALLED HIM MR.

She frowned and called him Mr.
Because in sport he kr.
   And so in spite
   That very night
This Mr. kr. sr.

THE LITTLE MAN WHO WASN'T THERE
Hughes Mearns

As I was going up the stair
   I met a man who wasn't there;
He wasn't there again today!
   I wish, I *wish* he'd stay away.

LITTLE WILLIE

Willie saw some dynamite,
Couldn't understand it quite;
Curiosity seldom pays:
It rained Willie seven days.

CARELESS WILLIE

Willie, with a thirst for gore,
Nailed his sister to the door.
Mother said, with humor quaint:
"Now, Willie dear, don't scratch the paint."

SISTER NELL

In the family drinking well
Willie pushed his sister Nell.
She's there yet, because it kilt her—
Now we have to buy a filter.

STATELY VERSE

If Mary goes far out to sea,
　By wayward breezes fanned,
I'd like to know—can you tell me?—
　Just where would Maryland?

If Tenny went high up in air
　And looked o'er land and lea,
Looked here and there and everywhere,
　Pray what would Tennessee?

I looked out of the window and
　Saw Orry on the lawn;
He's not there now, and who can tell
　Just where has Oregon?

Two girls were quarrelling one day
　With garden tools, and so
I said, "My dears, let Mary rake
　And just let Idaho."

An English lady had a steed.
　She called him 'Ighland Bay.
She rode for exercise, and thus
　Rhode Island every day.

THE KITTEN
Ogden Nash

　　　The trouble with a kitten is
　　　THAT
　　　Eventually it becomes a
　　　CAT.

A CANNER, EXCEEDINGLY CANNY
Carolyn Wells

A canner, exceedingly canny,
One morning remarked to his granny,
   "A canner can can
   Anything that he can,
But a canner can't can a can, can he?"

CELERY
Ogden Nash

Celery, raw,
Develops the jaw,
But celery stewed,
Is more quietly chewed.

MOTHER, MAY I GO OUT TO SWIM?

"Mother, may I go out to swim?"
"Yes, my darling daughter,
But hang your clothes on a hickory limb,
And don't go near the water."

THE SWAN

Swan swam over the sea—
   Swim, swan, swim;
Swan swam back again,
   Well swam, swan.

ON DIGITAL EXTREMITIES
Gelett Burgess

> I'd Rather have Fingers than Toes;
> I'd Rather have Eyes than a Nose;
> And As for my hair,
> I'm Glad it's all there;
> I'll be Awfully Sad, when it Goes!

THE PURPLE COW
Gelett Burgess

> I never saw a Purple Cow,
> I never hope to see one,
> But I can tell you, anyhow,
> I'd rather see than be one!

PEAS

> I eat my peas with honey,
> I've done it all my life.
> It makes the peas taste funny,
> But it keeps them on my knife.

THE FLEA AND THE FLY

> A flea and a fly got caught in a flue.
> Said the fly, "Let us flee."
> Said the flea, "Let us fly."
> So together they flew through a flaw in the flue.

365

My Fancy and I

GOBLIN FEET
J. R. R. Tolkien

I am off down the road
Where the fairy lanterns glowed
And the little pretty flitter-mice are flying:
A slender band of gray
It runs creepily away
And the hedges and the grasses are a-sighing.
The air is full of wings,
And of blundery beetle-things
That warn you with their whirring and their humming.
O! I hear the tiny horns
Of enchanted leprechauns
And the padded feet of many gnomes a-coming!

O! the lights! O! the gleams! O! the little tinkly sounds!
O! the rustle of their noiseless little robes!
O! the echo of their feet—of their happy little feet!
O! their swinging lamps in little starlit globes.

I must follow in their train
Down the crooked fairy lane
Where the coney-rabbits long ago have gone,
And where silvery they sing
In a moving moonlit ring
All a-twinkle with the jewels they have on.
They are fading round the turn
Where the glow-worms palely burn
And the echo of their padding feet is dying!
O! it's knocking at my heart—
Let me go! O! let me start!
For the little magic hours are all a-flying.

O! the warmth! O! the hum! O! the colours in the dark!
O! the gauzy wings of golden honey-flies!
O! the music of their feet—of their dancing goblin feet!
O! the magic! O! the sorrow when it dies.

SOMEONE
Walter de la Mare

Someone came knocking
  At my wee, small door;
Someone came knocking,
  I'm sure—sure—sure;
I listened, I opened,
  I looked to left and right,
But nought there was a-stirring
  In the still, dark night;
Only the busy beetle
  Tap-tapping in the wall,
Only from the forest
  The screech owl's call,
Only the cricket whistling
  While the dewdrops fall,
So I know not who came knocking,
  At all, at all, at all.

THE POINTED PEOPLE
Rachel Field

> I don't know who they are,
> But when it's shadow time
> In woods where the trees crowd close,
> With bristly branches crossed,
> From their secret hiding places
> I have seen the Pointed People
> Gliding through brush and bracken.
> Maybe a peaked cap
> Pricking out through the leaves,
> Or a tiny pointed ear
> Up-cocked, all brown and furry,
> From ferns and berry brambles,
> Or a pointed hoof's sharp print
> Deep in the tufted moss,
> And once a pointed face
> That peered between the cedars,
> Blinking bright eyes at me
> And shaking with silent laughter.

MR. MOON
A Song of the Little People
Bliss Carman

> O Moon, Mr. Moon,
> When you comin' down?
> Down on the hilltop,
> Down in the glen,
> Out in the clearin',
> To play with little men?
> Moon, Mr. Moon,
> When you comin' down?
>
> .   .   .   .   .   .

O Mr. Moon,
Hurry up along!
The reeds in the current
Are whisperin' slow;
The river's a-wimplin'
To and fro.
Hurry up along,
Or you'll miss the song!
Moon, Mr. Moon,
When you comin' down?

.   .   .   .   .   .

O Moon, Mr. Moon,
When you comin' down?
Down where the Good Folk
Dance in a ring,
Down where the Little Folk
Sing?
Moon, Mr. Moon,
When you comin' down?

CORNISH MAGIC
Ann Durell

Pixies, slipping, dipping, stealing;
Elf-bells, ringing, swinging, peeling;
Mermaids, giants, tin-mine fairies,
Piskies, wiskies, maids in dairies;
Moonlight in a fairy ring;
Breezes in a frenzied fling;
Bronze, bare mountains, rolling high;
Druids' heaps and sea gulls' cry;
Magic-made, when time began,
The Cornish coast, enchanted land.

BUGLE SONG
Alfred Tennyson

The splendor falls on castle walls
  And snowy summits old in story:
The long light shakes across the lakes,
  And the wild cataract leaps in glory.
Blow, bugle, blow; set the wild echoes flying,
Blow, bugle; answer, echoes, dying, dying, dying.

O hark, O hear! how thin and clear,
  And thinner, clearer, farther going!
O sweet and far from cliff and scar
  The horns of Elfland faintly blowing!
Blow, let us hear the purple glens replying:
Blow, bugle; answer, echoes, dying, dying, dying.

O love, they die in yon rich sky,
  They faint on hill or field or river:
Our echoes roll from soul to soul,
  And grow forever and forever.
Blow, bugle, blow; set the wild echoes flying,
And answer, echoes, answer, dying, dying, dying.

THE ELVES' DANCE
Thomas Ravenscroft

Round about, round about
  In a fair ring-a,
Thus we dance, thus we dance
  And thus we sing-a,
Trip and go, to and fro
  Over this green-a,
All about, in and out,
  For our brave Queen-a.

373

VERY NEARLY
Queenie Scott-Hopper

I never quite saw fairyfolk
  A-dancing in the glade,
Where, just beyond the hollow oak,
  Their broad green rings are laid;
But, while behind that oak I hid,
One day I very nearly did!

I never quite saw mermaids rise
  Above the twilight sea,
When sands, left wet, 'neath sunset skies,
  Are blushing rosily:
But—all alone, those rocks amid—
One day I very nearly did!

I never quite saw Goblin Grim,
  Who haunts our lumber room
And pops his head above the rim
  Of that oak chest's deep gloom:
But once—when mother raised the lid—
I very, very nearly did!

THE MAN WHO HID HIS OWN FRONT DOOR
Elizabeth MacKinstry

There was a little, Elvish man
  Who lived beside a moor,
A shy, secretive, furtive soul
  Who hid his own front door.

He went and hid his door beneath
  A pink laburnum bush:
The neighbors saw the curtains blow,
  They heard a singing thrush.

The Banker came and jingled gold,
  It did not serve him there;
The honey-colored walls uprose
  Unbroken and foresquare.

The Mayor called, the Misses Pitt
  With cordials and game pie;
There was not any door at all,
  They had to pass him by!

But ah! my little sister.
  Her eyes were wild and sweet,
She wore blue faded calico,
  And no shoes on her feet.

She found the wandering door in place
  And easily went through
Into a strange and mossy Hall
  Where bowls of old Delft blue

Held feasts of blackberries, like gems
  In webs of shining dew—
There stood that little Elvish man
  And smiled to see her, too!

THE FAIRIES
William Allingham

Up the airy mountain,
  Down the rushy glen,
We daren't go a-hunting
  For fear of little men;
Wee folk, good folk,
  Trooping all together;
Green jacket, red cap,
  And white owl's feather!

Down along the rocky shore
  Some make their home,
They live on crispy pancakes
  Of yellow tide-foam;
Some in the reeds
  Of the black mountain-lake,
With frogs for their watch-dogs,
  All night awake.

High on the hill-top
  The old King sits;
He is now so old and gray
  He's nigh lost his wits.
With a bridge of white mist
  Columbkill he crosses
On his stately journeys
  From Slieveleague to Rosses;
Or going up with music
  On cold, starry nights,
To sup with the Queen
  Of the gay Northern Lights.

They stole little Bridget
  For seven years long;
When she came down again
  Her friends were all gone.
They took her lightly back,
  Between the night and morrow;
They thought that she was fast asleep,
  But she was dead with sorrow.
They have kept her ever since
  Deep within the lake,
On a bed of flag-leaves,
  Watching till she wake.

By the craggy hill-side,
  Through the mosses bare,
They have planted thorn-trees
  For pleasure here and there.

Is any man so daring
  As dig them up in spite,
He shall find their sharpest thorns
  In his bed at night.

Up the airy mountain,
  Down the rushy glen,
We daren't go a-hunting
  For fear of little men;
Wee folk, good folk,
  Trooping all together;
Green jacket, red cap,
  And white owl's feather!

THE FAIRIES
Rose Fyleman

There are fairies at the bottom of our garden!
  It's not so very, very far away;
You pass the gardener's shed and you just keep straight ahead—
  I do so hope they've really come to stay.
There's a little wood, with moss in it and beetles,
  And a little stream that quietly runs through;
You wouldn't think they'd dare to come merrymaking there—
          Well, they do.

There are fairies at the bottom of our garden!
  They often have a dance on summer nights;
The butterflies and bees make a lovely little breeze,
  And the rabbits stand about and hold the lights.
Did you know that they could sit upon the moonbeams
  And pick a little star to make a fan,
And dance away up there in the middle of the air?
          Well, they can.

There are fairies at the bottom of our garden!
  You cannot think how beautiful they are;
They all stand up and sing when the Fairy Queen and King
  Come gently floating down upon their car.
The King is very proud and *very* handsome;
  The Queen—now can you guess who that could be?
(She's a little girl all day, but at night she steals away)
        Well—it's *me!*

STOCKING FAIRY
Winifred Welles

In a hole of the heel of an old brown stocking,
A little old Fairy sits rocking and rocking,
And scolding and pointing and squeaking and squinting,
Brown as a nut, a bright eye glinting,
She tugs at a thread, she drags up a needle,
She stamps and she shrills, she commences to wheedle,
To whine of the cold, in a fine gust of temper
She beats on my thumb, and then with a whimper
She sulks in her shawl, she says I've forgotten
I promised to make her a lattice of cotton,
A soft, woven window, cozy yet airy,
Where she could sit rocking and peeking—Hush, Fairy,
Tush, Fairy, sit gently, look sweetly,
I'll do what I said, now, and close you in neatly.

THE LIGHT-HEARTED FAIRY

Oh, who is so merry, so merry, heigh ho!
As the light-hearted fairy? heigh ho,
   Heigh ho!
  He dances and sings
  To the sound of his wings,
With a hey and a heigh and a ho!

Oh, who is so merry, so airy, heigh ho!
As the light-hearted fairy? heigh ho,
   Heigh ho!
  His nectar he sips
  From the primroses' lips,
With a hey and a heigh and a ho!

Oh, who is so merry, so merry, heigh ho!
As the light-hearted fairy? heigh ho!
   Heigh ho!
  The night is his noon
  And his sun is the moon,
With a hey and a heigh and a ho!

THE FAIRIES HAVE NEVER A PENNY TO SPEND
Rose Fyleman

The fairies have never a penny to spend,
  They haven't a thing put by;
But theirs is the dower of bird and of flower,
  And theirs are the earth and the sky.

And though you should live in a palace of gold
  Or sleep in a dried-up ditch,
You could never be poor as the fairies are,
  And never as rich.

Since ever and ever the world began
  They have danced like a ribbon of flame,
They have sung their song through the centuries long,
  And yet it is never the same.

And though you be foolish or though you be wise,
  With hair of silver or gold,
You could never be young as the fairies are,
  And never as old.

A FAIRY IN ARMOR
Joseph Rodman Drake

He put his acorn helmet on;
It was plumed of the silk of the thistle down;
The corslet plate that guarded his breast
Was once the wild bee's golden vest;
His cloak, of a thousand mingled dyes,
Was formed of the wings of butterflies;
His shield was the shell of a lady-bug green,
Studs of gold on a ground of green;
And the quivering lance which he brandished bright,
Was the sting of a wasp he had slain in fight.
Swift he bestrode his fire-fly steed;
   He bared his blade of the bent-grass blue;
He drove his spurs of the cockle-seed,
   And away like a glance of thought he flew,
To skim the heavens, and follow far
The fiery trail of the rocket-star.

I'D LOVE TO BE A FAIRY'S CHILD
Robert Graves

Children born of fairy stock
Never need for shirt or frock,
Never want for food or fire,
Always get their heart's desire:
Jingle pockets full of gold,
Marry when they're seven years old.
Every fairy child may keep
Two strong ponies and ten sheep;
All have houses, each his own,
Built of brick or granite stone;
They live on cherries, they run wild—
I'd love to be a Fairy's child.

BUTTERCUPS
Wilfrid Thorley

There must be fairy miners
　Just underneath the mould,
Such wondrous quaint designers
　Who live in caves of gold.

They take the shining metals
　And beat them into shreds;
And mould them into petals,
　To make the flowers' heads.

Sometimes they melt the flowers
　To tiny seeds like pearls,
And store them up in bowers
　For little boys and girls.

And still a tiny fan turns
　Above a forge of gold,
To keep, with fairy lanterns,
　The world from growing old.

FAIRY LULLABY
William Shakespeare

FIRST FAIRY

You spotted snakes with double tongue,
　Thorny hedgehogs be not seen;
Newts, and blind-worms, do no wrong;
　Come not near our fairy queen.

Philomel with melody
　Sing in our sweet lullaby;
Lulla, lulla, lullaby; lulla, lulla, lullaby!
Never harm, nor spell, nor charm,
　Come our lovely lady nigh!
　So good-night, with lullaby.

Weaving spiders, come not here;
   Hence, you long-legged spinners, hence;
Beetles black, approach not near;
   Worm, nor snail, do no offense.

FAIRY'S WANDER-SONG
William Shakespeare

Over hill, over dale,
   Thorough bush, thorough brier,
Over park, over pale,
   Thorough flood, thorough fire.
I do wander everywhere,
Swifter than the moone's sphere;
And I serve the fairy queen,
To dew her orbs upon the green.
The cowslips tall her pensioners be;
In their gold coats spots you see,
Those be rubies, fairy favors,
   In those freckles live their savors:
I must go seek some dewdrops here,
And hang a pearl in every cowslip's ear.

QUEEN MAB
William Shakespeare

Oh, then, I see Queen Mab hath been with you.
She is the fairies' midwife, and she comes
In shape no bigger than an agate stone
On the forefinger of an alderman,
Drawn with a team of little atomies
Athwart men's noses as they lie asleep;

Her wagon spokes made of long spinners' legs,
The cover of the wings of grasshoppers,
The traces of the smallest spider's web,
The collars of the moonshine's watery beams,
Her whip of cricket's bone, the lash of film,
Her wagoner a small, grey-coated gnat,
Not half so big as a round little worm
Prick'd from the lazy finger of a maid;
Her chariot is an empty hazelnut
Made by the joiner squirrel or old grub,
Time out o' mind the fairies' coachmakers.

And in this state she gallops night by night
Through lovers' brains, and then they dream of love;
O'er courtiers' knees, that dream in court'sies straight;
O'er lawyers' fingers, who straight dream in fees;
O'er ladies' lips, who straight on kisses dream,
Which oft the angry Mab with blisters plagues,
Because their breaths with sweetmeats tainted are.
Sometimes she gallops o'er a courtier's nose,
And then he dreams of smelling out a suit;
And sometimes comes she with a tithe pig's tail
Tickling a parson's nose as he lies asleep,
Then dreams he of another benefice.

Sometimes she driveth o'er a soldier's neck,
And then dreams he of cutting foreign throats,
Of breaches, ambuscades, Spanish blades,
Of healths five fathoms deep; and then anon
Drums in his ear, at which he starts and wakes,
And being thus frighted swears a prayer or two
And sleeps again. This is that very Mab
That plaits the manes of horses in the night
And bakes the elf locks in foul sluttish hairs,
Which once untangled much misfortune bodes,
This is she.

THE FAIRIES
Robert Herrick

If ye will with Mab find grace,
Set each platter in his place;
Rake the fire up, and get
Water in, ere sun be set.
Wash your pails and cleanse your dairies,
Sluts are loathsome to the fairies;
Sweep your house: Who doth not so,
Mab will pinch her by the toe.

A MUSICAL INSTRUMENT
Elizabeth Barrett Browning

What was he doing, the great god Pan,
    Down in the reeds by the river?
Spreading ruin, and scattering ban,
Splashing and paddling with hoofs of a goat,
And breaking the golden lilies afloat
    With the dragon-fly on the river.

He tore out a reed, the great god Pan,
    From the deep, cool bed of the river,
The limpid water turbidly ran,
And the broken lilies a-dying lay,
And the dragon-fly had fled away.
    Ere he brought it out of the river.

High on the shore sat the great god Pan,
    While turbidly flowed the river,
And hacked and hewed as a great god can,
With his hard bleak steel at the patient reed,
Till there was not a sign of the leaf indeed
    To prove it fresh from the river.

He cut it short, did the great god Pan,
   (How tall it stood in the river!)
Then drew the pith, like the heart of a man,
Steadily from the outside ring,
And notched the poor, dry, empty thing
   In holes as he sat by the river.

"This is the way," laughed the great god Pan,
   (Laughed while he sat by the river),
"The only way, since gods began
To make sweet music, they could succeed."
Then, dropping his mouth to a hole in the reed,
   He blew in power by the river.

Sweet, sweet, sweet, O Pan,
   Piercing sweet by the river!
Blinding sweet, O great god Pan,
The sun on the hill forgot to die,
And the lilies revived, and the dragon-fly
   Came back to dream on the river.

Yet half a beast is the great god Pan,
   To laugh as he sits by the river,
Making a poet out of a man:
The true gods sigh for the cost and pain—
For the reed which grows nevermore again
   As a reed with the reeds in the river.

THE GNOME
Harry Behn

I saw a Gnome
As plain as plain
Sitting on top
Of a weathervane.

He was dressed like a crow
In silky black feathers,
And there he sat watching
All kinds of weathers.

He talked like a crow too,
Caw caw caw,
When he told me exactly
What he saw,

Snow to the north of him
Sun to the south,
And he spoke with a beaky
Kind of a mouth.

But he wasn't a crow,
That was plain as plain
'Cause crows never sit
On a weathervane.

What I saw was simply
A usual gnome
Looking things over
On his way home.

IN THE HOURS OF DARKNESS
James Flexner

When the night is cloudy,
  And mists hang on the hill,
There are ghostly footsteps
  And voices, thin and shrill;
Nothing will your looking
  Show you in the dark
If the door is opened,
  But harken, harken, hark!

In the hours of darkness
    Thronging from their camp
Dark and ghostly goblins
    Flicker by the lamp;
Listen to their laughter
    As they flicker by the lamp!

When the rain is falling,
    And the night is bleak,
Something moves the knocker
    And makes the hinges creak;
Sometimes on the window
    A waving shadow falls;
Sometimes clammy whispers
    Echo through the halls.

They lure you with sweet voices
    When you should be in bed;
Something creaks behind you,
    Something creaks ahead,
Something gazes at you
    From behind a tree,
But if you look around you,
    Nothing will you see.

In the hours of darkness
    Thronging from their camp
Dark and ghostly goblins
    Flicker by the lamp;
Listen to their laughter
    As they flicker by the lamp.

HOW TO TELL GOBLINS FROM ELVES
Monica Shannon

The Goblin has a wider mouth
  Than any wondering elf.
The saddest part of this is that
  He brings it on himself.
For hanging in a willow clump
  In baskets made of sheaves,
You may see the baby goblins
  Under coverlets of leaves.

They suck a pink and podgy foot,
  (As human babies do),
And then they suck the other one,
  Until they're sucking two.
And so it is that goblins' mouths
  Keep growing very round.
So you can't mistake a goblin,
  When a goblin you have found.

OVERHEARD ON A SALTMARSH
Harold Monro

Nymph, nymph, what are your beads?

Green glass, goblin. Why do you stare at them?

Give them me.

      No.

Give them me. Give them me.

      No.

Then I will howl all night in the reeds,
Lie in the mud and howl for them.

Goblin, why do you love them so?

They are better than stars or water,
Better than voices of winds that sing,
Better than any man's fair daughter,
Your green glass beads on a silver ring.

Hush, I stole them out of the moon.

Give me your beads, I want them.

                              No.

I will howl in a deep lagoon
For your green glass beads, I love them so.
Give them me. Give them.

                    No.

FAITH, I WISH I WERE A LEPRECHAUN
Margaret Ritter

Faith, I wish I were a leprechaun
Beneath a hawthorn tree,
A-cobblin' of wee, magic boots,
A-eatin' luscious, lovely fruits;
Oh, fiddle-dum, oh, fiddle-dee,
I wish I were a leprechaun
Beneath a hawthorn tree!

Faith, I wish I were a leprechaun
Beneath a hawthorn tree,
A-throwin' snuff into the eyes
Of young and old and dull and wise;
Oh, fiddle-dum, oh, fiddle-dee,
I wish I were a leprechaun
Beneath a hawthorn tree!

Faith, I wish I were a leprechaun
Beneath a hawthorn tree,
With no more irksome thing to do
Than sew a small, bewitchin' shoe;
Oh, fiddle-dum, oh, fiddle-dee,
I wish I were a leprechaun
Beneath a hawthorn tree!

COULD IT HAVE BEEN A SHADOW?
Monica Shannon

What ran under the rosebush?
   What ran under the stone?
Could it have been a shadow,
   Running away alone?
Maybe a fairy's shadow,
   Slipping away at dawn
To guard a gleaming pot of gold
   For a busy leprechaun.

THE MERMAID
Alfred Tennyson

I

Who would be
A mermaid fair,
Singing alone,
Combing her hair
Under the sea,
In a golden curl
With a comb of pearl,
On a throne?

II

I would be a mermaid fair;
I would sing to myself the whole of the day;
With a comb of pearl I would comb my hair;
And still as I comb'd I would sing and say,
"Who is it loves me? Who loves not me?"
I would comb my hair till my ringlets would fall
      Low adown, low adown,
From under my starry sea-bud crown
      Low adown, low adown,
And I should look like a fountain of gold
      Springing alone
    With a shrill inner sound,
      Over the throne
      In the midst of the hall;
Till the great sea snake under the sea
From his coiled sleeps in the central deeps
Would slowly trail himself sevenfold
Round the hall where I sate, and look in at the gate
With his large, calm eyes for the love of me.
And all the mermen under the sea
Would feel their immortality
Die in their hearts for the love of me.

III

But at night I would wander away, away,
    I would fling on each side my low-flowing locks,
And lightly vault from the throne and play
    With the mermen in and out of the rocks;
We would run to and fro, and hide and seek,
    On the broad seawolds in the crimson shells,
Whose silvery spikes are nighest the sea.
But if any came near I would call, and shriek,
And adown the steep like a wave I would leap
    From the diamond ledges that jut from the dells;
For I would not be kiss'd by all who would list
Of the bold, merry mermen under the sea.

They would sue me, and woo me, and flatter me,
In the purple twilights under the sea;
But the king of them all would marry me,
Woo me, and win me, and marry me,
In the branching jaspers under the sea.
Then all the dry pied things that be
In the hueless mosses under the sea
Would curl round my silver feet silently,
All looking up for the love of me.
And if I should carol aloud, from aloft
All things that are forked, and horned, and soft
Would lean out from the hollow sphere of the sea,
All looking down for the love of me.

THE MERMAN
Alfred Tennyson

I

Who would be
A merman bold,
Sitting alone,
Singing alone
Under the sea,
With a crown of gold,
On a throne?

II

I would be a merman bold;
I would sit and sing the whole of the day;
I would fill the sea-halls with a voice of power
But at night I would roam abroad and play
With the mermaids in and out of the rocks,
Dressing their hair with the white seaflower;

And holding them back by their flowing locks
I would kiss them often under the sea,
And kiss them again till they kiss'd me
    Laughingly, laughingly;
And then we would wander away, away,
To the pale sea-groves straight and high
    Chasing each other merrily.

THE SEA WOLF
Violet McDougal

The fishermen say, when your catch is done
    And you're sculling in with the tide,
You must take great care that the Sea Wolf's share
    Is tossed to him overside.

They say that the Sea Wolf rides, by day,
    Unseen on the crested waves,
And the sea mists rise from his cold green eyes
    When he comes from his salt sea caves.

The fishermen say, when it storms at night
    And the great seas bellow and roar,
That the Sea Wolf rides on the plunging tides,
    And you hear his howl at the door.

And you must throw open your door at once,
    And fling your catch to the waves,
Till he drags his share to his cold sea lair,
    Straight down to his salt sea caves.

Then the storm will pass, and the still stars shine,
    In peace—so the fishermen say—
But the Sea Wolf waits by the cold Sea Gates
    For the dawn of another day.

THE UNICORN
Ella Young

While yet the Morning Star
Flamed in the sky
A Unicorn went mincing by,
Whiter by far than blossom of the thorn:
His silver horn
Glittered as he danced and pranced
Silver-pale in the silver-pale morn.

The folk that saw him, ran away.
Where he went, so gay, so fleet,
Star-like lilies at his feet
Flowered all day,
Lilies, lilies in a throng,
And the wind made for him a song:

But he dared not stay
Over-long!

THE RIDE-BY-NIGHTS
Walter de la Mare

Up on their brooms the Witches stream,
Crooked and black in the crescent's gleam,
One foot high, and one foot low,
Bearded, cloaked, and cowled, they go.
'Neath Charlie's Wane they twitter and tweet,
And away they swarm 'neath the Dragon's feet,
With a whoop and a flutter they swing and sway,
And surge pell-mell down the Milky Way.
Between the legs of the glittering Chair
They hover and squeak in the empty air.

Then round they swoop past the glimmering Lion
To where Sirius barks behind huge Orion;
Up, then, and over to wheel amain
Under the silver, and home again.

THE BROOMSTICK TRAIN
FROM THE BROOMSTICK TRAIN
Oliver Wendell Holmes

Look out! Look out, boys! Clear the track!
The witches are here! They've all come back!
They hanged them high,—No use! No use!
What cares a witch for the hangman's noose?
They buried them deep, but they wouldn't lie still,
For cats and witches are hard to kill;
They swore they shouldn't and wouldn't die,—
Books said they did, but they lie! they lie!

THE PLUMPUPPETS
Christopher Morley

When little heads weary have gone to their bed,
When all the good nights and the prayers have been said,
Of all the good fairies that send bairns to rest
The little Plumpuppets are those I love best.

If your pillow is lumpy, or hot, thin, and flat,
The little Plumpuppets know just what they're at:
They plump up the pillow, all soft, cool, and fat—
  The little Plumpuppets plump-up it!

The little Plumpuppets are fairies of beds;
They have nothing to do but to watch sleepyheads;
They turn down the sheets and they tuck you in tight,
And they dance on your pillow to wish you good night!

395

No matter what troubles have bothered the day,
Though your doll broke her arm or the pup ran away;
Though your handies are black with the ink that was spilt—
Plumpuppets are waiting in blanket and quilt.

If your pillow is lumpy, or hot, thin, and flat,
The little Plumpuppets know just what they're at:
They plump up the pillow, all soft, cool, and fat—
The little Plumpuppets plump-up it!

FOR GOOD LUCK
Juliana Horatia Ewing

Little Kings and Queens of May,
If you want to be,
Every one of you, very good,
In this beautiful, beautiful, beautiful wood,
Where the little birds' heads get so turned with delight
That some of them sing all night:
Whatever you pluck,
Leave some for good luck!

Picked from the stalk or pulled by the root,
From overhead or under foot,
Water-wonders of pond or brook—
Wherever you look,
And whatever you find,
Leave something behind:
Some for the Naiads,
Some for the Dryads,
And a bit for the Nixies and Pixies!

FANCY
William Shakespeare

Tell me where is Fancy bred,
Or in the heart or in the head?
How begot, how nourished?
    Reply, reply.
It is engender'd in the eyes,
With gazing fed; and Fancy dies
In the cradle where it lies.
    Let us all ring Fancy's knell:
    I'll begin it,—Ding, dong, bell.
Ding, dong, bell.

FAIRY SONG
John Keats

Shed no tear! O, shed no tear!
The flower will bloom another year.
Weep no more! O, weep no more!
Young buds sleep in the root's white core.
Dry your eyes! Oh! dry your eyes!
For I was taught in Paradise
To ease my breast of melodies—Shed no tear.
Overhead! look overhead!
'Mong the blossoms white and red—
Look up, look up. I flutter now
On this flush pomegranate bough.
See me! 'tis this silvery bell
Ever cures the good man's ill.
Shed no tear! O, shed no tear!
The flowers will bloom another year.
Adieu, adieu—I fly, adieu,
I vanish in the heaven's blue—Adieu, adieu!

397

Sign of my nation,
great and strong

THE STAR-SPANGLED BANNER
Francis Scott Key

O say, can you see, by the dawn's early light,
What so proudly we hailed at the twilight's last gleaming?
Whose broad stripes and bright stars, through the perilous fight,
O'er the ramparts we watched were so gallantly streaming!
And the rockets' red glare, the bombs bursting in air,
Gave proof through the night that our flag was still there:
O say, does that star-spangled banner yet wave
O'er the land of the free and the home of the brave?

On the shore, dimly seen through the mists of the deep,
Where the foe's haughty host in dread silence reposes,
What is that which the breeze, o'er the towering steep,
As it fitfully blows, half conceals, half discloses?
Now it catches the gleam of the morning's first beam,
In full glory reflected now shines on the stream.
'Tis the star-spangled banner! O long may it wave
O'er the land of the free and the home of the brave!

And where is that band who so vauntingly swore
That the havoc of war and the battle's confusion
A home and a country should leave us no more?
Their blood has washed out their foul footsteps' pollution.
No refuge could save the hireling and slave
From the terror of flight, or the gloom of the grave:
And the star-spangled banner in triumph doth wave
O'er the land of the free and the home of the brave!

O thus be it ever, when freemen shall stand
Between their loved homes and the war's desolation!
Blest with victory and peace, may the heaven-rescued land
Praise the Power that hath made and preserved us a nation.
Then conquer we must, when our cause it is just,
And this be our motto: "In God is our trust,"
And the star-spangled banner in triumph shall wave
O'er the land of the free and the home of the brave!

AMERICA THE BEAUTIFUL
Katharine Lee Bates

O beautiful for spacious skies,
　For amber waves of grain,
For purple mountain majesties
　Above the fruited plain!
　　　America! America!
　God shed His grace on thee,
And crown thy good with brotherhood
　From sea to shining sea!

O beautiful for pilgrim feet,
　Whose stern, impassioned stress
A thoroughfare for freedom beat
　Across the wilderness!
　　　America! America!
　God mend thine every flaw,
Confirm thy soul in self-control,
　Thy liberty in law!

O beautiful for heroes proved
　In liberating strife,
Who more than self their country loved,
　And mercy more than life!
　　　America! America!
　May God thy gold refine
Till all success be nobleness
　And every gain divine!

O beautiful for patriot dream
　That sees beyond the years
Thine alabaster cities gleam
　Undimmed by human tears!
　　　America! America!
　God shed His grace on thee
And crown thy good with brotherhood
　From sea to shining sea!

COLUMBUS
Joaquin Miller

Behind him lay the gray Azores,
   Behind the Gates of Hercules;
Before him not the ghost of shores,
   Before him only shoreless seas.
The good mate said: "Now must we pray,
   For lo! the very stars are gone.
Brave Admiral, speak, what shall I say?"
   "Why, say 'Sail on! sail on! and on!'"

"My men grow mutinous day by day;
   My men grow ghastly wan and weak."
The stout mate thought of home; a spray
   Of salt wave washed his swarthy cheek.
"What shall I say, brave Admiral, say,
   If we sight naught but seas at dawn?"
"Why, you shall say at break of day,
   'Sail on! sail on! sail on! and on!'"

They sailed and sailed, as winds might blow,
   Until at last the blanched mate said,
"Why, now not even God would know
   Should I and all my men fall dead.
These very winds forget their way,
   For God from these dread seas is gone.
Now speak, brave Admiral, speak and say"—
   He said: "Sail on! sail on! and on!"

They sailed. They sailed. Then spake the mate:
   "This mad sea shows his teeth tonight.
He curls his lip, he lies in wait,
   With lifted teeth, as if to bite!
Brave Admiral, say but one good word:
   What shall we do when hope is gone?"
The words leapt like a leaping sword:
   "Sail on! sail on! sail on! and on!"

Then, pale and worn, he kept his deck,
    And peered through darkness. Ah, that night
Of all dark nights! And then a speck—
    A light! a light! a light! a light!
It grew, a starlit flag unfurled!
    It grew to be Time's burst of dawn.
He gained a world; he gave that world
    Its grandest lesson: "On! sail on!"

SONNET
J. C. Squire

There was an Indian, who had known no change,
    Who strayed content along a sunlit beach
Gathering shells. He heard a sudden strange
    Commingled noise: looked up; and gasped for speech.
For in the bay, where nothing was before,
    Moved on the sea, by magic, huge canoes,
With bellying clothes on poles, and not one oar,
    And fluttering colored signs and clambering crews.

And he, in fear, this naked man alone
    His fallen hands forgetting all their shells,
His lips gone pale, knelt low behind a stone,
    And stared, and saw, and did not understand,
Columbus's doom-burdened caravels
    Slant to the shore, and all their seamen land.

HIAWATHA'S CHILDHOOD
FROM THE SONG OF HIAWATHA
Henry Wadsworth Longfellow

By the shores of Gitchee Gumee,
By the shining Big-Sea-Water,
Stood the wigwam of Nokomis
Daughter of the Moon, Nokomis.
Dark behind it rose the forest,
Rose the black and gloomy pine trees,
Rose the firs with cones upon them;
Bright before it beat the water,
Beat the clear and sunny water,
Beat the shining Big-Sea-Water.

There the wrinkled old Nokomis
Nursed the little Hiawatha,
Rocked him in his linden cradle,
Bedded soft in moss and rushes,
Safely bound with reindeer sinews;
Stilled his fretful wail by saying,
"Hush! the Naked Bear will hear thee!"
Lulled him into slumber, singing,
"Ewa-yea! my little owlet!
Who is this that lights the wigwam?
With his great eyes lights the wigwam?
Ewa-yea! my little owlet!"

Many things Nokomis taught him
Of the stars that shine in heaven;
Showed him Ishkoodah, the comet,
Ishkoodah, with fiery tresses;
Showed the Death-Dance of the spirits,
Warriors with their plumes and war-clubs,
Flaring far away to Northward
In the frosty nights of Winter;

Showed the broad white road in heaven,
Pathway of the ghosts, the shadows,
Running straight across the heavens,
Crowded with the ghosts, the shadows.

At the door on Summer evenings
Sat the little Hiawatha;
Heard the whispering of the pine trees,
Heard the lapping of the waters.
Sounds of music, words of wonder;
"Minne-wawa!" said the pine trees,
"Mudway-aushka!" said the water.

Saw the firefly, Wah-wah-taysee,
Flitting through the dusk of evening,
With the twinkle of its candle
Lighting up the brakes and bushes,
And he sang the song of children,
Sang the song Nokomis taught him:
"Wah-wah-taysee, little firefly,
Little, flitting, white-fire insect,
Little, dancing, white-fire creature,
Light me with your little candle,
Ere upon my bed I lay me,
Ere in sleep I close my eyelids!"

Saw the moon rise from the water
Rippling, rounding from the water,
Saw the flecks and shadows on it,
Whispered, "What is that, Nokomis?"
And the good Nokomis answered:
"Once a warrior, very angry,
Seized his grandmother, and threw her
Up into the sky at midnight;
Right against the moon he threw her;
'Tis her body that you see there."

Saw the rainbow in the heaven,
In the eastern sky, the rainbow,
Whispered, "What is that, Nokomis?"
And the good Nokomis answered:
" 'Tis the heaven of flowers you see there;
All the wild flowers of the forest,
All the lilies of the prairie,
When on earth they fade and perish
Blossom in that heaven above us."

When he heard the owls at midnight,
Hooting, laughing in the forest,
"What is that?" he cried in terror.
"What is that," he said, "Nokomis?"
And the good Nokomis answered:
"That is but the owl and owlet,
Talking in their native language,
Talking, scolding at each other."

Then the little Hiawatha
Learned of every bird its language,
Learned their names and all their secrets,
How they built their nests in Summer,
Where they hid themselves in Winter,
Talked with them whene'er he met them,
Called them "Hiawatha's Chickens."

Of all beasts he learned the language,
Learned their names and all their secrets,
How the beavers built their lodges,
Where the squirrels hid their acorns,
How the reindeer ran so swiftly,
Why the rabbit was so timid,
Talked with them whene'er he met them,
Called them "Hiawatha's Brothers."

POCAHONTAS
William Makepeace Thackeray

Wearied arm and broken sword
   Wage in vain the desperate fight;
Round him press a countless horde,
   He is but a single knight.
Hark! a cry of triumph shrill
   Through the wilderness resounds,
   As, with twenty bleeding wounds,
Sinks the warrior, fighting still.

Now they heap the funeral pyre,
   And the torch of death they light;
Ah! 'tis hard to die by fire!
   Who will shield the captive knight?
Round the stake with fiendish cry
   Wheel and dance the savage crowd,
   Cold the victim's mien and proud,
And his breast is bared to die.

Who will shield the fearless heart?
   Who avert the murderous blade?
From the throng with sudden start
   See, there springs an Indian maid.
Quick she stands before the knight:
   "Loose the chain, unbind the ring!
   I am daughter of the king,
And I claim the Indian right!"

Dauntlessly aside she flings
   Lifted axe and thirsty knife,
Fondly to his heart she clings,
   And her bosom guards his life!
In the woods of Powhatan,
   Still 'tis told by Indian fires
   How a daughter of their sires
Saved a captive Englishman.

THE LANDING OF THE PILGRIM FATHERS
Felicia Dorothea Hemans

The breaking waves dashed high
On a stern and rock-bound coast,
And the woods, against a stormy sky,
Their giant branches tossed;

And the heavy night hung dark
The hills and waters o'er,
When a band of exiles moored their bark
On a wild New England shore.

Not as the conqueror comes,
They, the true-hearted, came;
Not with the roll of the stirring drums,
And the trumpet that sings of fame;

Not as the flying come,
In silence and in fear;—
They shook the depths of the desert's gloom
With their hymns of lofty cheer.

Amidst the storm they sang,
And the stars heard, and the sea;
And the sounding aisles of the dim woods rang
To the anthem of the free!

The ocean-eagle soared
From his nest by the white wave's foam,
And the rocking pines of the forest roared;
This was their welcome home!

There were men with hoary hair
Amidst that pilgrim band;
Why had they come to wither there,
Away from their childhood's land?

There was woman's fearless eye,
Lit by her deep love's truth;
There was manhood's brow, serenely high,
And the fiery heart of youth.

What sought they thus afar?
Bright jewels of the mine?
The wealth of seas, the spoils of war?—
They sought a faith's pure shrine!

Aye, call it holy ground,
The soil where first they trod!
They left unstained what there they found—
Freedom to worship God!

FIRST THANKSGIVING OF ALL
Nancy Byrd Turner

Peace and Mercy and Jonathan,
And Patience (very small),
Stood by the table giving thanks
The first Thanksgiving of all.
There was very little for them to eat,
Nothing special and nothing sweet;
Only bread and a little broth,
And a bit of fruit (and no tablecloth);
But Peace and Mercy and Jonathan
And Patience, in a row,
Stood up and asked a blessing on
Thanksgiving, long ago.
Thankful they were their ship had come
Safely across the sea;
Thankful they were for hearth and home,
And kin and company;
They were glad of broth to go with their bread,
Glad their apples were round and red,
Glad of mayflowers they would bring
Out of the woods again next spring.

So Peace and Mercy and Jonathan,
And Patience (very small),
Stood up gratefully giving thanks
The first Thanksgiving of all.

THE WILDERNESS IS TAMED
Elizabeth Coatsworth

The axe has cut the forest down,
The laboring ox has smoothed all clear,
Apples now grow where pine trees stood,
And slow cows graze instead of deer.

Where Indian fires once raised their smoke
The chimneys of a farmhouse stand,
And cocks crow barnyard challenges
To dawns that once saw savage land.

The axe, the plow, the binding wall,
By these the wilderness is tamed,
By these the white man's will is wrought,
The rivers bridged, the new towns named.

SCHOOL DAYS IN NEW AMSTERDAM
Arthur Guiterman

Our city's sons and daughters,
    When old New York was new,
Explored Manhattan's waters
    And hills and valleys, too,
For strong they were and ruddy
    And made for sport and play;
And still they had to study,
    As children must, today.

No pedagogue was sterner
  Than theirs—the profiteer
Who charged for every learner
  Two beaver skins a year!
The windows needed glasses,
  The benches needed pads
For the burghers' winsome lasses
  And the burghers' lively lads.

From sum-books and from hornbooks
  They learned to add and spell;
From other worn and torn books
  They learned to read as well.
They lunched on "oly koekies."
  In Spring, the boys were much
Too fond of "cutting hoekies."
  That's "truancy" in Dutch.
But those abandoned sinners
  With dunderpates who tripped
In "Latin for Beginners"
  Were roundly, soundly whipped.
They had no dancing classes
  Or other frills and fads—
The burghers' hearty lasses
  And the burghers' sturdy lads.

In mild September weather
  Began the master's rule:
In pairs and groups together
  The pupils trudged to school
Till June, with rosy garlands,
  Came in and set them free
To range our near and far lands,
  Our glens, our woods, our sea.
No streets were dark and sooty,
  No squares were racked with din—
Oh, isle of banished beauty,
  How dear it must have been

Your ferny ways or grassy
 To wander, free and glad,
A burgher's laughing lassie
 Or a burgher's happy lad!

WASHINGTON
Nancy Byrd Turner

He played by the river when he was young,
He raced with rabbits along the hills,
He fished for minnows, and climbed and swung,
And hooted back at the whippoorwills.
Strong and slender and tall he grew—
And then, one morning, the bugles blew.

Over the hills the summons came,
Over the river's shining rim.
He said that the bugles called his name,
He knew that his country needed him,
And he answered, "Coming!" and marched away
For many a night and many a day.

Perhaps when the marches were hot and long
He'd think of the river flowing by
Or, camping under the winter sky,
Would hear the whippoorwill's far-off song.
Boy or soldier, in peace or strife,
He loved America all his life!

LEETLA GIORGIO WASHEENTON
Thomas Augustine Daly

You know w'at for ees school keep out
    Dees holiday, my son?
Wal, den, I gona tal you 'bout
    Dees Giorgio Washeenton.

Wal, Giorgio was leetla keed
    Ees leeve long time ago,
An' he gon' school for learn to read
    An' write hees nam', you know.
He moocha like for gona school
    An' learna hard all day,
Baycause he no gat time for fool
    Weeth bada keeds an' play.
Wal, wan cold day w'en Giorgio
    Ees steel so vera small,
He start from home, but he ees no
    Show up een school at all!
Oh, my! hees Pop ees gatta mad
    An' so he tal hees wife:
"Som' leetla boy ees gon' feel bad
    Today, you bat my life!"
An' den he grab a beega steeck
    An' gon' out een da snow
An' lookin' all aroun' for seek
    Da leetla Giorgio.
Ha! w'at you theenk? Firs' theeng he see
    Where leetla boy he stan'
All tangla up een cherry tree,
    Weeth hatchet een hees han'.
"Ha! w'at you do?" hees Pop he say,
    "W'at for you busta rule
An' stay away like dees for play
    Eenstead for gon' to school?"

Da boy ees say; "I no can lie,
   An' so I speaka true.
I stay away from school for try
   An' gat som' wood for you.
I theenka deesa cherry tree
   Ees gooda size for chop,
An' so I cut heem down, you see,
   For justa help my Pop."
Hees Pop he no can gatta mad,
   But looka please' an' say:
"My leetla boy, I am so glad
   You taka holiday."
Ees good for leetla boy, you see,
   For be so bright an' try
For help hees Pop; so den he be
   A granda man bimeby.
So now you gatta holiday
   An' eet ees good, you know,
For you gon' do da sama way
   Like leetla Giorgio.
Don't play so mooch, but justa stop,
   Eef you want be som' good,
An' justa help your poor old Pop
   By carry home some wood;
An' mebbe so like Giorgio
   You grow for be so great
You gona be da Presidant
   Of dese Unita State'.

YOUNG WASHINGTON
Arthur Guiterman

Tie the moccasin, bind the pack,
Sling your rifle across your back,
Up! and follow the mountain track,
   Tread the Indian Trail.

North and west is the road we fare
Toward the forts of the Frenchmen, where
"Peace or War!" is the word we bear,
    Life and Death in the scale.

The leaves of October are dry on the ground,
The sheaves of Virginia are gathered and bound,
Her fallows are glad with the cry of the hound,
    The partridges whirr in the fern;
But deep are the forests and keen are the foes
Where Monongahela in wilderness flows;
We've labors and perils and torrents and snows
    To conquer before we return.

Hall and council-room, farm and chase,
Coat of scarlet and frill of lace
All are excellent things in place;
    Joy in these if ye can.
Mine be hunting-shirt, knife, and gun,
Camp aglow on the sheltered run,
Friend and foe in the checkered sun;
    That's the life for a man!

GEORGE WASHINGTON
Rosemary and Stephen Vincent Benét

Sing hey! for bold George Washington,
That jolly British tar,
King George's famous admiral
From Hull to Zanzibar!
No—wait a minute—something's wrong—
George *wished* to sail the foam.
But, when his mother thought, aghast,
Of Georgie shinning up a mast,
Her tears and protests flowed so fast
That George remained at home.

416

Sing ho! for grave Washington,
The staid Virginia squire,
Who farms his fields and hunts his hounds
And aims at nothing higher!
Stop, stop, it's going wrong again!
George *liked* to live on farms,
But, when the Colonies agreed
They could and should and would be freed,
They called on George to do the deed
And George cried "Shoulder arms!"

Sing ha! for Emperor Washington,
That hero of renown,
Who freed his land from Britain's rule
To win a golden crown!
No, no, that's what George *might* have won
But didn't, for he said,
"There's not much point about a king,
They're pretty but they're apt to sting
And, as for crowns—the heavy thing
Would only hurt my head."

Sing ho! for our George Washington!
(At last I've got it straight.)
The first in war, the first in peace,
The goodly and the great.
But, when you think about him now,
From here to Valley Forge,
Remember this—he might have been
A highly different specimen,
And, where on earth would we be, then?
I'm glad that George was George.

PAUL REVERE'S RIDE
Henry Wadsworth Longfellow

Listen, my children, and you shall hear
Of the midnight ride of Paul Revere,
On the eighteenth of April, in Seventy-five;
Hardly a man is now alive
Who remembers that famous day and year.

He said to his friend, "If the British march
By land or sea from the town tonight,
Hang a lantern aloft in the belfry arch
Of the North Church tower as a signal light—
One, if by land, and two, if by sea;
And I on the opposite shore will be,
Ready to ride and spread the alarm
Through every Middlesex village and farm,
For the country folk to be up and to arm."

Then he said, "Good night!" and with muffled oar
Silently rowed to the Charlestown shore,
Just as the moon rose over the bay,
Where swinging wide at her moorings lay
The *Somerset*, British man-of-war;
A phantom ship, with each mast and spar
Across the moon like a prison bar,
And a huge black hulk, that was magnified
By its own reflection in the tide.

Meanwhile, his friend, through alley and street,
Wanders and watches, with eager ears,
Till in the silence around him he hears
The muster of men at the barrack door,
And the measured tread of the grenadiers,
Marching down to their boats on the shore.

Then he climbed to the tower of the Old North Church,
By the wooden stairs, with stealthy tread,
To the belfry-chamber overhead,
And startled the pigeons from their perch
On the somber rafters, that round him made
Masses and moving shapes of shade—
By the trembling ladder, steep and tall,
To the highest window in the wall,
Where he paused to listen and look down
A moment on the roofs of the town,
And the moonlight flowing over all.

Beneath in the churchyard, lay the dead,
In their night-encampment on the hill,
Wrapped in silence so deep and still
That he could hear, like a sentinel's tread,
The watchful night-wind, as it went
Creeping along from tent to tent,
And seeming to whisper, "All is well!"
A moment only he feels the spell
Of the place and the hour, and the secret dread
Of the lonely belfry and the dead;
For suddenly all his thoughts are bent
On a shadowy something far away,
Where the river widens to meet the bay—
A line of black that bends and floats
On the rising tide, like a bridge of boats.

Meanwhile, impatient to mount and ride,
Booted and spurred, with a heavy stride
On the opposite shore walked Paul Revere.
Now he patted his horse's side,
Now gazed at the landscape far and near,
Then, impetuous, stamped the earth,
And turned and tightened his saddle girth;
But mostly he watched with eager search
The belfry tower of the Old North Church,
As it rose above the graves on the hill,
Lonely and spectral and somber and still.

And lo! as he looks, on the belfry's height
A glimmer, and then a gleam of light!
He springs to the saddle, the bridle he turns,
But lingers and gazes, till full on his sight
A second lamp in the belfry burns!

A hurry of hoofs in a village street,
A shape in the moonlight, a bulk in the dark,
And beneath, from the pebbles, in passing, a spark
Struck out by a steed flying fearless and fleet:
That was all! And yet, through the gloom and the light,
The fate of a nation was riding that night;
And the spark struck out by that steed, in his flight,
Kindled the land into flame with its heat.

He has left the village and mounted the steep,
And beneath him, tranquil and broad and deep,
Is the Mystic, meeting the ocean tides;
And under the alders that skirt its edge,
Now soft on the sand, now loud on the ledge,
Is heard the tramp of his steed as he rides.

It was twelve by the village clock,
When he crossed the bridge into Medford town.
He heard the crowing of the cock,
And the barking of the farmer's dog,
And felt the damp of the river fog,
That rises after the sun goes down.
It was one by the village clock,
When he galloped into Lexington.
He saw the gilded weathercock
Swim in the moonlight as he passed,
And the meeting-house windows, blank and bare,
Gaze at him with a spectral glare,
As if they already stood aghast
At the bloody work they would look upon.

It was two by the village clock,
When he came to the bridge in Concord town.
He heard the bleating of the flock,
And the twitter of birds among the trees,
And felt the breath of the morning breeze
Blowing over the meadows brown.
And one was safe and asleep in his bed
Who at the bridge would be first to fall,
Who that day would be lying dead,
Pierced by a British musket-ball.

You know the rest. In the books you have read
How the British Regulars fired and fled—
How the farmers gave them ball for ball,
From behind each fence and farmyard wall,
Chasing the red-coats down the lane,
Then crossing the fields to emerge again
Under the trees at the turn of the road,
And only pausing to fire and load.

So through the night rode Paul Revere;
And so through the night went his cry of alarm
To every Middlesex village and farm—
A cry of defiance and not of fear,
A voice in the darkness, a knock at the door,
And a word that shall echo for evermore!
For, borne on the night-wind of the Past,
Through all our history, to the last,
In the hour of darkness and peril and need,
The people will awaken and listen to hear
The hurrying hoof-beats of that steed,
And the midnight message of Paul Revere.

CONCORD HYMN
Ralph Waldo Emerson

By the rude bridge that arched the flood,
    Their flag to April's breeze unfurled,
Here once the embattled farmers stood,
    And fired the shot heard round the world.

The foe long since in silence slept;
    Alike the conqueror silent sleeps;
And Time the ruined bridge has swept
    Down the dark stream which seaward creeps.

On this green bank, by this soft stream,
    We set today a votive stone;
That memory may their deed redeem,
    When, like our sires, our sons are gone.

Spirit, that made those heroes dare
    To die, and leave their children free,
Bid Time and Nature gently spare
    The shaft we raise to them and thee.

YANKEE DOODLE

Father and I went down to camp,
Along with Cap'n Goodwin,
And there we saw the men and boys,
As thick as hasty puddin'!

Yankee Doodle, keep it up,
Yankee Doodle dandy,
Mind the music and the step,
And with the girls be handy!

And there we see a thousand men,
As rich as Squire David;
And what they wasted ev'ry day,
I wish it could be saved.

And there I see a swamping gun,
Large as a log of maple,
Upon a deuced little cart,
A load for father's cattle.

And every time they shoot it off,
It takes a horn of powder,
And makes a noise like father's gun,
Only a nation louder.

I went as nigh to one myself,
As 'Siah's underpinning;
And father went as nigh ag'in,
I thought the deuce was in him.

We saw a little barrel, too,
The heads were made of leather;
They knocked upon it with little clubs,
And called the folks together.

And there they'd fife away like fun,
And play on cornstalk fiddles,
And some had ribbons red as blood,
All bound around their middles.

The troopers, too, would gallop up
And fire right in our faces;
It scared me almost to death
To see them run such races.

AMERICA
Samuel Francis Smith

My country, 'tis of thee,
Sweet land of liberty,
    Of thee I sing;
Land where my fathers died,
Land of the Pilgrims' pride,
From every mountain-side
    Let Freedom ring.

My native country, thee,
Land of the noble free—
　　Thy name I love;
I love thy rocks and rills,
Thy woods and templed hills:
My heart with rapture thrills
　　Like that above.

Let music swell the breeze,
And ring from all the trees
　　Sweet Freedom's song;
Let mortal tongues awake,
Let all that breathe partake,
Let rocks their silence break—
　　The sound prolong.

Our fathers' God, to Thee,
Author of liberty,
　　To Thee we sing;
Long may our land be bright
With Freedom's holy light;
Protect us by Thy might,
　　Great God, our King.

BENJAMIN FRANKLIN
Rosemary and Stephen Vincent Benét

Ben Franklin munched a loaf of bread while walking down the
　　street
And all the Philadelphia girls tee-heed to see him eat,
A country boy come up to town with eyes as big as saucers
At the ladies in their furbelows, the gempmun on their horses.

Ben Franklin wrote an almanac, a smile upon his lip,
It told you when to plant your corn and how to cure the pip,
But he salted it and seasoned it with proverbs sly and sage,
And people read "Poor Richard" till Poor Richard was the rage.

Ben Franklin made a pretty kite and flew it in the air
To call upon a thunderstorm that happened to be there,
—And all our humming dynamos and our electric light
Go back to what Ben Franklin found, the day he flew his kite.

Ben Franklin was the sort of man that people like to see,
For he was very clever but as human as could be.
He had an eye for pretty girls, a palate for good wine,
And all the court of France were glad to ask him in to dine.

But it didn't make him stuffy and he wasn't spoiled by fame
But stayed Ben Franklin to the end, as Yankee as his name.
"He wrenched their might from tyrants and its lightning from the
    sky."
And oh, when he saw pretty girls, he had a taking eye!

THOMAS JEFFERSON
Rosemary and Stephen Vincent Benét

Thomas Jefferson,
What do you say
Under the gravestone
Hidden away?

"I was a giver,
I was a molder,
I was a builder
With a strong shoulder."

Six feet and over,
Large-boned and ruddy,
The eyes grey-hazel
But bright with study.

The big hands clever
With pen and fiddle
And ready, ever,
For any riddle.

From buying empires
To planting 'taters,
From Declarations
To trick dumb-waiters.

"I liked the people,
The sweat and crowd of them,
Trusted them always
And spoke aloud of them.

"I liked all learning
And wished to share it
Abroad like pollen
For all who merit.

"I liked fine houses
With Greek pilasters,
And built them surely,
My touch a master's.

"I liked queer gadgets
And secret shelves,
And helping nations
To rule themselves.

"Jealous of others?
Not always candid?
But huge of vision
And open-handed.

"A wild-goose-chaser?
Now and again,
Build Monticello,
You little men!

"Design my plow, sirs,
They use it still,
Or found my college
At Charlottesville.

"And still go questing
New things and thinkers,
And keep as busy
As twenty thinkers."

"While always guarding
The people's freedom—
You need more hands, sir?
I didn't need 'em.

"They call you rascal?
They called me worse.
You'd do grand things, sir,
But lack the purse?

"I got no riches.
I died a debtor.
I died free-hearted
And that was better.

"For life was freakish
But life was fervent,
And I was always
Life's willing servant.

"Life, life's too weighty?
Too long a haul, sir?
I lived past eighty.
I liked it all, sir."

SONG OF THE SETTLERS
Jessamyn West

Freedom is a hard-bought thing—
A gift no man can give,
For some, a way of dying,
For most, a way to live.

Freedom is a hard-bought thing—
A rifle in the hand,
The horses hitched at sunup,
A harvest in the land.

Freedom is a hard-bought thing—
A massacre, a bloody rout,
The candles lit at nightfall,
And the night shut out.

Freedom is a hard-bought thing—
An arrow in the back,
The wind in the long corn rows,
And the hay in the rack.

Freedom is a way of living,
A song, a mighty cry.
Freedom is the bread we eat;
Let it be the way we die!

DANIEL BOONE
Arthur Guiterman

Daniel Boone at twenty-one
Came with his tomahawk, knife, and gun
Home from the French and Indian War
To North Carolina and the Yadkin shore.
He married his maid with a golden band,
Builded his house and cleared his land;
But the deep woods claimed their son again
And he turned his face from the homes of men.
Over the Blue Ridge, dark and lone,
The Mountains of Iron, the Hills of Stone,
Braving the Shawnee's jealous wrath,
He made his way on the Warrior's Path.

Alone he trod the shadowed trails;
But he was lord of a thousand vales
As he roved Kentucky, far and near,
Hunting the buffalo, elk, and deer.
What joy to see, what joy to win
So fair a land for his kith and kin,
Of streams unstained and woods unhewn!
"Elbow room!" laughed Daniel Boone.

On the Wilderness Road that his axmen made
The settlers flocked to the first stockade;
The deerskin shirts and the coonskin caps
Filed through the glens and the mountain gaps;
And hearts were high in the fateful spring
When the land said "Nay!" to the stubborn king.
While the men of the East of farm and town
Strove with the troops of the British Crown,
Daniel Boone from a surge of hate
Guarded a nation's westward gate.
Down in the fort in a wave of flame
The Shawnee horde and the Mingo came,
And the stout logs shook in a storm of lead;
But Boone stood firm and the savage fled.
Peace! And the settlers flocked anew,
The farm lands spread, the town lands grew;
But Daniel Boone was ill at ease
When he saw the smoke in his forest trees.
"There'll be no game in the country soon.
Elbow room!" cried Daniel Boone.

Straight as a pine at sixty-five—
Time enough for a man to thrive—
He launched his bateau on Ohio's breast
And his heart was glad as he oared it west;
There was kindly folk and his own true blood
Where great Missouri rolls his flood;
New woods, new streams, and room to spare,
And Daniel Boone found comfort there.

Yet far he ranged toward the sunset still,
Where the Kansas runs and the Smoky Hill,
And the prairies toss, by the south wind blown;
And he killed his bear on the Yellowstone.
But ever he dreamed of new domains
With vaster woods and wider plains;
Ever he dreamed of a world-to-be
Where there are no bounds and the soul is free.
At fourscore-five, still stout and hale,
He heard a call to a farther trail;
So he turned his face where the stars are strewn;
"Elbow room!" sighed Daniel Boone.

Down the Milky Way in its banks of blue
Far he has paddled his white canoe
To the splendid quest of the tameless soul—
He has reached the goal where there is no goal.
Now he rides and rides an endless trail
On the hippogriff of the flaming tail
Or the horse of the stars with the golden mane,
As he rode the first of the blue-grass strain.
The joy that lies in the search he seeks
On breathless hills with crystal peaks;
He makes his camp on heights untrod,
The steps of the shrine, alone with God.
Through the woods of the vast, on the plains of space
He hunts the pride of the mammoth race
And the dinosaur of the triple horn,
The manticore and the unicorn,
As once by the broad Missouri's flow
He followed the elk and the buffalo.
East of the sun and west of the moon,
"Elbow room!" laughs Daniel Boone.

JOHNNY APPLESEED
FROM JOHNNY APPLESEED
Vachel Lindsay

1.

"Johnny Appleseed, Johnny Appleseed,"
Chief of the fastnesses, dappled and vast,
In a pack on his back,
In a deer-hide sack,
The beautiful orchards of the past,
The ghosts of all the forests and the groves—
In that pack on his back,
In that talisman sack,
Tomorrow's peaches, pears and cherries,
Tomorrow's grapes and red raspberries,
Seeds and tree-souls, precious things.

2.

Hawthorn and crab-thorn bent, rain-wet,
And dropped their flowers in his night-black hair;
And the soft fawns stopped for his perorations;
And his black eyes shone through the forest-gleam,
And he plunged young hands into the new-turned earth,
And prayed dear orchard boughs into birth;
And he ran with the rabbit and slept with the stream,
And he ran with the rabbit and slept with the stream,
And he ran with the rabbit and slept with the stream,
And so for us he made great medicine,
And so for us he made great medicine,
And so for us he made great medicine,
In the days of President Washington.

THE OREGON TRAIL: 1843
Arthur Guiterman

Two hundred wagons, rolling out to Oregon,
   Breaking through the gopher holes, lurching wide and free,
Crawling up the mountain pass, jolting, grumbling, rumbling on,
   Two hundred wagons, rolling to the sea.

From East and South and North they flock, to muster, row on row,
A fleet of tenscore prairie ships beside Missouri's flow.
The bullwhips crack, the oxen strain, the canvas-hooded files
Are off upon the long, long trail of sixteen hundred miles.

The women hold the guiding lines; beside the rocking steers
With goad and ready rifle walk the bearded pioneers
Through clouds of dust beneath the sun, through floods of sweeping
    rain
Cross the Kansas prairie land, across Nebraska's plain.

Two hundred wagons, rolling out to Oregon,
   Curved round the campfire flame at halt when day is done,
Rest awhile beneath the stars, yoke again and lumber on,
   Two hundred wagons, rolling with the sun.

Among the barren buttes they wind beneath the jealous view
Of Blackfoot, Pawnee, Omaha, Arapahoe, and Sioux.
No savage threat may check their course, no river deep and wide;
They swim the Platte, they ford the Snake, they cross the Great
    Divide.

They march as once from India's vales through Asia's mountain
    door
With shield and spear on Europe's plain their fathers marched be-
    fore.
They march where leap the antelope and storm the buffalo
Still westward as their fathers marched ten thousand years ago.

Two hundred wagons, rolling out to Oregon,
   Creeping down the dark defile below the mountain crest,
Surging through the brawling stream, lunging, plunging, forging on,
   Two hundred wagons, rolling toward the West.

Now toils the dusty caravan with swinging wagon-poles
Where Walla Walla pours along, where broad Columbia rolls.
The long-haired trapper's face grows dark and scowls the painted
    brave;
Where now the beaver builds his dam the wheat and rye shall wave.

The British trader shakes his head and weighs his nation's loss,
For where those hardy settlers come the Stars and Stripes will toss.
Then block the wheels, unyoke the steers; the prize is his who dares;
The cabins rise, the fields are sown, and Oregon is theirs!

        They will take, they will hold,
        By the spade in the mold,
        By the seed in the soil,
        By the sweat and the toil,
        By the plow in the loam,
        By the school and the home!

Two hundred wagons, rolling out to Oregon,
   Two hundred wagons, ranging free and far,
Two hundred wagons, rumbling, grumbling, rolling on,
   Two hundred wagons, following a star!

THE FLOWER-FED BUFFALOES
Vachel Lindsay

        The flower-fed buffaloes of the spring
        In the days of long ago,
        Ranged where the locomotives sing
        And the prairie flowers lie low;
        The tossing, blooming, perfumed grass
        Is swept away by wheat,
        Wheels and wheels and wheels spin by
        In the spring that still is sweet.
        But the flower-fed buffaloes of the spring
        Left us long ago.

433

They gore no more, they bellow no more,
They trundle around the hills no more:—
With the Blackfeet lying low,
With the Pawnees lying low.

THE COWBOY
John Antrobus

"What care I, what cares he,
What cares the world of the life we know?
Little they reck of the shadowless plains,
The shelterless mesa, the sun and the rains,
The wild, free life, as the winds that blow."
  With his broad sombrero,
  His worn chaparajos,
    And clinking spurs,
  Like a Centaur he speeds,
  Where the wild bull feeds;
And he laughs, ha, ha!—who cares, who cares!

Ruddy and brown—careless and free—
A king in the saddle—he rides at will
O'er the measureless range where rarely change
The swart gray plains so weird and strange,
Treeless, and streamless, and wondrous still!
  With his slouch sombrero,
  His torn chaparajos,
    And clinking spurs,
  Like a Centaur he speeds,
  Where the wild bull feeds;
And he laughs, ha, ha!—who cares, who cares!

Swift and strong, and ever alert,
Yet sometimes he rests on the dreary vast;
And his thoughts, like the thoughts of other men
Go back to his childhood days again,
And to many a loved one in the past.

434

With his gay sombrero,
His rude chaparajos,
    And clinking spurs,
He rests a while,
With a tear and a smile,
Then he laughs, ha, ha!—who cares, who cares!

WHOOPEE TI YI YO, GIT ALONG, LITTLE DOGIES
John A. Lomax

As I walked out one morning for pleasure,
I spied a cowpuncher a-ridin' alone;
His hat was throwed back and his spurs was a-jinglin',
As he approached me a-singin' this song,

> *Whoopee ti yi yo, git along, little dogies,*
> *It's your misfortune, and none of my own.*
> *Whoopee ti yi yo, git along, little dogies,*
> *For you know Wyoming will be your new home.*

Early in the spring we round up the dogies,
Mark 'em and brand 'em and bob off their tails;
Round up our horses, load up the chuck-wagon,
Then throw the dogies upon the old trail.

It's whooping and yelling and driving the dogies;
Oh, how I wish you would go on!
It's whooping and punching and "Go on little dogies,
For you know Wyoming will be your new home."

Some boys goes up the trail for pleasure,
But that's where you get it most awfully wrong;
For you haven't any idea the trouble they give us
While we go driving them all along.

When the night comes on and we hold them on the bedground,
These little dogies that roll on so slow;
Roll up the herd and cut out the strays,
And roll the little dogies that never rolled before.

Your mother she was raised way down in Texas,
Where the jimson weed and sandburs grow;
Now we'll fill you up on prickly pear and cholla
Till you are ready for the trail to Idaho.

Oh, you'll be soup for Uncle Sam's Injuns,—
It's "beef, heap beef," I hear them cry.
Git along, git along, git along, little dogies,
You're going to be beef steers by and by.

>   *Whoopee ti yi yo, git along, little dogies,*
>   *It's your misfortune, and none of my own.*
>   *Whoopee ti yi yo, git along, little dogies,*
>   *For you know Wyoming will be your new home.*

SPANISH JOHNNY
Willa Cather

The old West, the old time,
   The old wind singing through
The red, red grass a thousand miles—
   And, Spanish Johnny, you!
He'd sit beside the water ditch
   When all his herd was in,
And never mind a child, but sing
   To his mandolin.

The big stars, the blue night,
   The moon-enchanted lane;
The olive man who never spoke,
   But sang the songs of Spain.
His speech with men was wicked talk—
   To hear it was a sin;
But those were golden things he said
   To his mandolin.

The gold songs, the gold stars,
　　The word so golden then;
And the hand so tender to a child—
　　Had killed so many men.
He died a hard death long ago
　　Before the Road came in—
The night before he swung, he sang
　　To his mandolin.

THE RAILROAD CARS ARE COMING

The great Pacific railway,
　　For California hail!
Bring on the locomotive,
　　Lay down the iron rail;
Across the rolling prairies
　　By steam we're bound to go,
The railroad cars are coming, humming
　　Through New Mexico,
The railroad cars are coming, humming
　　Through New Mexico.

The little dogs in dog-town
　　Will wag each little tail;
They'll think that something's coming
　　A-riding on a rail.
The rattlesnake will show its fangs,
　　The owl tu-whit, tu-who,
The railroad cars are coming, humming
　　Through New Mexico,
The railroad cars are coming, humming
　　Through New Mexico.

NANCY HANKS
Rosemary and Stephen Vincent Benét

If Nancy Hanks
Came back as a ghost,
Seeking news
Of what she loved most,
She'd ask first
"Where's my son?
What's happened to Abe?
What's he done?

"Poor little Abe,
Left all alone
Except for Tom,
Who's a rolling stone;
He was only nine
The year I died.
I remember still
How hard he cried.

"Scraping along
In a little shack,
With hardly a shirt
To cover his back,
And a prairie wind
To blow him down,
Or pinching times
If he went to town.

"You wouldn't know
About my son?
Did he grow tall?
Did he have fun?
Did he learn to read?
Did he get to town?
Do you know his name?
Did he get on?"

LINCOLN
Nancy Byrd Turner

There was a boy of other days,
A quiet, awkward, earnest lad,
Who trudged long weary miles to get
A book on which his heart was set—
And then no candle had!

He was too poor to buy a lamp
But very wise in woodmen's ways.
He gathered seasoned bough and stem,
And crisping leaf, and kindled them
Into a ruddy blaze.

Then as he lay full length and read,
The firelight flickered on his face,
And etched his shadow on the gloom,
And made a picture in the room,
In that most humble place.

The hard years came, the hard years went,
But, gentle, brave, and strong of will,
He met them all. And when today
We see his pictured face, we say,
"There's light upon it still."

DIXIE
FROM DIXIE
Daniel Decatur Emmett

I wish I was in de land ob cotton,
Old times dar am not forgotten;
    Look away, look away, look away, Dixie land!
In Dixie land whar I was born in,
Early on one frosty mornin',
    Look away, look away, look away, Dixie land!

439

Den I wish I was in Dixie! Hooray! Hooray!
In Dixie's land we'll take our stand, to lib an' die in Dixie,
Away, away, away down south in Dixie!
Away, away, away down south in Dixie!

Dis world was made in jis' six days,
An' finished up in various ways.
    Look away! look away! look away! Dixie land!
Dey den make Dixie trim and nice,
And Adam called it "Paradise."
    Look away! look away! look away! Dixie land!

Dar's buckwheat cakes and Injun batter,
Makes you fat er a little fatter;
    Look away, look away, look away, Dixie land!
Den hoe it down an' scratch your grabbel,
To Dixie's land I'm bound to trabbel;
    Look away, look away, look away, Dixie land!

NEGRO SPIRITUALS
Rosemary and Stephen Vincent Benét

We do not know who made them.
The lips that gave them birth
Are dust in the slaves' burying ground,
Anonymous as earth.

The poets, the musicians,
Were bondsmen bred and born.
They picked the master's cotton,
They hoed the master's corn.

The load was heavy on their backs,
The way was long and cold,
—But out of stolen Africa,
The singing river rolled,
And David's hands were dusky hands,
But David's harp was gold.

SWING LOW, SWEET CHARIOT
A Negro Spiritual

I looked over Jordan an' what did I see,
    Comin' for to carry me home,
A band of angels comin' after me,
    Comin' for to carry me home.

    Swing low, sweet chariot,
    Comin' for to carry me home,
    Swing low, sweet chariot,
    Comin' for to carry me home.

If you get there before I do,
    Comin' for to carry me home,
Tell all my friends I'm comin' there too,
    Comin' for to carry me home.

    Swing low, sweet chariot,
    Comin' for to carry me home,
    Swing low, sweet chariot,
    Comin' for to carry me home.

BATTLE-HYMN OF THE REPUBLIC
Julia Ward Howe

Mine eyes have seen the glory of the coming of the Lord;
He is trampling out the vintage where the grapes of wrath are stored;
He hath loosed the fateful lightning of His terrible swift sword;
    His truth is marching on.

I have seen Him in the watch-fires of a hundred circling camps;
They have builded Him an altar in the evening dews and damps;
I can read His righteous sentence by the dim and flaring lamps;
    His day is marching on.

441

I have read a fiery gospel, writ in burnished rows of steel:
"As ye deal with my contemners, so with you my grace shall deal;
Let the Hero, born of woman, crush the serpent with his heel,
    Since God is marching on."

He has sounded forth the trumpet that shall never call retreat;
He is sifting out the hearts of men before His judgment-seat:
Oh, be swift, my soul, to answer Him! be jubilant my feet!
    Our God is marching on.

In the beauty of the lilies Christ was born across the sea,
With a glory in His bosom that transfigures you and me;
As He died to make men holy, let us die to make men free,
    While God is marching on.

BARBARA FRIETCHIE
John Greenleaf Whittier

Up from the meadows rich with corn,
Clear in the cool September morn,

The clustered spires of Frederick stand
Green-walled by the hills of Maryland.

Round about them orchards sweep,
Apple and peach tree fruited deep,

Fair as the garden of the Lord
To the eyes of the famished rebel horde,

On that pleasant morn of the early fall
When Lee marched over the mountain-wall;

Over the mountains winding down,
Horse and foot, into Frederick town.

Forty flags with their silver stars,
Forty flags with their crimson bars,

Flapped in the morning wind; the sun
Of noon looked down and saw not one.

Up rose old Barbara Frietchie then,
Bowed with her fourscore years and ten;

Bravest of all in Frederick town,
She took up the flag the men hauled down;

In her attic window the staff she set,
To show that one heart was loyal yet.

Up the street came the rebel tread,
Stonewall Jackson riding ahead.

Under his slouched hat left and right
He glanced; the old flag met his sight.

"Halt!"—the dust-brown ranks stood fast.
"Fire!"—out blazed the rifle-blast.

It shivered the window, pane and sash;
It rent the banner with seam and gash.

Quick, as it fell, from the broken staff
Dame Barbara snatched the silken scarf.

She leaned far out on the window-sill,
And shook it forth with a royal will.

"Shoot, if you must, this old gray head,
But spare your country's flag," she said.

A shade of sadness, a blush of shame,
Over the face of the leader came;

The nobler nature within him stirred
To life at that woman's deed and word;

"Who touches a hair of yon gray head
Dies like a dog! March on!" he said.

All day long through Frederick street
Sounded the tread of marching feet:

All day long that free flag tossed
Over the heads of the rebel host.

Ever its torn folds rose and fell
On the loyal winds that loved it well;

And through the hill-gaps sunset light
Shone over it with a warm good-night.

Barbara Frietchie's work is o'er,
And the Rebel rides on his raids no more.

Honor to her! and let a tear
Fall, for her sake, on Stonewall's bier.

Over Barbara Frietchie's grave,
Flag of Freedom and Union, wave!

Peace and order and beauty draw
Round thy symbol of light and law;

And ever the stars above look down
On thy stars below in Frederick town!

THE FLAG GOES BY
Henry Holcomb Bennett

Hats off!
Along the street there comes
A blare of bugles, a ruffle of drums,
A flash of color beneath the sky:
Hats off!
The flag is passing by!

Blue and crimson and white it shines,
Over the steel-tipped, ordered lines.
Hats off!
The colors before us fly;
But more than the flag is passing by:
Sea-fights and land-fights, grim and great,
Fought to make and to save the State;
Weary marches and sinking ships;
Cheers of victory on dying lips;

Days of plenty and years of peace;
March of a strong land's swift increase;
Equal justice, right and law,
Stately honor and reverend awe;

Sign of a nation great and strong
To ward her people from foreign wrong;
Pride and glory and honor—all
Live in the colors to stand or fall.

　Hats off!
Along the street there comes
A blare of bugles, a ruffle of drums;
And loyal hearts are beating high:
　Hats off!
The flag is passing by!

THE GETTYSBURG ADDRESS
DELIVERED AT GETTYSBURG, PENNSYLVANIA
NOVEMBER 19, 1863
Abraham Lincoln

Fourscore and seven years ago
our fathers brought forth upon this continent
a new nation,
conceived in liberty,
and dedicated to the proposition
that all men are created equal.
Now we are engaged in a great civil war,
testing whether that nation,
or any nation so conceived and so dedicated,
can long endure.
We are met on a great battlefield
of that war.

We have come to dedicate
a portion of that field
as a final resting place
for those who here gave their lives
that that nation might live.
It is altogether fitting and proper
that we should do this.
But in a larger sense
we cannot dedicate,
we cannot consecrate,
we cannot hallow this ground.
The brave men, living and dead,
who struggled here,
have consecrated it
far above our poor power to add or detract.
The world will little note,
nor long remember,
what we say here;
but it can never forget
what they did here.
It is for us, the living,
rather to be dedicated here
to the unfinished work
which they who fought here
have thus far so nobly advanced.
It is rather for us to be here dedicated
to the great task remaining before us,
that from these honored dead
we take increased devotion
to that cause for which they gave
the last full measure of devotion;
that we here highly resolve
that these dead shall not have died in vain;
that this nation, under God,
shall have a new birth of freedom,
and that government
of the people, by the people, and for the people,
shall not perish from the earth.

O CAPTAIN! MY CAPTAIN!
Walt Whitman

O Captain! my Captain! our fearful trip is done,
The ship has weather'd every rack, the prize we sought is won,
   The port is near, the bells I hear, the people all exulting,
   While follow eyes the steady keel, the vessel grim and daring;

        But O heart! heart! heart!
          O the bleeding drops of red,
        Where on the deck my Captain lies,
          Fallen cold and dead.

O Captain! my Captain! rise up and hear the bells;
Rise up—for you the flag is flung—for you the bugle trills,
   For you bouquets and ribbon'd wreaths—for you the shores
     a-crowding,
   For you they call, the swaying mass, their eager faces turning;

        Here, Captain! dear father!
          This arm beneath your head!
        It is some dream that on the deck,
          You've fallen cold and dead.

My Captain does not answer, his lips are pale and still,
My father does not feel my arm, he has no pulse nor will,
   The ship is anchor'd safe and sound, its voyage closed and done,
   From fearful trip the victor ship comes in with object won;

        Exult, O shores! and ring, O bells!
          But I, with mournful tread,
        Walk the deck my Captain lies,
          Fallen cold and dead.

THE NEW COLOSSUS
ENGRAVED ON A PLAQUE IN THE STATUE OF LIBERTY
Emma Lazarus

Not like the brazen giant of Greek fame,
With conquering limbs astride from land to land;
Here at our sea-washed, sunset gates shall stand
A mighty woman with a torch, whose flame
Is the imprisoned lightning, and her name
Mother of Exiles. From her beacon-hand
Glows world-wide welcome; her mild eyes command
The air-bridged harbor that twin cities frame.
"Keep, ancient lands, your storied pomp!" cries she
With silent lips. "Give me your tired, your poor,
Your huddled masses yearning to breathe free,
The wretched refuse of your teeming shore.
Send these, the homeless, tempest-tost to me,
I lift my lamp beside the golden door!"

I AM AN AMERICAN
Elias Lieberman

I am an American.
My father belongs to the Sons of the Revolution;
My mother, to the Colonial Dames.
One of my ancestors pitched tea overboard in Boston Harbor;
Another stood his ground with Warren;
Another hungered with Washington at Valley Forge.
My forefathers were America in the making:
They spoke in her council halls;
They died on her battle-fields;
They commanded her ships;
They cleared her forests.
Dawns reddened and paled.
Staunch hearts of mine beat fast at each new star
In the nation's flag.

Keen eyes of mine foresaw her greater glory:
The sweep of her seas,
The plenty of her plains,
The man-hives in her billion-wired cities.
Every drop of blood in me holds a heritage of patriotism.
I am proud of my past.
I am an AMERICAN.

I am an American.
My father was an atom of dust,
My mother a straw in the wind,
To His Serene Majesty.
One of my ancestors died in the mines of Siberia;
Another was crippled for life by twenty blows of the knout.
Another was killed defending his home during the massacres.
The history of my ancestors is a trail of blood
To the palace-gate of the Great White Czar.
But then the dream came—
The dream of America.
In the light of the Liberty torch
The atom of dust became a man
And the straw in the wind became a woman
For the first time.
"See," said my father, pointing to the flag that fluttered near,
"That flag of stars and stripes is yours;
It is the emblem of the promised land.
It means, my son, the hope of humanity.
Live for it—die for it!"
Under the open sky of my new country I swore to do so;
And every drop of blood in me will keep that vow.
I am proud of my future.
I am an AMERICAN.

INDIAN NAMES
Lydia Huntley Sigourney

Ye say they all have passed away,
    That noble race and brave;
That their light canoes have vanished
    From off the crested wave;
That, mid the forests where they roamed,
    There rings no hunters' shout;
But their name is on your waters,
    Ye may not wash it out.

'Tis where Ontario's billow
    Like ocean's surge is curled,
Where strong Niagara's thunders wake
    The echo of the world,
Where red Missouri bringeth
    Rich tribute from the west,
And Rappahannock sweetly sleeps
    On green Virginia's breast.

Ye say their conelike cabins,
    That clustered o'er the vale,
Have disappeared, as withered leaves
    Before the autumn's gale;
But their memory liveth on your hills,
    Their baptism on your shore,
Your everlasting rivers speak
    Their dialect of yore.

Old Massachusetts wears it
    Within her lordly crown,
And broad Ohio bears it
    Amid his young renown.
Connecticut hath wreathed it
    Where her quiet foliage waves,
And bold Kentucky breathes it hoarse
    Through all her ancient caves.

Wachusett hides its lingering voice
   Within its rocky heart,
And Alleghany graves its tone
   Throughout his lofty chart.
Monadnock, on his forehead hoar,
   Doth seal the sacred trust,
Your mountains build their monument,
   Though ye destroy their dust.

I HEAR AMERICA SINGING
Walt Whitman

I hear America singing, the varied carols I hear,
Those of mechanics, each one singing his as it should be, blithe and
   strong.
The carpenter singing his as he measures his plank or beam,
The mason singing as he makes ready for work, or leaves off work,
The boatman singing what belongs to him in the boat, the deckhand
   singing on the steamboat deck,
The shoemaker singing as he sits on his bench, the hatter singing
   as he stands,

The woodcutter's song, the ploughboy's on his way in the morning,
   or at noon intermission, or at sundown,
The delicious singing of the mother, or of the young wife at work,
   or of the girl singing or washing,
Each singing what belongs to him or her and to none else,
The day that belongs to the day—at night the party of young fellows,
   robust, friendly,
Singing with open mouths their strong, melodious songs.

A NATION'S STRENGTH
Ralph Waldo Emerson

> Not gold, but only man can make
>   A people great and strong;
> Men who, for truth and honor's sake,
>   Stand fast and suffer long.
>
> Brave men who work while others sleep,
>   Who dare while others fly—
> They build a nation's pillars deep
>   And lift them to the sky.

WASHINGTON MONUMENT BY NIGHT
Carl Sandburg

1

The stone goes straight.
A lean swimmer dives into night sky,
Into half-moon mist.

2

Two trees are coal black.
This is a great white ghost between.
It is cool to look at.
Strong men, strong women, come here.

3

Eight years is a long time
To be fighting all the time.

4

The republic is a dream.
Nothing happens unless first a dream.

5

The wind bit hard at Valley Forge one Christmas.
Soldiers tied rags on their feet.
Red footprints wrote on the snow . . .
. . . and stone shoots into stars here
. . . into half-moon mist tonight.

6

Tongues wrangled dark at a man.
He buttoned his overcoat and stood alone.
In a snowstorm, red hollyberries, thoughts, he stood alone.

7

Women said: He is lonely
. . . fighting . . . fighting . . . eight years . . .

8

The name of an iron man goes over the world.
It takes a long time to forget an iron man.

ABRAHAM LINCOLN WALKS AT MIDNIGHT
IN SPRINGFIELD, ILLINOIS
Vachel Lindsay

It is portentous, and a thing of state
    That here at midnight, in our little town
A mourning figure walks, and will not rest,
    Near the old courthouse pacing up and down,

Or by his homestead, or in shadowed yards
    He lingers where his children used to play,
Or through the market, on the well-worn stones,
    He stalks until the dawn-stars burn away.

A bronzed, lank man! His suit of ancient black,
    A famous high top-hat and plain, worn shawl
Make him the quaint great figure that men love,
    The prairie lawyer, master of us all.

He cannot sleep upon his hillside now,
    He is among us—as in times before!
And we who toss and lie awake for long,
    Breathe deep, and start, to see him pass the door.

His head is bowed. He thinks of men and kings.
    Yea, when the sick world cries, how can he sleep?
Too many peasants fight, they know not why;
    Too many homesteads in black terror weep.

The sins of all the war-lords burn his heart.
    He sees the dreadnaughts scouring every main.
He carries on his shawl-wrapped shoulders now
    The bitterness, the folly, and the pain.

He cannot rest until a spirit-dawn
    Shall come—the shining hope of Europe free:
The league of sober folk, the Workers' earth,
    Bringing long peace to Cornland, Alp and Sea.

It breaks his heart that kings must murder still,
    That all his hours of travail here for men
Seem yet in vain. And who will bring white peace
    That he may sleep upon his hill again?

SAIL ON, O SHIP OF STATE!

FROM THE BUILDING OF THE SHIP

Henry Wadsworth Longfellow

Thou, too, sail on, O Ship of State!
Sail on, O Union, strong and great!
Humanity with all its fears,
With all its hopes of future years,
Is hanging breathless on thy fate!
We know what Master laid thy keel,
What Workmen wrought thy ribs of steel,
Who made each mast, and sail, and rope,
What anvils rang, what hammers beat,
In what a forge and what a heat
Were shaped the anchors of thy hope!
Fear not each sudden sound and shock,
'Tis of the wave and not the rock;
'Tis but the flapping of the sail,
And not a rent made by a gale!
In spite of rock and tempest's roar,
In spite of false lights on the shore,
Sail on, nor fear to breast the sea!
Our hearts, our hopes, are all with thee,
Our hearts, our hopes, our prayers, our tears,
Our faith, triumphant o'er our fears,
Are all with thee,—are all with thee!

From all the world
to me

TRAVEL
Robert Louis Stevenson

I should like to rise and go
Where the golden apples grow;
Where below another sky
Parrot Islands anchored lie,
And, watched by cockatoos and goats,
Lonely Crusoes building boats;
Where in sunshine reaching out
Eastern cities, miles about,
Are with mosque and minaret
Among sandy gardens set,
And the rich goods from near and far
Hang for sale in the bazaar;
Where the Great Wall round China goes,
And on one side the desert blows,
And with bell and voice and drum,
Cities on the other hum;
Where are forests, hot as fire,
Wide as England, tall as a spire,
Full of apes and coconuts
And the Negro hunters' huts;
Where the knotty crocodile
Lies and blinks in the Nile,
And the red flamingo flies
Hunting fish before his eyes;

Where in jungles, near and far,
Man-devouring tigers are,
Lying close and giving ear
Lest the hunt be drawing near,
Or a comer-by be seen
Swinging in a palanquin;
Where among the desert sands
Some deserted city stands,
All its children, sweep and prince,
Grown to manhood ages since,
Not a foot in street or house,
Not a stir of child or mouse,
And when kindly falls the night,
In all the town no spark of light.
There I'll come when I'm a man
With a camel caravan;
Light a fire in the gloom
Of some dusty dining room;
See the pictures on the walls,
Heroes, fights, and festivals;
And in a corner find the toys
Of the old Egyptian boys.

FROM ENGLAND:
HOME THOUGHTS FROM ABROAD
Robert Browning

Oh! to be in England
   Now that April's there,
And whoever wakes in England
   Sees, some morning, unaware,
That the lowest boughs and the brushwood sheaf
Round the elm-tree bole are in tiny leaf,
While the chaffinch sings on the orchard bough
In England—now!

And after April, when May follows,
And the whitethroat builds, and all the swallows—
Hark! where my blossomed pear-tree in the hedge
   Leans to the field and scatters on the clover
Blossoms and dew-drops—at the bent spray's edge—
   That's the wise thrush; he sings each song twice over,
Lest you should think he never could recapture
The first fine careless rapture!
And though the fields look rough with hoary dew,
All will be gay when noon-tide wakes anew
The buttercups, the little children's dower—
Far brighter than this gaudy melon-flower.

A SONG OF SHERWOOD
Alfred Noyes

Sherwood in the twilight, is Robin Hood awake?
Gray and ghostly shadows are gliding through the brake,
Shadows of the dappled deer, dreaming of the morn,
Dreaming of a shadowy man that winds a shadowy horn.

Robin Hood is here again: all his merry thieves
Hear a ghostly bugle-note shivering through the leaves,
Calling as he used to call, faint and far away,
In Sherwood, in Sherwood, about the break of day.

Merry, merry England has kissed the lips of June:
All the wings of fairyland were here beneath the moon,
Like a flight of rose-leaves fluttering in a mist
Of opal and ruby and pearl and amethyst.

Merry, merry England is waking as of old,
With eyes of blither hazel and hair of brighter gold:
For Robin Hood is here again beneath the bursting spray
In Sherwood, in Sherwood, about the break of day.

461

Love is in the greenwood building him a house
Of wild rose and hawthorn and honeysuckle boughs;
Love is in the greenwood; dawn is in the skies;
And Marian is waiting with a glory in her eyes.

Hark! The dazzled laverock climbs the golden steep!
Marian is waiting: is Robin Hood asleep?
Round the fairy grass-rings frolic elf and fay,
In Sherwood, in Sherwood, about the break of day.

Oberon, Oberon, rake away the gold,
Rake away the red leaves, roll away the mould,
Rake away the gold leaves, roll away the red,
And wake Will Scarlett from his leafy forest bed.

Friar Tuck and Little John are riding down together
With quarter-staff and drinking-can and gray goose-feather.
The dead are coming back again; the years are rolled away
In Sherwood, in Sherwood, about the break of day.

Softly over Sherwood the south wind blows.
All the heart of England hid in every rose
Hears across the greenwood the sunny whisper leap,
Sherwood in the red dawn, is Robin Hood asleep?

Hark, the voice of England wakes him as of old
And, shattering the silence with a cry of brighter gold,
Bugles in the greenwood echo from the steep,
Sherwood in the red dawn, is Robin Hood asleep?

Where the deer are gliding down the shadowy glen
All across the glades of fern he calls his merry men—
Doublets of the Lincoln green glancing through the May
In Sherwood, in Sherwood, about the break of day—

Calls them and they answer: from aisles of oak and ash
Rings the *Follow! Follow!* and the boughs begin to crash;
The ferns begin to flutter and the flowers begin to fly;
And through the crimson dawning the robber band goes by.

Robin! Robin! Robin! All his merry thieves
Answer as the bugle-note shivers through the leaves;
Calling as he used to call, faint and far away,
In Sherwood, in Sherwood, about the break of day.

FROM SCOTLAND:
LULLABY OF AN INFANT CHIEF
Walter Scott

O, hush thee, my baby, thy sire was a knight,
Thy mother a lady, both lovely and bright;
The woods and the glens, from the towers which we see,
They all are belonging, dear baby, to thee.

O, fear not the bugle, though loudly it blows,
It calls but the warders that guard thy repose;
Their bows would be bended, their blades would be red,
Ere the step of a foeman draws near to thy bed.

O, hush thee, my baby, the time soon will come,
When thy sleep shall be broken by trumpet and drum;
Then hush thee, my darling, take rest while you may,
For strife comes with manhood, and waking with day.

FROM SCOTLAND:
MY HEART'S IN THE HIGHLANDS
Robert Burns

My heart's in the Highlands, my heart is not here;
My heart's in the Highlands a-chasing the deer;
Chasing the wild deer, and following the roe,
My heart's in the Highlands wherever I go.

Farewell to the Highlands, farewell to the North,
The birthplace of valour, the country of worth;
Wherever I wander, wherever I rove,
The hills of the Highlands forever I love.

Farewell to the mountains high covered with snow;
Farewell to the straths and green valleys below;
Farewell to the forests and wild-hanging woods;
Farewell to the torrents and loud-pouring floods.

My heart's in the Highlands, my heart is not here;
My heart's in the Highlands, a-chasing the deer;
Chasing the wild deer, and following the roe,
My heart's in the Highlands wherever I go!

FROM IRELAND:
THE LAKE ISLE OF INNISFREE
W. B. Yeats

I will arise and go now, and go to Innisfree,
And a small cabin build there, of clay and wattles made;
Nine bean rows will I have there, a hive for the honey bee,
        And live alone in the bee-loud glade.

And I shall have some peace there, for peace comes dropping slow,
Dropping from the veils of the morning to where the cricket sings;
There midnight's all a glimmer, and noon a purple glow,
        And evening full of the linnet's wings.

I will arise and go now, for always night and day
I hear lake waters lapping with low sounds by the shore;
While I stand on the roadway, or on the pavements gray,
        I hear it in the deep heart's core.

A PIPER
Seumas O'Sullivan

> A piper in the streets today
> Set up, and tuned, and started to play,
> And away, away, away on the tide
> Of his music we started; on every side
> Doors and windows were opened wide,
> And men left down their work and came,
> And women with petticoats colored like flame,
> And little bare feet that were blue with cold,
> Went dancing back to the age of gold,
> And all the world went gay, went gay,
> For half an hour in the street today.

FROM WALES:
WE WHO WERE BORN
Eiluned Lewis

> We who were born
> In country places
> Far from cities
> And shifting faces,
> We have a birthright
> No man can sell,
> And a secret joy
> No man can tell.
>
> For we are kindred
> To lordly things:
> The wild duck's flight
> And the white owl's wings,
> The pike and the salmon,
> The bull and the horse,
> The curlew's cry
> And the smell of gorse.

Pride of trees,
Swiftness of streams,
Magic of frost
Have shaped our dreams.
No baser vision
Their spirit fills
Who walk by right
On the naked hills.

ALL THROUGH THE NIGHT

Sleep, my babe, lie still and slumber,
All through the night,
Guardian angels God will lend thee,
All through the night;
Soft, the drowsy hours are creeping,
Hill and vale in slumber steeping,
Mother, dear, her watch is keeping,
All through the night.

CRADLE SONG
Carl Michael Bellman

Lullaby, my little one,
   Go to sleep, little baby.
Pussy's playing in the sun;
   Go to sleep, little baby.
Mama's busy spinning yarn,
Daddy's working in the barn,
   Lullaby, my baby.

THE TREE
Björnstjerne Björnson
Translated by Professor Palmer

The tree's early leaf buds were bursting their brown:
"Shall I take them away?" said the frost, sweeping down.
    "No, dear; leave them alone
    Till blossoms here have grown,"
Prayed the tree, while it trembled from rootlet to crown.

The tree bore its blossoms, and all the birds sung:
"Shall I take them away?" said the wind, as it swung.
    "No, dear; leave them alone
    Till berries here have grown,"
Said the tree, while its leaflets quivering hung.

The tree bore its fruit in the midsummer glow:
Said the girl, "May I gather thy berries or no?"
    "Yes, dear, all thou canst see;
    Take them; all are for thee,"
Said the tree, while it bent its laden boughs low.

THERE IS A CHARMING LAND
Adam Oehlenschlager
Translated by Robert Hillyer

    There is a charming land
    Where grow the wide-armed beeches
    By the salt eastern Strand.
    Old Denmark, so we call
    These rolling hills and valleys,
    And this is Freia's Hall.

Here sat in days of yore
The warriors in armor,
Well rested from the war.
They scattered all their foes,
And now beneath great barrows
Their weary bones repose.

The land is lovely still,
With blue engirdling ocean
And verdant vale and hill,
Fair women, comely maids,
Strong men and lads are dwelling
In Denmark's island glades.

FROM FRANCE:
THE GOOD JOAN
Lizette Woodworth Reese

Along the thousand roads of France,
Now there, now here, swift as a glance,
A cloud, a mist blown down the sky,
Good Joan of Arc goes riding by.

In Domremy at candlelight,
The orchards blowing rose and white
About the shadowy houses lie;
And Joan of Arc goes riding by.

On Avignon there falls a hush,
Brief as the singing of a thrush
Across old gardens April-high;
And Joan of Arc goes riding by.

The women bring the apples in,
Round Arles when the long gusts begin,
Then sit them down to sob and cry;
And Joan of Arc goes riding by.

Dim fall the hoofs down old Calais;
In Tours a flash of silver-gray,
Like flaw of rain in a clear sky;
And Joan of Arc goes riding by.

Who saith that ancient France shall fail,
A rotting leaf driv'n down the gale?
Then her sons know not how to die;
Then good God dwells no more on high!

Tours, Arles, and Domremy reply!
For Joan of Arc goes riding by.

THE SKY IS UP ABOVE THE ROOF
Paul Verlaine
Translated by Ernest Dowson

> The sky is up above the roof
>   So blue, so soft.
> A tree there, up above the roof,
>   Swayeth aloft.
>
> A bell within that sky we see,
>   Chimes low and faint;
> A bird upon that tree we see,
>   Maketh complaint.
>
> Dear God, is not life up there
>   Simple and sweet?
> How peacefully are borne up there
>   Sounds of the street.

THE CHILD READS AN ALMANAC
Francis Jammes
Translated by Ludwig Lewisohn

> The child reads on; her basket of eggs stands by.
> She sees the weather signs, the Saints with awe,
> And watches the fair houses of the sky:
> The *Goat*, the *Bull*, the *Ram*, et cetera.
>
> And so the little peasant maiden knows
> That in the constellations we behold,
> Are markets like the one to which she goes
> Where goats and bulls and rams are bought and sold.
>
> She reads about the market in the sky.
> She turns a page and sees the *Scales* and then
> Says that in Heaven, as at the grocery,
> They weigh salt, coffee and the souls of men.

THE GIRAFFE
FROM THE GIRAFFE
Nikolai Gumileo
Translated by Bowra

> Listen:
> There roams, far away, by the waters of Clead,
> An exquisite beast, the giraffe.
> He moves like a ship in the vastness and stillness of space;
> Approaching, he seems to bewitch all the creatures around;
> His sails are inflated with winds of adventure and grace;
> He scarcely touches the ground.
>
> He is kingly and straight, and his movements incredibly light;
> His skin is the play of the sun on the murmuring wave.
> I know that the ostriches witness a wonderful sight
> When at nightfall he hides in his emerald cave.

SPRING'S ARRIVAL
A Folk Poem

> All the birds have come again,
> Hear the happy chorus!
> Robin, bluebird, on the wing,
> Thrush and wren this message bring.
>> Spring will soon come marching in,
>> Come with joyous singing.

FROM GERMANY:
SLEEP, BABY, SLEEP

> Sleep, baby, sleep!
> Thy father watches the sheep;
> Thy mother is shaking the dreamland tree,
> And down falls a little dream on thee:
> Sleep, baby, sleep!

> Sleep, baby, sleep!
> The large stars are the sheep;
> The wee stars are the lambs, I guess,
> The fair moon is the shepherdess:
> Sleep, baby, sleep!

FROM BELGIUM:
TO THE SUN FROM A FLOWER
Guido Gezelle
Translated by Jethro Bithell

> O Sun, when I stand in my green leaves,
>> With my petals full of dew,
> And you fare forth in your splendor,
>> My blossoming heart looks to you.

471

When, on the red dawn throning,
   The world at your feet you view,
Forget not the little flower
   That waits and watches for you.

FROM HOLLAND:
ROBINSON CRUSOE RETURNS TO AMSTERDAM
FROM AMSTERDAM
Francis Jammes
Translated by Jethro Bithell

The pointed houses lean so you would swear
That they were falling. Tangled vessel masts
Like leafless branches lean against the sky
Amid a mass of green, and red, and rust,
Red herrings, sheepskins, coal along the quays.

Robinson Crusoe passed through Amsterdam,
(At least I think he did), when he returned
From the green isle shaded with cocoa-trees.

What were the feelings of his heart before
These heavy knockers and these mighty doors! . . . .

Did he look through the window-panes and watch
The clerks who write in ledgers all day long?
Did tears come in his eyes when he remembered
His parrot, and the heavy parasol
Which shaded him in the sad and clement isle?

"Glory to thee, good Lord," he would exclaim,
Looking at chests with tulip-painted lids.
But, saddened by the joy of the return,
He must have mourned his kid left in the vines
Alone, and haply on the island dead.

THE FISHERMAN
A Folk Poem
English version by Anne Higginson Spicer

> Fisher, in your bright bark rowing,
> Whither fishing are you going?
> > All is lovely, all is lovely,
> > All is lovely, fisherman.
>
> See you not that last star hiding
> In a cloud, as you are riding?
> > Take your sail in, take your sail in,
> > Take your sail in, fisherman.
>
> If your net you are entangling,
> Sail and oar soon will be dangling.
> > O be wary, O be wary,
> > O be wary, fisherman.
>
> Danger lurks for him who listens
> Where the singing mermaid glistens,
> > Gaze not on her, gaze not on her,
> > Gaze not on her, fisherman.
>
> Fisher, in your bright bark rowing,
> Turn your prow, you'd best be going,
> > Flee from danger, flee from danger,
> > Flee from danger, fisherman.

FROM SPAIN:
SHE WAS A PRETTY LITTLE GIRL
Ramon Perez de Ayala
Translated by Alida Malkus

> She was a pretty little girl.
> They spoke to her with all tenderness,
> And gave her sweet caresses.

473

This little girl had a doll.
The doll was very fair
and her name, without question, was Cordelia.

Once upon a time, this is how it was.

The doll, of course, did not speak.
She said nothing to the little girl.
"Why do you not talk like everyone else,
And say tender words to me?"
The little girl asked the doll.
The doll answered not a word.

The little girl, angry, flew into a temper.
She threw the doll upon the floor
and she stamped on it, and broke it.

And then, by a miracle, before she died,
the doll spoke:
"I loved you more than anyone,
but I was not able to tell it."

Once upon a time, this is how it was.

FROM ITALY:
ITALIAN LULLABY

Hush-a-by, baby,
Your name is so lovely.
He who gave it to you is a gallant fellow.
Bo, bo, bo, bo, bo.
Hush-a-by, darling.

Hush-a-by, baby,
May sleep come to my darling,
Let it come swiftly, not on foot, but on horseback.
Bo, bo, bo, bo, bo.
Hush-a-by, my lovely child.

FROM ITALY:
CINCIRINELLA HAD A MULE
Translated by Maria Cimino

> Cincirinella had a mule in his stall,
> All day long he kept it on the go,
> Cart and saddle and bridle and all,
> Trot trot Cincirinella. Ho!
>
> He trotted on the mountain, he trotted on the plain,
> He'd be trotting still, if he hadn't dropped.
> With pennies in his pocket and pennies to gain
> Cincirinella never never stopped.

FROM SARDINIA:
SLEEP, BABY BOY

> Oh! ninna and anninia!
> Sleep, baby boy;
> Oh! ninna and anninia!
> God give thee joy.
> Oh! ninna and anninia!
> Sweet joy be thine;
> Oh! ninna and anninia!
> Sleep, brother, mine.

FROM GREECE:
THE SWAN AND THE GOOSE
Aesop
Rendered into verse by William Ellery Leonard

> A rich man bought a Swan and Goose—
> That for song, and this for use.
> It chanced his simple-minded cook
> One night the Swan for Goose mistook.

475

But in the dark about to chop
The Swan in two above the crop,
He heard the lyric note, and stayed
The action of the fatal blade.

And thus we see a proper tune
Is sometimes very opportune.

FROM GREECE:
THE CHILDREN'S SONG
A Folk Poem

The swallow has come again
Across the wide, white sea;
She sits and sings through the falling rain,
"O March, my beloved March!
And thou, sad February,
Though still you may cover with snow the plain,
You yet smell sweet of the Spring!"

FROM ISRAEL:
THE GRASSHOPPER'S SONG
H. N. Bialik
Translated by Jessie Sampter

A scraping sound: The grasshopper
In the field does purr and whir-r-r.

"Come forth, grasshoppers, come to dance,
And chant to God your lovely chants.

"Let all who can, be heard and seen
With pirouette and tambourine.

"For none shall hide where grass is deep,
But if you've legs, arise and leap!

"All that are here, respond, proclaim:
Blessed is He and blessed His name!

"Blessed be God who for our sake
This happy summertime did make.

"A plenteous feast in field and fen,
Enough for all.—Amen, amen!"

FROM JORDAN:
MY LITTLE BIRDS
A Folk Poem
Translated by Henrietta Siksek-Su'ad

You have your water and your grain,
You have your fields all full of grass,
You have horizons far and wide.
Flutter along, my little birds.
Flutter along. . . . Flutter along. . . .
And sing me a song, my little birds.

Come fly around me, little birds.
Do not fear a hunter's gun.
I am no hunter you can see.
Flutter along, my little birds.
Flutter along. . . . Flutter along.
And sing me a song, my little birds.

Your children are inside the nest,
Tucked in between feather and straw.
Your children will sleep undisturbed by me.
Flutter along, my little birds.
Flutter along. . . . Flutter along.
And sing me a song, my little birds.

DATES
Translated by E. Powys Mathers

> We grow to the sound of the wind
> Playing his flutes in our hair,
>
> Palm tree daughters,
> Brown flesh Bedouin,
> Fed with light
> By our gold father;
>
> We are loved of the free-tented,
> The sons of space, the hall-forgetters,
> The wide-handed, the bright sworded
> Masters of horses.
>
> Who has rested in the shade of our palms
> Shall hear us murmur ever above his sleep.

FROM EGYPT:
ADORATION OF THE DISK
King Akhnaten and Princess Nefer Neferiu Aten
Translated by Robert Hillyer

> The cattle roam again across the fields;
> Birds flutter in the marsh, and lift their wings
> Also in adoration, and the flocks
> Run with delight through all the pleasant meadows.
>
> Both north and south along the dazzling river,
> Ships raise their sails and take their course before thee;
> And in the ocean, all the deep sea fish
> Swim to the surface to drink in thy light.
>
> The chick within the egg, whose breath is thine,
> Who runneth from its shell, chirping its joy,
> And dancing on its small unsteady legs,
> To greet the splendor of the rising sun.

478

FROM PERSIA:
WAKE!
FROM THE RUBÁIYÁT
Omar Khayyám
Translated by Edward FitzGerald

Wake! For the Sun, who scatter'd into flight
The Stars before him from the Field of Night,
    Drives Night along with them from Heav'n, and strikes
The Sultan's Turret with a Shaft of Light.

FROM SOUTH AFRICA:
THE WILDEBEEST
June Daly

You who like a boulder stand
    In your brown, beloved land;
All a wild ox ought to be:
    Long of nuzzle, lean of knee,
    Vigilant of restless eye,
    Taut and sinewy of thigh,
    Shaggy-bearded, mane-adorned,
    Massive-shouldered, vicious-horned . . .
You who stand to watch us pass
Fetlock deep in tawny grass,

Watch in peace! For not today
Menace comes your browsing way.
Watch in peace! And when we pass,
Cross again the golden grass
That billows round you like a sea.
    Many may your seasons be
    In these pastures' pleasant length,
    Rugged monument to strength.

ICAN DANCE
ton Hughes

The low beating of the tom-toms,
The slow beating of the tom-toms,
Low . . . slow
Slow . . . low—
Stirs your blood.

Dance!
A night-veiled girl
Whirls softly into a
Circle of light.
Whirls softly . . . slowly,
Like a wisp of smoke around the fire—
And the tom-toms beat,
And the tom-toms beat,
And the low beating of the tom-toms
Stirs your blood.

FROM CHINA:
THE LITTLE RAIN
Tu Fu
Translated by L. Cranmer-Byng

Oh! she is good, the little rain! and well she knows our need
Who cometh in the time of spring to aid the sun-drawn seed;
She wanders with a friendly wind through silent nights unseen,
The furrows feel her happy tears, and lo! the land is green.

Last night cloud-shadows gloomed the path that winds to my abode,
And the torches of the river-boats like angry meteors glowed.
To-day fresh colors break the soil, and butterflies take wing
Down broidered lawns all bright with pearls in the garden of the
King.

FROM CHINA:
DANCING
Yang Kuei-Fei
Translated by Florence Ayscough and Amy Lowell

Wide sleeves sway.
Scents,
Sweet scents
Incessantly coming.

It is red lilies,
Lotus lilies,
Floating up,
And up,
Out of autumn mist.

Thin clouds
Puffed,
Fluttered,
Blown on a rippling wind
Through a mountain pass.

Young willow shoots
Touching,
Brushing
The water
Of the garden pool.

FROM JAPAN:
RIVER-FOG
Fukayabu Kiyowara
Translated by Arthur Waley

Because river-fog
Hiding the mountain base
Has risen,
The autumn mountain looks as though it hung in the sky.

481

So sweet the plum trees smell!
Would that the brush that paints the flower
Could paint the scent as well.

I come to look, and lo,
The plum tree petals scatter down
A fall of purest snow.

FROM SIBERIA:
HEY! MY PONY!
A TARTAR CHILD'S SONG
Eleanor Farjeon

What will you ride on?
I'll ride a nut-brown pony!
Hempen halter, iron bit,
Round the field I'll ride on it!
    Hey! my nut-brown pony!

What will you ride on?
I'll ride a coal-black pony!
Scarlet saddle, silken reins,
I will cross Sahara's plains.
    Hey! my coal-black pony!

What will you ride on?
I'll ride a snow-white pony!
Silver bridle, golden girth,
I will travel round the earth.
    Hey! My snow-white pony!

482

IN THE BAZAARS OF HYDERABAD
Sarojini Naidu

What do you sell, O ye merchants?
Richly your wares are displayed.
Turbans of crimson and silver,
Tunics of purple brocade,
Mirrors with panels of amber,
Daggers with handles of jade.

What do you weigh, O ye vendors?
Saffron and lentil and rice.
What do you grind, O ye maidens?
Sandalwood, henna, and spice.
What do you call, O ye pedlars?
Chessmen and ivory dice.

What do you make, O ye goldsmiths?
Wristlet and anklet and ring,
Bells for the feet of blue pigeons,
Frail as a dragon-fly's wing,
Girdles of gold for the dancers,
Scabbards of gold for the king.

What do you cry, O ye fruitmen?
Citron, pomegranate, and plum.
What do you play, O musicians?
Cither, sarangi, and drum.
What do you chant, O magicians?
Spells for aeons to come.

What do you weave, O ye flower-girls
With tassels of azure and red?
Crowns for the brow of a bridegroom,
Chaplets to garland his bed,
Sheets of white blossoms new-gathered
To perfume the sleep of the dead.

VOCATION
Rabindranath Tagore
Who was awarded the Nobel Prize for Literature

When the gong sounds ten in the morning and I walk to school by
    our lane,
Every day I meet the hawker crying, "Bangles, crystal bangles!"
There is nothing to hurry him on, there is no road he must take, no
    place he must go to, no time when he must come home.
I wish I were a hawker, spending my day in the road, crying,
    "Bangles, crystal bangles!"

When at four in the afternoon I come back from the school,
I can see through the gate of that house the gardener digging the
    ground.
He does what he likes with his spade, he soils his clothes with dust,
    nobody takes him to task if he gets baked in the sun or gets wet.
I wish I were a gardener digging away at the garden with nobody to
    stop me from digging.

Just as it gets dark in the evening and my mother sends me to bed,
I can see through my open window the watchman walking up and
    down.
The lane is dark and lonely and the street lamp stands like a giant
    with one red eye in its head.
The watchman swings his lantern and walks with his shadow at his
    side, and never once goes to bed in his life.
I wish I were a watchman walking the streets all night, chasing the
    shadows with my lantern.

FUN WITH FISHING
Eunice Tietjens

Ten South Sea Island boys
Went fishing for their dinner.
One caught a long gray eel
To keep from growing thinner.

484

Nine South Sea Island boys
Went fishing with a spear.
One saw a fish with stripes
And speared it straight and clear.

Eight South Sea Island boys
Went diving after shell.
One found an oyster pearl
And liked it very well.

Seven South Sea Island boys
Went fishing on the coral.
One caught a parrot fish.
They cooked it up with laurel.

Six South Sea Island boys
Were splashing as they could,
One caught an octopus—
He thought it tasted good.

Five South Sea Island boys
Went fishing on the reef.
One caught a bright red fish.
Its life was very brief.

Four South Sea Island boys
Were fishing in the creek.
The shrimps went darting quickly by,
But one was just as quick.

Three South Sea Island boys
Set out their lobster traps.
One found a lobster there,
The wicked sort that snaps.

Two South Sea Island boys
Fished with fire at night.
One saw two shining eyes
And stabbed, and hit it right.

One South Sea Island boy
Went fishing with a net.
A sword-fish cut his net in two.
That boy is fishing yet!

FROM AUSTRALIA:
WHEN I WAS SIX
Zora Cross

When I was only six years old,
  Heigh-ho! for Folly O!
I wandered in a fairy fold,
  Heigh holly! to and fro.

I rode upon a blossom's back
  Up hill and over sea,
And all the little pixie pack
  For fun would follow me.

O, golden was the gown I wore
  Of buttercups and air,
And twenty diamond stars or more
  Were pinned upon my hair.

All day I chased the laughing sky
  Above the busy town,
But when the moon unwinked her eye,
  Ho, ho! I hurried down.

And then within the baby's shoe
  I hid my lady's pearls,
From maid to merry maid I flew
  And knotted all their curls.

And when the children were abed,
  I tapped the window pane,
And laughed as someone softly said:
  "Whist, goblins there again!"

Ho, ho! I flitted here and there
   Amid my elfin band,
While on the green in frolic fair,
   We tripped it hand in hand.

As air and moonlight I was free
   Within that fairy fold,
For all the world belonged to me
   When I was six years old.

FROM PUERTO RICO:
THE HURRICANE
Pales Matos
Translated by Alida Malkus

When the hurricane unfolds
Its fierce accordion of winds,
On the tip of its toes,
Agile dancer, it sweeps whirling
Over the carpeted surface of the sea
With the scattered branches of the palm.

FROM CUBA:
PROPOSITION
Nicolás Guillén
Translated by Langston Hughes

Tonight
when the moon comes out
I shall change it
into money.

487

But I'd be sorry
if people knew about it,
for the moon
is an old family treasure.

FROM MEXICO:
THE INDIANS COME DOWN FROM MIXCO
Miguel Angel Asturias
Translated by D.D.W.

The Indians come down from Mixco
laden with deep blue
and the city with its frightened
streets receives them
with a handful of lights
that, like stars, are extinguished
when daybreak comes.

A round of heartbeats
is in their hands that stroke
the wind like two oars;
and from their feet fall
prints like little soles
in the dust of the road.

The stars that peep out
at Mixco stay in Mixco
because the Indians catch them
for baskets that they fill
with chickens and the big white flowers
of the golden Spanish bayonet.

The life of the Indians
is quieter than ours,
and when they come down from Mixco
they make no sound but the panting
that sometimes hisses on their lips
like a silken serpent.

488

THOUGHTS OF A LITTLE GIRL
María Enriqueta
Translated by Emma Gutiérrez Suárez

> I think flowers can see
> and clouds play a game,
> that when the wind whispers,
> the leaves understand.
> They sway and they dance
> in the mad-cap breeze.
>
> Sometimes in the morning
> to the meadow I go,
> where the daisies are playing
> in the wind.
>
> First the wind whispers,
> then runs, jumps, and tickles their feet.
> And the daisies, their heads sweetly nodding,
> laugh, sway, and shiver in glee.

FROM BRAZIL:
CRADLE SONG OF THE ELEPHANTS
Adriano del Valle
Translated by Alida Malkus

> The little elephant was crying
> because it did not want to sleep . . .
> Go to sleep, my little elephant,
> the moon is going to hear you weep.
>
> Papa elephant is near.
> I hear him bellowing among the mangoes.
> Go to sleep, my little elephant,
> the moon will hear my little fellow . . .

489

FROM HONDURAS:
I HAVE LOST MY SHOES
Constantino Suasnavar
Translated by M.L.

> I have lost my shoes
> in the great Valley of Sula.
>
> Crossing over rivers
> by slumbering bridges
> under the cloak of the moon.
>
> To the rustling of banana groves
> and the roars of the puma
> here I come, *caramba!*,
>
> here I come, shoeless,
> to San Pedro Sula.

FROM VENEZUELA:
THE SOWER
R. Olivares Figueroa
Translated by D.F.

> On a white field,
> black little seeds . . .
> *Let it rain! rain!*
>
> "Sower, what do you sow?"
> How the furrow sings!
> *Let it rain! rain!*
>
> "I sow rainbows,
> dawns and trumpets!"
> *Let it rain! rain!*

THE LITTLE GIRL THAT LOST A FINGER
Gabriela Mistral
Who was awarded the Nobel Prize for Literature
Translated by M.L.

> And a clam caught my little finger,
> and the clam fell into the sand,
> and the sand was swallowed by the sea,
> and the whales caught it in the sea,
> and the whales arrived at Gibraltar,
> and in Gibraltar the fishermen sing:
> "News of the earth we drag up from the sea,
> news of a little girl's finger:
> let her who lost it come get it!"
>
> Give me a boat to go fetch it,
> and for the boat give me a captain,
> for the captain give me wages,
> and for his wages let him ask for the city:
> Marseilles with towers and squares and boats,
> in all the wide world the finest city,
> which won't be lovely with a little girl
> that the sea robbed of her finger,
> and that whalers chant for like town criers,
> and that they're waiting for on Gibraltar . . .

THE WRECK OF THE "JULIE PLANTE"
A Legend of Lac St. Pierre
William Henry Drummond

> On wan dark night on Lac St. Pierre,
>   De win' she blow, blow, blow,
> An' de crew of de wood scow *Julie Plante*
>   Got scar't an' run below—

For de win' she blow lak hurricane,
  Bimeby she blow some more,
An' de scow bus' up on Lac St. Pierre
  Wan arpent from de shore.

De captinne walk on de front deck,
  An' walk de hin' deck too—
He call de crew from up de hole,
  He call de cook also.
De cook she's name was Rosie,
  She come from Montreal,
Was chambermaid on lumber barge
  On de Grande Lachine Canal.

De win' she blow from nor'-eas'-wes',
  De sout' win' she blow too,
W'en Rosie cry, "Mon cher captinne,
  Mon cher, w'at I shall do?"
De captinne t'row de beeg ankerre,
  But still de scow she dreef:
De crew he can't pass on de shore,
  Becos he los' hees skeef.

De night was dark lak wan black cat,
  De wave run high an' fas',
W'en de captinne tak' de Rosie girl
  An' tie her to de mas'.
Den he also tak' de life preserve,
  An' jomp off on de lak',
An' say, "Good-bye, ma Rosie dear,
  I go drown for your sak'!"

Nex' mornin' very early
  'Bout ha'f pas' two—t'ree—four—
De captinne—scow—an' de poor Rosie
  Was corpses on de shore.
For de win' she blow lak hurricane,
  Bimeby she blow some more,
An' de scow bus' up on Lac St. Pierre,
  Wan arpent from de shore.

Now all good wood scow sailor man,
   Tak' warning by dat storm,
An' go an' marry some nice French girl
   An' leev on wan beeg farm.
De win' can blow lak hurricane,
   An' s'pose she blow some more,
You can't get drown' on Lac St. Pierre
   So long you stay on shore.

FROM CANADA:
THE SONG MY PADDLE SINGS
E. Pauline Johnson

West wind, blow from your prairie nest,
Blow from the mountains, blow from the west.
The sail is idle, the sailor too;
O wind of the west, we wait for you!

Blow, blow!
I have wooed you so,
But never a favor you bestow.
You rock your cradle the hills between,
But scorn to notice my white lateen.

I stow the sail and unship the mast:
I wooed you long, but my wooing's past;
My paddle will lull you into rest:
O drowsy wind of the drowsy west,
Sleep, sleep!
By your mountains steep,
Or down where the prairie grasses sweep,
Now fold in slumber your laggard wings,
For soft is the song my paddle sings.

493

Be strong, O paddle! be brave, canoe!
The reckless waves you must plunge into.
Reel, reel,
On your trembling keel,
But never a fear my craft will feel.

We've raced the rapids; we're far ahead:
The river slips through its silent bed.
Sway, sway,
As the bubbles spray
And fall in tinkling tunes away.

And up on the hills against the sky,
A fir tree rocking its lullaby
Swings, swings,
Its emerald wings,
Swelling the song that my paddle sings.

FROM CANADA:
PAUL BUNYAN
FROM PAUL BUNYAN
Arthur S. Bourinot

He came,
striding
over the mountain,
the moon slung on his back,
like a pack,
a great pine
stuck on his shoulder
swayed as he walked,
as he talked
to his blue ox
Babe;

a huge, looming shadow
of a man,
clad
in a mackinaw coat,
his logger's shirt
open at the throat
and the great mane of hair
matching,
meeting
the locks of night,
the smoke from his cauldron pipe
a cloud on the moon
and his laugh
rolled through the mountains
like thunder
on a summer night
while the lightning of his smile
split the heavens
asunder.

LET THE NATIONS BE GLAD
The Bible: from Psalm 67

God be merciful unto us, and bless us;
    And cause his face to shine upon us;
That thy way may be known upon earth,
    Thy saving health among all nations.
Let the people praise thee, O God;
Let all the people praise thee.

O let the nations be glad and sing for joy:
For thou shalt judge the people righteously,
    And govern the nations upon earth.
Let the people praise thee, O God;
Let all the people praise thee.

Story time

is a special time

THE HIGHWAYMAN
Alfred Noyes

PART I

The wind was a torrent of darkness among the gusty trees,
The moon was a ghostly galleon tossed upon cloudy seas,
The road was a ribbon of moonlight over the purple moor,
And the highwayman came riding—
   Riding—riding—
The highwayman came riding, up to the old inn-door.

He'd a French cocked-hat on his forehead, a bunch of lace at his
   chin,
A coat of the claret velvet, and breeches of brown doe-skin;
They fitted with never a wrinkle; his boots were up to the thigh!
And he rode with a jeweled twinkle,
   His pistol butts a-twinkle,
His rapier hilt a-twinkle, under the jeweled sky.

Over the cobbles he clattered and clashed in the dark inn-yard,
And he tapped with his whip on the shutters, but all was locked and
   barred:
He whistled a tune to the window, and who should be waiting there
But the landlord's black-eyed daughter,
   Bess, the landlord's daughter,
Plaiting a dark red love-knot into her long black hair.

And dark in the dark old inn-yard a stable-wicket creaked
Where Tim the ostler listened; his face was white and peaked;
His eyes were hollows of madness, his hair like moldy hay,
But he loved the landlord's daughter,
   The landlord's red-lipped daughter,
Dumb as a dog he listened, and he heard the robber say—

"One kiss, my bonny sweetheart, I'm after a prize tonight,
But I shall be back with the yellow gold before the morning light;
Yet, if they press me sharply, and harry me through the day,
Then look for me by moonlight,
   Watch for me by moonlight,
I'll come to thee by moonlight, though hell should bar the way."

He rose upright in the stirrups; he scarce could reach her hand,
But she loosened her hair i' the casement! His face burned like a
     brand
As the black cascade of perfume came tumbling over his breast;
And he kissed its waves in the moonlight,
   (Oh, sweet black waves in the moonlight!)
Then he tugged at his rein in the moonlight, and galloped away to
     the West.

PART II

He did not come in the dawning; he did not come at noon;
And out o' the tawny sunset, before the rise o' the moon,
When the road was a gipsy's ribbon, looping the purple moor,
A red-coat troop came marching—
   Marching—marching—
King George's men came marching, up to the old inn-door.

They said no word to the landlord, they drank his ale instead,
But they gagged his daughter and bound her to the foot of her
     narrow bed;
Two of them knelt at her casement, with muskets at their side!

There was death at every window;
  And hell at one dark window;
For Bess could see, through her casement, the road that *he* would
    ride.

They had tied her up to attention, with many a sniggering jest;
They had bound a musket beside her, with the barrel beneath her
    breast!
"Now keep good watch!" and they kissed her. She heard the dead
    man say—
Look for me by moonlight;
  Watch for me by moonlight;
I'll come to thee by moonlight, though hell should bar the way!

She twisted her hands behind her; but all the knots held good!
She writhed her hands till her fingers were wet with sweat or blood!
They stretched and strained in the darkness, and the hours crawled
    by like years,
Till now, on the stroke of midnight,
  Cold, on the stroke of midnight,
The tip of one finger touched it! The trigger at least was hers!

The tip of one finger touched it; she strove no more for the rest!
Up, she stood up to attention, with the barrel beneath her breast,
She would not risk their hearing: she would not strive again;
For the road lay bare in the moonlight;
  Blank and bare in the moonlight;
And the blood of her veins in the moonlight throbbed to her love's
    refrain.

Tlot-tlot; tlot-tlot! Had they heard it? The horse-hoofs ringing clear;
Tlot-tlot, tlot-tlot, in the distance? Were they deaf that they did not
    hear?
Down the ribbon of moonlight, over the brow of the hill,
The highwayman came riding,
  Riding, riding!
The red-coats looked to their priming! She stood up, straight and
    still!

Tlot-tlot, in the frosty silence! *Tlot-tlot*, in the echoing night!
Nearer he came and nearer! Her face was like a light!
Her eyes grew wide for a moment; she drew one last deep breath,
Then her finger moved in the moonlight,
   Her musket shattered the moonlight,
Shattered her breast in the moonlight and warned him—with her
    death.

He turned; he spurred to the westward; he did not know who stood
Bowed, with her head o'er the musket, drenched with her own red
    blood!
Not till the dawn he heard it, his face grew gray to hear
How Bess, the landlord's daughter,
   The landlord's black-eyed daughter,
Had watched for her love in the moonlight, and died in the darkness
    there.

Back he spurred like a madman, shrieking a curse to the sky,
With the white road smoking behind him, and his rapier brandished
    high!
Blood-red were his spurs in the golden moon; wine-red was his velvet
    coat,
When they shot him down on the highway,
   Down like a dog on the highway,
And he lay in his blood on the highway, with a bunch of lace at his
    throat.

. . . .

And still of a winter's night, they say, when the wind is in the trees,
When the moon is a ghostly galleon tossed upon cloudy seas,
When the road is a ribbon of moonlight over the purple moor,
A highwayman comes riding—
   Riding—riding—
A highwayman comes riding, up to the old inn-door.

Over the cobbles he clatters and clangs in the dark inn-yard;
And he taps with his whip on the shutters, but all is locked and
      barred;
He whistles a tune to the window, and who should be waiting there
   But the landlord's black-eyed daughter,
     Bess, the landlord's daughter,
   Plaiting a dark red love-knot into her long black hair.

ANNABEL LEE
Edgar Allan Poe

    It was many and many a year ago,
      In a kingdom by the sea
    That a maiden there lived, whom you may know
      By the name of Annabel Lee;
    And this maiden she lived with no other thought
      Than to love and be loved by me.

    I was a child and *she* was a child,
      In this kingdom by the sea,
    But we loved with a love that was more than love—
      I and my Annabel Lee—
    With a love that the wingèd seraphs of heaven
      Coveted her and me.

    And this was the reason that, long ago,
      In this kingdom by the sea,
    A wind blew out of a cloud, chilling
      My beautiful Annabel Lee;
    So that her highborn kinsmen came
      And bore her away from me,
    To shut her up in a sepulcher
      In this kingdom by the sea.

The angels, not half so happy in heaven,
  Went envying her and me—
Yes!—that was the reason (as all men know,
  In this kingdom by the sea)
That the wind came out of the cloud by night,
  Chilling and killing my Annabel Lee.

But our love it was stronger by far than the love
  Of those who were older than we—
  Of many far wiser than we—
And neither the angels in heaven above,
  Nor the demons down under the sea,
Can ever dissever my soul from the soul
  Of the beautiful Annabel Lee:

For the moon never beams, without bringing me dreams
  Of the beautiful Annabel Lee;
And the stars never rise, but I feel the bright eyes
  Of the beautiful Annabel Lee:
And so, all the night-tide, I lie down by the side
Of my darling—my darling—my life and my bride,
  In the sepulcher there by the sea—
  In her tomb by the sounding sea.

LOCHINVAR
Walter Scott

O, young Lochinvar is come out of the west,
Through all the wide Border his steed was the best,
And save his good broadsword he weapons had none;
He rode all unarmed, and he rode all alone.
So faithful in love, and so dauntless in war,
There never was knight like the young Lochinvar.

He stayed not for brake, and he stopped not for stone,
He swam the Eske river where ford there was none;
But, ere he alighted at Netherby gate,
The bride had consented, the gallant came late:
For a laggard in love, and a dastard in war,
Was to wed the fair Ellen of brave Lochinvar.

So boldly he entered the Netherby hall,
Among bride's-men and kinsmen, and brothers and all;
Then spoke the bride's father, his hand on his sword
(For the poor craven bridegroom said never a word),
"O come ye in peace here, or come ye in war,
Or to dance at our bridal, young Lord Lochinvar?"

"I long wooed your daughter, my suit you denied;—
Love swells like the Solway, but ebbs like its tide—
And now I am come, with this lost love of mine,
To lead but one measure, drink one cup of wine.
There are maidens in Scotland more lovely by far,
That would gladly be bride to the young Lochinvar."

The bride kissed the goblet; the knight took it up,
He quaffed off the wine, and he threw down the cup,
She looked down to blush, and she looked up to sigh,
With a smile on her lips and a tear in her eye.
He took her soft hand, ere her mother could bar,—
"Now tread we a measure!" said young Lochinvar.

So stately his form, and so lovely her face,
That never a hall such a galliard did grace;
While her mother did fret, and her father did fume,
And the bridegroom stood dangling his bonnet and plume;
And the bride-maidens whispered, " 'Twere better by far
To have matched our fair cousin with young Lochinvar."

One touch to her hand, and one word in her ear,
When they reached the hall door, and the charger stood near;

So light to the croupe the fair lady he swung,
So light to the saddle before her he sprung!
"She is won! we are gone, over bank, bush, and scaur;
They'll have fleet steeds that follow," quoth young Lochinvar.

There was mounting 'mong Græmes of the Netherby clan;
Forsters, Fenwicks, and Musgraves, they rode and they ran;
There was racing, and chasing, on Cannobie Lee,
But the lost bride of Netherby ne'er did they see.
So daring in love, and so dauntless in war,
Have ye e'er heard of gallant like young Lochinvar?

THE DORCHESTER GIANT
Oliver Wendell Holmes

There was a giant in times of old,
    A mighty one was he;
He had a wife, but she was a scold,
So he kept her shut in his mammoth fold;
    And he had children three.

It happened to be an election day,
    And the giants were choosing a king;
The people were not democrats then,
They did not talk of the rights of men,
    And all that sort of thing.

Then the giant took his children three,
    And fastened them in the pen;
The children roared; quoth the giant, "Be still!"
And Dorchester Heights and Milton Hill
    Rolled back the sound again.

Then he brought them a pudding stuffed with plums,
    As big as the State House dome;
Quoth he, "There's something for you to eat;
So stop your mouths with your 'lection treat,
    And wait till your dad comes home."

So the giant pulled him a chestnut stout,
    And whittled the boughs away;
The boys and their mother set up a shout,
Said he, "You're in, and you can't get out,
    Bellow as loud as you may."

Off he went, and he growled a tune
    As he strode the fields along;
'Tis said a buffalo fainted away,
And fell as cold as a lump of clay,
    When he heard the giant's song.

But whether the story's true or not,
    It isn't for me to show;
There's many a thing that's twice as queer
In somebody's lectures that we hear,
    And those are true you know.

What are those lone ones doing now,
    The wife and the children sad?
Oh, they are in a terrible rout,
Screaming, and throwing their pudding about,
    Acting as they were mad.

They flung it over to Roxbury hills,
    They flung it over the plain,
And all over Milton and Dorchester too
Great lumps of pudding the giants threw;
    They tumbled as thick as rain.

Giant and mammoth have passed away,
    For ages have floated by;
The suet is hard as a marrowbone,
And every plum is turned to a stone,
    But there the puddings lie.

And if, some pleasant afternoon,
    You'll ask me out to ride,
The whole of the story I will tell,
And you shall see where the puddings fell,
    And pay for the punch beside.

LORD LOVEL

Lord Lovel he stood at his castle-gate
   Combing his milk-white steed;
When up came Lady Nancy Belle,
   To wish her lover good speed, speed,
   To wish her lover good speed.

"Where are you going, Lord Lovel?" she said,
   "Oh! where are you going?" said she;
"I'm going, my Lady Nancy Belle,
   Strange countries for to see, to see,
   Strange countries for to see."

"When will you be back, Lord Lovel?" she said;
   "Oh! when will you come back?" said she;
"In a year or two—or three, at the most,
   I'll return to my fair Nancy-cy,
   I'll return to my fair Nancy."

But he had not been gone a year and a day,
   Strange countries for to see,
When languishing thoughts came into his head,
   Lady Nancy Belle he would go see, see,
   Lady Nancy Belle he would go see.

So he rode and he rode on his milk-white steed,
   Till he came to London town,
And there he heard St. Pancras' bells,
   And the people all mourning, round, round,
   And the people all mourning round.

"Oh! what is the matter?" Lord Lovel he said,
   "Oh! what is the matter?" said he;
"A lord's lady is dead," a woman replied,
   "And some call her Lady Nancy-cy,
   And some call her Lady Nancy."

So he order'd the grave to be open'd wide,
  And the shroud he turnèd down,
And there he kiss'd her clay-cold lips,
  Till the tears came trickling down, down,
  Till the tears came trickling down.

Lady Nancy she died as it might be to-day,
  Lord Lovel he died as to-morrow;
Lady Nancy she died out of pure, pure grief,
  Lord Lovel he died out of sorrow, sorrow,
  Lord Lovel he died out of sorrow.

Lady Nancy was laid in St. Pancras' church,
  Lord Lovel was laid in the choir;
And out of her bosom there grew a red rose,
  And out of her lover's a brier, brier,
  And out of her lover's a brier.

They grew, and they grew, to the church-steeple top,
  And then they could grow no higher:
So there they entwined in a true-lover's knot,
  For all lovers true to admire-mire,
  For all lovers true to admire.

THE RAGGLE, TAGGLE GYPSIES

There were three gypsies a-come to my door,
  And downstairs ran this lady, O.
One sang high and another sang low,
  And the other sang "Bonnie, Bonnie Biskay, O."

Then she pulled off her silken gown,
  And put on hose of leather, O.
With the ragged, ragged rags about her door
  She's off with the Raggle, Taggle Gypsies, O.

'Twas late last night when my lord came home,
    Inquiring for his lady, O.
The servants said on every hand,
    "She's gone with the Raggle, Taggle Gypsies, O."

"Oh, saddle for me my milk-white steed,
    Oh, saddle for me my pony, O,
That I may ride and seek my bride
    Who's gone with the Raggle, Taggle Gypsies, O."

Oh, he rode high and he rode low,
    He rode through woods and copses, O,
Until he came to an open field,
    And there he espied his lady, O.

"What makes you leave your house and lands?
    What makes you leave your money, O?
What makes you leave your new-wedded lord
    To go with the Raggle, Taggle Gypsies, O?"

"What care I for my house and lands?
    What care I for my money, O?
What care I for my new-wedded lord?
    I'm off with the Raggle, Taggle Gypsies, O."

"Last night you slept on a goose-feather bed,
    With the sheet turned down so bravely, O.
Tonight you will sleep in the cold, open field,
    Along with the Raggle, Taggle Gypsies, O."

"What care I for your goose-feather bed,
    With the sheet turned down so bravely, O?
For tonight I shall sleep in a cold, open field,
    Along with the Raggle, Taggle Gypsies, O."

THE SANDS OF DEE
Charles Kingsley

"O Mary, go and call the cattle home,
    And call the cattle home,
    And call the cattle home
  Across the sands of Dee!"
The western wind was wild and dank with foam,
  And all alone went she.

The western tide crept up along the sand,
    And o'er and o'er the sand,
    And round and round the sand,
  As far as eye could see.
The rolling mist came down and hid the land,
  And never home came she.

"Oh! is it weed, or fish, or floating hair—
    A tress of golden hair,
    A drownèd maiden's hair
  Above the nets at sea?
Was never salmon yet that shone so fair
  Among the stakes on Dee."

They rowed her in across the rolling foam,
    The cruel crawling foam,
    The cruel hungry foam,
  To her grave beside the sea:
But still the boatmen hear her call the cattle home
  Across the sands of Dee.

THE DESTRUCTION OF SENNACHERIB
Lord Byron

The Assyrian came down like the wolf on the fold,
And his cohorts were gleaming in purple and gold;
And the sheen of their spears was like stars on the sea,
When the blue wave rolls nightly on deep Galilee.

Like the leaves of the forest when Summer is green,
That host with their banners at sunset were seen:
Like the leaves of the forest when Autumn hath flown,
That host on the morrow lay withered and strown.

For the Angel of Death spread his wings on the blast,
And breathed in the face of the foe as he passed;
And the eyes of the sleepers waxed deadly and chill,
And their hearts but once heaved, and forever grew still.

And there lay the steed with his nostril all wide,
But through it there rolled not the breath of his pride;
And the foam of his gasping lay white on the turf,
And cold as the spray of the rock-beating surf.

And there lay the rider distorted and pale,
With the dew on his brow, and the rust on his mail;
And the tents were all silent, the banners alone,
The lances unlifted, the trumpet unblown.

And the widows of Ashur are loud in their wail,
And the idols are broke in the temple of Baal;
And the might of the Gentile, unsmote by the sword,
Hath melted like snow in the glance of the Lord!

MEG MERRILIES
John Keats

Old Meg she was a Gipsy,
   And liv'd upon the Moors:
Her bed it was the brown heath turf,
   And her house was out of doors.

Her apples were swart blackberries,
   Her currants pods o' broom;
Her wine was dew of the wild white rose,
   Her book a churchyard tomb.

Her Brothers were the craggy hills,
Her Sisters larchen trees—
Alone with her great family
She liv'd as she did please.

No breakfast had she many a morn,
No dinner many a noon,
And 'stead of supper she would stare
Full hard against the Moon.

But every morn of woodbine fresh
She made her garlanding,
And every night the dark glen Yew
She wove, and she would sing.

And with her fingers old and brown
She plaited Mats o' Rushes,
And gave them to the Cottagers
She met among the Bushes.

Old Meg was brave as Margaret Queen
And tall as Amazon:
An old red blanket cloak she wore;
A chip hat had she on.
God rest her agèd bones somewhere—
She died full long agone!

THE LISTENERS
Walter de la Mare

"Is there anybody there?" said the Traveler,
Knocking on the moonlit door;
And his horse in the silence champed the grasses
Of the forest's ferny floor.
And a bird flew up out of the turret,
Above the Traveler's head:
And he smote upon the door again a second time;
"Is there anybody there?" he said.

But no one descended to the Traveler;
  No head from the leaf-fringed sill
Leaned over and looked into his gray eyes,
  Where he stood perplexed and still.
But only a host of phantom listeners
  That dwelt in the lone house then
Stood listening in the quiet of the moonlight
  To that voice from the world of men:
Stood thronging the faint moonbeams on the dark stair
  That goes down to the empty hall,
Hearkening in an air stirred and shaken
  By the lonely Traveler's call.
And he felt in his heart their strangeness,
  Their stillness answering his cry,
While his horse moved, cropping the dark turf,
  'Neath the starred and leafy sky;
For he suddenly smote on the door, even
  Louder, and lifted his head:—
"Tell them I came, and no one answered,
  That I kept my word," he said.
Never the least stir made the listeners,
  Though every word he spake
Fell echoing through the shadowiness of the still house
  From the one man left awake:
Aye, they heard his foot upon the stirrup,
  And the sound of iron on stone,
And how the silence surged softly backward,
  When the plunging hoofs were gone.

SPANISH WATERS
John Masefield

Spanish waters, Spanish waters, you are ringing in my ears,
Like a slow sweet piece of music from the gray forgotten years;
Telling tales, and beating tunes, and bringing weary thoughts to me
Of the sandy beach at Muertos, where I would that I could be.

There's a surf breaks on Los Muertos, and it never stops to roar,
And it's there we came to anchor, and it's there we went ashore,
Where the blue lagoon is silent amid snags of rotting trees,
Dropping like the clothes of corpses cast up by the seas.

We anchored at Los Muertos when the dipping sun was red,
We left her half-a-mile to sea, to west of Nigger Head;
And before the mist was on the Cay, before the day was done,
We were ashore on Muertos with the gold that we had won.

We bore it through the marshes in a half-score battered chests,
Sinking, in the sucking quagmires, to the sunburn on our breasts,
Heaving over tree trunks, gasping, damning at the flies and heat,
Longing for a long drink, out of silver, in the ship's cool lazareet.

The moon came white and ghostly as we laid the treasure down,
There was gear there'd make a beggarman as rich as Lima Town,
Copper charms and silver trinkets from the chests of Spanish crews,
Gold doubloons and double moidores, louis d'ors and portagues,

Clumsy yellow-metal earrings from the Indians of Brazil,
Uncut emeralds out of Rio, bezoar stones from Guayaquil,
Silver, in the crude and fashioned, pots of old Arica bronze,
Jewels from the bones of Incas desecrated by the Dons.

We smoothed the place with mattocks, and we took and blazed the
        tree,
Which marks yon where the gear is hid that none will ever see,
And we laid aboard the ship again, and south away we steers,
Through the loud surf of Los Muertos which is beating in my ears.

I'm the last alive that knows it. All the rest have gone their ways
Killed, or died, or come to anchor in the old Mulatas Cays,
And I go singing, fiddling, old and starved and in despair,
And I know where all that gold is hid, if I were only there.

It's not the way to end it all. I'm old, and nearly blind,
And an old man's past's a strange thing, for it never leaves his mind.
And I see in dreams, awhiles, the beach, the sun's disk dipping red,
And the tall ship, under topsails, swaying in past Nigger Head.

I'd be glad to step ashore there. Glad to take a pick and go
To the lone blazed coco-palm tree in the place no others know,
And lift the gold and silver that has moldered there for years
By the loud surf of Los Muertos which is beating in my ears.

THE GLOVE AND THE LIONS
Leigh Hunt

King Francis was a hearty king, and loved a royal sport,
And one day, as his lions fought, sat looking on the court;
The nobles fill'd the benches, and the ladies in their pride,
And 'mongst them sat the Count de Lorge, with one for whom he
    sigh'd;
And truly 'twas a gallant thing to see that crowning show—
Valour and love, and a king above, and the royal beasts below.

Ramped and roared the lions, with horrid, laughing jaws;
They bit, they glared, gave blows like beams, a wind went with their
    paws;
With wallowing might and stifled roar they rolled one on another,
Till all the pit, with sand and mane, was in a thundrous smother;
The bloody foam above the bars came whisking through the air;
Said Francis, then, "Faith, gentlemen, we're better here than there!"

De Lorge's love o'erheard the King, a beauteous, lively dame,
With smiling lips, and sharp, bright eyes, which always seemed the
    same:
She thought, "The Count my lover, is as brave as brave can be,
He surely would do wondrous things to show his love for me!
King, ladies, lovers, all look on, the occasion is divine;
I'll drop my glove to prove his love, great glory will be mine!"

She dropped her glove to prove his love, then looked at him and
    smiled;
He bowed, and in a moment leaped among the lions wild;
The leap was quick; return was quick; he has regained his place,
Then threw the glove, but not with love, right in the lady's face!
"In truth!" cried Francis, "rightly done!" and he rose from where he
    sat;
"No love," quoth he, "but vanity, sets love a task like that."

LADY CLARE
Alfred Tennyson

It was the time when lilies blow,
    And clouds are highest up in air,
Lord Ronald brought a lily-white doe
    To give his cousin, Lady Clare.

I trow they did not part in scorn;
    Lovers long-betroth'd were they;
They two will wed the morrow morn;
    God's blessing on the day!

"He does not love me for my birth,
    Nor for my lands so broad and fair;
He loves me for my own true worth,
    And that is well," said Lady Clare.

In there came old Alice the nurse,
    Said, "Who was this that went from thee?"
"It was my cousin," said Lady Clare,
    "Tomorrow he weds with me."

"O God be thank'd!" said Alice the nurse,
    "That all comes round so just and fair:
Lord Ronald is heir of all your lands,
    And you are not the Lady Clare."

"Are ye out of your mind, my nurse, my nurse,"
  Said Lady Clare, "that ye speak so wild?"
"As God's above," said Alice the nurse,
  "I speak the truth: you are my child.

"The old Earl's daughter died at my breast;
  I speak the truth, as I live by bread!
I buried her like my own sweet child,
  And put my child in her stead."

"Falsely, falsely have ye done,
  O mother," she said, "if this be true,
To keep the best man under the sun
  So many years from his due."

"Nay now, my child," said Alice the nurse,
  "But keep the secret for your life,
And all you have will be Lord Ronald's,
  When you are man and wife."

"If I'm a beggar born," she said,
  "I will speak out, for I dare not lie.
Pull off, pull off, the brooch of gold,
  And fling the diamond necklace by."

"Nay now, my child," said Alice the nurse,
  "But keep the secret all ye can."
She said, "Not so: but I will know
  If there be any faith in man."

"Nay now, what faith?" said Alice the nurse,
  "The man will cleave unto his right."
"And he shall have it," the lady replied,
  "Tho' I should die tonight."

"Yet give one kiss to your mother dear!
  Alas! my child, I sinn'd for thee."
"O mother, mother, mother," she said,
  "So strange it seems to me.

"Yet here's a kiss for my mother dear,
    My mother dear, if this be so,
And lay your hand upon my head,
    And bless me, mother, ere I go."

She clad herself in a russet gown,
    She was no longer Lady Clare:
She went by dale, and she went by down,
    With a single rose in her hair.

The lily-white doe Lord Ronald had brought
    Leapt up from where she lay,
Dropt her head in the maiden's hand,
    And follow'd her all the way.

Down stept Lord Ronald from his tower,
    "O Lady Clare, you shame your worth!
Why come you drest like a village maid,
    That are the flower of the earth?"

"If I come drest like a village maid,
    I am but as my fortunes are:
I am a beggar born," she said,
    "And not the Lady Clare."

"Play me no tricks," said Lord Ronald,
    "For I am yours in words and in deed.
Play me no tricks," said Lord Ronald,
    "Your riddle is hard to read."

O and proudly stood she up!
    Her heart within her did not fail:
She look'd into Lord Ronald's eyes,
    And told him all her nurse's tale.

He laugh'd a laugh of merry scorn:
    He turn'd and kiss'd her where she stood.
"If you are not the heiress born,
    And I," said he, "the next in blood—

"If you are not the heiress born,
    And I," said he, "the lawful heir,
We two will wed tomorrow morn,
    And you shall still be Lady Clare."

LORD ULLIN'S DAUGHTER
Thomas Campbell

A Chieftain to the Highlands bound
    Cries, "Boatman, do not tarry!
And I'll give thee a silver pound
    To row us o'er the ferry!"

—"Now, who be ye, would cross Lochgyle
    This dark and stormy water?"
—"O I'm the chief of Ulva's isle,
    And this, Lord Ullin's daughter.

"And fast before her father's men
    Three days we've fled together,
For should he find us in the glen,
    My blood would stain the heather.

"His horsemen hard behind us ride—
    Should they our steps discover,
Then who will cheer my bonny bride
    When they have slain her lover?"

Out spoke the hardy Highland wight,
    "I'll go, my chief, I'm ready:
It is not for your silver bright,
    But for your winsome lady:—

"And by my word! the bonny bird
    In danger shall not tarry;
So though the waves are raging white,
    I'll row you o'er the ferry."

By this the storm grew loud apace,
  The water-wraith was shrieking;
And in the scowl of heaven each face
  Grew dark as they were speaking.

But still as wilder blew the wind,
  And as the night grew drearer,
Adown the glen rode armèd men,
  Their trampling sounded nearer.

"O haste thee, haste!" the lady cries,
  "Though tempest round us gather;
I'll meet the raging of the skies,
  But not an angry father!"

The boat has left a stormy land,
  A stormy sea before her—
When, O! too strong for human hand
  The tempest gather'd o'er her.

And still they row'd amidst the roar
  Of waters fast prevailing:
Lord Ullin reach'd that fatal shore,—
  His wrath was changed to wailing.

For, sore dismayed, through storm and shade
  His child he did discover:—
One lovely hand she stretch'd for aid,
  And one was round her lover.

"Come back! come back!" he cried in grief,
  "Across this stormy water:
And I'll forgive your Highland chief:—
  My daughter!—O my daughter!"

'Twas vain: the loud waves lash'd the shore,
  Return or aid preventing;
The waters wild went o'er his child,
  And he was left lamenting.

From the family

scrapbook

THE STAR
Jane Taylor

Twinkle, twinkle, little star,
How I wonder what you are,
Up above the world so high,
Like a diamond in the sky.

When the blazing sun is set,
And the grass with dew is wet,
Then you show your little light,
Twinkle, twinkle, all the night.

Then the traveler in the dark
Thanks you for your tiny spark,
He could not see where to go
If you did not twinkle so.

In the dark blue sky you keep,
And often through my curtains peep,
For you never shut your eye
Till the sun is in the sky.

As your bright and tiny spark
Lights the traveler in the dark,
Though I know not what you are,
Twinkle, twinkle, little star.

I LOVE LITTLE PUSSY
Jane Taylor

I love little Pussy.
   Her coat is so warm,
And if I don't hurt her,
   She'll do me no harm.
So I'll not pull her tail,
   Or drive her away,
But Pussy and I
   Very gently will play,
She will sit by my side,
   And I'll give her her food,
And she'll like me because
   I am gentle and good.

I'll pat little Pussy,
   And then she will purr,
And thus show her thanks
   For my kindness to her;
I'll not pinch her ears,
   Nor tread on her paws,
Lest I should provoke her
   To use her sharp claws;
I never will vex her,
   Nor make her displeased,
For Pussy can't bear
   To be worried or teased.

THE THREE LITTLE KITTENS
Eliza Lee Follen

Three little kittens lost their mittens;
   And they began to cry,
     "Oh, mother dear,
     We very much fear
That we have lost our mittens."

"Lost your mittens!
You naughty kittens!
Then you shall have no pie!"
    "Mee-ow, mee-ow, mee-ow."
"No, you shall have no pie."
    "Mee-ow, mee-ow, mee-ow."

The three little kittens found their mittens;
  And they began to cry,
    "Oh, mother dear,
    See here, see here!
See, we have found our mittens!"
    "Put on your mittens,
    You silly kittens,
And you may have some pie."
    "Purr-r, purr-r, purr-r,
Oh, let us have the pie!
    Purr-r, purr-r, purr-r."

The three little kittens put on their mittens,
  And soon ate up the pie;
    "Oh, mother dear,
    We greatly fear
That we have soiled our mittens!"
    "Soiled your mittens!
    You naughty kittens!"
Then they began to sigh,
    "Mee-ow, mee-ow, mee-ow."
Then they began to sigh,
    "Mee-ow, mee-ow, mee-ow."

The three little kittens washed their mittens,
  And hung them out to dry;
    "Oh, mother dear,
    Do not you hear
That we have washed our mittens?"

"Washed your mittens!
Oh, you're good kittens!
But I smell a rat close by,
        Hush, hush! Mee-ow, mee-ow."
"We smell a rat close by,
        Mee-ow, mee-ow, mee-ow."

THE BABY
George Macdonald

Where did you come from, baby dear?
Out of the everywhere into the here.

Where did you get your eyes so blue?
Out of the sky as I came through.

What makes the light in them sparkle and spin?
Some of the starry spikes left in.

Where did you get that little tear?
I found it waiting when I got here.

What makes your forehead so smooth and high?
A soft hand stroked it as I went by.

What makes your cheek like a warm white rose?
Something better than anyone knows.

Whence that three-cornered smile of bliss?
Three angels gave me at once a kiss.

Where did you get that pearly ear?
God spoke, and it came out to hear.

Where did you get those arms and hands?
Love made itself into hooks and bands.

Feet, whence did you come, you darling things?
From the same box as the cherubs' wings.

How did they all just come to be you?
God thought about me, and so I grew.

But how did you come to us, you dear?
God thought of you, and so I am here.

MARY'S LAMB
Sarah Josepha Hale

Mary had a little lamb,
  Its fleece was white as snow;
And everywhere that Mary went,
  The lamb was sure to go.

He followed her to school one day,
  Which was against the rule;
It made the children laugh and play
  To see a lamb at school.

And so the teacher turned him out,
  But still he lingered near,
And waited patiently about
  Till Mary did appear.

Then he ran to her, and laid
  His head upon her arm,
As if he said, "I'm not afraid—
  You'll keep me from all harm."

"What makes the lamb love Mary so?"
  The eager children cried.
"Oh, Mary loves the lamb, you know,"
  The teacher quick replied.

And you each gentle animal
  In confidence may bind,
And make them follow at your will,
  If you are only kind.

THE MOUNTAIN AND THE SQUIRREL
Ralph Waldo Emerson

The mountain and the squirrel
Had a quarrel,
And the former called the latter "Little prig";
Bun replied,
"You are doubtless very big;
But all sorts of things and weather
Must be taken in together
To make up a year,
And a sphere.
And I think it no disgrace
To occupy my place.
If I'm not so large as you,
You are not so small as I,
And not half so spry.
I'll not deny you make
A very pretty squirrel track.
Talents differ; all is well and wisely put;
If I cannot carry forests on my back,
Neither can you crack a nut!"

THE SPIDER AND THE FLY
Mary Howitt

"Will you walk into my parlor?" said the Spider to the Fly,
" 'Tis the prettiest little parlor that ever you did spy;
The way into my parlor is up a winding stair,
And I have many curious things to show when you are there."
"Oh no, no," said the little Fly, "to ask me is in vain;
For who goes up your winding stair can ne'er come down again."

"I'm sure you must be weary, dear, with soaring up so high;
Will you rest upon my little bed?" said the Spider to the Fly.
"There are pretty curtains drawn around, the sheets are fine and thin;
And if you like to rest awhile, I'll snugly tuck you in!"
"Oh no, no," said the little Fly, "for I've often heard it said
They never, never wake again, who sleep upon your bed!"

Said the cunning Spider to the Fly, "Dear friend, what can I do
To prove the warm affection I've always felt for you?
I have within my pantry, good store of all that's nice;
I'm sure you're very welcome—will you please to take a slice?"
"Oh no, no," said the little Fly, "kind sir, that cannot be,
I've heard what's in your pantry, and I do not wish to see!"

"Sweet creature," said the Spider, "you're witty and you're wise;
How handsome are your gauzy wings, how brilliant are your eyes!
I have a little looking-glass upon my parlor shelf;
If you'll step in one moment, dear, you shall behold yourself."
"I thank you, gentle sir," she said, "for what you're pleased to say,
And bidding you good-morning now, I'll call another day."

The Spider turned him round about, and went into his den,
For well he knew the silly Fly would soon come back again;
So he wove a subtle web in a little corner sly,
And set his table ready to dine upon the Fly.
Then he came out to his door again, and merrily did sing,
"Come hither, hither, pretty Fly, with the pearl and silver wing;
Your robes are green and purple, there's a crest upon your head;
Your eyes are like the diamond bright, but mine are dull as lead."

Alas, alas! how very soon this silly little Fly,
Hearing his wily, flattering words, came slowly flitting by;
With buzzing wings she hung aloft, then near and nearer drew,—
Thinking only of her brilliant eyes, and green and purple hue;
Thinking only of her crested head—poor foolish thing! At last,
Up jumped the cunning Spider, and fiercely held her fast.
He dragged her up his winding stair, into his dismal den
Within his little parlor—but she ne'er came out again!

And now, dear little children, who may this story read,
To idle, silly, flattering words, I pray you ne'er give heed;
Unto an evil counsellor close heart, and ear, and eye,
And take a lesson from this tale of the Spider and the Fly.

LITTLE ORPHANT ANNIE
James Whitcomb Riley

Little Orphant Annie's come to our house to stay,
An' wash the cups and saucers up, an' brush the crumbs away,
An' shoo the chickens off the porch, an' dust the hearth, an' sweep,
An' make the fire, an' bake the bread, an' earn her board-an'-keep;
An' all us other children, when the supper things is done,
We set around the kitchen fire an' has the mostest fun
A-list'nin' to the witch tales 'at Annie tells about,
An' the Gobble-uns 'at gits you
    Ef you
     Don't
      Watch
       Out!

Onc't they was a little boy wouldn't say his prayers,—
So when he went to bed at night, away upstairs,
His Mammy heerd him holler, an' his Daddy heerd him bawl,
An' when they turn't the kivvers down, he wasn't there at all!
An' they seeked him in the rafter room, an' cubbyhole, an' press,
An' seeked him up the chimbly flue, an' ever'wheres, I guess;
But all they ever found was thist his pants an' roundabout:—
An' the Gobble-uns 'll git you
    Ef you
     Don't
      Watch
       Out!

An' one time a little girl 'ud allus laugh an' grin,
An' make fun of ever'one, an' all her blood an' kin;
An' onc't, when they was "company," an' ole folks was there,
She mocked 'em an' shocked 'em, an' said she didn't care!
An' thist as she kicked her heels, an' turn't to run an' hide,
They was two great big Black Things a-standin' by her side,
An' they snatched her through the ceilin' 'fore she knowed what
    she's about!
An' the Gobble-uns 'll git you
            Ef you
              Don't
                Watch
                  Out!

An' little Orphant Annie says, when the blaze is blue,
An' the lamp-wick sputters, an' the wind goes *woo-oo!*
An' you hear the crickets quit, an' the moon is gray,
An' the lightnin' bugs in dew is all squenched away,—
You better mind yer parents, and yer teachers fond an' dear,
An' churish them 'at loves you, an' dry the orphant's tear,
An' he'p the pore an' needy ones 'at clusters all about,
Er the Gobble-uns 'll git you
            Ef you
              Don't
                Watch
                  Out!

THE RAGGEDY MAN
James Whitcomb Riley

O The Raggedy Man! He works fer Pa;
An' he's the goodest man ever you saw!
He comes to our house every day,
An' waters the horses, an' feeds 'em hay;
An' he opens the shed—an' we all ist laugh
When he drives out our little, old, wobble-ly calf;

An' nen—ef our hired girl says he can—
He milks the cow fer 'Lizabuth Ann—
  Ain't he a' awful good Raggedy Man?
    Raggedy! Raggedy! Raggedy Man!

W'y, The Raggedy Man—he's ist so good
He splits the kindlin' an' chops the wood;
An' nen he spades in our garden, too,
An' does most things 'at *boys* can't do—
He clumbed clean up in our big tree
An' shooked a' apple down fer me—
An' 'nother 'n,' too, fer 'Lizabuth Ann—
An' 'nother 'n,' too, fer The Raggedy Man—
  Ain't he a' awful kind Raggedy Man?
    Raggedy! Raggedy! Raggedy Man!

An' The Raggedy Man, he knows most rhymes
An' tells 'em, if I be good, sometimes:
Knows 'bout Giunts, an' Griffuns, an' Elves,
An' the Squidgicum Squees 'at swallers therselves!
An' wite by the pump in our pasture-lot,
He showed me the hole 'at the Wunks is got,
'At lives 'way deep in the ground, 'an can
Turn into me, er 'Lizabuth Ann!
Er Ma, er Pa, er The Raggedy Man!
  Ain't he a funny old Raggedy Man?
    Raggedy! Raggedy! Raggedy Man!

The Raggedy Man—one time when he
Wuz makin' a little bow-'n'-orry fer me,
Says, "When *you're* big like your Pa is,
Air you go' to keep a fine store like his—
An' be a rich merchunt—an' wear fine clothes?—
Er what *air* you go' to be, goodness knows!"
An' nen he laughed at 'Lizabuth Ann,
An' I says "'M go' to be a Raggedy Man!—
  I'm ist go' to be a nice Raggedy Man!"
    Raggedy! Raggedy! Raggedy Man!

LITTLE GUSTAVA
Celia Thaxter

Little Gustava sits in the sun,
Safe in the porch, and the little drops run
From the icicles under the eaves so fast,
For the bright spring sun shines warm at last,
   And glad is little Gustava.

She wears a quaint little scarlet cap,
And a little green bowl she holds in her lap,
Filled with bread and milk to the brim,
And a wreath of marigolds round the rim.
   "Ha, ha!" laughs little Gustava.

Up comes her little gray coaxing cat
With her little pink nose, and she mews, "What's that?"
Gustava feeds her,—she begs for more;
And a little brown hen walks in at the door.
   "Good-day!" cries little Gustava.

She scatters crumbs for the little brown hen.
There comes a rush and a flutter, and then
Down fly her little white doves so sweet,
With their snowy wings and their crimson feet.
   "Welcome!" cries little Gustava.

So dainty and eager they pick up the crumbs.
But who is this through the doorway comes?
Little Scotch terrier, little dog Rags,
Looks in her face, and his funny tail wags.
   "Ha, ha!" laughs little Gustava.

"You want some breakfast too?" and down
She sets her bowl on the brick floor brown;
And little dog Rags drinks up her milk,
While she strokes his shaggy locks, like silk.
   "Dear Rags!" says little Gustava.

Waiting without stood sparrow and crow,
Cooling their feet in the melting snow:
"Won't you come in, good folk?" she cried.
But they were too bashful, and stayed outside,
    Though "Pray come in!" cried Gustava.

So the last she threw them, and knelt on the mat
With doves and biddy and dog and cat.
And her mother came to the open house-door.
"Dear little daughter, I bring you some more.
    My merry little Gustava!"

Kitty and terrier, biddy and doves,
All things harmless Gustava loves.
The shy, kind creatures 'tis joy to feed,
And oh, her breakfast is sweet indeed
    To happy little Gustava!

LITTLE BOY BLUE
Eugene Field

The little toy dog is covered with dust,
    But sturdy and staunch he stands;
And the little toy soldier is red with rust,
    And his musket moulds in his hands.
Time was when the little toy dog was new,
    And the soldier was passing fair;
And that was the time when our Little Boy Blue
    Kissed them and put them there.

"Now, don't you go till I come," he said,
    "And don't you make any noise!"
So, toddling off to his trundle-bed,
    He dreamt of the pretty toys;
And, as he was dreaming, an angel song
    Awakened our Little Boy Blue—
Oh! the years are many, the years are long,
    But the little toy friends are true!

Aye, faithful to Little Boy Blue they stand,
  Each in the same old place—
Awaiting the touch of a little hand,
  The smile of a little face;
And they wonder, as waiting the long years through
  In the dust of that little chair,
What has become of our Little Boy Blue,
  Since he kissed them and put them there.

"ONE, TWO, THREE!"
Henry Cuyler Bunner

It was an old, old, old, old lady,
  And a boy that was half-past three;
And the way that they played together
  Was beautiful to see.

She couldn't go romping and jumping,
  And the boy no more could he;
For he was a thin little fellow,
  With a thin little twisted knee.

They sat in the yellow sunlight,
  Out under the maple tree;
And the game they played I'll tell you,
  Just as it was told to me.

It was hide-and-go-seek they were playing,
  Though you'd never have known it to be—
With an old, old, old, old lady,
  And a boy with a twisted knee.

The boy would bend his face down
  On his little sound right knee,
And he guessed where she was hiding
  In guesses One, Two, Three.

537

"You are in the china closet!"
   He would laugh and cry with glee—
It wasn't the china closet,
   But he still had Two and Three.

"You are up in Papa's big bedroom,
   In the chest with the queer old key!"
And she said: "You are *warm* and *warmer*;
   But you're not quite right," said she.

"It can't be the little cupboard
   Where Mamma's things used to be—
So it must be in the clothespress, Gran'ma!"
   And he found her with his Three.

Then she covered her face with her fingers,
   That were wrinkled and white and wee,
And she guessed where the boy was hiding,
   With a One and a Two and a Three.

And they never had stirred from their places
   Right under the maple tree—
This old, old, old, old lady,
   And the boy with the lame little knee—
This dear, dear, dear old lady,
   And the boy who was half-past three.

JEST 'FORE CHRISTMAS
Eugene Field

Father calls me William, sister calls me Will,
Mother calls me Willie, but the fellers call me Bill!
Mighty glad I ain't a girl—ruther be a boy,
Without them sashes, curls, an' things that's worn by Fauntleroy!
Love to chawnk green apples an' go swimmin' in the lake—
Hate to take the castor-ile they give for belly-ache!
'Most all the time, the whole year round, there ain't no flies on me,
But jest 'fore Christmas I'm as good as I kin be!

Got a yeller dog named Sport, sic him on the cat;
First thing she knows she doesn't know where she is at!
Got a clipper sled, an' when us kids goes out to slide,
'Long comes the grocery cart, an' we all hook a ride!
But sometimes when the grocery man is worried an' cross,
He reaches at us with his whip, an' larrups up his hoss,
An' then I laff an' holler, "Oh, ye never teched *me!*"
But jest 'fore Christmas I'm as good as I kin be!

Gran'ma says she hopes that when I git to be a man,
I'll be a missionarer like her oldest brother, Dan,
As was et up by the cannibuls that lives in Ceylon's Isle,
Where every prospeck pleases, an' only man is vile!
But Gran'ma she has never been to see a Wild West show,
Nor read the Life of Daniel Boone, or else I guess she'd know
That Buff'lo Bill an' cowboys is good enough for me!
Excep' jest 'fore Christmas, when I'm good as I kin be!

And then old Sport he hangs around, so solemn-like an' still,
His eyes they keep a-sayin': "What's the matter, little Bill?"
The old cat sneaks down off her perch an' wonders what's become
Of them two enemies of hern that used to make things hum!
But I am so perlite an' 'tend so earnestly to biz,
That Mother says to Father: "How improved our Willie is!"
But Father, havin' been a boy hisself, suspicions me
When, jest 'fore Christmas, I'm as good as I kin be!

For Christmas, with its lots an' lots of candies, cakes, an' toys,
Was made, they say, for proper kids, an' not for naughty boys;
So wash yer face an' bresh yer hair, an' mind yer p's and q's,
An' don't bust out yer pantaloons, and don't wear out yer shoes;
Say "Yessum" to the ladies, an' "Yessur" to the men,
An' when they 's company, don't pass yer plate for pie again;
But, thinkin' of the things yer'd like to see upon that tree,
Jest 'fore Christmas be as good as yer kin be!

TRY, TRY AGAIN
T. H. Palmer

'Tis a lesson you should heed,
    Try, try again;
If at first you don't succeed,
    Try, try again;
Then your courage should appear,
For, if you will persevere,
You will conquer, never fear;
    Try, try again.

LITTLE THINGS
FROM LITTLE THINGS
Julia A. F. Carney

Little drops of water,
    Little grains of sand,
Make the mighty ocean
    And the pleasant land.

Little deeds of kindness,
    Little words of love,
Make our earth an Eden,
    Like the heaven above.

FOUR-LEAF CLOVER
Ella Higginson

I know a place where the sun is like gold,
    And the cherry blossoms burst with snow,
And down underneath is the loveliest nook,
    Where the four-leaf clovers grow.

One leaf is for hope, and one is for faith,
  And one is for love, you know,
And God put another in for luck—
  If you search, you will find where they grow.

But you must have hope, and you must have faith,
  You must love and be strong—and so
If you work, if you wait, you will find the place
  Where the four-leaf clovers grow.

COME, LITTLE LEAVES
George Cooper

"Come, little leaves," said the wind one day,
"Come o'er the meadows with me and play;
Put on your dresses of red and gold,
For summer is gone and the days grow cold."

Soon as the leaves heard the wind's loud call,
Down they came fluttering, one and all;
Over the brown fields they danced and flew,
Singing the glad little songs they knew.

"Cricket, good-by, we've been friends so long,
Little brook, sing us your farewell song;
Say you are sorry to see us go;
Ah, you will miss us, right well we know.

"Dear little lambs in your fleecy fold,
Mother will keep you from harm and cold;
Fondly we watched you in vale and glade,
Say, will you dream of our loving shade?"

Dancing and whirling, the little leaves went,
Winter had called them, and they were content;
Soon, fast asleep in their earthy beds,
The snow laid a coverlid over their heads.

I REMEMBER, I REMEMBER
Thomas Hood

I remember, I remember,
　The house where I was born,
The little window, where the sun
　Came peeping in at morn:
He never came a wink too soon,
　Nor brought too long a day,
But now I often wish the night
　Had borne my breath away!

I remember, I remember,
　The roses, red and white,
The violets, and the lily-cups,
　Those flowers made of light!
The lilacs, where the robin built,
　And where my brother set
The laburnum on his birthday:
　The tree is living yet!

I remember, I remember,
　Where I was used to swing,
And thought the air must rush as fresh,
　To swallows on the wing.
My spirit flew in feathers then,
　That is so heavy now;
And summer pools could hardly cool
　The fever on my brow!

I remember, I remember,
　The fir-trees, dark and high;
I used to think their slender tops
　Were close against the sky:
It was a childish ignorance:
　But now, 'tis little joy
To know I'm further off from heaven
　Than when I was a boy.

THE OLD OAKEN BUCKET
FROM THE OLD OAKEN BUCKET
Samuel Woodworth

How dear to this heart are the scenes of my childhood,
    When fond recollection presents them to view!
The orchard, the meadow, the deep-tangled wildwood,
    And every loved spot which my infancy knew;
The wide-spreading pond, and the mill that stood by it;
    The bridge and the rock where the cataract fell;
The cot of my father, the dairy-house nigh it,
    And e'en the rude bucket which hung in the well!
The old oaken bucket, the iron-bound bucket,
    The moss-covered bucket which hung in the well.

IN SCHOOL-DAYS
FROM IN SCHOOL-DAYS
John Greenleaf Whittier

Still sits the schoolhouse by the road,
    A ragged beggar sleeping;
Around it still the sumachs grow,
    And blackberry-vines are creeping.

Within, the master's desk is seen,
    Deep scarred by raps official;
The warping floor, the battered seats,
    The jackknife's carved initial;

The charcoal frescoes on its wall;
    Its door's worn sill, betraying
The feet that, creeping slow to school,
    Went storming out to playing!

Long years ago a winter sun
    Shone over it at setting;
Lit up its western windowpanes,
    And low eaves' icy fretting.

543

It touched the tangled golden curls,
    And brown eyes full of grieving,
Of one who still her steps delayed
    When all the school were leaving.

For near her stood the little boy
    Her childish favor singled:
His cap pulled low upon a face
    Where pride and shame were mingled.

Pushing with restless feet the snow
    To right and left, he lingered;—
As restlessly her tiny hands
    The blue-checked apron fingered.

He saw her lift her eyes; he felt
    The soft hand's light caressing,
And heard the tremble of her voice,
    As if a fault confessing.

"I'm sorry that I spelt the word:
    I hate to go above you,
Because"—the brown eyes lower fell—
    "Because, you see, I love you!"

THE BAREFOOT BOY
FROM THE BAREFOOT BOY
John Greenleaf Whittier

Blessings on thee, little man,
Barefoot boy, with cheek of tan!
With thy turned-up pantaloons,
And thy merry whistled tunes;
With thy red lips, redder still
Kissed by strawberries on the hill;
With the sunshine on thy face,
Through thy torn brim's jaunty grace;
From my heart I give thee joy,—
I was once a barefoot boy!

THE VILLAGE BLACKSMITH
Henry Wadsworth Longfellow

Under a spreading chestnut-tree
The village smithy stands;
The smith, a mighty man is he,
With large and sinewy hands;
And the muscles of his brawny arms
Are strong as iron bands.

His hair is crisp, and black, and long,
His face is like the tan;
His brow is wet with honest sweat,
He earns whate'er he can,
And looks the whole world in the face,
For he owes not any man.

Week in, week out, from morn till night,
You can hear his bellows blow;
You can hear him swing his heavy sledge,
With measured beat and slow,
Like a sexton ringing the village bell,
When the evening sun is low.

And children coming home from school
Look in at the open door;
They love to see the flaming forge,
And hear the bellows roar,
And catch the burning sparks that fly
Like chaff from a threshing-floor.

He goes on Sunday to the church,
And sits among his boys;
He hears the parson pray and preach,
He hears his daughter's voice,
Singing in the village choir,
And it makes his heart rejoice.

It sounds to him like her mother's voice,
Singing in Paradise!
He needs must think of her once more,
How in the grave she lies;
And with his hard, rough hand he wipes
A tear out of his eyes.

Toiling—rejoicing—sorrowing,
Onward through life he goes;
Each morning sees some task begun,
Each evening sees it close;
Something attempted, something done,
Has earned a night's repose.

Thanks, thanks to thee, my worthy friend,
For the lesson thou hast taught!
Thus at the flaming forge of life
Our fortunes must be wrought;
Thus on its sounding anvil shaped
Each burning deed and thought!

WOODMAN, SPARE THAT TREE
FROM WOODMAN, SPARE THAT TREE
George Pope Morris

Woodman, spare that tree!
  Touch not a single bough!
In youth it sheltered me,
  And I'll protect it now.
'Twas my forefather's hand
  That placed it near his cot;
There, woodman, let it stand,
  Thy axe shall harm it not!

When but an idle boy
  I sought its grateful shade;
In all their gushing joy
  Here, too, my sisters played.

My mother kissed me here;
    My father pressed my hand—
Forgive this foolish tear,
    But let that old oak stand!

My heart-strings round thee cling,
    Close as thy bark, old friend!
Here shall the wild-bird sing,
    And still thy branches bend.
Old tree! the storm still brave!
    And, woodman, leave the spot;
While I've a hand to save,
    Thy axe shall harm it not.

SEA MEMORIES
Henry Wadsworth Longfellow

Often I think of the beautiful town
    That is seated by the sea;
Often in thought go up and down
The pleasant streets of that dear old town,
    And my youth comes back to me.
        And a verse of a Lapland song
        Is haunting my memory still:
        "A boy's will is the wind's will,
And the thoughts of youth are long, long thoughts."

I can see the shadowy lines of its trees,
    And catch, in sudden gleams,
The sheen of the far-surrounding seas,
And islands that were the Hesperides
    Of all my boyish dreams.
        And the burden of that old song,
        It murmurs and whispers still:
        "A boy's will is the wind's will,
And the thoughts of youth are long, long thoughts."

I remember the black wharves and the ships,
    And the sea tides tossing free;
And the Spanish sailors with bearded lips,
And the beauty and mystery of the ships,
    And the magic of the sea.
        And the voice of that wayward song
        Is singing and saying still:
        "A boy's will is the wind's will,
And the thoughts of youth are long, long thoughts."

OLD IRONSIDES
WRITTEN IN PROTEST AGAINST THE PROPOSED
BREAKING UP OF THE FRIGATE CONSTITUTION.
Oliver Wendell Holmes

Ay, tear her tattered ensign down!
    Long has it waved on high,
And many an eye has danced to see
    That banner in the sky;
Beneath it rung the battle shout,
    And burst the cannon's roar;—
The meteor of the ocean air
    Shall sweep the clouds no more.

Her deck, once red with heroes' blood,
    Where knelt the vanquished foe,
When winds were hurrying o'er the flood,
    And waves were white below,
No more shall feel the victor's tread,
    Or know the conquered knee;—
The harpies of the shore shall pluck
    The eagle of the sea!

Oh, better that her shattered hulk
    Should sink beneath the wave;
Her thunders shook the mighty deep,
    And there should be her grave;

Nail to the mast her holy flag,
  Set every threadbare sail,
And give her to the god of storms,
  The lightning and the gale!

CASEY AT THE BAT
Ernest Lawrence Thayer

The outlook wasn't brilliant for the Mudville nine that day;
The score stood four to two with but one inning more to play.
And then when Cooney died at first and Barrows did the same,
A sickly silence fell upon the patrons of the game.

A straggling few got up to go in deep despair. The rest
Clung to the hope which springs eternal in the human breast;
They thought if only Casey could but get a whack at that—
We'd put up even money now with Casey at the bat.

But Flynn preceded Casey, as did also Jimmy Blake,
And the former was a lulu and the latter was a cake;
So upon that stricken multitude grim melancholy sat,
For there seemed but little chance of Casey's getting to the bat.

But Flynn let drive a single, to the wonderment of all,
And Blake, the much despisèd, tore the cover off the ball;
And when the dust had lifted, and the men saw what had occurred,
There was Jimmy safe at second and Flynn a-hugging third.

Then from five thousand throats and more there rose a lusty yell;
It rumbled through the valley, it rattled in the dell;
It knocked upon the mountain and recoiled upon the flat,
For Casey, mighty Casey, was advancing to the bat.

There was ease in Casey's manner as he stepped into his place;
There was pride in Casey's bearing and a smile on Casey's face.
And when, responding to the cheers, he lightly doffed his hat,
No stranger in the crowd could doubt 'twas Casey at the bat.

Ten thousand eyes were on him as he rubbed his hands with dirt;
Five thousand tongues applauded when he wiped them on his shirt.
Then while the writhing pitcher ground the ball into his hip,
Defiance gleamed in Casey's eye, a sneer curled Casey's lip.

And now the leather-covered sphere came hurtling through the air,
And Casey stood a-watching it in haughty grandeur there.
Close by the sturdy batsman the ball unheeded sped—
"That ain't my style," said Casey. "Strike one," the umpire said.

From the benches, black with people, there went up a muffled roar,
Like the beating of the storm waves on a stern and distant shore.
"Kill him! Kill the umpire!" shouted someone on the stand;
And it's likely they'd have killed him had not Casey raised his hand.

With a smile of Christian charity great Casey's visage shone;
He stilled the rising tumult; he bade the game go on;
He signaled to the pitcher, and once more the spheroid flew;
But Casey still ignored it, and the umpire said, "Strike two."

"Fraud!" cried the maddened thousands, and echo answered, "Fraud!"
But one scornful look from Casey and the audience was awed.
They saw his face grow stern and cold, they saw his muscles strain,
And they knew that Casey wouldn't let that ball go by again.

The sneer is gone from Casey's lip, his teeth are clenched in hate;
He pounds with cruel violence his bat upon the plate.
And now the pitcher holds the ball, and now he lets it go,
And now the air is shattered by the force of Casey's blow.

Oh, somewhere in this favored land the sun is shining bright;
The band is playing somewhere, and somewhere hearts are light,
And somewhere men are laughing, and somewhere children shout;
But there is no joy in Mudville—mighty Casey has struck out.

THE LITTLE BLACK-EYED REBEL

The heroine's name was Mary Redmond, and she lived in Philadelphia. During the occupation of that town by the British, she was ever ready to aid in the secret delivery of the letters written home by the husbands and fathers fighting in the Continental Army.

Will Carleton

A boy drove into the city, his wagon loaded down
With food to feed the people of the British-governed town;
And the little black-eyed rebel, so innocent and sly,
Was watching for his coming from the corner of her eye.

His face looked broad and honest, his hands were brown and tough,
The clothes he wore upon him were homespun, coarse, and rough;
But one there was who watched him, who long time lingered nigh
And cast at him sweet glances from the corner of her eye.

He drove up to the market, he waited in the line;
His apples and potatoes were fresh and fair and fine;
But long and long he waited, and no one came to buy,
Save the black-eyed rebel, watching from the corner of her eye.

"Now who will buy my apples?" he shouted, long and loud;
And "Who wants my potatoes?" he repeated to the crowd;
But from all the people round him came no word of a reply,
Save the black-eyed rebel, answering from the corner of her eye.

For she knew that 'neath the lining of the coat he wore that day,
Were long letters from the husbands and the fathers far away,
Who were fighting for the freedom that they meant to gain or die;
And a tear like silver glistened in the corner of her eye.

But the treasures—how to get them? crept the question through her
    mind,
Since keen enemies were watching for what prizes they might find;
And she paused a while and pondered, with a pretty little sigh;
Then resolve crept through her features, and a shrewdness fired her
    eye.

551

So she resolutely walked up to the wagon old and red;
"May I have a dozen apples for a kiss?" she sweetly said:
And the brown face flushed to scarlet; for the boy was somewhat shy,
And he saw her laughing at him from the corner of her eye.

"You may have them all for nothing, and more, if you want," quoth
    he.
"I will have them, my good fellow, but can pay for them," said she;
And she clambered on the wagon, minding not who all were by.
With a laugh of reckless romping in the corner of her eye.

Clinging round his brawny neck, she clasped her fingers white and
    small,
And then whispered, "Quick! the letters! thrust them underneath
    my shawl!
Carry back again *this* package, and be sure that you are spry!"
And she sweetly smiled upon him from the corner of her eye.

Loud the motley crowd were laughing at the strange, ungirlish freak,
And the boy was scared and panting, and so dashed he could not
    speak;
And, "Miss, I have good apples," a bolder lad did cry;
But she answered, "No, I thank you," from the corner of her eye.

With the news of loved ones absent to the dear friends they would
    greet,
Searching them who hungered for them, swift she glided through the
    street.
"There is nothing worth the doing that it does not pay to try,"
Thought the little black-eyed rebel, with a twinkle in her eye.

CASABIANCA
Felicia Dorothea Hemans

    The boy stood on the burning deck,
      Whence all but him had fled;
    The flame that lit the battle's wreck,
      Shone round him o'er the dead.

Yet beautiful and bright he stood,
  As born to rule the storm;
A creature of heroic blood,
  A proud, though childlike form.

The flames roll'd on—he would not go
  Without his father's word;
That father, faint in death below,
  His voice no longer heard.

He call'd aloud—"Say, father, say
  If yet my task be done!"
He knew not that the chieftain lay
  Unconscious of his son.

"Speak, father!" once again he cried,
  "If I may yet be gone!"
And but the booming shots replied,
  And fast the flames roll'd on.

Upon his brow he felt their breath,
  And in his waving hair;
And look'd from that lone post of death,
  In still, yet brave despair;

And shouted but once more aloud,
  "My father! must I stay?"
While o'er him fast, through sail and shroud,
  The wreathing fires made way.

They wrapt the ship in splendour wild,
  They caught the flag on high,
And stream'd above the gallant child,
  Like banners in the sky.

There came a burst of thunder sound—
  The boy—oh! where was he?
Ask of the winds that far around
  With fragments strewed the sea,

With mast, and helm, and pennon fair,
    That well had borne their part;
But the noblest thing that perished there
    Was that young faithful heart.

THE LEAK IN THE DIKE
Phoebe Cary

The good dame looked from her cottage
    At the close of the pleasant day,
And cheerily called to her little son
    Outside the door at play:
"Come, Peter, come! I want you to go,
    While there is yet light to see,
To the hut of the blind old man who lives
    Across the dike, for me;
And take these cakes I made for him—
    They are hot and smoking yet;
You have time enough to go and come
    Before the sun is set."

Then the good-wife turned to her labor,
    Humming a simple song,
And thought of her husband, working hard
    At the sluices all day long;
And set the turf a-blazing,
    And brought the coarse, black bread;
That he might find a fire at night,
    And see the table spread.

And Peter left the brother,
    With whom all day he had played,
And the sister who had watched their sports
    In the willow's tender shade;

And told them they'd see him back before
    They saw a star in sight—
Though he wouldn't be afraid to go
    In the very darkest night!
For he was a brave, bright fellow,
    With eye and conscience clear;
He could do whatever a boy might do,
    And he had not learned to fear.
Why, he wouldn't have robbed a bird's nest,
    Nor brought a stork to harm,
Though never a law in Holland
    Had stood to stay his arm!

And now, with his face all glowing,
    And eyes as bright as the day
With the thoughts of his pleasant errand,
    He trudged along the way;
And soon his joyous prattle
    Made glad a lonesome place—
Alas! if only the blind old man
    Could have seen that happy face!
Yet he somehow caught the brightness
    Which his voice and presence lent;
And he felt the sunshine come and go
    As Peter came and went.

And now, as the day was sinking,
    And the winds began to rise,
The mother looked from her door again,
    Shading her anxious eyes,
And saw the shadows deepen,
    And birds to their homes come back,
But never a sign of Peter
    Along the level track.
But she said: "He will come at morning,
    So I need not fret or grieve—
Though it isn't like my boy at all
    To stay without my leave."

But where was the child delaying?
　　On the homeward way was he,
And across the dike while the sun was up
　　An hour above the sea.
He was stopping now to gather flowers;
　　Now listening to the sound,
As the angry waters dashed themselves
　　Against their narrow bound.
"Ah! well for us," said Peter,
　　"That the gates are good and strong,
And my father tends them carefully,
　　Or they would not hold you long!
You're a wicked sea," said Peter;
　　"I know why you fret and chafe;
You would like to spoil our lands and homes;
　　But our sluices keep you safe!"

But hark! through the noise of waters
　　Comes a low, clear, trickling sound;
And the child's face pales with terror,
　　And his blossoms drop to the ground.
He is up the bank in a moment,
　　And, stealing through the sand,
He sees a stream not yet so large
　　As his slender, childish hand.
'Tis a leak in the dike! He is but a boy,
　　Unused to fearful scenes;
But, young as he is, he has learned to know
　　The dreadful thing that means.
A *leak in the dike!* The stoutest heart
　　Grows faint that cry to hear,
And the bravest man in all the land
　　Turns white with mortal fear.
For he knows the smallest leak may grow
　　To a flood in a single night;
And he knows the strength of the cruel sea
　　When loosed in its angry might.

And the boy! He has seen the danger,
    And, shouting a wild alarm,
He forces back the weight of the sea
    With the strength of his single arm!
He listens for the joyful sound
    Of a footstep passing nigh;
And lays his ear to the ground, to catch
    The answer to his cry.
And he hears the rough winds blowing,
    And the waters rise and fall,
But never an answer comes to him,
    Save the echo of his call.
He sees no hope, no succor,
    His feeble voice is lost;
Yet what shall he do but watch and wait,
    Though he perish at his post!

So, faintly calling and crying
    Till the sun is under the sea;
Crying and moaning till the stars
    Come out for company;
He thinks of his brother and sister,
    Asleep in their safe, warm bed;
He thinks of his father and mother;
    Of himself as dying, and dead;
And of how, when the night is over,
    They must come and find him at last!
But he never thinks he can leave the place
    Where duty holds him fast.

The good dame in the cottage
    Is up and astir with the light,
For the thought of her little Peter
    Has been with her all the night.
And now she watches the pathway,
    As yester-eve she had done;
But what does she see so strange and black
    Against the rising sun?

Her neighbors are bearing between them
    Something straight to her door;
Her child is coming home, but not
    As he ever came before!

"He is dead!" she cries; "my darling!"
    And the startled father hears,
And comes and looks the way she looks,
    And fears the thing she fears:
Till a glad shout from the bearers
    Thrills the stricken man and wife—
"Give thanks, for your son has saved our land,
    And God has saved his life!"
So, there in the morning sunshine
    They knelt about the boy;
And every head was bared and bent
    In tearful, reverent joy.

'Tis many a year since then; but still,
    When the sea roars like a flood,
Their boys are taught what a boy can do
    Who is brave and true and good.
For every man in that country
    Takes his son by the hand,
And tells him of little Peter,
    Whose courage saved the land.

They have many a valiant hero,
    Remembered through the years:
But never one whose name so oft
    Is named with loving tears.
And his deed shall be sung by the cradle,
    And told to the child on the knee,
So long as the dikes of Holland
    Divide the land from the sea!

CURFEW MUST NOT RING TONIGHT
Rosa Hartwick Thorpe

Slowly England's sun was setting o'er the hilltops far away,
Filling all the land with beauty at the close of one sad day;
And the last rays kissed the forehead of a man and maiden fair,
He with footsteps slow and weary, she with sunny floating hair;
He with bowed head, sad and thoughtful, she with lips all cold and
  white,
Struggling to keep back the murmur, "Curfew must not ring to-
  night!"

"Sexton," Bessie's white lips faltered, pointing to the prison old,
With its turrets tall and gloomy, with its walls, dark, damp and
  cold—
"I've a lover in the prison, doomed this very night to die
At the ringing of the curfew, and no earthly help is nigh.
Cromwell will not come till sunset"; and her face grew strangely
  white
As she breathed the husky whisper, "Curfew must not ring tonight!"

"Bessie," calmly spoke the sexton—and his accents pierced her heart
Like the piercing of an arrow, like a deadly poisoned dart—
"Long, long years I've rung the curfew from that gloomy, shadowed
  tower;
Every evening, just at sunset, it has told the twilight hour;
I have done my duty ever, tried to do it just and right—
Now I'm old I still must do it: Curfew, girl, must ring tonight!"

Wild her eyes and pale her features, stern and white her thoughtful
  brow,
And within her secret bosom Bessie made a solemn vow.
She had listened while the judges read, without a tear or sigh,
"At the ringing of the curfew, Basil Underwood must die."
And her breath came fast and faster, and her eyes grew large and
  bright,
As in undertone she murmured, "Curfew must not ring tonight!"

With quick step she bounded forward, sprang within the old church
   door,
Left the old man threading slowly paths he'd often trod before;
Not one moment paused the maiden, but with eye and cheek aglow
Mounted up the gloomy tower, where the bell swung to and fro
As she climbed the dusty ladder, on which fell no ray of light,
Up and up, her white lips saying, "Curfew shall not ring tonight!"

She has reached the topmost ladder, o'er her hangs the great dark
   bell:
Awful is the gloom beneath her like the pathway down to hell;
Lo, the ponderous tongue is swinging. 'Tis the hour of curfew now,
And the sight has chilled her bosom, stopped her breath and paled
   her brow;
Shall she let it ring? No, never! Flash her eyes with sudden light,
And she springs and grasps it firmly: "Curfew shall not ring tonight!"

Out she swung, far out; the city seemed a speck of light below;
She 'twixt heaven and earth suspended as the bell swung to and fro;
And the sexton at the bell rope, old and deaf, heard not the bell,
But he thought it still was ringing fair young Basil's funeral knell.
Still the maiden clung more firmly, and, with trembling lips and
   white,
Said, to hush her heart's wild beating, "Curfew shall not ring to-
   night!"

It was o'er; the bell ceased swaying, and the maiden stepped once
   more
Firmly on the dark old ladder, where for hundred years before
Human foot had not been planted; but the brave deed she had done
Should be told long ages after—often as the setting sun
Should illume the sky with beauty, aged sires, with heads of white,
Long should tell the little children, "Curfew did not ring that night."

O'er the distant hills came Cromwell; Bessie sees him, and her brow,
Full of hope and full of gladness, has no anxious traces now.

At his feet she tells her story, shows her hands all bruised and torn;
And her face so sweet and pleading, yet with sorrow pale and worn,
Touched his heart with sudden pity—lit his eye with misty light;
"Go, your lover lives!" said Cromwell; "Curfew shall not ring to-
    night!"

THE WRECK OF THE HESPERUS
Henry Wadsworth Longfellow

It was the schooner Hesperus,
    That sailed the wintry sea;
And the skipper had taken his little daughter,
    To bear him company.

Blue were her eyes, as the fairy-flax,
    Her cheeks like the dawn of day,
And her bosom white as the hawthorn buds,
    That ope in the month of May.

The skipper he stood beside the helm,
    His pipe was in his mouth;
And he watched how the veering flaw did blow
    The smoke now West, now South.

Then up and spake an old Sailor,
    Had sailed the Spanish Main:
"I pray thee, put into yonder port,
    For I fear a hurricane.

"Last night, the moon had a golden ring,
    And tonight no moon we see!"
The skipper, he blew a whiff from his pipe,
    And a scornful laugh laughed he.

Colder and louder blew the wind,
    A gale from the North-east;
The snow fell hissing in the brine,
    And the billows frothed like yeast.

Down came the storm, and smote amain
  The vessel in its strength;
She shuddered and paused, like a frightened steed,
  Then leaped her cable's length.

"Come hither! come hither! my little daughter,
  And do not tremble so;
For I can weather the roughest gale,
  That ever wind did blow."

He wrapped her warm in his seaman's coat,
  Against the stinging blast;
He cut a rope from a broken spar
  And bound her to the mast.

"O father! I hear the church-bells ring,
  O say, what may it be?"
" 'Tis a fog-bell on a rock-bound coast!"—
  And he steered for the open sea.

"O father! I hear the sound of guns,
  O say, what may it be?"
"Some ship in distress, that cannot live
  In such an angry sea!"

"O father! I see a gleaming light,
  O say, what may it be?"
But the father answered never a word,
  A frozen corpse was he.

Lashed to the helm, all stiff and stark,
  With his face turned to the skies;
The lantern gleamed through the gleaming snow
  On his fixed and glassy eyes.

Then the maiden clasped her hands, and prayed
  That savèd she might be;
And she thought of Christ, who stilled the waves,
  On the Lake of Galilee.

And fast through the midnight dark and drear,
  Through the whistling sleet and snow,
Like a sheeted ghost, the vessel swept
  Towards the reef of Norman's Woe.

And ever the fitful gusts between
  A sound came from the land;
It was the sound of the trampling surf,
  On the rocks and the hard sea-sand.

The breakers were right beneath her bows,
  She drifted a weary wreck,
And a whooping billow swept the crew
  Like icicles from her deck.

She struck where the white and fleecy waves
  Looked soft as carded wool,
But the cruel rocks, they gored her side,
  Like the horns of an angry bull.

Her rattling shrouds, all sheathed in ice,
  With the masts, went by the board;
Like a vessel of glass, she stove and sank,
  Ho! ho! the breakers roared!

At daybreak, on the bleak sea-beach,
  A fisherman stood aghast,
To see the form of a maiden fair,
  Lashed close to a drifting mast.

The salt sea was frozen on her breast,
  The salt tears in her eyes;
And he saw her hair, like the brown sea-weed,
  On the billows fall and rise.

Such was the wreck of the Hesperus,
  In the midnight and the snow!
Christ save us all from a death like this,
  On the reef of Norman's Woe!

THE CHARGE OF THE LIGHT BRIGADE
Alfred Tennyson

Half a league, half a league,
Half a league onward,
All in the valley of Death
    Rode the six hundred.
"Forward the Light Brigade!
Charge for the guns!" he said.
Into the valley of Death
    Rode the six hundred.

"Forward, the Light Brigade!"
Was there a man dismayed?
Not though the soldier knew
    Some one had blundered.
Theirs not to make reply,
Theirs not to reason why,
Theirs but to do and die.
Into the valley of Death
    Rode the six hundred.

Cannon to right of them,
Cannon to left of them,
Cannon in front of them
    Volleyed and thundered;
Stormed at with shot and shell,
Boldly they rode and well,
Into the jaws of Death,
Into the mouth of hell
    Rode the six hundred.

Flashed all their sabres bare,
Flashed as they turned in air
Sabring the gunners there,
Charging an army, while
    All the world wondered.

Plunged in the battery-smoke
Right through the line they broke;
Cossack and Russian
Reeled from the sabre-stroke
    Shattered and sundered.
Then they rode back, but not,
    Not the six hundred.

Cannon to right of them,
Cannon to left of them,
Cannon behind them
    Volleyed and thundered;
Stormed at with shot and shell,
While horse and hero fell,
They that had fought so well
Came through the jaws of Death,
Back from the mouth of hell,
All that was left of them,
    Left of six hundred.

When can their glory fade?
Oh, the wild charge they made!
    All the world wondered.
Honor the charge they made!
Honor the Light Brigade,
    Noble six hundred!

ABOU BEN ADHEM AND THE ANGEL
Leigh Hunt

Abou Ben Adhem (may his tribe increase)
Awoke one night from a deep dream of peace,
And saw, within the moonlight of the room,
Making it rich, and like a lily in bloom,

An angel writing in a book of gold:—
Exceeding peace had made Ben Adhem bold,
And to the presence in the room he said,
"What writest thou?" The vision rais'd his head,
And with a look made of all sweet accord,
Answer'd, "The names of those who love the Lord."
"And is mine one?" said Abou. "Nay, not so,"
Replied the angel. Abou spoke more low,
But cheerly still; and said: "I pray thee then,
Write me as one that loves his fellow men."

The angel wrote, and vanish'd. The next night
It came again with a great wakening light,
And show'd the names whom love of God had bless'd
And lo! Ben Adhem's name led all the rest.

EXCELSIOR
Henry Wadsworth Longfellow

The shades of night were falling fast,
As through an Alpine village passed
A youth, who bore, 'mid snow and ice,
A banner, with the strange device,
 Excelsior!

His brow was sad; his eye beneath
Flashed like a faulchion from its sheath,
And like a silver clarion rung
The accents of that unknown tongue,
 Excelsior!

In happy homes he saw the light
Of household fires gleam warm and bright;
Above, the spectral glaciers shone,
And from his lips escaped a groan,
 Excelsior!

"Try not the Pass!" the old man said,
"Dark lowers the tempest overhead,
The roaring torrent is deep and wide!"
And loud that clarion voice replied,
    Excelsior!

"O stay!" the maiden said, "and rest
Thy weary head upon this breast!"
A tear stood in his bright blue eye,
But still he answered, with a sigh,
    Excelsior!

"Beware the pine-tree's withered branch!
Beware the awful avalanche!"
This was the peasant's last good-night!
A voice replied, far up the height,
    Excelsior!

At break of day, as heavenward
The pious monks of Saint Bernard
Uttered the oft-repeated prayer,
A voice cried through the startled air,
    Excelsior!

A traveler, by the faithful hound,
Half-buried in the snow, was found,
Still grasping in his hand of ice
That banner, with the strange device
    Excelsior!

There, in the twilight cold and grey,
Lifeless, but beautiful, he lay,
And from the sky, serene, and far,
A voice fell, like a falling star,
    Excelsior!

ACKNOWLEDGMENTS

THE EDITOR AND DOUBLEDAY & COMPANY herewith render thanks to the following authors, publishers, and agents whose interest, co-operation, and permission to reprint poems have made possible the publication of *Favorite Poems Old and New—Selected for Boys and Girls.*

All possible care has been taken to trace the ownership of every selection included and to make full acknowledgment of its use. If any errors have inadvertently occurred, they will be corrected in subsequent editions, provided notification is sent to the publisher. Many of the poems here included are traditional, with the author unknown.

American-Scandinavian Foundation, The, New York, for "The Tree" from *Arne* from *Poems and Songs* by Björnstjerne Björnson, translated by Professor Palmer; and "There Is a Charming Land" by Adam Oehlenschlager, translated by Robert Hillyer.

Angus & Robertson Ltd., Sydney, Australia, for "When I Was Six" by Zora Cross from *Book of Australian and New Zealand Verse.*

Appleton-Century-Crofts, Inc., for "The Ingenious Little Old Man" by John Bennett, "This and That" by Florence Boyce Davis (copyright 1928 by Century Company), "The Peppery Man" by Arthur Macy (copyright 1908 by Century Company), and "A Pop Corn Song" by Nancy Byrd Turner, all from *St. Nicholas Magazine;* "The Elf and the Dormouse" by Oliver Herford from *St. Nicholas Book of Verse,* copyright 1923 by Century Company; and "The Flower-Fed Buffaloes" from *Going to the Stars,* by Vachel Lindsay, copyright 1926 by D. Appleton & Company.

Artists and Writers Guild, Inc., for "Noonday Sun" and "Open Range" from the Giant Golden Book Tenggren's *Cowboys and Indians* by Kathryn and Byron Jackson, copyright 1948 by Simon and Schuster, Inc., and Artists and Writers Guild, Inc.

Basil Blackwell, Oxford, England, for "Goblin Feet" by J. R. R. Tolkien.

Bobbs-Merrill Company, The, Inc., for "Be Different to Trees" from *The Skyline Trail,* by Mary Carolyn Davies, copyright © 1924, 1952, used by special permission of the publishers; "Little Orphant Annie," "The Beetle," and "The Raggedy Man" from *Rhymes of Childhood,* and "Extremes" from *The Book of Joyous Children,* copyright © 1902, 1930, both by James Whitcomb Riley, used by special permission of the publishers.

Brandt & Brandt for "Benjamin Franklin," "George Washington," "Nancy Hanks," "Negro Spirituals," and "Thomas Jefferson" from *A Book of Americans* by Rosemary and Stephen Vincent Benét, published by Rinehart & Company, Inc., copyright 1933 by Rosemary and Stephen Vincent Benét; "Chanson Innocente" from *Poems 1923–1954,* by e. e. Cummings, copyright 1923, 1951 by e. e. Cummings,

568

published by Harcourt, Brace and Company; "Afternoon on a Hill," "City Trees," "Portrait by a Neighbor," and "Travel" from *Collected Poems*, by Edna St. Vincent Millay, copyright 1917, 1920, 1921 by Edna St. Vincent Millay, copyright renewed 1945, 1948, 1949 by Edna St. Vincent Millay, published by Harper & Brothers.

Bruce Humphries, Inc., for "Wild Geese" from *The City and Other Poems* by Elinor Chipp.

Jonathan Cape Ltd., London, and Mrs. H. M. Davies for "Leisure" from *The Collected Poems of W. H. Davies.*

Wm. Collins Sons & Co., Ltd., London, for "Bobby Blue" and "Washing" from *More about Me* by John Drinkwater.

Coward-McCann, Inc., for "The Mouse" and "The Bad Kittens" from *Compass Rose*, by Elizabeth Coatsworth, copyright 1929 by Coward-McCann, Inc.

Curtis Brown Ltd., New York, for "Jonathan Bing" from *Jonathan Bing and Other Verses*, by Beatrice Curtis Brown, copyright © 1936 by Beatrice Curtis Brown.

Dial Press, The, Inc., for "Song of the Pop Bottlers" from *A Bowl of Bishop* by Morris Bishop, copyright 1954 by Morris Bishop.

Dodd, Mead & Company, Inc., for "The Octopussycat" from *Mixed Beasts* by Kenyon Cox; "The Birthday Child" from *Round the Mulberry Bush* by Rose Fyleman; "The Sea Gypsy" by Richard Hovey from *More Songs from Vagabondia* by Bliss Carman and Richard Hovey; "The Sky Is Up above the Roof" by Paul Verlaine; and "How to Tell the Wild Animals" by Carolyn Wells.

Dodd, Mead & Company, Inc., and William Heinemann Ltd., London, for "Cradle Song" and "In the Bazaars of Hyderabad" by Sarojini Naidu.

Dodd, Mead & Company, Inc., and McClelland & Stewart Ltd., Canada, for "Mr. Moon" and "Vagabond Song" by Bliss Carman.

Dodd, Mead & Company, Inc., and Wood Lush & Company, London, for "The Field Mouse" and "The Wasp" from *Collected Poems* by William Sharp.

Doubleday & Company, Inc., for "At the Theater," "Barefoot Days," "The Ice-Cream Man," "The Playhouse Key," and "Taxis" from *Taxis and Toadstools*, by Rachel Field, copyright 1926 by Doubleday & Company, Inc.; "In the Hours of Darkness" by James Flexner from *Creative Youth* by Hughes Mearns, copyright 1925 by Doubleday & Company, Inc.; "archy, the cockroach, speaks" from *The Lives and Times of Archy and Mehitabel*, by Don Marquis, copyright 1927 by Doubleday & Company, Inc.; "Could It Have Been a Shadow," "Country Trucks," "How to Tell Goblins from Elves," "Only My Opinion," "Our Hired Man," and "The Tree Toad" from *Goose Grass Rhymes*, by Monica Shannon, copyright 1930 by Doubleday & Company, Inc.; "Sonnet" from *Poems: First Series*, by J. C. Squire, copyright 1919 by Doubleday & Company, Inc.; "Give Me the Splendid Silent Sun," "I Hear America Singing," "O Captain! My Captain," and "O Tan-Faced Prairie Boy" from *Leaves of Grass*, by Walt Whitman, copyright 1924 by Doubleday & Company, Inc.

Doubleday & Company, Inc., and The Society of Authors, London, for "Mice" from *Fifty-One New Nursery Rhymes*, by Rose Fyleman, copyright 1932 by Doubleday & Company, Inc.; "The Spring" from *The Fairy Green*, by Rose Fyleman, copyright 1923 by Doubleday & Company, Inc.; "The Child Next Door" from *Fairies and Chimneys*, by Rose Fyleman, copyright 1920 by Doubleday & Company, Inc.

Doubleday & Company, Inc., The Society of Authors and Punch Magazine, both of London, and Rose Fyleman, for "The Fairies" and "The Fairies Have Never a Penny to Spend" from *Fairies and Chimneys*, by Rose Fyleman, copyright 1920 by Doubleday & Company, Inc.

Doubleday & Company, Inc., and Messrs. Cassell & Co. and A. P. Watt & Son, both

571

573

575

INDEX OF TITLES

578

588

Spanish waters, Spanish waters, you are ringing in my ears, 514
Speak gently, Spring, and make no sudden sound; 173
Spring grass, there is a dance to be danced for you. 224
Spring is the morning of the year, 221
Stars over snow, 264
Still sits the schoolhouse by the road, 543
"Summer is coming, summer is coming, 294
Swan swam over the sea— 364
. . . Swarms of minnows show their little heads, 134
Sweet and low, sweet and low, 54
Swing, swing, 110

Tall people, short people, 247
Tell me where is Fancy bred, 397
Ten South Sea Island boys, 484
The apples are seasoned, 239
The Arctic moon hangs overhead; 179
The Assyrian came down like the wolf on the fold, 511
The axe has cut the forest down, 411
The birds go fluttering in the air, 140
The boy stood on the burning deck, 552
The breaking waves dashed high, 409
The cattle roam again across the fields; 478
The chameleon changes his color; 129
The child next door has a wreath on her hat; 302
The child reads on; her basket of eggs stands by. 470
The children were shouting together, 99
The city mouse lives in a house;— 138
The coach is at the door at last; 242
The cock is crowing, 69
The country vegetables scorn, 233
The day before April, 20
The earth abideth forever. 259
The earth is the Lord's, and the fulness thereof; 232
The fairies have never a penny to spend, 379
The fisherman goes out at dawn, 316
The fishermen say, when your catch is done, 393
The flower-fed buffaloes of the spring, 433

The fog comes, 82
The friendly cow all red and white, 164
The gingham dog and the calico cat, 348
The Goblin has a wider mouth, 388
The goldenrod is yellow; 78
The good dame looked from her cottage, 554
The grass so little has to do,— 223
The Grasshopper, the Grasshopper, 133
The great Pacific railway, 437
The hay appeareth, and the tender grass sheweth itself, 233
The heavens declare the glory of God, 267
The horses of the sea, 274
The Indians come down from Mixco, 488
The little elephant was crying, 489
The little Jesus came to town; 93
The little songs of summer are all gone today. 148
The little toy dog is covered with dust, 536
The long canoe, 113
The Lord in His wisdom made the fly, 357
The Lord is my shepherd; 25
The low beating of the tom-toms, 480
The maple is a dainty maid, 212
The midnight plane with its riding lights, 201
The Moon's the North Wind's cooky, 265
The morns are meeker than they were, 81
The mountain and the squirrel, 530
The night the green moth came for me, 139
The night was coming very fast; 281
The night will never stay, 263
The old West, the old time, 436
The one-l lama, 356
The only real airship, 198
The ostrich is a silly bird, 331
The outlook wasn't brilliant for the Mudville nine that day; 549
The Owl and the Pussycat went to sea, 354
The panther is like a leopard, 331
The Peppery Man was cross and thin; 319
The pointed houses lean so you would swear, 472

594

D. D. W. (Translator), 488
D. F. (Translator), 490
Daly, June, 479
Daly, Thomas Augustine, 304, 414
Davies, Mary Carolyn, 20, 111, 208
Davies, William H., 78
Davis, Fannie Stearns, 19
Davis, Florence Boyce, 311
de Ayala, Ramon Perez, 473
de la Mare, Walter, 5, 8, 42, 132, 138, 265, 308, 370, 394, 513
del Valle, Adriano, 489
Dickinson, Emily, 13, 81, 123, 187, 223, 261, 268, 279
Dorrance, Dick, 201
Dowson, Ernest (Translator), 469
Drake, Joseph Rodman, 380
Dresbach, Glenn Ward, 236
Drinkwater, John, 6, 7, 247, 262
Driscoll, Louise, 22
Drummond, William Henry, 491
Durell, Ann, 372

Eastman, Max, 252
Eastwick, Ivy O., 307
Eaton, Walter Prichard, 213
Edey, Marion, 124, 169
Eliot, T. S., 157
Emerson, Ralph Waldo; 125, 290, 422, 452, 530
Emmett, Daniel Decatur, 439
Enriqueta, María, 489
Ewing, Juliana Horatia, 143, 396
E-Yeh-Shure (Louise Abeita), 20

Farjeon, Eleanor, 39, 41, 79, 80, 130, 222, 233, 263, 303, 323, 482
Farrar, John, 106, 214
Field, Eugene, 55, 70, 348, 536, 538
Field, Rachel, 6, 107, 183, 184, 217, 229, 244, 245, 249, 252, 254, 309, 323, 371
Figueroa, R. Olivares, 490
Fisher, Aileen, 147
FitzGerald, Edward (Translator), 479
Fletcher—see Beaumont and Fletcher
Flexner, James, 386
Follen, Eliza Lee, 526
Francis of Assisi, Saint, 259
Freeman, Mary E. Wilkins, 331
Frost, Frances, 34, 167, 173, 201, 239
Frost, Robert, 67, 161, 230, 286

Fyleman, Rose, 50, 131, 136, 302, 377, 379

Garland, Hamlin, 268
Gezelle, Guido, 471
Gilbert, W. S., 349, 351
Grahame, Kenneth, 88, 282, 342
Graves, Robert, 100, 380
Greenaway, Kate, 38, 101, 105
Grider, Dorothy, 124, 169
Guillén, Nicolás, 487
Guiterman, Arthur, 411, 415, 428, 432
Gumileo, Nikolai, 470

Hale, Sarah Josepha, 529
Hall, Carolyn, 131
Helburn, Theresa, 31
Hemans, Felicia Dorothea, 409, 552
Herbert, A. P., 129
Herford, Oliver, 345
Herrick, Robert, 25, 77, 384
Higginson, Ella, 540
Hillyer, Robert, 113
Hillyer, Robert (Translator), 467, 478
Hodgson, Ralph, 61
Hogg, James, 301
Holmes, Oliver Wendell, 321, 395, 506, 548
Hood, Thomas, 36, 542
Hovey, Richard, 191
Howard, Winifred, 191
Howe, Julia Ward, 441
Howitt, Mary, 175, 530
Huff, Barbara A., 42, 250
Hughes, Langston, 74, 140, 216, 244, 480
Hughes, Langston (Translator), 487
Hugo, Victor, 53, 280
Hunt, Leigh, 516, 565

Ingelow, Jean, 50

Jackson, Byron, 161, 271
Jackson, Helen Hunt, 78
Jackson, Kathryn, 161, 271
Jackson, Leroy F., 45
Jammes, Francis, 470, 472
Johnson E. Pauline, 493
Joyce, James, 271
Justus, May, 310

598